ILLUMINATION

THE EVE SERIES - BOOK FOUR

A.L. WADDINGTON

Cover Design by Greg Simanson
Edited by Carol Farabee

This is a work of fiction. Names, characters, places, brands, media, and incidents are either the product of the author's imagination or are used fictitiously. Any resemblance to similarly named places or to persons living or deceased is unintentional.

PRINT ISBN: 978-1-948143-10-3
EPUB ISBN: 978-1-948143-11-0
Library of Congress Control Number: 2018956559

ACKNOWLEDGMENTS

I would like to thank the staff at Scarlett Ink Publishing who believed in my work and ultimately made this possible. Also, lots of love to my editor, Carol Farabee, for the countless hours of hard work she's invested to make my ramblings come to life.

I would also like to offer my heartfelt gratitude to Heather, Joe, Dale, and Sandy for listening and pushing me through this last year. I could not have made it without you all. And last but certainly not least, my deepest thanks to my readers for following along on Jocelyn and Jackson's journey. I truly appreciate your love and support in helping me bring them to life.

For my husband, Eric: Thanks for believing in me. None of this would have been possible without you. I love you!

And for my beautiful grandchildren: Landon, Jocelyn, Scarlett, & Stetson: You have brought so much job & love into my life.

DEDICATION

The EVE Series is dedicated to the loving memory to my grandfather,
Floyd E. Hyatt.
September 28, 1918 – May 1, 2015

My grandfather was a loving and devoted husband to his wife, Margaret, of sixty-seven years and a World War II Veteran in the Pacific campaign. He was a man of honor who was a kind, spiritual man, who was always there for anyone in need of anything. As a child with an overactive imagination, I used to read to him and my grandmother the silly little stories I would write. I will never forget the day I told him *Essence* was being published and how it made me feel when he told me how proud he was of me for chasing after my dreams of being an author. He leaves behind a legacy of four children, eleven grandchildren, twenty-seven great grandchildren, and eight great-great grandchildren, who love him dearly and will never forgot all the love, kindness, and generosity he bestowed upon us and the world. He was truly a great man.

The soul should always stand ajar. Ready to welcome the ecstatic experience.
~Emily Dickinson

CHAPTER ONE

SATURDAY, *March 27, 2010*

I sat at the desk by our bedroom window and stared at my childhood home across the street. The huge Civil War era-built estate loomed across the vast lawn in the mid-morning sky. I watched the porch swing swaying slightly in the breeze on the wrap-around porch and the rockers moving gently back and forth. There was a light drizzle clinging to the chilly air. The house looked hollow and unfriendly. I imagined my dad in his pajama bottoms and sweatshirt sitting in his recliner watching some documentary on the history channel. My mother was most likely in her office dictating patient charts and my younger brother, Ethan, was probably scavenging through the kitchen looking for something to snack on. It was just another typical Saturday morning in the Timmons's household with one exception ... me.

"Good morning, I brought you some coffee." A female voice breached the silence from the doorway behind me.

"Thank you. When did you arrive?" I got up and hugged my new sister-in-law, Phoebe.

"This morning. My parents picked me up about an hour ago at the airport." She handed me the mug and sat down on the corner of mine and Jackson's bed. She lightly patted the empty space beside her. "Sit down."

I filled the vacancy next to her and took a long sip, letting the warm liquid course through me. "I didn't know you were visiting us this weekend."

"It was a last-minute decision, actually. After talking to my mother last evening, I decided to come visit for the weekend." She smiled softly. "Everyone is very worried about you."

"I'm fine." Phoebe raised a questioning eyebrow. "Seriously, I am." I rolled my eyes at the floor and took another sip of coffee.

"It doesn't sound like it to me."

"Did you bring Wally with you?" I inquired with vain hopes of changing the subject.

"No, I left him home with Carson. They can survive a weekend without me."

"Oh, I was hoping he was with you. I miss him." Wally was Phoebe's son, who was just shy of his second birthday. I simply adored him and had not had the opportunity to see him since Christmas.

"You will see him over Easter." Phoebe sighed in exasperation. "I understand that the relationship with your family has deteriorated since your wedding over Christmas break."

"Deteriorated? Unfortunately, there was no relationship to deteriorate, with my mother or Ethan for that matter. We stopped all communication since Thanksgiving. And things with my dad are improving somewhat. He did wave to me yesterday when Jackson and I were leaving for school and he was off to work." I tried to sound more optimistic than I felt.

"Jocelyn, I know the last six months have been challenging for you. I honestly cannot imagine how difficult it must be to learn about *EVE*, be a newlywed, and be estranged from your family and most of your friends all while trying to complete your senior year of high school with the highest possible scores."

I fumbled internally over a couple of words I wanted to say in protest, but instead remained silent. There was no use fighting anything she had said. It was all true and we both knew it.

"Jackson told our mother that you cried all the way to school and that many nights when you believe him to be asleep, you cry."

I continued to stare down at my coffee mug. "He had no right to reveal something so personal. And if he had, he should have confided in me, not his mother." I got up and walked out of the room, ending our conversation.

I pulled my jacket and scarf out of the foyer closet and walked out the front door without saying a word to anyone. I felt so angry that Jackson had betrayed my confidence. *How dare he confide in his mother about his concerns! I am his wife. He has no right to speak to anyone about me behind my back.*

I stuffed my hands in my pockets as my feet reached the sidewalk. I didn't even bother to look back to see if anyone noticed my departure. I didn't care if they did or didn't. I followed the sidewalk down to the sports park. Thankfully, it had cleared up and the sun was fighting to break through the clouds. It was still chilly out, but everywhere I looked there were signs that nature was awakening after her long winter sleep.

I crossed over the soccer fields where the grass was still saturated from the periodic snows and rains so typical of our springs in Chicago. I walked aimlessly around the path to the playground by the baseball diamonds. I sat down on one of the swings and kicked off the ground. I pumped harder with my arms and legs and soared into the sky, leaving all my troubles on the ground below me.

"I figured this was where you were headed," a voice startled me from behind. "You always loved the swings." My dad sat down on the swing next to mine. "I saw you leave a little while ago and thought I would take advantage of the chance to speak to you alone."

I dragged my feet on the wet mulch to bring myself to a halt beside him. "I'm glad you did." I didn't know what to say to him. We had not spoken in almost three months.

"I wasn't sure you would be too happy to speak with me." He swayed a bit in the swing. "I'm not proud of my recent behavior. I know this hasn't been easy on any of us, but I want us to be a family again. I hate knowing you're right across the street and feeling like I can't speak to you."

"Daddy, you can speak to me any time you want to. Nothing has changed between us. I love you!" I leaned over and wrapped my arms around his neck, spilling my tears all over his shoulder. "I've missed you so much," I cried.

"I missed you too." He hugged me back. "Are you doing all right?"

I sat back in my swing and brushed the tears off my cheeks with a smile. "I'm doing much better now."

"How is married life treating you?" he inquired.

"Wonderful. He makes me very happy."

"I'm glad. How about your friends? Ethan told me that they have been giving you a lot of grief about your marriage." My dad tilted his head a bit and wrinkled his eyebrows in concern.

"He would know. He has caused a lot of it," I told him.

"I figured as much. I have tried to talk with him."

"Oh, don't worry about it. He is not the worst of them. Jenna actually puts

Ethan to shame. She has been truly horrible, and Hilary is not much better. Thankfully, basketball season is finally over. I never thought I would be happy to see the end of it, but I was. I decided that I am not going to play softball this year because of them."

"Why would you let them take that away from you? You love softball, and this is your final year to play. Who cares what they think?"

"They ruined basketball season for me, and I really don't want them to ruin softball for me also." I ran my sneakers over the mulch under the swing.

"So, don't let them. I've never known you to give up a fight, especially over something you love." He half laughed. "You're married, aren't you?"

"Yes," I accidently snorted and sidestepped the jibe. "But Caitlyn has been wonderful. So, has Zak. Most people are except for the ones who were supposed to be my best friends."

"I'm sorry, but you still should not let them dictate what you do," he reasoned.

"I don't know what I am going to do. Try-outs are a couple weeks away and I haven't decided on anything yet."

The sun warmed up the gentle breeze that brushed the clouds lightly across the sky just enough to take the morning chill out of the air. We laughed and talked on the swings for the next couple of hours. It felt like a load of worries had been lifted off my shoulders. My heart soared like a child again. It was so easy and natural to fall back into being Daddy's little girl again.

By noon I was sorry I had skipped breakfast. My stomach was growling relentlessly. Finally, I couldn't ignore it any longer.

"Hey, Dad, would you like to join me for lunch? I know Jackson would be thrilled to see you and his sister is visiting from Boston for the weekend. I would love for you to finally meet her. She is so amazing."

"I would enjoy that." I took my father's hand and led him back down the pathway towards home.

"I do admit that it is a little strange having a married daughter who is still in high school," he confessed, swinging our hands like we did when I was little.

"I know," I admitted weakly.

"You should hear some of the names your mother has come up with for Jackson." He chuckled and rolled his eyes.

"Should I even ask?" I hated to imagine.

"Well, for the first month after you married him, she called him 'the home wrecker.' One of the nurses at the hospital told me … you remember her, right? Anyway, I said something to your mom that evening, which as you can imagine went over very well, but at least she doesn't call him that anymore." I laughed. I couldn't help it. He shoved me playfully. "Now she refers to him as 'Jocelyn's first husband.'"

"Cute. It sounds like her," I giggled despite myself.

"I know and I'm sorry, but you know how she can be." He squeezed my hand tenderly.

"I am familiar with her work," I muttered under my breath.

We strolled up the walkway of the house that I now considered my home. The landscaping was awakening with tiny little buds beginning to break free of the soil and reach for the sky. The topiary was a lush green and the crimson was practically dripping off the burning bushes. It stood in perfect accent with the red bricks of the Chandler estate, which was complemented by the forest green shutters and black iron fences. The year may have been 2010, but the estate was from yesteryear.

"Are you sure they won't mind me simply dropping in uninvited?" My dad paused on the porch. "We haven't actually spoken since you returned from Boston and the last time I was here I punched your husband." He chuckled despite his best efforts not to.

"Of course. They will be fine with it. They are not the kind of people who hold a grudge." I grasped his hand and opened the front door with my other hand.

"There you are! Thank goodness you are all right. I was …" Jackson came to a halt in the foyer when he noticed my dad standing behind me. "Sir." He extended a hand to my father.

"Hello, Jackson." My dad shook his hand and pulled him into a hug. "How have you been, son?"

"Good sir, very good. And you?" Jackson smiled but glanced at me with a questioning look in his eyes.

"I went for a walk to get some air and he found me on the swings."

"I was cleaning the garage and saw her leave. She looked upset, so I knew where she was headed." He placed his hand on my shoulder. "It's where she always hides when something is bothering her." My dad gave me a knowing smile.

"Well, please come on in." Jackson led the way into the family room.

My dad and I took a seat on the couch and my new husband sat down on the loveseat across from us. Jackson smiled uncomfortably. "Can I get you a cup of coffee?"

"Thank you." Dad nodded.

"Would you like some also, Jocelyn?" Jackson offered as he stood up.

"Please. Would you like some help?" He shook his head with a grin.

"I thought I heard voices in here." Emily's voice rang out as she and Phoebe entered the room.

"Oh, hello." My dad stood up and shook hands with Emily. "It's nice to see you again."

"You also." Emily looked elegant in her beige slacks, silk tank, and violet half jacket. "I would like you to meet my daughter, Phoebe." The two shook hands.

"It's nice to finally meet you. I've heard a lot of good things about you. I'm Jocelyn's father, Shane." My dad smiled at her.

"Thank you. It's nice to meet you as well." Phoebe smiled gracefully. I could only imagine what she must have been thinking about my dad after all that had transpired in the last several months.

Jackson excused himself while his mother and sister took his place on the loveseat. Phoebe had all the professionalism only an attorney could muster in an uncomfortable situation. She crossed her legs nonchalantly, looking anything but casual in her stylish cream-colored jeans, light brown calf boots, soft teal sweater, and gray plaid scarf. Her long, thick brown curls were swept and pinned loosely over one shoulder.

"I'm sorry it took me so long to come over," my dad said, leaning forward a little. "I know it has been entirely past due."

"I understand this whole situation has been difficult on your family and I apologize for that," Emily said politely.

"I realize my wife and son have made things worse for the two of them and for that I am sorry. As for me," he took my hand and smiled, "my feelings were hurt because ever since you were born, I have dreaded the day I'd have to give you up. But I always thought I would be the one to give you away."

"I am sorry, Daddy. It all happened so fast and I wanted you there. You were the only thing missing." I leaned over and hugged him tightly.

Jackson reentered the room with his father, Robert, carrying a tray with a kettle of freshly brewed coffee, saucers and cups, sugar and cream, and a plate of finger sandwiches. "Is everything all right?" he asked, setting the tray on the coffee table.

"Yes, everything is wonderful." I released my father and wiped a few stray tears off my cheeks.

* * *

Jackson was propped up on some pillows reviewing his notes for a government test we had on Monday when I climbed into bed beside him. I took the papers out of his hand and tossed them on the floor. "I will have none of that in my bed." I crawled onto his lap and straddled him, leaning down and kissing him playfully.

"You seem to be feeling much better," he said with a sly grin and wrapped his arms around my waist.

"I am. It felt so good to talk with my dad again." I kissed him again.

"It does me good to see you acting like your old self. I am glad you two finally managed to talk things out." He reached over and turned out the lights. I giggled as he kissed me intensely and rolled over on top of me.

CHAPTER TWO

WEDNESDAY, April 2, 1879

The hours and days moved slowly by. I never thought I would miss being in school so much and spending time with my friends. I missed the trivial conversations shared during our lunch breaks and even studying and doing assignments. The days and weeks started blending together and time became meaningless. I longed for something … anything that would keep my mind occupied.

Jackson was consumed with work. Typically, he stayed late at the office and then once he came home, he would bury himself in his study and work until long after I retired for the evening. He said he was paying his dues and that he didn't want anyone to think the only reason he was hired in his father's office was because he was the boss's son. He said he had to prove he was good enough to be employed there.

Married life wasn't turning out to be everything I had thought it would be.

CHAPTER THREE

WEDNESDAY, *March 31, 2010*

Jackson and I arrived at school shortly before the first bell rang. We were both excited about the week being half over with and spring break only a couple days away. It had been a difficult semester thus far for both of us. We switched out our books at our lockers, kissed quickly, and hurried off to our first class of the day.

By noon, Caitlyn and I sat down at the table beside Zak and Jackson. The cafeteria was held to a medium roar. At the other end of our table sat Jenna, Hilary, Cody, Kyle, Ethan, Liang, Corbin, and Haley. They did their best to ignore us as we took our seats, but I could see Jenna watching everything we did. She glared at us with a disgusted expression on her face. It had been months since she and Hillary stormed out of my room when Jackson and I had returned from Christmas break, and I couldn't understand why she wouldn't simply leave me alone.

Zak and Jackson were discussing March Madness and arguing over which team was going to win the championship game.

"Seriously? This is what you idiots are talking about?" Caitlyn teased, nudging Zak playfully. "All you have talked about for the last two weeks is college basketball. Ahhh … I don't care anymore!" She threw her hands up for emphasis and we all laughed at her.

"Sorry, babe, you knew this was my illness when we started dating. Don't expect me to change, because it'll never happen." Zak gave her a cocky grin.

"I know." Caitlyn rolled her eyes in my direction. "Why you would voluntarily want to live with one of these," she nodded in Zak's direction with a grin, "is beyond me."

I put my head over on Jackson's shoulder. "He's kinda cute so I think I'll keep him," I laughed.

"Ah, thanks, sweetheart. I appreciate that." Jackson leaned over and gave me a quick peck on the cheek.

With five minutes left in our lunch period, Caitlyn and I excused ourselves to run to the lady's room. We were laughing and acting silly as we walked into the restroom closest to the cafeteria. Unfortunately, some routines are harder to break than some friendships and we bumped into Hilary and Jenna ogling their reflections in the mirrors.

"Oh look, Hilary, it's Mrs. Chandler," Jenna mocked.

"Knock it off, Jenna, it's gotten old." I brushed past her to the mirror at the end of the row.

"Where the hell do you get off telling me what to do?" Jenna spun to confront me.

Caitlyn walked up behind Jenna and lightly tapped her on the shoulder. "Hey, Jenna." Jenna turned her head to look at Caitlyn. "Do you recall what Jocelyn did to Taylor? That's gonna be nothing compared to what I'm going to do to you if you don't stop being a bitch and talking about Jocelyn behind her back." Then Caitlyn flashed her best fake smile.

"Why are you fighting her battles?" Hilary asked from her stance in front of the stalls.

"Why are you fighting hers?" Caitlyn fired back at Hilary.

"Look, Jenna, if you have something to say to me say it, because I am tired of this." I stepped closer to her.

"All right fine, I will." Jenna put her hands on her hips and tried to look superior. "I can't believe you would be so incredibly stupid as to get married while you're still in high school. Not to mention that you are so selfish you couldn't care less that your elopement has torn your entire family apart. Your mother was right, you're gonna get knocked up and drop out of college. And I'm gonna laugh when he leaves your ass and you end up on welfare." Jenna practically shouted in my face.

"Good Lord, Jenna. You do realize you don't need a husband to get knocked up in college. It happens to girls all the time, even high school girls. So be more concerned about your own life and keep the hell out of mine. Only, I can't help but notice how sad your life must be for you to still be so consumed with mine. I truly feel sorry for you," I said with pity. "Come on, Caitlyn, we have better company we can be in than these pathetic souls." I smirked once at Hilary before we exited the bathroom and busted out laughing.

* * *

I told Jackson about my altercation with Jenna on our way home. He got a kick out of my response to her.

"I mean if she does not want to be friends any longer, that is fine, but do not harass me every time you bump into me just to show off to your friends," I ranted.

"Jocelyn … honey, let it go. If she wants to behave like a child, let her. Do not stoop to her level and play her petty games."

"I know, you're right. She just aggravates the hell out of me. I wish she would just leave me alone." I sighed audibly and looked out the window.

"Have you given any thought about where you would like to go for spring break?" He smiled attempting to change the subject.

"Where would you like to go?"

"Saint Thomas. They have the most beautiful white sand beaches and the best fresh fruit margaritas of any place I have ever been." He grinned over at me before pulling into our driveway.

"Can we go anywhere?" I asked, opening my door and climbing out of his CRV.

"Sure." Jackson grabbed his backpack and followed me up the walkway.

I paused on the porch for a moment and turned to look at my husband. "Well, I was thinking … my dad mentioned last Saturday that Sidney was coming home for spring break next week. She should be here Friday evening. He said she was having a rough semester and could really use the break. I would put money on it that her night terrors are getting worse and more vivid. She is probably close to a nervous breakdown if she is experiencing anything remotely close to what I was. What if we take her down to Uncle Nicholas's for a few days and explain *EVE* to her? Then we can go to Florida for a couple days or something. What do you think?"

"Do you really think she is ready to be told?" Jackson opened the front door for us.

I laid my backpack in the foyer beside the stairs with his and followed him into the kitchen. "Yes, I would imagine so. It has been months since her night terrors began. I remember very well the mental and physical toll it took on me. I can't imagine trying to deal with all that and go to college at the same time as you both did. I could not even make it to my classes *there*."

Jackson opened the refrigerator and grabbed a of couple oranges and tossed me one. He set his down on the island and took a seat on one of the barstools. "It was rough, I can tell you that. But how are you going to convince her to go with us? It's not like you can openly tell her we are going to see your uncle."

I sat down on the stool beside his and began peeling my orange. "Well, that is why I think we should also go somewhere warm for a couple days. That could be our cover story and then once we are on the road, I can say we are going to stop by his place along the way. Knowing Sidney, this is going to be extremely difficult on her. She is going to take this way worse than I did."

Jackson peeled his orange and bit into a wedge. "I do not see how that is possible." He stifled a laugh before reaching for a banana.

"At least I handled it better *here* than I did *there*." I stole the banana from him playfully. It was hard to argue with him when he was right.

He was about to respond when Emily entered the kitchen. "Good afternoon, kids, how were your classes today?"

"Fabulous, as always." Jackson slid off his stool. "I guess we had better get started on our homework." He smiled over at his mother. "The joys of high school," he muttered on his way out of the kitchen.

"Yes, dear," I giggled and followed him up to our room.

CHAPTER FOUR

*F*RIDAY, *April 4, 1879*

I awoke to silence and unease. I had become accustomed to Cora waking me up around seven every morning, but today she was strangely absent. Slightly confused, I got up and put on my robe. I looked up at the clock on the mantel, it was shortly after eight. I washed my face, brushed my teeth, and sat down at the vanity to brush my hair when there was a soft knock on my bedroom door.

"Cuse' me, mam, may I come in?" Our cook Tamesha's voice echoed through the door.

"Yes, of course," I called back, turning towards the door.

Tamesha walked in hesitantly, twisting her apron over and over in her hands. She looked as if she were about to burst into tears. "Mam, I sorry to bother ya this mornin' but I think ya better come downstairs."

My stomach immediately tightened into a knot. I got up quickly and approached her, placing my hands over hers to stop her fiddling with her apron. "Tamesha, what is wrong?"

"Mam, letz get ya dressed first," she offered, scurrying over to my armoire and flipping through my gowns.

I kept quiet simply because her nervousness was making me more uneasy. Terrible things were running through my mind while she pulled on the strings of my corset and got me into my gown. I had no idea what was going on and why it was Tamesha in my room this morning and not Cora.

Although I did not look exactly like my normal self, I headed downstairs to investigate what was going on under my roof that I did not know about. As my foot hit the bottom step, our front door opened and Jackson and Davonte, who was our houseman and Tamesha's husband, walked in. I saw Jackson's eyes scan over me then turn towards Tamesha, who shook her head quietly.

I paused in my steps, looking between the three of them. I hated being excluded from whatever everyone else was in on. "What is going on, Jackson? I demand to know."

"My dear, Davonte picked me up at the office this morning. Your father asked him to." His face looked forlorn.

"Why?"

"Come with me," Jackson said quietly and took my hand, leading me out onto our front porch. The sun was bouncing brightly off the early morning dew. I felt nauseated as I watched Jackson struggle to find the right words to say.

"Jackson, you are scaring me. What is going on?" I searched his tormented face for clues.

He placed his arms gently around my waist. "Sweetheart, I wanted to be the one to tell you." He took a deep breath and looked like he wanted to be anywhere else other than right here at this moment. "Mimi passed away last night in her sleep." My body went numb and a scream from deep inside my soul escaped without my knowledge. I felt my knees go out from under me as Jackson's grip on my waist kept me from collapsing on the porch.

"No! No! No ..." Tears rushed from my eyes as I fought to tear myself away from Jackson. All I wanted to do was run to my parents' home next door.

"Jocelyn ..." Jackson struggled to keep a hold of me, but I pushed him away. I rushed down the steps completely forgetting the heavy gown that enveloped me. I lifted the front of my skirt and ran as fast as I could across the vast lawns, barely aware of Emily and Robert climbing out of their carriage at the foot of my parents' front steps. Nor did I turn when they called out my name.

I threw open the door and stopped dead in my steps. The house held an eerie tone of audible sadness. The grandfather clock had stopped and the mirror in the foyer was covered with a black cloth. Jackson came to a halt beside me, putting his arm around my waist, while his parents stood slightly behind us.

"Mother ... Mother ..." I sobbed.

"Oh, Jocelyn ..." My mother entered the foyer from the kitchen with open arms that I immediately rushed into. My father was right behind her, wrapping both of us in the safety of his strong arms.

"Please, tell me it isn't true. She can't be gone. She can't ..." I cried like a small child in their arms.

"I am so sorry, my love." My mother stroked my hair with tears rolling down her cheeks. "You know she loved you so."

"I loved her so much. I cannot imagine this house without her." I wept uncontrollably.

"She went peacefully in her sleep, dear." My father wiped tears off his own cheeks.

I was unaware of the amount of time the six of us stood there silently crying for the loss of the woman who had been the beating heart of my childhood home. I didn't care. All I could think about was the sound of her cheerful voice filling my mornings. Her reflection in my vanity mirror every day of my life until I was married. Her skillful hands working magic on my hair. Her pulling my corset strings telling me to "suck it in, child." Her loving arms holding me when my world was falling apart, and all those nights she sat in the rocker beside my bed when I was ill or had night terrors. I would never again feel the solace and safety of her arms.

My mind refused to let reality sink in, it was too unimaginable. She could not be gone.

"Come." Emily's soft voice reached into the cocoon that engulfed me. I felt her tender touch guide us into the parlor. I sat down on the lounge with my mother beside me and Jackson and my father kneeling in front of us.

Jackson took out his handkerchief and wiped the tears from my face. I looked over at my father with pleading eyes. "Why? How did this happen?"

"I believe her heart simply gave out while she was sleeping," Father replied.

"How is Cora? Eddie? Where are they?" I looked between my parents.

"Cora is upstairs in their living quarters with Eddie. Sarah went over to your house at dawn and brought her to Eddie. He is torn up. I have never seen him in such a state. She is doing her best to take care of him. I was up there right before you arrived bringing them some tea and toast. Neither of them is doing well," Mother said.

"I must go to them," I told them.

I got up in a fog, unable to feel my body, and wandered up the two flights of stairs to Eddie and Mimi's living quarters. Tears were blurring my vision as I traced my hand lightly over the sturdy walls of the home I loved so dearly. I knocked softly on the door and waited for a response.

"Come in,'" Cora's voice cracked in response.

I hesitated a moment, my heart breaking in two for the woman I dearly loved as my mother, my closest confidante, and strongest ally. The blinds were closed. The few candles that adorned the room offered a soft warm glow. Cora and Eddie were sitting in the rockers with the hearth between them. Mimi was lying still on the bed she and Eddie had occupied throughout their lives together. The father and daughter sat there solemnly sheathed in grief.

I slowly approached the two of them and knelt in front of Cora, wrapping my arms around her. "I am so very sorry." I sobbed along with the woman I had grown up with. Cora was about the closest person I had to a sister except for probably Olivia.

"I can't believe she's gone," Cora cried on my shoulder.

Cora and I cried and held each other until we were both exhausted. Eddie sat silently rocking in the chair with the glow from the hearth beside him shining off his tears as he stared at Mimi as if he was expecting her to awaken at any moment. He had never been a man of many words but was always a warm soul. His eyes were filled with disbelief and pain. I had no words of comfort to offer him. His loss was unimaginable.

Finally, I pulled myself together as best I could. I found the strength to stand on my own two feet and the courage to face Mimi. She was lying peacefully with her arms across her chest. Her eyes were closed and someone, most likely Eddie, had placed two coins over her eyes. I choked back the scream welling up in my chest. She appeared to be sleeping. I kept waiting for her chest to rise and fall. I reached out and placed my hand over hers … those hands that had held me so often with tender love, brushed my hair, helped me dress, took care of me in every possible way for eighteen years, were cold and stiff.

I hastily brushed the tears off my face with Jackson's handkerchief and leaned over and kissed Mimi on the cheek. "Thank you so much for taking such good care of me, for always being there for me, for your wisdom, your sense of humor, and for loving me. I am going to miss you every day for the rest of my life. I love you, Mimi," I whispered in her ear.

I turned around and hugged Eddie. This silent tower of a man turned into a frail shell and fell apart in my arms. He hugged me so tightly and let out a sob that had been brewing deep down in his soul. I held him while he cried and mumbled incoherently against my shoulder. I struggled to hold myself together, as I had never in all my life seen Eddie in such as state.

By midafternoon I wandered back downstairs. There were hushed whispers in every corner. My brothers and their families had joined our parents in the parlor. Jackson met me at the bottom of the stairs with open arms. I reached out to him and wrapped myself in the warmth of his muscular arms.

"How are you holding up?" he asked in a soft voice.

"Not well," I whispered into his chest.

"You need to eat something. Tamesha said you did not eat breakfast." Jackson leaned over and kissed my forehead. "You need to keep your strength."

"I am not hungry."

"At least have some tea. Sarah is not doing well so Tamesha is in the kitchen cooking up something. I am not sure what." He took my hand and led me into the parlor with everyone else. I was immediately surrounded by my brothers. Only William was absent, although I did overhear Olivia tell Rachel that she had called him earlier to tell him what had happened.

My brothers James and Jonathon were both in tears while Patrick II was calm and stoic as per his personality. He hugged me briefly then rejoined his wife, Katherine. She was the only one in attendance who did not seem bothered by Mimi's death. It made me hate her even more as I glared at her sitting in the rocker examining her nails. I felt like walking over there and smacking her smug face. I knew it would make me feel better.

The afternoon floated into evening. The sun drew behind the trees and rested beneath the houses. Long shadows fell over the halls, yet no one moved to light the oil lamps until it was difficult to see across the parlor. Hushed tones were heard from every corner. It felt wrong, disrespectful to speak aloud. Tamesha and Bertina had filled the dining room table with various dishes and desserts. Family members drifted by throughout the day picking up little things here and there, yet no one ate much of anything.

By late evening everyone was drained. Tears had been shed steadily by almost everyone, leaving the household covered in a mournful cloud. I leaned heavily on my brothers and Jackson throughout the evening hours. I almost collapsed before ever making it back over to my own house at the end of the exhausting day.

As I finally crawled into bed and curled up in a ball all I could think about was never seeing Mimi's smile again or hearing her motherly voice or boisterous laughter. I felt as if a huge hole had been torn straight through my heart. Every memory I had from my childhood had her in it. Mimi was always my voice of reason when I was too stubborn to admit I was wrong. She dried my tears, scolded me for the mistakes I made, and praised me for my accomplish-ments. She knew my darkest secrets and never told a soul.

I had considered many times discussing *EVE* with her. I couldn't help but wonder what she would have thought of it. Or if she had ever heard of it. She was so wise and had always seemed to know about mysterious things from her mother and grandmother. Mimi had always been very superstitious and had a weird way of just knowing. It always made me want to confide in her, but I never could bring myself to do it. I was still grasping it all myself and never knew how to begin explaining it to her in a way that wouldn't make me sound mad. Now I wished I had figured out a way because it honestly wouldn't have surprised me if she'd known something about it.

Jackson crawled into bed beside me and wrapped me in his arms. I rolled over and rested my head on his bare chest. The warmth of his skin was sooth-ing, as was the strong, steady rhythm of his heartbeat. He leaned down and kissed the top of my head but remained silent. Tonight, there were no words that would bring me any peace.

CHAPTER FIVE

Friday, April 2, 2010

Sidney was already at our parents' home by the time Jackson and I pulled in the driveway after school. Her little lime green bug was parked in the spot where my car used to sit a short time ago. Now it sat mainly idle in the driveway of my new home at the Chandler Estate, which had been aptly titled Cobblestone Trail when it was built.

"Sidney's here." I nodded towards her bug from our front porch.

"Have you spoken with her yet?" Jackson asked, unlocking the front door.

"No need." I tugged the sleeve of his jacket. "Here she comes."

My older sister was indeed on her way across the front yard of our parents' home and headed in our direction. She smiled big and waved at the two of us.

"Jocelyn ..." She picked up her pace. "Hey, Jocelyn ... Jackson, wait a moment."

We stood frozen in our steps. I wasn't sure what type of reception to expect from her. I had not spoken to her since Thanksgiving and she had not contacted me when she'd learned Jackson and I had gotten married over Christmas vacation.

"Oh my God, Jocelyn! I can't believe you're married." She jogged up on our porch and threw her arms around me. "I'm so happy for you!"

"Thank you, Sid." I laughed, completely stunned by her reaction and wrapped my arms around her.

She released me and grabbed ahold of Jackson. "That goes for you too, little brother." She reached up and kissed him on the cheek. I giggled at the shocked expression on Jackson's face, not to mention the fact that he was two years older than her.

"Please, come on inside. I want to hear all about school." I pulled her off my husband and shoved her in the front door.

Sidney and I took a seat on the couch in the family room. Jackson excused himself to get us some refreshments. My sister smiled pleasantly until my new husband was out of the room, then she scooted closer to me and placed her nervous hands over mine. "So, tell me the truth, what in the world possessed you to run off and get married during your senior year? Mom had a conniption fit when Dad told her what you did. She called me up screaming to high heaven about you."

"I can only imagine," I muttered.

"So why did you do it? Are you pregnant?"

"No," I laughed. "Of course not. Do you remember what the house was like when you came home over Thanksgiving?" She nodded. "Well, it got a lot worse. Ethan and I were fighting all the time and Mom acted like I did not even exist. The tension was so thick I couldn't breathe. It was like walking around on eggshells all the time. My nerves were shot, and I couldn't take it any longer. So, Jackson and I decided to move the wedding up six months." I leaned in a little closer and whispered, "There is a little more to it than just that, but I will tell you all about that later."

Sidney's eyes got huge. "You *are* pregnant?"

"Sidney!" *Always the first assumption.*

"Are you?"

"No, of course not. I am not that stupid."

Jackson reentered the room with glasses of iced tea, chips, and cheese dip and set the tray down on the coffee table. "So how have you been, Sidney?"

"I'm doing well. Glad spring break is finally here. This semester has been rough. My classes are kicking my butt." She grinned to cover her exhaustion that was now evident through the dark circles under her eyes.

"And you think coming home is going to give you the relaxing break you need?" I raised an eyebrow with sarcasm.

"Probably not, but I had to get away from campus and couldn't afford to migrate to Florida." She flopped back against the couch.

Jackson looked over at me with a look that told me this was the perfect time to suggest a trip to her. I nodded slightly back before turning towards Sidney. "Where is Landon? Did he come home with you?"

"No, he and some of his fraternity brothers left yesterday for Fort Lauderdale. None of them were bringing their girlfriends so I decided I really didn't want to be the only one. Besides, I really couldn't afford it anyway."

"Well, how would you like to go on a trip with us?"

Sidney glanced between the two of us as if we'd lost our minds. "Where?"

I locked eyes with Jackson. We had not decided on a destination yet. So, I was a little surprised when Jackson spoke up. "We were thinking of heading down to New Orleans for a few days. Jocelyn has never seen the French Quarter before and I thought it would be fun to get away from all the stress around here. You are more than welcome to come with us. Our treat."

"Are you serious?" She looked at me with hesitation.

"Come with us, it will be fun." I grabbed her hands enthusiastically.

"How can you afford something like that?" I could hear the skepticism in her voice.

"Did your sister not tell you that she married a trust fund baby?" Jackson laughed.

I did my best to keep my face placid. How could I possibly have told her when I did not know myself? I knew that the Chandlers were financially stable, but I had no clue as to how stable they were. Money was just something Jackson and I had never discussed.

"No, she failed to mention it. But anyway, I don't want to intrude on your little get-a-way. You two have been married such a short while and would have more fun if I wasn't tagging along with you."

"Shut up, you are coming with us. I insist," I chimed in.

"Well … I could use the distraction. It's been a rough semester. Are you sure you don't mind?" Sidney inquired.

"Of course not. Don't be silly," I said playfully.

"All right, when do we leave?"

"Tomorrow morning. Can you be ready to leave about five?" Jackson piped up.

"Sure, I haven't unpacked anything yet so I'm ready whenever you are."

"Wonderful, just make sure you are here on time," I added, knowing how she was notorious for being late to everything.

"I will." She stuck out her tongue at me.

* * *

Later that evening, I scrambled around trying to make sure I didn't forget to pack anything. I put Uncle Monte's journal in a small leather satchel along with the ancient photo album documenting mine and Jackson's life together in the latter half of the nineteenth century. My brain was frantic. I wished I had something … a photo or letter or something that would provide Sidney with tangible memorabilia that *she* was a part of *EVE*.

I sat down on the corner of our bed trying to figure out how I was even going to broach the subject with my sister. *This would be so much easier if we were close and shared things with each other. But we never have been.*

"How am I going to do this?" I muttered aloud to myself.

"Very carefully." Emily stood quietly in our doorway in her evening robe. "I am sorry, I did not mean to intrude. I was coming up here to see if you needed any help."

"Thank you, but I believe I have everything packed. I just cannot figure out how I am going to raise the subject of *EVE* with Sidney. If she is experiencing anything remotely close to what I can recall going through *there*, then this is going to be extremely difficult," I complained.

Emily sat down on the bed beside me. "Try not to worry so much. I know you will find the right words when the time comes." Her voice was soft and comforting.

"I hope you are right." I sighed and looked down at my hands. "Mimi passed away."

"Yes, I was not sure if you knew, so I did not want to bring it up." Emily placed her hands gently over mine. "How much are you remembering?"

"Almost all of it." The vivid memories stabbed me in the heart and brought tears to my eyes. "I kept pushing it out of my mind all day, but it has not been easy. I loved her very much."

"I know you did. We all did. It is difficult to imagine her not around. She was such a loving woman, and boy, could she keep your brothers in line." Emily chuckled. "I have never known anyone like her."

"Neither have I. I will miss you so much." I forced myself to smile.

"I know you will, my dear. And as difficult as it may be, you must force yourself to focus on Sidney for the time being. She is going to need you now

24

more than ever before. Remember what it felt like when you were experiencing the same symptoms?" My mother-in-law looked up at me with the kindest eyes. I nodded empathetically. "Try to get some sleep." She patted my hand. "I will see you in the morning."

I crawled into bed alone. Jackson was downstairs in the study going over travel arrangements with his father. I had no idea what time he would make it to bed, but my head hurt and all I wanted to do was sleep. My mind was a whirlwind of scenarios. None of which were good. I couldn't decide if I should wait until we got down to Uncle Nicholas's house and let him explain *EVE* to her or if I should attempt to start the conversation with her once we were well on our way. I decided the only thing I could do was play it by ear and see how it went. Either way, I knew this spring break was going to be anything but relaxing.

CHAPTER SIX

SATURDAY, *April 5, 1879*

Jackson stayed close by me trying to block the cold gusts of wind that tore around us as we stood on the outskirts of our family plot. It was gray and misting with a low fog that hovered over the ground. My family huddled closely around the rosewood coffin that held our beloved Mimi. Cora and Eddie clung to each other at the head of our gathering.

William stood beside me, holding his young wife tightly. Our parents, siblings, and family members stood as a large black cloud without a dry eye amongst us. It was clear how dearly loved Mimi was by all.

Everyone gathered at our home afterwards where Tamesha and Bertina had fixed another round of various foods to feed our depression. I slumped on the loveseat in the parlor next to Jackson until midafternoon. Finally, I had reached the end of my tears and could no longer stand to have everyone around me. I waited until Jackson excused himself to fix a plate and escaped out the back door.

My house was empty, cold, and dreary. I ran upstairs to my room and threw myself across my bed. The embers were faded to almost nothing in the hearth, and I did not know how to properly stoke the fire to bring it back to life. I didn't bother to even light an oil lamp. I didn't want to invite any light into my somber existence.

I pulled the duvet up over my head, curled up in a ball, and let the tears flow freely. My heart physically ached. The grief was overwhelming. I wrapped my arms around myself and fought the urge to scream out my despair. The corner foundation of my existence was gone and a part of me with her.

CHAPTER SEVEN

Saturday, *April 3, 2010*

We crossed the state line into Indiana by five thirty in the morning. Jackson was wide awake and talking a mile a minute about all the places he wanted us to visit while in New Orleans. Sidney was sprawled out across the back seat curled up with a pillow and a blanket, happily asleep. I was doing my best to stay awake and comment generally on Jackson's enthusiasm. I was afraid if I fell asleep he would have a hard time staying awake himself. I envied Sidney sleeping soundly in the back seat. We chatted about various superficial topics, trying to avoid the possibility of Sidney overhearing anything we hadn't been prepared for her to hear in case she was only pretending to be asleep behind us.

Sidney sat up just as we were passing through downtown Indianapolis. The sky was bright and cloudless, and the spring air drifted in through the cracked windows.

"Where are we?" She leaned in between the front seats.

"Indianapolis," Jackson answered.

"Is that all? I was hoping we were farther along than that." She sighed deeply.

"Sorry." He glanced over at me. He was not used to Sidney's outspoken ways.

As we made our way from Interstate 65 to 70 in downtown Indy, I marveled over the jumble of highway intersections. It was a concrete mess with high-rises jutting through the twists and turns about the skyline. I watched the signs and held my breath as Jackson navigated our way over several lanes of Saturday traffic.

"This is ridiculous," I noted as we switched lanes again.

"It's called the Spaghetti Bowl. I would hate to have to drive this during rush hour traffic." He tried to laugh it off. "Whoever designed this part of the city must have been on drugs."

As we followed Interstate 70 out of the city I began to relax again. I knew my time was drawing short as we were probably forty minutes from Uncle Nicholas's house. I had emailed him the night before and told him about our arrival. We had consulted with him frequently regarding the situation with Sidney and her continuous night terrors. He was extremely supportive and had agreed to help us in any way possible when we explained the gift of *EVE*.

We took the Bloomington exit and headed towards the campus of Indiana University. We would have to pass through it on our way to his house. The campus was just as enticing as I remembered it being.

"Are we stopping to eat?" Sidney put the book she had been reading aside and looked out the window. "Where are we?"

"IU," I said and turned towards her. "Do you remember our Uncle Nicholas, Dad's younger brother?"

"Vaguely, why?" Her eyes narrowed a bit.

"He is a professor at IU and lives around here."

"So ..." Sidney hesitated.

"I told him we would stop by," I said as casually as possible.

"I thought he and Dad were no longer on speaking terms. When have you talked to him?" Curiosity mixed with surprise was clearly written across her face.

"They aren't, but I got in touch with him shortly before Christmas. He has been a wonderful help to me in a lot of ways and I wanted you to meet him," I explained.

"Okay, I'm confused." She leaned forward anxiously as Jackson pulled up in front of the old Victorian home.

"You'll see," I said and opened the car door.

Uncle Nicholas's house was even more beautiful than I remembered. The flowerbeds were beginning to awaken, and little buds were peeking up towards the sky. The leaf buds on the trees were prominent on every branch that swayed slightly in the gentle breeze. The house itself stood as a beautiful beacon of days gone by.

Uncle Nicholas stepped out on the porch before we even shut the car doors.

"Good morning, you must have made good time." He walked out to greet us. It was barely nine o'clock.

"Yes, traffic was not too bad." Jackson approached my uncle and shook his hand. "At least until we hit Indianapolis."

I ran up and gave Uncle Nicholas a big hug. "It's so good to see you again. I've missed you."

"I missed you too, dear." He squeezed me tightly.

Sidney hung back clearly confused about my relationship with our uncle. I had not mentioned to her that I had seen him. I probably should have told her more before we arrived.

"Uncle Nicholas, I would like to introduce you to my sister, Sidney." I turned, gesturing towards my sister standing alone and looking awkward. "Sidney, this is our Uncle Nicholas." I motioned for her to come forward.

Her step was steady but slow. She looked as if she was reluctant to shake his hand, but she finally did. "Hello," she said in almost a whisper.

"How do you do?" He shook her hand with a gentleman's style. "It is a pleasure to see you again."

"Yes, it's been a long time." The tension began to ease from her face. I suppose she had decided that perhaps he was not as crazy as our father had always told us he was.

"Please, come on in." He waved towards his home. "I have just made something to eat. I hope you are all hungry."

"Famished," Jackson replied and followed him into the house.

Sidney hesitated a moment and grabbed my arm. "See you again? When was the last time you saw him?"

"I saw him a couple times in December," I said casually and hurried into the house before she could question me any further.

The men were already gathered in the kitchen putting lunch on the table when I joined them. There was fresh fruit, a huge bowl of spinach salad with a light rosemary dressing, cottage cheese, homemade bread, and real butter. Healthy and organic. Everything screamed Uncle Nicholas. I smiled and helped him set the table and poured everyone a tall glass of green tea with fresh lemon wedges.

We made small talk about school and how my parents were reacting to our marriage, very superficial nonsense. Finally, Uncle Nicholas looked pointedly at Sidney and asked the question I wasn't prepared for quite so soon in our visit.

"Sidney, your sister told me you have been having difficulty sleeping," he pointedly stated.

She played with her bread and stared a hole straight through me. My palms began to sweat, and I failed to meet her eye. "Oh, it's nothing. Just stress from school." She did her best to blow off his inquiry.

"What are you seeing in these dreams that is frightening you so much that you are waking up in a state of terror?" He pushed her a little.

"Nothing really. My imagination is working overtime." I heard her mimic the same words I had used in another time to excuse my behavior away.

"Hmmmm ... I suppose you are feeling terrified because you feel a strong kinship with the people who have reoccurring roles in your dreams. The places and people begin to overlap and feel more like a memory than a dream with you in the starring role." Sidney's eyes got wide, but she remained silent. "Are you screaming because when the light begins to fade, you know there is nothing you can do to hold onto that world? Rather you are thrust back into this one."

Sidney's face went pale and her hands began to shake almost violently. "How do you know that?" she barely whispered. "You cannot possibly know that." Even seated beside her I hardly heard her words. Silent tears escaped from the corner of her eyes. "I don't understand ..."

"Sidney," our uncle began in a soft, comforting voice as he placed his hand over hers. "Everyone at this table has experienced the same thing you are going through. The fear, the strong desire for your dreams to be real, the pull towards the people there and the relationship you have with them."

"But how ... I don't understand," she interrupted, despair lacing her voice.

"My dear, do you know why your sister and her husband got in touch with me again?" he asked in a fatherly voice. Sidney stared at him speechless.

"Sidney, you have a very special gift, just like your sister, Jackson, his entire family, and a few other members of your own family." He smiled lovingly at her.

She stared blankly at the three of us. She appeared to be somewhere between hysterics and sheer terror. My heart went out to her. I knew exactly what she was experiencing. I reached over and took her shaking hand in mine.

"It is okay, Sidney. Trust me, I know how you feel. Please just listen to him and let him explain everything to you," I tried to assure her.

"Jocelyn ..." She looked at me with big tears falling down her cheeks. "What's wrong with me?" she pleaded.

"Nothing ... there is nothing wrong with you. I promise. Please listen to him, he can help you," I begged.

Sidney slowly looked over at Uncle Nicholas. She was pasty, sweaty, and her face was streaked with silent tears. Her expression was that of a frightened young child. I felt horrible. This was the part I was dreading.

Uncle Nicholas stood up and walked over to Sidney holding out his hand. "Sidney, please come with me. The family room is more comfortable than the kitchen table." He took her hand and nodded towards Jackson and me to join them.

"I know this is very difficult for you to believe and a lot of what I have to say will sound a tad on the insane side, but you have to trust me and keep an open mind." Uncle Nicholas sat down in his recliner.

"I don't think anything can surprise me at this point. I feel like I'm losing my mind. I don't know what is real and what is not anymore. I am having so much trouble in school because I can't concentrate on anything." She sank back in the couch.

"I am going to get our things from the car," Jackson said to the room and disappeared out the front door. I knew he was going after the journals and the photo albums. I nodded at him and sat down on the couch beside my distraught sister.

"I know exactly how you feel. I went through the same thing last fall. I know you are going to find this hard to believe but you and I and possibly Ethan as well, inherited a very special gift from Uncle Nicholas and Uncle Monte ... do you remember him?"

"A little bit. He died a long time ago." She looked over at our uncle. "I believe that was when you and our dad had a fight ... at his funeral. Am I right?"

"Yes, unfortunately I haven't spoken to Shane since. I tried to explain to him the truth behind our brother's death and he found it difficult to believe to say the least." Nicholas let out a hollow chuckle.

"Truth about what?" Sidney implored.

Jackson returned with my leather satchel in hand and sat down beside me. "Sidney, do you *want* to know why your sister and I got married so quickly?" He smiled and scooted closer to me.

"No," she squeaked.

The three of us spent the entire afternoon explaining to Sidney everything we knew about *EVE*, the truth about Uncle Monte's death, and my relationship with Jackson. The journals were a little much for her to handle, but she really came unglued when Jackson showed her the photo album of us in the nineteenth century. She freaked out and fell apart in front of us. Visual proof was a little more than she was ready for.

All in all, Sidney handled everything better than I did … at least better than I did in 1878. When all was said and done, she sat there calmly and absorbed it all. The three of us remained silent while her brain processed the life changing information. She held our album on her lap and lightly traced her fingers over the photo of Jackson and me at the gazebo with our three children.

"This is unbelievable. This is really you guys … and you have beautiful children. What year is this?" She turned her eyes to us and asked with a voice that was barely a whisper.

"I believe it is sometime in the 1890s. Jackson and I waited until I finished graduate school *here* before we had our children," I explained.

"Why is my time different than yours?" She looked between the three of us with big frightened eyes. "I don't know anyone or recognize anyone from our family during that time period."

"Do you know what year it is in your alternate time?" Jackson asked.

"I know I live in a little town called Braintree Highlands. It's in Massachusetts. I know it is not too far from Boston. I know it's shortly after the Revolutionary War and I live with my grandmother. Her name is Marissa Timmons and she …"

"Wait a minute." Our uncle jumped from his recliner. "Did you say Marissa Timmons?"

"Yes … why?" Sidney was shocked by his excitement.

"Marissa Timmons—she has blond hair, brown eyes, petite woman, very sharp. Am I right?" Uncle Nicholas rambled.

"Yes," Sidney replied as the three of us looked at him stunned and confused.

"Marissa Timmons was my grandmother. She is our father, Walter's mom. And she is your grandmother in your other time?" Sidney nodded slowly. "Wait just a minute." He rushed from the room to the back of the house toward his office.

"What was that all about?" She looked over at us confused.

"I'm not sure. I think he's trying to figure out how it is all interlocked." I guessed because that is what I was thinking. I looked over at Jackson and he just shrugged.

"How do you deal with all this? Isn't it confusing? How do you know what is real and what is not?" Sidney eyed the two of us.

"I could not have gotten through it without my family," Jackson answered. "I was just like you, in college, when the barrier started deteriorating and I did not handle it well. It was hard even after I knew about *EVE*. But I promise it does get easier with time."

"My barrier is still not completely down yet either, but I am able to recall most things from one place to the other. I still get confused a lot and have to have Jackson or his parents clarify things for me," I explained.

"How do you keep everyone and everything straight? I mean you have two families, plus this family and the time periods are drastically different. Doesn't it drive you crazy?" She looked exhausted.

"The fact that my lives are so vastly different I think makes it easier in a way. In one life I play sports, am a middle child, and have a poor relationship with my mother and brother. In the other, I have four older brothers, servants, and a wonderful relationship with my family. It is an amazing life, but one filled with limited opportunity for me as a woman. Therefore, it is hard to confuse the two. The main issue I have is getting Jackson's siblings spouses straight from one time to the other." I laughed, looking over at Jackson.

Uncle Nicholas reentered the family room with an old notebook that looked as if it had seen better days. He kneeled in front of the three of us on the couch and placed it on my lap.

"Look." He pointed to a name in the middle of the page. "Marissa Simone Timmons, our grandmother. I mean my grandmother, but yes, she is yours as well. We have the same father *there*, Walter Mitchell Timmons. Our father was married once before to a woman named Julia, your mother, before he married my mother, Bethany. From what my grandmother wrote, your mother passed away during childbirth. Our father was distraught with grief over your mother. Therefore, Marissa raised you. It says that when he remarried, he asked you if you wanted to live with him and my mother. You were six years old and very close with Marissa. You refused to leave her. Patrick, Jocelyn's *other* father, was born a year later."

"Oh my God, so in one life I am your niece and your older sister in another?" Sidney shook her head in disbelief.

"That means you are my sister in one life and my aunt in another." I turned towards Sidney and had to laugh at the strangeness of it all.

"Yes, it is unreal. But we are all interlocked because of *EVE*." He smiled.

"So, if I find you there, will you know me?" Sidney asked.

Uncle Nicholas was silent for a moment then looked pointedly at her. "How old are you now?"

"Twenty."

"Let me see, if you were seven when Patrick was born, and he is seven years older than I. No, I am only six in your time and my barrier is completely up. From what I remember I know my father has a daughter from his first wife, but we do not see her very often. I know that I grew up in Boston with my parents and my brothers. I remember you, visiting you and you giving me candy." He sighed. "I cannot believe I never put it together before ... that you were *that* Sidney! It just never occurred to me."

"This is too much." Renewed tears slid down her cheeks. "I have you *there* with me, but I don't because you don't know me."

I wrapped my arms around her. She put her head down on my shoulder and sobbed. I knew the overwhelming feelings that haunted her. It was such a short while ago I was in the same place and experiencing the rush of emotions and terrors she was now fighting. I held her tightly and let her cry it out.

It was growing dark outside. I knew it was past dinnertime, but no one mentioned it and food was the last thing on our minds.

CHAPTER EIGHT

Sunday, April 6, 1879

Jackson went to church services along with our families. I left the
blinds closed and stayed in bed. I just wanted to be left alone. I couldn't imagine
going over to my parents' house for Sunday dinner with the family and Mimi
not being there, always in the background but still in the forefront of all activities. It was too heartbreaking, and I wasn't ready to face everyone.

My room was dreary and dark with just a splash of light sneaking through
my shuttered windows. Davonte kept the fire roaring in the hearth to add some
warmth to my sorrow. I rolled over and looked at the empty pillow beside me. I
traced my fingers lightly over the soft blue linen where a few short hours ago
Jackson's head had been.

I closed my eyes and tried to concentrate on what had transpired in my
other world just to distract me from my current hell. I thought about my sister
Sidney and how her world was suddenly flipped on its side the way mine had
been just a short while ago. My heart went out to her. I wished she was here
with me now. As much as I truly loved Phoebe and Olivia, I really wished I had
at least one sister instead of four older brothers. But it seemed to me in my gut
that I knew that even in my life *there* I was just learning how to really be a
sister. Sidney and I were only now beginning to build a relationship between us
and it was a new experience for both of us. Phoebe and Olivia both were more
like sisters to me *here* than Sidney had been throughout my life *there*. A tear

rolled down my face and I wiped it away with haste, thinking how my relationship with my closest friend, Jenna, had deteriorated since Jackson and I got married. For the life of me I could not understand how some aspects of my life had fallen completely apart just as others were finally coming together.

* * *

"Sweetheart, are you all right?" Jackson rubbed my shoulder waking me. I opened my eyes to find my gorgeous husband sitting on the side of our bed still in his Sunday suit looking stunningly handsome. "It is almost two in the afternoon. Do you feel like joining us for super at your parents' house?"

"Do I have to?" I stretched and laced my fingers through his.

"No, but it would make everyone happy if you would make an appearance. Your family is worried about you."

"I really do not feel like seeing anyone," I whispered.

"I think it would do you some good to get out of the house and see your family. I know they are having a hard time also and would love to see you." He stood up and pulled back the covers. "Please … for me?"

"For you." I climbed out of bed and straight into the security of his arms.

* * *

The sunlight was blinding when we stepped out onto the front porch. There was a cool breeze blowing white puffy clouds across the sky. The flowerbeds were beginning to show signs of life and I noticed tiny little buds sprouting out along the naked tree branches as we made our way down our cobblestone driveway. I held onto Jackson's arm and slightly adjusted the new spring hat upon my brow. The wind mixed with the sun felt comforting on my face as I turned towards the immense sky above.

We arrived next door shortly before three in the afternoon. Jonathon and his family were there along with my uncles, Nicholas and Monte, and their families. My other two brothers, Patrick II and James, were visiting their wives' families. Still, despite being full of people, the house clung to an air of sorrow. Voices were lowered, laughter felt hushed, and the mirrors were still shrouded in black cloths.

Olivia and William were sitting in the parlor talking with Uncle Monte and Aunt Vivian. Jackson excused himself to speak with his father leaving me standing there feeling somewhat out of place. I wandered over to the piano and sat down. My fingers traced lightly over the keys, but the music in them seemed to remain silent. All I felt like doing was crying being here in this house without Mimi. My hands fell silent in my lap.

"Good afternoon, Mrs. Chandler." Uncle Nicholas placed his hand on my shoulder. "May I join you?"

"Of course." I tried to sound better than I felt.

"How are you?" He sat down on the bench beside me.

"I have been better. How are you doing?"

"I am doing well." He leaned in a little closer and whispered. "I was just thinking about our conversation last evening with Sidney. I think all in all it went fairly well, don't you?"

A smile crept across my lips. "Yes, I believe it did. I was thinking about that earlier as well. I was also wishing that she and I shared the same planes. Is it not strange that we do not?"

"Honestly, after talking with her and learning her role in her *other* life has raised more questions than ever about how we are all linked through *EVE*. It baffles me that on one plane she is my niece yet on the other, my sister."

I shook my head sharing his dismay. "It makes me wonder if others in our family share this trait, but we are unaware simply because we exist on a different plane other than them. Does that make sense?"

"No, but I understand what you mean." He chuckled.

"Do you think she will be all right? I mean it is a lot to adjust to and I have you, Uncle Monte, and all the Chandlers to lean on. Sidney is alone in this."

"How do you figure?" he asked.

"Well, on her *other* plane both you and Monte still have your barriers up, so you do not know her *there*," I explained.

"You have almost full knowledge across planes, correct?" I nodded. "Sidney will too, in time, and once she does, she will have you to share it with. Until then, she has you to help guide her. Plus, she will have Jackson and his family as well I am sure."

"True, I know they will do all they can for her as well. Have you told Uncle Monte yet about her?" I asked.

"No. Actually I was waiting until you and I could tell him together. I thought it would be more appropriate." He smiled. "Shall we?" He gestured towards Monte sitting across the room.

"Now? Are you serious? What about supper?" I questioned.

"We will go for a short walk. It is a lovely afternoon and we still have a little time before we eat."

"All right," I said with hesitation, following Nicholas.

The three of us excused ourselves and headed down the pathway towards the park without uttering a word. I walked in between them with an arm linked to each. I was waiting for Nicholas to start the conversation since I had no clue how to begin to explain yesterday or rather the yesterday that was two centuries from now.

"So, are either of you going to explain to me what is so important that you had to drag me out of the house to tell me?" Monte asked shortly before we turned on the walkway to the little white gazebo in the middle of the park.

I glanced up at Nicholas hoping he would begin, but he only smiled and nodded at me. "I am sure you remember my sister, Sidney," I said. Monte nodded.

"Is she all right?" he inquired.

"She will be. She started having night terrors sometime last fall. When she came home for Thanksgiving, she startled us all by waking up screaming. The similarities between what I had experienced *here* and her behavior *there* was too much of a coincidence." I rambled on for the next thirty minutes, bringing him up to the events through yesterday *there*. Monte sat down on a bench and rubbed his chin thoughtfully, absorbing my words in silence for several minutes after I had finished speaking.

"I'll be damned," he muttered more to himself than to either of us. "I cannot believe it. She is our older sister, Sidney?"

"Wait a minute!" A light bulb flashed across my mind. I could not believe it did not occur to me before this moment. "Your sister … my aunt! Where is she now?" I nearly shouted. "My God, how old is she *here*?" My mind was buzzing so fast I couldn't think about the math.

The two men looked between one another. Finally, Monte said, "In her fifties."

"Where is she? I want to see her!" I gushed.

"As you stated, Sidney was raised by our grandmother, Marissa. We really do not know her that well. She is older than us and by the time we were old enough to understand who she was, she was married and starting her own family. We only saw her on holidays or special occasions," Monte explained.

"But where is she?" I couldn't understand why they wouldn't just tell me.

"Jocelyn, you have to understand. When I was about ten, we moved from Boston to Chicago. Sidney was already married by then and had a couple of children of her own. I only talk to her a couple times a year, typically around the holidays, Christmas and Easter. We exchange letters, but that is about all the communication I have with her," Monte explained.

"So, she is in Boston?" I clarified. "Tell me what you know about her."

"Yes, she is still in Boston. She is married with four children and I think she has around ten or so grandchildren. I have lost count over the years," Monte informed me. "Her last name is now Marshall. She married a man named Keifer back when she was twenty. They have a beautiful home close to Boston. The last time we were there was for her youngest son's wedding and that was probably five or six years ago."

"That was certainly a festive affair. I have never seen such an outlandish wedding," Nicholas added.

I sat down on the bench beside Monte and contemplated all the information. I could not imagine my sister not only married with children, but a grandmother as well. I was dying to see her, talk to her, and ask her all she knew about our *other* world that she had certainly seen well beyond my years.

"I want to meet her," I said mainly to myself.

"Understandable." Nicholas took a seat beside me and placed his hand over mine and gave it a gentle squeeze. "However, it is a long way to Boston by train and this is something you should definitely discuss with your husband."

"Yes, I will. Thank you both for everything." I tried my best to remain composed and remember where I was. I hated the fact that in this time I had to discuss every little thing with Jackson as if I was incapable of making any decision on my own.

Uncle Monte stood up. "Well, I believe we should head back. I am starving for some of Sarah's good cooking." He patted his belly with a smile.

Jackson crawled into bed and flopped back against the pillows. "I am beat," he announced heavily. "I finally finished the draft on the Finley case. I can file the paperwork first thing in the morning."

"You work too hard." I leaned over his chest. "You are supposed to relax on the weekend. That is what it is for ... remember?" I gave him a coy grin.

"Right, as if I can afford to relax. My father rides me harder than anyone else in the office," Jackson complained, wrapping his arms around me.

I reached up and kissed him softly. "That is only because he knows you can handle anything he throws at you," I whispered back.

"Oh yeah ..." Jackson leaned in and kissed me intensely. Laughing, I tried to squirm away from him, but he rolled over on top of me. "What are you going to do now, Mrs. Chandler?" He moved his lips down over my neck to my shoulder. I could feel his hot breath on my skin and I completely forgot to mention my earlier conversation with my uncles.

CHAPTER NINE

SUNDAY, *April 4, 2010*

The dawn broke over the horizon in a blaze of pink, purple, and shades of gold. I sat on the porch swing feeling a deep sadness within me and a hollowness in my chest. I rocked gently and pulled the fleece blanket up around my neck. It was a brisk, beautiful morning, yet I was filled with sorrow from losing Mimi. I could recall my *other* world more clearly with each passing day and I knew she was the rock and foundation of my household. Her death was devastating.

"Good morning." Jackson approached with two mugs of coffee in his hands. "What are you doing up so early?" He handed me a mug and sat down beside me, putting his arm around me and pulling me close to him.

"Thank you." I took a sip of the coffee, loving the warmth that flowed through my body. "I needed that." As soon as the words fell out of my mouth the tears rolled down my cheeks. "I cannot believe she is gone," I sobbed.

"I know darling, I know," he whispered and kissed me gently on the forehead. "I was not sure how much you were aware of what had happened *there.*"

"Most of it." I snuggled in closer to him. "I know Mimi was the center of my world. She was always there for me. She dressed me, brought me breakfast every morning, wiped my tears, and tucked me in every night. I can remember her laughter, the warmth of her hugs and her words of comfort or sometimes scolding me." I sighed audibly. "I cannot imagine my life *there* without her."

"I realize this has got to be incredibly hard for you. I know how much you love her," he spoke softly.

"Sometimes, I wish the barrier would never come down." I shook my head in dismay.

"I am in touch with that emotion." He closed his eyes briefly, and I knew he was hurting just as much as I was, possibly even more since his memories were crystal clear whereas mine were still slightly muddled.

"There you both are." Uncle Nicholas stood on the porch holding onto the screen door. "I was wondering why the kitchen was empty, but the coffee maker was on." He smiled and took a sip from his mug. "Good morning, may I join you?"

"Of course," Jackson welcomed him. "I am afraid Jocelyn is having a bit of trouble with Mimi's death."

"Yes, I was wondering if you were recalling any of that." He took a seat in one of the rockers by the swing. "I am so sorry for your loss. She was an amazing lady." He chuckled softly as if remembering something. "She was brutally honest and kept everyone in line. I will miss her very much."

"Me too." I smiled faintly at him.

"Is Sidney still sleeping?" Uncle Nicholas inquired.

"I believe so. I have not seen her yet. And on the bright side, I did not hear any screaming last night either," I said.

"Yes, I noticed that as well. I think maybe after our long day yesterday she may have gotten the first good night's sleep she's had in a long time," my uncle observed.

"I remember how well I slept that first night after I found out. It was heavenly." I was not exaggerating one bit.

We chatted for the next several hours over coffee and fresh fruit about what courses I was considering taking in the fall. It felt wonderful to have such a normal conversation about such typical things. Uncle Nicholas was wonderful at offering advice on various classes and Jackson told me which professors I should take and which ones I should avoid.

Sidney appeared downstairs in the kitchen shortly before noon. She looked haphazard but well rested. I had forgotten how she could look so beautiful by simply rolling out of bed. Her long blond hair hung loosely around her shoulders like a golden halo, and her sapphire blue eyes sparkled in the morning sunlight. I watched her walk down the steps with her graceful long legs exactly like Amy's and remembered how jealous I always was of everything about her.

"How are you feeling?" I asked her while I poured her a cup of coffee and fixed myself another.

"Better. I actually slept through the night for the first time in I don't know how long." She inhaled deeply and jumped gracefully on the counter next to the coffee maker. "So, is this the only big secret you've been hiding or is there something else?" She laughed and kicked her feet back and forth like a child.

"Nope, that was it." I smiled and handed her the mug.

"Good, because I really don't think I could take anymore." Her smile was intoxicating.

"I know how you feel. It is a tad overwhelming. I have known about it for almost six months and it only gets harder ... at least some of the time." I hated myself for the tear that escaped from the corner of my eye. "I am sorry, one of my dearest friends just passed away *there* and it has not been easy dealing with it on either plane."

"Oh my God, Jocelyn. I am so sorry. Who was it?" She leaped down and put her arm around me.

"Mimi." I took a seat down at the table. "She was the kindest person I have ever known." Sidney sat down in the chair beside me and placed her hand over mine. I wiped another tear off my cheek and spilled my heart out. I rambled on and on about my *other* life and the world that I was only beginning to understand.

"I am so very sorry, sis. I had no idea what your *other* world was like. I guess I never considered it actually." She lowered her eyes. "I have been so consumed with trying to figure out my *other* life. I never really heard what you had said about yours."

"It's all right ... really. I know exactly how you feel," I assured her.

"I just wish our time periods were the same. I would feel so much better if you were *there* with me."

"I do too. I don't know what I would do without Jackson and his family. Plus, Uncle Nicholas has been wonderful. I have leaned on them a great deal in the last six months. Stranger still, I have gotten the opportunity to know our Uncle Monte."

"I still cannot believe you got back in touch with Uncle Nicholas *here*. He's sweet. I wish he and Dad could work out their differences." Sidney grinned.

"Can you imagine the look on Dad's face when Nicholas tried to explain *EVE* to him?" I laughed. "That would have been priceless."

"Yes, I imagine it was. He must truly believe his brother is mad." She giggled.

"Oh, there is something else you should probably know." I fiddled with my mug. "Do you remember how I told you that Jackson and his family pulled a surprise wedding on me?"

"Yes. I know it was all so romantic." Sidney smirked and rolled her eyes.

"Well, there was one thing I failed to mention. Mainly because I had not told you we were back in touch with each other, but the Chandlers had one more surprise for me. They invited Uncle Nicholas also so that I would have at least one family member in attendance. I was hesitant to mention it because I know Dad would really be hurt if he found out, because Uncle Nicholas sort of gave me away," I tried to explain.

"Ouch," she whistled lowly. "That would be a slap in the face. You know how Dad feels about him."

"I know, but I was so happy to have him there. Of course, I wish it was Dad who could have given me away, but since he could not, I was thrilled to have Uncle Nicholas stand in," I admitted.

"Understandable," Sidney agreed. "Don't you find it a little comical how many similarities there are between the two of them?"

"Just a smidge," I laughed and pinched my fingers almost all the way together.

"It's almost eerie, don't you think?" We leaned together, giggling like we had a decade earlier.

It was so wonderful to have a moment of happiness with someone in my family. Now that my father and I were trying to work things out between us, it felt amazing to finally connect with Sidney too. It was something we had never shared and now finally had the opportunity to.

* * *

We spent the day touring the IU campus. Later, after dinner was cleaned up and dishes put away Uncle Nicholas and Sidney disappeared into his study. He wanted to explain all the theories and hypotheses that he'd expressed to Jackson's family and me just a few short months ago. Jackson and I retreated upstairs to our room. I pulled out our night clothes and bath things and took his hand in mine, smiling at the silly grin on his face as I led him down the hallway to the bathroom.

I turned on the hot water and poured some bubble bath into the running stream. I began to undress when Jackson's reflection caught my eye in the mirror. He was unbuttoning his shirt and sliding it off his broad shoulders. His chest and abdomen were sculpted with just a small amount of hair. I turned around and traced my fingers over his warm skin down to the top of his jeans. I grinned up at him and unfastened his jeans. He kissed me passionately and helped me out of my shirt. We quickly got ourselves tangled together in a heated frenzy of groping and grabbing.

Jackson leaned over me, pushing me back against the edge of the bathtub. The bathmat slipped beneath my feet and went out from under me. I let out a sudden scream and tightened my grip around Jackson's shoulder, but it was no use and we lost complete footing and tumbled half clothed, into the water and bubbles in a tangled mess.

We landed in the tub with Jackson awkwardly on top of me. I was laughing so hard I could barely catch my breath. Our clothes were soaked through and we had managed to splash half of the water all over the floor. The bathroom was a mess and we couldn't have cared less. It felt amazing to let go and laugh out the tension that had been stuck in my chest for what felt like an eternity.

"Oh my God!" I laughed. "I cannot—" But before I could finish my sentence Jackson pressed his lips on mine with a kiss that was full of hunger and laughter. He undid the clasp on the front of my bra and slid it back off my shoulders. A cocky grin slid over his shapely lips and his bright green eyes shone with devilish fever.

"Is everything all right in there? We heard a loud thump … sounded like you guys were falling through the ceiling." Uncle Nicholas knocked and hollered through the door.

It was as if he had thrown a bucket of cold water on us in our hot steamy bubble bath. "Sorry, we slipped and fell in the tub. We're fine," I hollered back as Jackson climbed out of the water. There were bubbles sticking to his jeans and his bare chest and shoulders. He had never looked so sexy.

"Just um … clean up your mess and try to keep it down." I could hear the chuckle in his voice as he tried to scold us.

"How embarrassing," I snickered, climbing out of the tub myself.

Jackson leaned against the sink and struggled to peel his jeans off. I unfastened my own and hopped around the bathroom myself trying to remove the second layer of skin that seemed glued to my body. It was ridiculous.

"You realize I have been waiting all day for you to bring up your conversation with your uncles?" Jackson tossed his soaked jeans in the sink alongside his socks.

"Boy, you know how to kill a mood." I sat down on the edge of the tub and pulled my jeans the rest of the way off and tossed them on top of his. "We are standing here naked in front of one another with a romantic bubble bath waiting for us and you want to discuss this now?" I put my hands on my hips and tried to act cross but failed miserably. I tossed my semi-wet hair over my shoulder with a wink and climbed back into the water.

"So where did you and your uncles disappear to yesterday?" He climbed in behind me. I leaned my body against his as he enveloped me in his arms.

I rested my head back against his shoulder and felt the water soothe every muscle in my body. "We walked down to the park. Uncle Nicholas and I wanted to talk with Monte about Sidney." I turned my head to look up at my husband's loving face. "I guess he did not even realize that *my* sister was also *his* sister. How messed up is this?"

"It is weird, I will grant you that." He dipped a washcloth in the water and ran it up my arm, letting the water flow off my skin.

"Did you know that Sidney *there* is living in Boston with her husband, four children, and ten-plus grandchildren? I would not even know how to tell her something like that."

"I don't think you should." He continued running the water over my shoulders.

"I am sure it is only a matter of time before she asks. It will not be long before she realizes that her older self is a part of our lives *there*. And what should we tell her when she does?"

"Nothing. Tell her absolutely nothing. It would amount to the same as you discovering the photo album. It is too dangerous to know about one's future. It could ultimately change the course her life is on now. She could marry the wrong man, have an accident, or numerous other things that could alter events," Jackson explained.

"But she's already married if she's twenty."

"Where is she living?"

"Boston. Our uncles only exchange letters with her at Christmas and Easter. They rarely see her." Jackson poured some water over my head and began to lather up some shampoo through my hair. "I remember my father having an older sister, but they were never close like he is with his brothers. I just never imagined it was also *my* sister." I leaned my head back while he rinsed my hair. The warm water felt incredible running down my back. It was almost carrying my trouble away with the suds. "For the life of me I shall never be able to wrap my brain around the enormity of *EVE*."

"I believe that when Sidney asks us we should be as honest as we can and say that she lives in Boston and that she has very little contact with her brothers. Trust me, it is the right thing to do."

"I know, you're right. I will keep the details to myself." I leaned over my shoulder and kissed him lightly on the lips.

"Come on now, we need to finish up before we are so pruned, we look eighty years old." He started washing his own hair while I lathered up his torso.

CHAPTER TEN

TUESDAY, April 8, 1879

I sat on the porch swing with a copy of Jackson's old book of poems by Walt Whitman that I'd found in one of the bookcases in his study. The late morning sun was shining brightly but offered little warmth. I adjusted the afghan around my shoulders and took another sip of coffee. My heavy gown billowed out about me in a shimmering wave of pale blue satin trimmed in ivory lace. The bodice was cut in the same material but had alternate stripes of a rich ivory. It was an elegant design given to me by Emily. She had made it for me for Easter last year, and I absolutely loved it.

I rested the book on my lap and gazed out at the trees that dotted our vast front lawn. Tiny little leaves were beginning to appear. The birds were chirping high above, bringing a peaceful calm to the world around them. For the last two days all I could think about was visiting Sidney in Boston. After my conversation with Jackson in the tub I hadn't dared broach the subject with him again. I was afraid he would reason me out of it. A part of me knew he was right, that I shouldn't meddle with things, but I knew I could answer so many questions for her, and that she could answer so many for me as well.

"Good morning, my dear." Emily greeted from the porch steps. It wasn't until I heard her voice that I realized that my mind had been wandering elsewhere. I hadn't even noticed her approaching.

"Good morning. How are you today?" I smiled warmly. "Please, join me. I was just enjoying the morning air and the works of Whitman."

"Thank you." She sat down in the rocker by the swing. Bertina came out with a fresh pot of coffee. She refilled mine and poured a cup for my mother-in-law.

"I saw you sitting over here looking as beautiful as a painting," Emily remarked when Bertina disappeared back into the house.

"Thank you." I took a long sip of my coffee, letting the steaming liquid warm my body.

"Robert told me about Sidney."

"Yes, I figured Jackson had discussed it with him. He has not brought the subject up *here* since we discussed it Sunday evening *there*," I explained. "I want to visit her."

"I thought as much. I am sure you recall that my sister and her family still reside in Boston. Therefore, you and I could take a trip for a visit." She smiled coyly.

"Do you think Jackson would allow me to go?"

"If I ask him, he would not dare say no." I loved the way her mind worked.

"No, he would not, but I am sure in private he would voice his objections to me," I said with certainty. "He can be quite stubborn you know."

"I have no doubt you can handle my son." Emily smirked.

"He will fuss, I am sure." I shook my head slowly, dreading that upcoming conversation. "He will not be pleased."

"He also cannot take time away from the office to make the journey with you. Robert sings praises of Jackson's hard work. He claims our son is a very talented attorney and I would imagine that Robert is throwing everything at Jackson right now to see how he handles it." Emily took another drink and set her cup down on the small porch table.

"Yes, he is. Jackson is putting in extremely long hours both at the office and at home. I feel as if I never see him. I spent more time with him when he was studying at Northwestern," I observed with obvious displeasure.

"I told Robert he was working him too hard and that Jackson needed to be spending more time with you, but he believes that Jackson needs to work hard now so that he may play later. I believe there should be a balance." She sighed heavily. "But alas, I am overruled. Robert is determined to make his son the best criminal attorney in Chicago."

"If this is the way to reach that goal then I am positive he will be there within no time at all. Jackson wants to make his father proud, so he works until he literally drops at the end of every day," I informed his mother.

"Do not worry. Jackson can handle anything Robert puts him through. He is a strong man," she assured me.

"Yes, I know. But do you honestly believe Jackson is going to allow me to accompany you to Boston?" I gave her a quizzical look.

Emily sighed heavily, deep in thought. "Before we get ahead of ourselves and upset Jackson, I will write the necessary letters to my sister, Elaina. I am sure she and her husband, Samuel, would be more than happy to receive us." She stood up and brushed out her skirt. "Thank you for the coffee. I had better hurry home, so I can send the letter out today."

I fidgeted around the house, unable to concentrate on anything. My mind kept wandering off to Boston. It was impossible for me to imagine Sidney middle-aged and married with children, even grandchildren. The only Sidney I could envision was the one that was starting to become clearer and clearer in my memories. That Sidney was thin, petite, with long, gorgeous blonde hair and an almost bubbly personality. I knew she was popular in high school and a cheerleader in both high school and college. And she was smart also, a pre-med student at Northwestern University. In the far reaches of my mind I seemed to recall her reference marriage as "not a ball and chain but rather a noose around your neck." This *other* Sidney, this older one, was a literal stranger to me and, truth be told, scared the daylights out of me.

I had Davonte saddle up Cheyenne in the early afternoon. I wanted to take a ride to try and clear my thoughts. I sat sidesaddle with my gown flowing around me and led her down the brick-lined street to the meadows just outside of town. The sun was shining brightly above, and the spring air had warmed up a smidge since morning. My mind was a whirlwind of thought but still, focus escaped me.

I always loved riding horses when I was a child. William and I had spent hours together galloping through the woods and meadows surrounding our little section of the world. There was something carefree and comforting about it that no matter what was going on, horseback riding always relaxed me. There was a comfort in the sound of hooves hitting the ground, the feel of her strong muscles flexing beneath me, the speed at which she ran. It cleared my head and gave me peace.

I felt the breeze brushing past my cheeks causing a few strands of hair to escape my riding cap. The green was beginning to return to the straw yellow of the winter grass. It was as if the world was beginning to wake up after a long nap.

* * *

Jackson didn't return home until well past supper. I was sitting by the hearth crocheting a piece that I hoped to put on a pillow when it was finished. I wasn't nearly as talented as my mother or Olivia when it came to any form of needle-point, but I tried. Mimi had spent many hours trying to perfect my technique but unfortunately, the skill had managed to escape me. It had almost become a joke between us because nothing I ever attempted remotely resembled what it was supposed to be.

"Good evening, my love. How was your day?" Jackson leaned down and kissed me softly on the cheek before warming his hands on the fire.

"Lovely. I went for a ride this afternoon on Cheyenne." I gazed upon his stunning profile against the flames.

"Alone?" He turned and questioned.

"Yes." I couldn't understand why such a thing would upset him.

"Out in the meadows beyond town?" He turned back towards the fire and asked.

"Yes. Why?"

"I do not want you out riding alone anymore. It is not safe for a lady to be out galloping about on her own." His voice took on an almost fatherly tone.

"I have never had any problems before."

Jackson came over and knelt in front of me and placed his hands over mine. He looked up at me with eyes full of sorrow and concern. "Just the same. I would feel much better if you took Davonte with you hereafter. Chicago is not as small a community as you would like to believe. Industry is pushing farther north and with it comes some unsavory characters. It is not safe for you to be out riding alone."

"As you wish, my dear."

I wasn't sure why he was making such a big deal over me riding alone. I had been doing it for years without any consequences. It seemed that working in the city and witnessing the worst of what was out there had changed his outlook on life and not in a positive way. Therefore, I promised just to appease him if for no other reason than it wasn't something that was worth arguing over. There were other, more important battles waiting on the horizon.

As I sat at the vanity a short time later brushing out my hair and watching

Jackson undress for bed in the reflection of the mirror, I still could not bring myself to bring up the subject of Sidney again. He was already upset and starting a conversation about her would only intensify his mood.

For tonight I would hold my tongue and wait until his head was a bit clearer. I set the brush down and crawled into our bed. Jackson added a couple more logs on the fire and stoked it with the poker until he seemed satisfied it would burn. He turned down the oil lamps on the mantle then climbed into bed beside me. I immediately went to him and rested my head down upon his bare chest. He wrapped his arms around me and kissed the top of my head.

"I know you think I am being overprotective, Jocelyn. But I do not know what I would do if something ever happened to you," he whispered in the dark.

"Sweetheart, nothing is going to happen to me. You already know that." I patted the side of his chest.

"I do not believe in tempting fate." His words were barely loud enough for me to hear him and I picked up on the small choke in his voice. I leaned up and looked at him.

"Jackson, what is wrong?" I stared up at his silhouette that was barely visible but only for the glow of the embers from the hearth.

"I went to court today and they brought in a man who was arrested about ten miles from here for raping and beating three different women. He did not even know them. They were merely out and about going on with their daily lives and he dragged them into alleys off the streets. It terrifies me to think of something like that happening to you. So please, just humor me and do not go anywhere alone. Take Davonte with you if you go shopping or riding." He squeezed me a little tighter and kissed me again.

"I will, I promise." His words gave me the chills. Thinking that something so horrible had happened so close to our home left me feeling more than a little nervous about how much time I spent home without him. I was so thankful that we had such wonderful people in our home taking care of us.

CHAPTER ELEVEN

Tuesday, *April 6, 2010*

The New Orleans skyline loomed before us in all its majestic glory. Twilight broke through the horizon in its pink and purple brilliance. It was a stunning sight to behold. I was driving with Sidney in the passenger seat and Jackson was snoring softly across the seat behind us. It had been a very long drive from Bloomington to New Orleans. The three of us took turns driving and drove straight through with the intent of having more time to relax and enjoy the city. We had promised Uncle Nicholas we would stop back by on our way home and spend the night.

We pulled in front of the *Lanuax Mansion* shortly before six in the evening. Uncle Nicholas had stayed there during his visit several years ago and highly recommended it. He even set up the reservations for us. He'd said it was in the heart of the city and within walking distance to literally everything. The place was a stunning sight, like something I was looking at in my *other* world. I stood beside Jackson's CRV completely in awe of the ambiance around me.

Sidney settled into The Weiland Room on the main floor. It opened onto the colorful Victorian garden dressed in an orchestra of color. The room was a cornflower blue on two walls with the other two covered in wallpaper with delicate blue flowers. There was an enormous brick inlaid fireplace on the back wall surrounded by the original flooring and stove's tole hood. The ceiling was at least fourteen feet tall and the floors were hardwood. There was a comfortable love seat facing towards fireplace, a wrought iron bed on the opposite wall, an old-fashioned rocker in the corner, oil lamps on the night table, and period pieces that took me back to yesteryear.

The hostess was a charming woman who gave us a little tour through the common areas of the house. She informed us that attorney Charles Andrew Johnson, a lifelong bachelor, had built the 11,000 square-foot mansion in 1879. She gestured towards a portrait above the mantel. "And this is Mr. Johnson. It was painted in 1884 by *Maria Brooks*, a member of the Royal Academy. She is also listed in the Women in History Museum in New York and passed away in 1906." The three of us followed her into the next room. "Another interesting tidbit was that Mr. Johnson was a close friend of Confederate General Robert E. Lee. Plus, this home was one of the settings for Brad Pitt's movie, *The Curious Case of Benjamin Button*," she said with obvious pride. "The house is currently owned by Mrs. Ruth Bodenheimer, who is only the fourth owner. Many of the rooms, which are not open to the public or guests, still maintain the home's original wallpaper, locks and furnishings, including the grand Victorian dining room set."

She led us through the back door onto a breathtaking veranda resting amidst the Victorian garden and across a little cobblestone pathway to a small building on the back corner of the property. "And here is the Enchanted Cottage." She unlocked the door, handed Jackson the brass key, and stepped aside. "Please let me know if there is anything you need," she said warmly with a thick southern drawl.

"Thank you." Jackson and I both shook her hand.

"Enjoy your stay." She smiled and departed, leaving us alone to make ourselves at home.

Jackson set our luggage down in the corner before collapsing across the oversized wicker bed. Sidney immediately crawled up on the lounge near the window overlooking the garden. They looked exhausted. I leaned against the wall by the door and closed my eyes for a moment. I wanted nothing more than a hot shower and a good night's sleep, but my stomach was rumbling, and I knew I would never sleep until I got something to eat.

"Is anyone hungry?" I walked over to the window and pulled the floral drapes together and turned on the oil shaped lamp on the bedside table. The light offered a soft glow off the creamy yellow walls that were both comforting and easy on the eyes.

"Starved," Sidney replied as she literally fell over sideways on the lounge and curled up in the fetal position. "But I don't want to move. Do you think they deliver pizza around here?" she mumbled half into the pillow.

"I would imagine so," Jackson called from his spot on the bed.

"Seriously?" I flopped down beside him and gave him a playful kiss on the cheek. "We are in New Orleans and you want pizza?"

"I would put money on it that it's fabulous down here." Sidney half snickered.

"I would bet you're right," Jackson concluded.

"I do not want pizza. Not tonight anyway. I want real food. Please…"

"Fine, we will get cleaned up and go have some dinner. I am sure there is something close by." Jackson begrudgingly climbed off the bed and retrieved his suitcase.

"Fine," Sidney grumbled and peeled herself off the lounge. "I'll go shower and meet you both back here in thirty minutes."

"Sounds good," I responded, watching her stumble out the door and across the garden.

* * *

We all felt better after we'd eaten some real food. We walked back to our lodging, exhausted, but in good spirits. As we rounded the corner Sidney reached out and touched my arm. "Would you mind coming to my room for a minute?"

"Sure." I leaned up and kissed Jackson on the cheek. "I will be there in a minute."

"Take your time." He hugged me tightly. "Goodnight, Sidney." We watched as Jackson rounded the corner of the house and disappeared behind the garden gate.

"What's up?" I turned towards my sister.

"I just wanted to talk." I followed her into the house and back into her room. I flopped down on the corner of her bed, and she curled up with one of the pillows.

"Aren't you tired?" I was about to fall asleep where I sat.

"No, not really," she said in a low voice. Then it clicked. She was going through the same apprehension I was when I found out.

"Scared to fall asleep." I reached over and took her hand. She nodded. "I understand. I remember being terrified to sleep. I would do anything to try to stay awake." I scooted up towards the head of the bed beside her. "It will get easier, I promise," I said softly.

"I don't know how you do it. This whole thing is so demented there aren't even words to describe it." Sidney exhaled loudly, leaning her head back against her pillow.

"I know, but it is not a matter of how you do it, you just do it because you don't have any choice in the matter. We do not have any say in it." I lay back against the other pillow. "It happens without our permission, but once you adjust to the shock of the differences between your two worlds it really is a blessing in disguise."

"I don't see how. I wish I could turn it off. Do you think Uncle Monte was right for what he did?" she pondered. "I can understand why he did it."

"I thought about it," I admitted. "I actually talked with Uncle Monte about it on Thanksgiving. Problem was I wanted to leave that plane, not this one, but apparently since we're all interrelated, if I chose to do that then I wouldn't even exist here."

"I don't understand."

"Well, we're all interrelated. I am supposed to be my great-great-grand-mother's daughter. I am actually a descendent of my own daughter, Alyssa, in that time period," I admitted.

"Are you serious?" She creased her forehead and looked at me with her head tilted slightly.

"Yes, and I would be lying if I said that information didn't screw with me for a long time. Even thinking about it now … it's just plain creepy. I am a direct descendent of my own daughter, of myself. How messed up is that?" I snorted.

"That is pretty screwed up." She laughed at me. "So, if you did what Uncle Monte did … *there*, you would never exist on this plane? Wouldn't you just exist *here* as you but not the you with *EVE*?"

"Huh? That is a good question. Uncle Monte did not seem to think so, but that does actually make sense, more so than I would just never be."

"How did you ever adjust to this?" Sidney leaned over and brushed my bangs away from my eyes.

"Who ever said I have adjusted to it?" I smiled over at her weary face. "Look, Sidney, I wish I could tell you that once everything becomes clearer it will be so much easier. But I would be lying if I told you that."

"Great," she muttered.

"No, seriously, listen to me." I put my hand reassuringly on her arm. "I still struggle with this every day, but honestly, it is so amazing. Look what we can do, get to witness. All those things that others get to read about in textbooks and biographies, we get to experience it firsthand. It is pretty fabulous if you ask me," I confessed.

"Yeah, I have thought about that and it is pretty amazing. However, even though you may have been born during the Civil War, I get to live through it and from what I can recall, that was not exactly fabulous."

"But you live in Boston. And you are a woman. I think it is fairly safe to say you are going to come through it all right." I tried not to make light of it. "But I honestly do not know." And that was the truth.

"And if you did, you wouldn't tell me anyway." She rolled her eyes at me.

"That is not fair. And seriously, I honestly do not know."

"All right, fine." She pouted. "Well, thanks for staying up and talking with me. I appreciate it. It really helped. "Sidney leaned up and hugged me.

"Any time, you know that." I squeezed her tightly and patted her back. "I'm always here if you need me."

"Thanks." She surprised me by kissing me on the cheek when she let me go. "Don't be upset if you get that sobbing hysterical call at three in the morning."

"Of course." I stood up and walked to the door. "Try not to think about it. Just close your eyes and drift away."

"I will, thanks again." My sister climbed under the covers. "Goodnight, Jocelyn."

"Goodnight, Sidney. Sweet dreams." I closed her door behind me.

CHAPTER TWELVE

THURSDAY, *April 10, 1879*

Emily came by shortly before noon to join me for lunch. We sat down at the little table on the veranda overlooking the back gardens. Davonte had eagerly begun working on them, planting new shrubbery, bushes, and adding little pathways. It still seemed odd to me when I glanced over the lawn how different it appeared from this world to the one that was becoming clearer to me with each passing day. This yard, Jenna's yard, was one I had trampled over hundreds of times throughout my youth. Even as Olivia's former yard, I had spent many long hours running across its lush grass. But the views were so vastly different. This one had the stables and carriage house, a fence bordered the property, and the trees were much younger. The other claimed a storage shed, a large wooden swing set in the opposite corner, had no restrictions on the border, mature trees throughout, and had a large barbeque built into the corner of the veranda.

Emily was wearing a beautiful pale sage gown with a light shawl draped over her shoulders. Her bonnet had soft looking plum feathers on the right side and accented her outfit perfectly. She sat down gracefully and took a sip of her tea.

"I mailed the letter to my sister yesterday. Robert was none too thrilled with the idea of us traveling unaccompanied. So, to appease him, I thought perhaps we should take Davonte and Tamesha with us. I know he would feel much better if we had a man traveling with us for security."

"Yes, I believe Jackson would share his views. I will ask them once we hear back from your sister and the arrangements have been finalized."

"That will be fine."

"Has Robert said anything else to you about being out by yourself recently?" I inquired, thinking back to my conversation with Jackson the other evening.

"Yes, in fact, he has. He was insistent that I go nowhere unaccompanied by one of the household staff and most preferably, Barnaby." She gave me a puzzled look. "Why? Did my son say something to you?"

"On Monday evening I casually mentioned that I had gone riding along the outskirts of town by myself and he was very unhappy with me for doing so. He insisted that I never go riding without Davonte with me. He said it was no longer safe for me to be out alone. Did Robert mention to you the man that was arrested? He had done unspeakable things to several ladies and it all happened about ten miles from here. It really upset Jackson," I explained.

"I am afraid Robert did not elaborate a great deal on the subject. He only mentioned that some individuals with questionable character had migrated to the area recently."

"Jackson said something very similar."

"Any idea of what they were referring to?" I asked, stirring my tomato basil soup.

"Not really. I did hear Mr. Cain telling Mr. Donaldson of some problems he has had recently when I stopped at the mercantile yesterday for some household supplies. He was saying that some rough looking men had given his wife a difficult time when they visited the store on Monday morning. I did not get the details, but I am assuming that our husbands must have heard about it also."

"That would certainly explain why they do not want us out by ourselves. Jackson told me that there has been an uprising in migration towards the city and that the living conditions were deplorable in the more industrial areas. I have not seen them myself, nor do I have any desire to travel to such an area."

"I believe they are working on a case involving someone from that district. I know they have been down there recently because of their client." She shook her head slightly and took another sip of her tea. "Sometimes it scares me knowing the types of people they have to encounter because of their profession."

"You do not believe we are in any real danger, do you?" The thought made me a bit uneasy.

"No, I trust they are just being overly cautious. If we were in any real danger, I believe they would have told us." I felt better with the confidence I heard in her voice.

"Either way, perhaps this would be a good time to visit Boston for a while." I wanted to change the subject.

"Perhaps you are right. It would be so nice to see my sister and her family. It has been a long while since I got the opportunity to spend some time with them. Hopefully, we will hear back from her shortly. Elaina has always been prompt when replying to my letters in the past," she assured me with a smile.

* * *

Jackson came home well after dark again. He looked tired after another long day at the office. I hated what these long hours were doing to him. I told Tamesha to warm up some dinner for him and joined him beside the hearth.

"Hello, my darling. How was your day?" He kissed me lightly on the cheek and sat down on the lounge.

"Better than yours, I am guessing." I tried to smile and handed him the evening paper. "Long day?"

"Very. And I still have some briefs to go over before I turn in." He sighed heavily.

"Can they not wait until tomorrow? I believe you have done enough for one day." I sat down beside him.

"No. I have a meeting first thing in the morning. So, I must finish them tonight." He ran his hand wearily through his hair. "I also heard that you plan on going to Boston with my mother." He looked at me out of the corner of my eye.

"Yes. For a brief visit with your Aunt Elaina. Your mother invited me to join her."

"I am sure she did." He looked more annoyed than anything. "And I suppose this has nothing to do with your sister?"

"Jackson—" I began, but he cut me off.

"Never mind." He stood. "I am hungry and have work to do," he said before exiting the room.

I sat there alone. I was positive that his entire mood was not directed at me, but I was sure some of it was. I debated on following him to the kitchen to assure him that we would not be traveling alone, but a part of me told me that now was not the time for that conversation. Jackson hated it when I made plans about things without discussing them with him first and I knew he felt like I was defying his wishes regarding Sidney.

I picked up my copy of *Great Expectations* and tried to lose myself in Charles Dickens's words. But it proved pointless. I found myself listening to Jackson, Tamesha, and Betsy moving about in the kitchen until I finally heard his footsteps disappear down the hall and his office door shut quietly behind him.

I put the novel aside and made my way upstairs to get ready for bed.

CHAPTER THIRTEEN

Thursday, *April 8, 2010*

The smell of coffee woke me from a deep sleep. Jackson was showered, dressed, and sitting at the antique desk overlooking the colorful Victorian garden. He was scribbling something down, lost in deep concentration. I watched him pause for a moment and take a sip of coffee. My brain was only beginning to process the world at a conscious level. I closed my eyes and tried to recall the events of the day before … in my *other* world.

I could see our beautiful home, the vast gardens awakening in the spring morning, and the fresh dew thick upon the grounds glistening in the early light. I could feel the heaviness of the gown I was wearing and the tightness of my corset. It was still such a foreign feeling to me but also one I was quickly adapting to in a weird sort of way. I could hear the chatter of Bertina and Cora in the rooms below as they went about their daily activities.

This peaceful world absent of all the hustle and bustle of the twenty-first century was a welcomed reprieve. I was beginning to understand the views of everyone in my family regarding this unusual way of living. There was a majestic calm that was impossible to find in my *other* life. Given the lifestyle the world had transitioned into over the last hundred and thirty-some odd years, I now understood the words Phoebe had said about the drastically different roles and how she had come to love her role in each of her lives.

* * *

We strolled down to the corner of Toulouse Rue and Bourbon Rue in the French Quarter. It was warm and musty out, but the morning rays were burning off the low-lying fog. I had thrown on a royal blue, long-sleeved, hooded T-shirt and a pair of gray express shorts with my converse. My hair was up in a ponytail and I had thrown on a little make-up for good measure. But as soon as I saw Sidney, I felt like one of Cinderella's ugly stepsisters. Her golden hair was flowing down across her shoulders and her make-up was perfectly applied. She was wearing a cute, little beige layered skirt and a dusty rose soft tank with a light grey kami that flattered her hourglass figure perfectly. I wanted desperately to rush back in and change when I saw her, but I couldn't without seeming petty.

The architecture up and down the street was brilliant and very old. There was so much to see my eyes couldn't absorb it all. It was as if the streets whispered of Anne Rice's undead characters. The lampposts were a staple of old-world era. Balconies adorned every building overlooking the traffic of people below. Vibrant colors clung from every surface in sight.

The shop windows that curbed the brick-lined streets were like nothing I had ever witnessed on the streets of Chicago. Windows displaying the arts of witchcraft, voodoo, bondage, and other various ideologies baffled me as we walked by. Sidney looked over at me occasionally and raised an eyebrow, but she kept her comments to herself for once. I stifled a giggle more than once as I strolled along holding Jackson's hand.

We ate brunch at a small café on the Quarter. We sat outside on some stiff iron chairs along the sidewalk and ate our croissants and sipped our coffee. We debated back and forth about where we wanted to visit first. Sidney wanted to visit the Art District. Jackson was dying to check out the infamous Lafayette Cemetery in the Garden District. I voted with Jackson more out of curiosity than anything else. So as soon as we were finished, we jumped a streetcar and took it down to Washington Avenue.

There was a large concrete wall surrounding the cemetery. I immediately got an eerie feeling as we passed through the wrought-iron fence. We walked slowly, looking at all the details of the different tombs and crypts. It was creepy and in desperate need of a weed eater. Several of the tombs were crumbling around the edges showing the true age of the area.

We stepped lightly through the overgrown grass. In the distance I could hear a lawn mower, but it had yet to make it over to this part of the cemetery. I noticed several people with pencils and paper making rubbings of names carved in stone. As we turned a corner, I stopped to read a plaque that said the cemetery was founded in 1833 and christened "cities of the dead." Apparently, there were immigrants from more than twenty-five countries and natives of twenty-six states buried there.

A short distance away was a crypt engraved with the Confederate flag and the words, Harry T. Hayes, 1820 – 1876. The inscription read: Civil War Brigadier General, 7th Louisiana Infantry, Confederate States Army.

I lightly ran my fingers over the dates on the warm stone. This man was a Confederate brigadier general during the Civil War. He could have fought against either of my uncles or even Jackson's father during the war. It seemed so odd to me that only yesterday I'd been eating dinner with a man who had fought in the battles of Gettysburg, Chancellorsville, and Fredericksburg. And yet, this man, this general had been gone from this world for well over a hundred years. I tried to imagine what he would think of the world as we know it now.

"Are you all right?" Jackson came up behind me and gently touched my shoulder.

"Yes, I am fine." I smiled up at his face through the glaring sunlight. "I was looking at the dates. This man was a brigadier general in the Confederate Army. I was just thinking I wonder if he ever fought against my uncles or your dad."

"I don't know, maybe. We could look him up and see what battles he fought in. Have you got a pen?"

"Yes." I dug around in my backpack for a pen and the small notepad I carried with me and handed them to him.

Jackson jotted down the name, rank, and dates for the soldier. "We can look him up when we get back to the cottage." He handed them back to me and I placed them securely in my backpack. "Are you sure you are feeling okay?"

"I guess it's hard for me to be fully in one place without considering all that happened before during our *other* lives. It's just weird. I don't know how you do it."

"Practice, I suppose. There is no secret to it."

He took my hand and we caught back up with Sidney. She was standing in front of a family tomb with a puzzled look on her face.

"Hey, what's wrong?" I asked as we approached.

"Nothing. It's just well ... I know this name, but I can't place it and it's driving me nuts."

"The Ferguson family? Judge Ferguson?" Jackson thought for a moment. "Judge Ferguson was the one who presided over the *Plessy vs. Ferguson,* 'separate but equal' case in 1896. It was not overturned until 1954's *Brown vs. Board of Education of Topeka."*

"How could you possibly know all this?" Sidney looked stunned.

"You're forgetting, Jackson's a lawyer," I said with pride.

"Maybe *there,* but the case he just recited hasn't occurred in your world yet." She smirked.

"True, but when I was studying to take the bar exam *there,* I may have glanced over some important cases that are relevant still today that I knew I would eventually have to know." Jackson gave her a smart-ass grin.

"You must be very proud of yourself." She gave him a sisterly shove.

"I am actually. Have you any idea how hard it is to take the bar and take high school classes at the same time? This year has been a royal pain."

"Was it worth it?" Sidney inquired, looking at each of us.

"Was what worth it?" Jackson asked.

"Leaving college and your life in Boston, hunting my sister down, and having to repeat your senior year?"

Jackson wrapped his arm tightly around my shoulder with a smile. "Most definitely."

"Agreed," I chimed in.

* * *

It was after eight before we finally returned to our cottage and finally got some alone time. I sat down at the antique desk and flipped open my laptop. I took out the little notepad that Jackson had written in earlier and typed in the name Harry T. Hays. Immediately, a black and white portrait appeared on the screen along with a short biography. It seemed that Mr. Hays had started out as a colonel of the 7th Louisiana Infantry in the Battle of Bull Run and the Shenandoah Campaign. Afterwards, he was promoted to a brigadier general in the summer of 1862, just in time to be assigned to the 1st Louisiana Infantry for the battles of Antietam, Fredericksburg, Chancellorsville, and even Gettysburg. However, during the battle of Spotsylvania in Virginia, he was wounded by shrapnel but survived the duration of the war to become Sheriff of Orleans Parish, Louisiana. He passed away a decade after the war ended.

"Jackson, look," I hollered over my shoulder. "This Brigadier General Hays did fight in the battle of Antietam, Chancellorsville, and Bull Run. He could have very well been fighting against Uncle Monte or your dad." I turned in the chair to face Jackson, who was lounging across the bed flipping through channels. "Isn't that strange?"

"Not really." He rolled over to face me. "The enormity of those battles throughout the war was something I believe is difficult for you to envision. There were thousands of men involved, all fighting for what they believed in. Some fought to preserve the Union, some for the right to leave it. It tore families, friends, and neighbors apart and pitted them against one another. It was a horrible time in history."

"History? That seems like a strange way of putting it, considering."

"I know, but I barely remember it. I was so young. I was only five when the war broke out. All I remember is my mother crying a lot and my father gone. My brother Alex remembers a lot more of it than I do."

"Was Robert ever injured in the war?"

"He was hit with shrapnel in his right leg. He has a deep scar from it. I believe he got it at Gettysburg. He also has a scar in his abdomen from where he was jabbed with a bayonet at Antietam. That put him in the hospital for almost a month. He could have come home but he refused to leave his unit. He received several medals for his service. You should ask him about it some time."

"I never realized," I whispered more to myself than to him. After reading most of my uncle's journals it was apparent how difficult the war had been on him and my family. It was almost unimaginable to me to think of Robert being in the same position.

Jackson climbed off the bed with renewed spirit. "Come on, sweetheart. Join me in the shower." He took me by the hand and dragged me off towards the bathroom.

Two hours later I had convinced Jackson to explore the night life in New Orleans. I had heard of the enticing jazz clubs, the big bands, the dancing, and I was eager to see it firsthand. I called Sidney's room and asked if she was up for a little nightlife and of course, she was. She told me she had taken a long, hot, bubble bath, and napped for the last couple hours. Now that she had her second wind, she was ready to experience New Orleans' nightlife. She asked for thirty minutes to get ready and then she'd meet us in front of the B & B.

I hopped off the phone and rushed over to the little armoire that served as our closet. I wanted to find something spectacular and sexy, especially after spending the day looking like the ugly stepsister. But I couldn't find one outfit of mine that would compare with anything that Sidney wore on a typical Tuesday.

I turned around towards Jackson. He was already dressed in jeans, a dark gray T-shirt, and an unbuttoned, untucked white dress shirt with thin black stripes. His black casual shoes and belt completed his outfit. He looked so handsome, the last thing I wanted to do was look drab standing next to him.

"Jackson, do you think it's possible that tomorrow we can go shopping for some new clothes for me? I really didn't bring anything special to wear out on the town." I didn't want to admit to him that I really didn't *own* anything to wear out on the town, but I was pretty sure he was already aware of it.

"We can do that." He got up from the desk and came up beside me. "What is bothering you? I have never seen you so uneasy or concerned about your wardrobe."

"You saw how Sidney dressed today. I looked like a bum in comparison and I know she's going to be dressed to the nines tonight and I have nothing like that," I confessed.

"Jocelyn, you are so beautiful regardless of what you wear. You have no cause to think that you look dull or drab or whatever in comparison to your sister." Jackson wrapped his arms around me and held me tight. "I wish you could see yourself through my eyes," he whispered. "Then you would see how gorgeous you truly are."

"Thank you." I gazed up into his emerald eyes.

"I love you just the way you are. Do not ever change." He smiled down at me.

"Okay, but can you help me pick out something to wear tonight?" I said lightly, but he knew I was also serious.

"If you would like me to." He let go of me and began looking through my clothes. He pulled out a plain, white T-shirt, a pair of faded jeans with a couple of strategically placed rips, my wide black belt with the large silver buckle, and my black blazer. He handed them over to me. "Try this on."

I slipped into them and stood in front of the full-length mirror. The T-shirt was about an inch-and-a-half shy of the top of my jeans showing just enough of my abdomen to add a little sex appeal. I rolled the sleeves of the blazer up about mid forearm and smoothed out the collar on it. Jackson came up behind me and fastened a thin white gold chain around my neck that held a little charm that interlocked two diamond hearts, one in black with horns and a pointed tail, the other with a halo. Jackson had given it to me a while back because apparently my horns hold up my halo. I thought it was too cute and wore it all the time.

"There." Jackson stood back and looked at me. "Gorgeous," he smiled. "Leave your hair down, add a few curls at the ends, and just a hint of make-up."

"You scare me. You know that don't you?" I turned back around toward the mirror. I hated to admit it, but he was right. "If I didn't know any better, I'd swear you were a gay man." I chuckled.

"I grew up with Phoebe, remember? She made me her little pet project to try to give me a sense of style. Please do not tell her it worked," he said as he sat back down at the desk.

I finished getting ready, and I had to admit I was rather pleased with the results. I looked both sexy and stylish. I added my large hoop earrings and several loose bracelets to complete the ensemble. I felt like a new lady as Jackson and I strolled through the garden around to the front of the building. The night air was warm and comforting. The stars littered the sky like sparkling fireflies a million miles away. The air was heavy with the aroma of rich spices. I linked my fingers through Jackson's and took a deep breath of the night air feeling better than I had in a long time.

Sidney was for once waiting on us when we arrived. And of course, as always, she looked stunning. She was wearing a royal blue short dress with strappy heels that wrapped around her ankles and tied in the back. Her hair was left loose and cascaded down her back and over her shoulders. She looked stunning.

The three of us headed down the crowded Bourbon Street to explore the nightlife. Music filled our ears, but I had no clue from where it originated. It seemed to be everywhere and from nowhere at the same time. People were dancing in the middle of the street and all along the sidewalks. There was a feeling of freedom and wildness in the air.

We saw the infamous House of Blues, ate a fabulous French creole dinner at the historic *Galatoire's Restaurant,* and then explored several jazz clubs or at least the curb appeal of them. I felt bad that they couldn't go inside because I was still underage. Thankfully, neither of them seemed to mind. Instead, we joined in with the other tourists and locals and let the sounds of the jazz music carry us away.

By the time we made it back to our little cottage, I was drenched in sweat from dancing for hours nonstop. I discovered that Jackson was an amazing dancer and could certainly hold his own. And there was no shortage of men waiting to sweep Sidney off her feet. It was almost comical. She barely had time to catch her breath before someone else asked her to dance. She was gracious to all of them. It was so wonderful to see her finally relax and have fun. This was exactly what she needed after the long months of stress, hallucinations, and fear of insanity.

I hugged and kissed her cheek goodnight as we parted ways at the entrance of the *Lanaux Mansion*. She was tired and worn down but still had a smile on her face. I watched her as she walked to the door. She turned and waved before closing the door behind her. Jackson put his arm around my shoulders and led me around to our little hideaway from the world outside.

CHAPTER FOURTEEN

SATURDAY, April 12, 1879

The early afternoon light shone warmly on the cobblestone bricks of our veranda. Cora and Tamesha had set up a buffet table along the back filled with delicious foods and delicate deserts. I had decided that Jackson needed a reprieve from his long hours and some quality time with our friends. Therefore, I invited our closest friends to an afternoon barbecue at our home in hopes of getting him out of his office for a few hours.

Although Jackson was not thrilled about hosting the party and claimed he needed to spend the time working, he had reluctantly agreed to attend.

Lee and Elizabeth were the first to arrive shortly before two o'clock. They were followed directly by Laurie and her fiancé, Theodore, and Christina with her fiancé, Thomas, who had chosen to ride together. Dimitri and Evelyn showed up next looking very happy and in high spirits. It was wonderful to see Dimitri looking so well after all that he'd went through with his break-up with Maryanne. Olivia and William were the last to arrive.

Olivia was trying to be more sociable, but it still had taken a lot of urging to get her to attend today. I had spent the better part of last evening next door trying to persuade her and only after William stepped in and assured her that everyone in attendance would be thrilled to see her and without judgment, did she finally relent.

The ladies discussed the upcoming weddings, the details, the preparations, and anxiety over making sure everything went smoothly. The gentlemen politely commented when necessary but appeared bored with the topic more than anything else. I noticed Elizabeth slip away from the group quietly and walk over to the dessert table. I squeezed Jackson's hand and joined her.

"When did we turn into our mothers?" I asked, stepping up beside her.

"I was just wondering the same thing," she smiled. "It is a lovely party."

"Thank you." I picked up a piece of angel food cake and handed it to Elizabeth.

"Did you think we would be here this quickly?" she asked.

"I could not wait to marry Jackson. I was so excited about playing the little wife, having a husband come home every evening that I could take care of, but I saw him a lot more when we were dating. He is so consumed with work and his cases that I rarely ever see him," I complained.

"Well, soon you will have a child to occupy your time." She smiled and sighed dreamily. "I cannot wait to have children with Lee."

"Yes, hopefully," was all I could manage to say as that uncomfortable knot formed in the pit of my stomach. I couldn't possibly tell her we were taking full measures to avoid pregnancy. Plus, a part of me truly envied her since I knew she'd enjoy being a mother long before I would.

"You must be so excited." Her cheerful tone only made me feel worse.

"I am." I offered her the best smile I could muster.

"Olivia is looking better. How is she feeling?" I was thankful she changed the subject.

"She has her good and bad days. Unfortunately, Mimi's recent passing has been hard on all of us and I think that just compounded her grief."

"I know how close you were with her. I'm so sorry, I did not mean to ..."

"It's been hard. We're all trying to deal with her loss." *This subject is worse than the last one.*

"Is Jackson enjoying his new position?" Elizabeth shifted uncomfortably.

"Very much so. He works long hours most nights, so I really do not get to see him as much as I would like, but he says he has to prove himself." I half smiled.

"It cannot be easy to be the boss' son. I'm sure he doesn't want his colleagues to believe he was only given the opportunity because of his father. That means he must work twice as hard as everyone else to prove he deserves his position," she reasoned.

"I understand." I took a bite of the cake before I continued. "I truly do. I just wish he wouldn't be so consumed with his work that he spends all waking hours on it." I shrugged and then straightened my shoulders again, remembering that I shouldn't shrug.

"I am sure that will change in time," Elizabeth assured me.

"And what are you hens cackling about?" Lee asked as he approached us and helped himself to a piece of cake.

"The long hours you and Jackson find it necessary to work." She smiled as he slipped his arm around her waist.

"It makes the time we get to spend with our lovely ladies even more special." Lee had a devilish charm about him, I realized.

I tried my best to stifle the laugh that was building in my chest. The part of my brain that was growing stronger every day containing all that I was aware of in my *other* life, tried not to choke on the laugh. That newly awakened portion of my brain giggled inwardly as I tried not to blurt out, "You're so full of it, Lee."

The afternoon sun was shining brightly on the veranda. The scene before me resembled the *last barbecue at Twelve Oaks,* but on a much smaller scale. The costumes were similar, although the hooped skirts were no longer as wide, and the cut of the gentlemen's jackets were altered a smidge. Yet, viewing it through the future eyes from twenty-first century, the slight variances in the last decade made no difference to the strange bewilderment of it all.

Thomas and Theodore were demonstrating something to the small group in the corner, invoking an uproar of laughter. Jackson glanced back at them over his shoulder as he approached the three of us.

"I believe everyone is having a good time." Jackson paused beside me kissing me lightly on the cheek. "You were right, I really needed this."

"You should never doubt me." I smiled, looking up into his beautiful emerald green eyes. He looked incredibly handsome with the sun sparkling off his wavy black hair.

"'Always listen to your wife,' my father used to say, 'because she always has your best interest at heart,'" Lee stated before taking another bite.

"Your father is a wise man," Elizabeth concluded.

Bertina and Tamara brought out the barbecued pork that Davonte had been preparing since yesterday morning. With it they served roasted red garlic pota-toes, corn bread, green beans, corn, and a spinach salad. The aroma immediately made me hungry, and I remembered I'd skipped breakfast that morning in my rush to see to all the party's preparations.

Everyone gathered around the long table set perfectly with fresh linens, china, and silver. Cora had truly outdone herself in her attention to the smallest details from the napkin rings to the placeholders. She was so much like her mother. I smiled to myself as I sat down thinking that in having her with me a part of Mimi was still with me as well.

Once everyone was seated Jackson stood up from his chair at the head of the table and tapped the side of his glass with the butter knife. "I want to thank you all for coming on this beautiful spring day. As we all begin this next journey in our lives, friends and family take on a whole new meaning." He raised his glass of white wine and the rest of us followed suit. "Here's to a blissful journey for us all and may we always share the love and friendship we have today." The party drank gleefully to Jackson's toast before he sat back down.

Soon everyone was talking excitedly about their expectations for the upcoming season. I ate quietly, absorbing the atmosphere around me. Laurie and Elizabeth were discussing their wedding details—the flowers, the dress patterns, the colors. I nodded and remarked cheerfully where appropriate. But in the back of my mind I couldn't shake the uneasiness of Elizabeth's words earlier ... I wanted a child so desperately I could almost cry. With Jackson consumed with work my hours were long and lonely. Even the necessity of waiting broke my heart. *There*, waiting was not only logical, it was necessary, or rather it made sense. But *here ... here*, I'd never wanted anything more.

I glanced around at my closest friends and family, a table full of couples, and realized that they would all most likely have children before Jackson and me. I smiled over at Laurie, nodding along with something she was yammering about and took another long drink of wine.

My heart sank a little further in my chest as I realized fully ... *this is your life*.

CHAPTER FIFTEEN

Saturday, April 10, 2010
Sunday, April 11, 2010

The long hours spent in the CRV were driving me batty. I loved New Orleans and hated leaving, but I was also very anxious to return home and sleep in my own bed. The endless highway stretched on forever with nothing much exciting to view. The day was overcast, which only added to the dreadful nausea I was feeling from sitting in the car for hours on end. Normally, I read on long car rides, but today not even a good book could make me focus. I leaned my head against the window and prayed we would reach Uncle Nicholas's house before I got sick in the car.

After almost fourteen hours in the CRV, we finally arrived in his driveway. Every muscle in my body was stiff and sore. It was close to ten o'clock and all I wanted was to soak in that big ol' tub upstairs. I stretched and yawned trying to get the blood flowing back into my extremities, but my body screamed out in protest. I leaned against the open door as my traveling companions who were experiencing similar difficulties stretched their aching muscles as well.

Upon hearing our moaning and groaning, my uncle appeared on the front porch with warm welcomes. He helped us in with our luggage after hugging each of us. It felt so good to see him again, and I noticed that Sidney seemed to relax a little more in his presence. I hesitated a moment as I watched the two of them walking into his home each with an arm loosely draped around the other. I couldn't have been more thrilled with how well Sidney warmed up to him.

A half hour later I found myself soaking in a tub full of steaming hot water with bubbles up to my chin. I'd left Jackson and Sidney downstairs with Uncle Nicholas as they told him about our little trip to New Orleans. The house was so quiet and peaceful. My muscles began to loosen in the water. I closed my eyes and rested my head against the back of the tub with a washcloth. I was so tired I could have easily fallen asleep in there.

* * *

It was almost noon by the time our band of travelers rolled out of bed to greet Uncle Nicholas. But our gracious host never flinched and instead had a pot of fresh coffee and a healthy breakfast waiting for us as we dragged our tired rears downstairs. I felt like a new person after my long soak in the tub and ten hours of sleep. Jackson and Sidney appeared renewed, full of smiles and smart remarks towards each other as if they'd been friends for years.

My uncle passed me a plate of fresh assorted melons and said, "Jackson tells me that you and Emily are taking a trip to Boston to see Sidney." Sidney's head whipped around mid-bite. Clearly, she hadn't been around when Jackson spilled the beans either.

My eyes narrowed in on my husband who was doing his best to look innocent. "Yes, we're going to visit her sister Elaina."

"And track down Sidney," Jackson added.

"You're making assumptions," I countered.

"Tell me you are not going to look her up while you are there," Jackson said with a challenge ringing in his voice.

"Jackson, we've covered this…" I suddenly lost my appetite.

"Jocelyn, please don't be upset with your husband. He was only seeking my advice on your decision," Uncle Nicholas explained.

"I did not say I was going there to interrogate her. I never said I was even going to confide in her who I am." I watched their expressions change. "Besides, are you telling me that you do not think Emily can be trusted? She is going to be with me the entire time." I raised my eyebrows at them.

"Yes, I trust Emily, but you are not thinking of this from the time perspective of *EVE*. Even if you do not *tell* Sidney who you are, she will recognize you immediately. Her two worlds will be completely adjoined just as yours soon will be, like Jackson's, his family … all of us. I am afraid I would have to agree with Jackson on this one, Jocelyn. Going to Boston is a bad idea. The temptation would be too great," Uncle Nicolas said.

"I agree. As much as I trust my mother, I believe the temptation would be overwhelming," Jackson added.

"Temptation?" Sidney looked confused.

"Yes, temptation." Jackson poured himself some more coffee and added in too much sugar and cream. "Thanks to the photo album your Uncle Monte left behind, Jocelyn and I now know when we'll have children, their gender, and their names. That's more information than either of us should know. With our general knowledge of history, we can piece together too much already. However, our life on this plane thirty years from now is completely unknown to us ... but not to you."

"What if I promise not to tell her anything? Can't I do that? Won't I have a memory of this conversation?" Sidney pleaded. "I really want to see Jocelyn and Emily. It would mean a lot to me."

"I really do not believe it would be a good idea," Uncle Nicholas said.

"Me neither," Jackson agreed.

"Don't I get a say in all this?" I was starting to get annoyed. "You two are acting like the last one hundred thirty years never happened and I have no right to control any aspect of my life."

"Well, if you want to be completely accurate about this situation, the last one hundred thirty years have not taken place and you do not have any rights." Jackson smirked.

"Are you forbidding me to go?" My eyes narrowed as I glared at him trying to control my anger.

"Jocelyn," my uncle said calmly. "It is not just your future Sidney can tell you about, it is everything. Sidney has information about world events for the next thirty years. Surely, you can understand the danger in that knowledge?"

"But what if she promises?" I couldn't believe how unreasonable they were being. "I mean, I *do not* care about world events. Everyone here knows I don't pay attention to the news. I just want to see my sister ..." I reached over and took Sidney's hand. "Or aunt or whatever she is *there*. You have my word I won't inquire about any future events about anything."

"I believe you, sweetheart. I honestly do. Still, I truly do not think it is a good idea. There are simply too many variables, accidents that can happen, unintentional things that could alter your perception," Uncle Nicholas reasoned.

"That's not fair!" I explained, feeling rather childish and hating how it sounded.

"Jocelyn, you know there are some precautions we need to take because of

EVE. This happens to be one of them. I am sorry, darling." Jackson tried to comfort me.

I sat there fuming while my sister remained stoic. I looked over at her blank expression and wished I knew her a little better. Perhaps if I did, if we were closer, I might have some clue what was going on behind her haunted blue eyes. But she remained silent on the subject.

* * *

After our late breakfast and heated debate Jackson and Sidney went down to the IU campus to explore. Finally, alone, Uncle Nicholas made us a tall glass of raspberry iced tea sweetened perfectly with just a smidgen of pure honey. He handed me a glass and I followed him out to the front porch. It was the perfect Midwestern afternoon. The sky was a light blue with thick fluffy marshmallow looking clouds. The air was warm with a barely detectable breeze that wasn't even strong enough to be noticeable. My uncle's carefully groomed flowerbeds were thriving under the recent rain. Tulips and Easter lilies were just beginning to open and reaching their little faces towards the sky. The grass across the massive front lawn had already regained some of its green lushness.

We sat together on the porch swing and spent the afternoon discussing how things were going at home. He was pleased that things seemed to be on the mend with my dad but disappointed with the fact that my mother and Ethan were still not speaking to me. I was touched by his genuine concern over my familial discord. I wished there was something I could do to fix his relationship with my dad. I knew it was something that weighed heavily on my uncle and that the way they left things still upset my dad.

"Do you think there is any way we could make him understand? What if me, Sidney, and the Chandlers all sat down with him with you and explained it all? Make him understand," I said.

"Jocelyn, I love your spirit." He chuckled heartily. "But you know how well the truth worked before on him."

"What if we showed him the album and explain it to him the way we did with Sidney? It wasn't easy, but she finally understood."

"Sidney was experiencing the depletion of her barrier. She was having night terrors, visions of her *other* life. That made all the difference in believing in *EVE.* My brother did not inherit *EVE.* It is almost incomprehensible for him," he explained.

"Why does everything about this have to be so complicated? For the last six months my world has been turned upside down and inside out. Black is white and white is … purple." I gestured wildly for emphasis and exhaled audibly. "Everything I thought I knew and understood turned out to be an illusion."

"I understand how you feel. Why do you think I have spent my entire adult life doing research? I realize to some it may seem ridiculous, but it gives my mind peace by connecting the dots between cultures, profits, medical conditions, and theories. Without it I believe I would have lost my mind years ago living this lifestyle."

"I can appreciate that. I have thought a great deal about your research and theories. I can understand why you find it necessary to put the pieces together. It helps you sleep at night."

"Isn't it strange how something can not only change your life in a matter of moments, but also manage to consume it for the remainder of your life?" His eyes drifted out over the lawn, but I knew he wasn't seeing anything but his own thoughts. His words were barely loud enough for me to hear him.

"Yes, it is. I cannot tell you how many nights I have lost sleep reading Uncle Monte's journals trying to understand the world at that time through his eyes. Or the many times I have sat down and jotted timelines, events, names, and dates trying to piece our heritage together from the things I have learned from you and the Chandlers and my sketchy memories." I sighed heavily and smiled over at him. "I miss being ordinary."

"Ordinary is boring and boring is death. You, Jocelyn Alyssa, are anything but ordinary." My uncle smiled and put his arm around my shoulder with a gentle squeeze.

"But I look at my friends at school. They are worried about grades, colleges, who is dating who, and what they are doing on Friday night. They take history class as a requirement of graduation and most them couldn't care less about it. I was even one of them my junior year. And now, here I am absorbing everything I can find on that time period and the surrounding eras. But I also find myself almost envious of everyone else's naivety of the world around them," I tried to explain.

"I understand. I know many of my colleagues believe I am … odd." He looked over at me and smiled. "They see a man, a lifelong bachelor who never dates, teaches history classes, speaks a little too properly, keeps an organic greenhouse behind his very carefully manicured Victorian home. I am not naïve or blind," he chuckled. "I hear them talk and debate about my sexuality, as if that is the only explanation for my peculiarities."

"And I am guessing you have never corrected them?" I shook my head with a smile.

"Of course not. It is more fun to let them speculate. Why should I destroy their delusions when they seem to enjoy gossiping about them so much?" He let out a hearty laugh.

"You have a devious streak in you I never would have guessed about."

"Well, without Lydia and my son's life can sometimes be a little dull. So sometimes I enjoy poking the noses at trivial matters. I know it is silly, but it is fun."

"True. After being around Alex and Phoebe and their rather unconventional choices, it makes me even more grateful that Jackson is with me. Did you ever consider what Alex and Phoebe have done?" I inquired.

"Like I said before, Lydia is the only lady I have ever loved or could imagine ever loving. She is the mother of my children and the light of my life. For me, there could never be anyone else. I know Alex and Phoebe do not believe what they are doing is adultery or polygamy, and that is fine for them. That is their choice. Personally, I could never do it with having full conscious awareness of both planes. However, I do not judge them for their decisions. We all do what we must, what we feel is best for us to live with this gift." My uncle's gaze shifted back over the lawn.

We sat in silence for a long time, each of us lost in our own thoughts and watching the afternoon sun drift across the sky. It made me sad that my uncle was living down here all alone with only his research to keep him company. I couldn't imagine what his life was like here when we were not around. He didn't have anyone to spend time with, confide in, and no one, but his family knew what a truly amazing man he was, what a kind and loving heart was hidden behind that tweed jacket and odd façade.

"Uncle Nicholas, are you truly happy *here*? Don't you get lonely?" I asked in a low voice and leaned my head against his shoulder.

"It has been lonelier since Monte left, but I manage to occupy my time."

"We will be moving to Boston in June after graduation. Why don't you come with us? There are so many universities in the East." I looked up at his face and noticed for the first time that he and my dad had the exact same eyes.

"I have thought about it since learning about you and the Chandlers. And now, knowing about Sidney too, that is just the icing on the cake, so to speak. I do love the university here. I love the staff and let us not forget I do have tenure." His smile broadened. "That is always a good thing. But perhaps it is time I consider expanding my horizons with my family on this plane as well."

"You mean you will consider it?" I sat up straight and turned towards him. "It would be so wonderful to have you close to us in Boston!"

"I think so too. I will make some inquiries after break." I threw my arms around him and hugged him tightly.

"Thank you!" I squealed.

Jackson and Sidney returned from campus. I couldn't wait to share the good news with them as I hopped down the porch steps to greet them. They were both as excited about the possibility as I was.

The four of us cooked an early dinner together. The image of us strongly reminded me of the everyday occurrence that took place in the Chandler household. Nicholas and Jackson thought nothing of it. Even I was becoming accustomed to it after living within their home for the last several months, but it was clear by Sidney's awkwardness that this experience was completely foreign to her. Still, through her amazement she took to it with high spirits and joined in with a willingness to learn how to prepare and cook a meal.

Sidney rambled on about her classes, cheerleading, and Landon. I could tell by the way she talked about him things were getting serious between them. I was happy for her, but I was also worried about how this gift would affect their relationship. Perhaps she would do as Phoebe and Alex. I knew she could never live in solitary like Uncle Nicholas. Sidney wasn't built that way. I also knew she was married to a man named Keifer Marshall in her *other* life ... at least her fifty-something-year-old self was. I had learned all sorts of things about her *other* life and in some small reaches of my heart I wanted to search her out *there* just to ask her if her fifty-something-year-old-self *here* was still with Landon Harrison. But I knew I wasn't going to be able to because my uncle and Jackson felt so strongly against the trip.

We headed home a little after six in the evening. I wanted to stay another night, but Sidney and Jackson wanted to have time to recuperate before classes started up again on Monday. I hated leaving my uncle. It felt as if every time I saw him, I spent more time saying goodbye to him than anything else. Still, a part of me was anxious to get home. There was nothing quite like crawling into my own bed and getting a good night's sleep. And it had been a long time since I'd been home.

CHAPTER SIXTEEN

MONDAY, April 14, 1879

Emily dropped by shortly after lunch waving an envelope and smiling happily.

"Jocelyn, it arrived. Elaina's letter." She sat down beside me on the lounge where I had been working on my needlepoint. "She is so excited. She cannot wait to see me and meet you."

I hadn't had the opportunity to speak with her alone since my exhaustive conversation with my uncle and Jackson. And truthfully, I had been avoiding speaking with her just because I knew how much she wanted to go also. "That is wonderful. I would love to meet her too. Unfortunately, I do not believe we will be making the trip." I set my needlework aside. "Jackson spoke with Uncle Nicholas *there* and he has forbidden me to go."

"Please, tell me he did not use that phrase?" Her expression darkened.

"Yes," I replied in a low voice.

"I see." Emily stood back up. "Please excuse me, Jocelyn. I need to have a conversation with my son ... and my husband."

And before I could even reply Emily was gone. I picked up my needlepoint and stared at it absentmindedly, not even seeing what was in front of me. I got the worst sick feeling in my stomach knowing what was surely to follow.

* * *

I puttered around the house for the remainder of the afternoon. I was tempted to call Jackson to see what had happened, but I quickly decided against it. A part of me wanted to take Cheyenne out for a ride to clear my head, but I didn't believe I would accomplish the same serenity as before if I had to be escorted by Davonte. There was literally nothing for me to do but sit here and wait.

I wandered from room to room wishing for something to occupy my time. I would have given anything for one of those blasted devices Jackson had told me about and I vaguely recalled, a television or a computer. Either of those would apparently suffice in helping me to waste countless hours. There was no simple and easy way to waste mind numbing hours *here*.

I found myself in the kitchen with Tamesha and Bertina. They were discussing the preparations for dinner when my presence interrupted them.

"Good afternoon, ladies. How is everything going today?" I greeted them.

"Very well, Mrs. Chandler. Is there anything I can do for ya?" Tamesha asked.

"Yes. There is. I would like to make a dessert for this evening. Do you know how to make an angel food cake with a light lemon frosting?"

"Yes, ma'am. I'll start it right away." She began moving over to the pantry.

"No. Tamesha, I am sorry. You misunderstood me. Can you *teach* me how to make one?" I said with a smile and a confidence I didn't feel in my gut.

"Ya want me to show ya how to make it?" I nodded. "Okay."

I spent the next couple hours in the kitchen with Tamesha whipping up egg whites until they stood in a stiff peek and taking advantage of the opportunity to get to know her a little better. I had never really spent much time alone with her before and was pleased to discover Tamesha was a very sweet woman. It took her a little while to feel comfortable with me but after I wore her down, she was soon acting as if we were lifelong friends. She was an excellent teacher, patient, and kind.

We finished up shortly before five. The cake didn't look nearly as beautiful as one Sarah or probably Tamesha could have made, but I was certainly proud of it. And the lemon frosting was heavenly.

I rushed upstairs to get cleaned up and changed my clothes before Jackson came home. Cora was already in my room with a basin of fresh water and was laying out a rose gown trimmed in ivory lace. She helped me undress quickly and freshen up my face and hair. I fussed with my gown. For some reason, most likely because I was in a hurry, it just wouldn't lay right. It was all twisted. I let out a deep breath of frustration followed by a laugh of exasperation. Cora looked at me strangely for a moment and then busted out laughing herself.

"This is ridiculous!" I declared. "I cannot get this thing straight."

"Arms up. Turn around."

I held my arms over my head while Cora twisted and pulled my gown straight. We giggled like two young schoolgirls. It was such a silly thing, two grown women struggling to put on a gown.

"There, how's that?" She grinned.

"Wonderful. Thank you."

I spun around to face the mirror while Cora fastened the eyelets on my dress. We both straightened it out and smoothed it down. It looked beautiful. The deep rose color brought out the blush in my cheeks and flattered my tiny figure. I turned sideways wishing for a half second that I had a tad bit larger chest just to enhance the bodice.

"Thank you, Cora." She handed me my shawl off the corner of my bed since there was a little chill in the air.

"Have a good evening, Mrs. Chandler."

"You too, Cora."

* * *

Jackson arrived home around a quarter after six. He handed Davonte his hat and jacket before pouring himself a brandy ... something he rarely did. I watched him silently knowing it best to keep my mouth shut and let him begin when he was ready. I remained on the lounge in the parlor pretending to read while watching him out of the corner of my eye.

After his third brandy he put the glass down and walked over near the hearth. He drummed his fingers on the mantle for a few moments before turning and facing me.

"My mother came down to the office this afternoon," he began. "She interrupted our day, pulled my father and me into his office, and lectured me for a solid hour." I could tell he was struggling to remain calm. "I have never been more humiliated in all my life. How could you tell my mother I forbade you to visit Boston?"

"Emily came over after lunch. She was very excited saying she had received a reply from her sister, Elaina. She said her sister was very happy to receive us and meet me. So, I told her that after your conversation with Uncle Nicholas, you forbade me to go. Is that not what you said at his house?" I said innocently.

"Jocelyn, you must understand. By telling my mother that I forbade you, you might as well tell her I beat you. She was livid."

"I am so sorry, Jackson. It was not my intent to get your mother upset with you," I tried to explain.

"But you did. I cannot recall ever seeing her so upset." He shook his head slightly.

"Did you expect me to lie to her? She asked me a question. I answered her honestly. Please, tell me what I did wrong?" I asked in a tone he was not familiar with from me.

"Don't be coy. You know good and well what you did and what the result would be." His eyes narrowed just a smidgen.

"So, you wanted me to lie. Is that what you're saying?" I said flatly.

"I expected you to be considerate of your husband." Jackson raised his voice a mere octave.

"I will not be told what ..." A knock on the front door ended my reply.

We stood in silence and listened to Davonte greet the visitors at our front door. His voice was followed directly by those of Robert and Emily. Moments later the two of them were standing in the doorway of our parlor. I immediately rose and pleasantly greeted them with smiles and hugs.

"Good evening, I apologize for interrupting your evening." Emily hugged me back and then whispered in my ear. "I am afraid I upset my son earlier and didn't want him to blame you for it."

"Please come in." I motioned towards the seats in the parlor. "Have you had dinner this evening?"

"Not yet." Robert sat down in a chair beside the fire. "My wife wanted to come here first."

"Then you must join us for dinner," I offered. "Excuse me for a moment. I must tell Tamesha to set two more settings." I hurried off to the kitchen.

Emily was a bit shocked when I informed her I was the baker of the angel food cake. She knew I was fairly helpless when it came to baking. She was pleased that my cook was such an easy-going, kind, and pleasant woman.

The table was set with an ivory tablecloth, two tear-lit candles, china dishes, and a bouquet of purple violets. Tamesha had prepared a lemon chicken on a bed of fluffy white rice, snow peas, and yeast rolls. Halfway through our delicious dinner, Emily broke the news I had been dreading.

"I got a letter from my sister, Elaina. She is very excited to see us," she mentioned casually.

"Is that the plan? Stay with Aunt Elaina and Uncle Samuel while you interrogate Sidney?" Jackson paused and looked directly at his mother.

"I beg your pardon. We are not going to interrogate anyone, least of all Sidney." Emily didn't miss a beat.

"You have an Uncle Sam?" I giggled.

"Yes," Jackson shot me a disapproving look.

"Sorry. I just thought it was ironic." I immediately shut up.

"I have to agree with your uncle on this. He does not believe this trip is a good idea. There are some things that are better left unknown. This trip is only going to cause problems, in *both* your worlds," Jackson continued.

"What exactly are your concerns, son?" Robert inquired.

"Sidney is around fifty right now, correct?"

"I believe so," I answered.

"Do you believe you will not be tempted whatsoever to inquire about your *other* life?" His eyes narrowed a little across the table at me.

"I am not following." I moved the food around on my plate to avoid his eyes. We both knew I was aware what he was thinking.

"Sidney can answer all types of questions about the future *there*. And not just your future either. I am referring to advancements in technology, medicine, world events, all of it. You believe you can resist the desire to know what the world you are only now beginning to slightly understand is like decades from what you currently know. Can you?" His eyes shifted towards his mother.

"I cannot deny it is intriguing." A slight grin slid across her lips. "But I do know how to restrain myself, Jackson."

"I am sorry. It is not that I do not trust your ability to restrain yourself. I simply believe the temptation may be too dangerous." He took another bit of his chicken.

"I am not a child, son. I think you are exaggerating a bit." Emily rolled her eyes in my direction with a slight grin.

"We shall see." Jackson smirked.

"Very nice. Very nice." Emily pointed at her son's plate. "Eat your vegetables."

Nothing was settled by the time dinner was over. The only thing we had managed to accomplish was aggravate each other even more than before. Jackson wouldn't budge from his point of view and for the first time in my life, I wouldn't either. Jackson was stunned by my attitude and I could tell he did not appreciate this newfound independence of mine. But I didn't care. I had spent my entire life being told what I could and could not do by the men in my life. For the first time ever, I decided I was going to stand up for myself and not let my life be dictated to me.

Jackson didn't speak to me after his parents left for the evening. As soon as the door closed behind them, he retreated to his office without saying a single word to me. I considered following him but then thought otherwise. I climbed up the stairs and got ready for bed. I did not see him the rest of the evening.

CHAPTER SEVENTEEN

Monday, April 12, 2010

I woke up early to the dreaded sound of the alarm clock blaring on Jackson's side of the bed. He rolled over and grumblingly smacked the button on top before rolling himself out of bed. He headed into the bathroom to start the shower while I pulled the covers up over my head, wishing I could sleep for a couple more hours. It had been such a long and mentally exhausting spring break and I felt anything but refreshed on our first day back at school. I could only hope that Sidney was faring better than I was.

She hadn't been doing so well when she departed for school last evening. Our stop over at Uncle Nicholas's on our way home seemed to ease her spirit some. It appeared to me that his presence had the same calming effect on her as it did on me. She was much more relaxed at his house than the entire time we'd spent in New Orleans. I wish we'd had more time with her to help her adjust. It reminded me again how thankful I was not only to have Jackson to help me but the support of his entire family also. Uncle Nicholas promised to keep in touch with her daily either by phone or email to make sure she was transitioning as best she could on her own. I knew the semester was only several more weeks longer, but I knew how terrified she was feeling and how alone those weeks were going to feel. She promised to call me often and did her best to be strong even though her eyes betrayed her.

* * *

Our first day back was creeping by ever so slowly. I missed New Orleans, Sidney, and my uncle, even the mindless humming of the wheels on the highway. Sitting in AP Lit was the last place I wanted to be. My teacher, Mrs. Killian, was rambling on about *Into the Wild* by Jon Krakauer. We were spending the entire semester writing various papers on this one single book. I had read it cover to cover so many times I was sick and tired of hearing about it. As much as I really liked Mrs. Killian, I could not bring myself to pay attention to another long-winded episode on the topic. I was doing my best just to stay awake.

The hallway was crowded as I pushed my way to my locker. Voices bounced off the walls with various tales of spring break adventures. Caitlyn rushed up beside me while I was stuffing my backpack in my locker. "You're not going to believe this … you're not going to be the only married girl in high school."

"What?" I slammed my locker shut and leaned up against it.

"Cody just told Zak that Hailey is pregnant." Caitlyn smirked. "Can you believe that?"

"Corbin's girlfriend? The blonde annoying one?"

I vaguely recalled my brother's best friend's girlfriend. She had been over to our house a few times with Corbin. She was always draped all over him. I knew that the relationship between Corbin and Hailey had caused some friction between Corbin and Ethan. Apparently, Corbin couldn't go anywhere or do anything without Hailey glued to his side. Plus, Liang and Hailey were very different and didn't exactly get along well.

"Yeah, the ditzy one who dresses in clothes two sizes too small and thinks she's so much prettier than she actually is." She rolled her eyes. "I remember Corbin used to hang out with Ethan all the time, but now …"

"How is Corbin taking it?"

"Like I said, I guess they're getting married," she laughed. "They're only seventeen!"

We pushed our way towards the cafeteria. "And pregnancy is a good reason to get married?"

"Not in my opinion. Plus, Hailey has the maturity level of a six-year-old. I actually feel sorry for Corbin."

"Why? It is not like she forced him into anything. He lost his entire identity once he got involved with her. It is kind of sad and pathetic," I remarked, rolling my eyes.

"I guess that's what happens when you have absolutely no self-esteem and daddy issues. Or mommy issues," Caitlyn concluded.

"Which one of them?" I entered the cafeteria.

"Take your pick…" Caitlyn followed me towards the food line.

The guys were already waiting at our usual table when we arrived. Caitlyn and I grabbed a slice of pizza and a chocolate chip cookie along with iced teas. I had gotten so use to eating healthy food at the Chandler's it made the pizza at school taste even worse.

I set my tray on the table and slid into the chair beside Jackson. Caitlyn sat down next to Zak across from us. I noticed Ethan sitting beside Liang and several of the other juniors at a table across the cafeteria. He looked up when he noticed me but didn't even bother to give me a nod.

"Did you hear the news?" Zak began.

"I just told her." Caitlyn took a bite of her pizza.

"Told her what?" Jackson inquired. He was picking at his food with little interest.

"Hailey's pregnant. She and Corbin are getting married," Zak informed him.

"Who is Hailey?" Jackson looked over at me.

"You remember her. She is the girl that is always hanging on Ethan's best friend, Corbin. They were at that party Ethan decided to throw at my parents' house last fall." I tried to jog his memory.

"The obnoxious blonde that was always giggling?" Jackson asked.

"That's the one." Caitlyn nodded.

"Wow. She is annoying." I looked over at Jackson, surprised at his words. He never really remarked on people in such a way.

"Okay, enough of the sad and immature. Have you decided whether or not you're going to try out for the softball team tomorrow?" Caitlyn dropped her pizza back on the tray with disgust.

"I haven't decided yet," I mumbled.

"I agree with your dad. You really should not let Jenna and Hillary keep you from playing. You love softball," Jackson said.

"You have to play. It's our senior year … our final year. We've played softball every year since we were five years old. You can't quit now. It wouldn't be right," Caitlyn pleaded.

"I know, it's just … well, I barely made it through basketball season because of those two and their smart-ass remarks."

"Come on, you play first base, Hillary will be buried behind the plate, and Jenna is out in left field. You'll never have to interact with either of them," Caitlyn pointed out.

"Just the entire time we're in the dug-out," I muttered, rolling my eyes at her.

"What position do you play?" Jackson inquired.

"Short stop," Zak answered for her. "She's bad-ass on the field." He smiled over at his girlfriend with pride.

"Softball is my favorite sport." Caitlyn blushed a bit. "Are you seriously going to let them win? I've never known you to walk away from a fight, especially when you're in the right."

"I know, I know." I let out a deep sigh. "All right, I will try out."

"Fabulous!" Caitlyn squealed with delight. "I knew you wouldn't let me down."

CHAPTER EIGHTEEN

TUESDAY, *April 15, 1878*

I walked down to Phoebe's house after a late lunch to visit with her and play with my nephew, Wallace. The Easter lilies and tulips were beginning to bloom in a variety of brilliant colors. Despite the slight chill in the air, it was a gorgeous day. The sound of my heels shuffling on the cobblestones and the swish of my gown were muffled greatly by the song being sung by the blue jay perched on a branch in the willow tree of Elizabeth's yard as I passed her home along the walkway.

Katie, Phoebe's housekeeper, greeted me upon my arrival. She was a small mousy woman with pale gray eyes. She had a kind demeanor and a soft voice. She stood back from the door wiping her hands on her apron. "Good afternoon, Mrs. Chandler. Please, come in. Mrs. Monroe is in the parlor."

"Thank you, Katie." I handed her my shawl and bonnet.

Phoebe was sitting in the rocking chair beside the hearth listening to the phonograph and knitting a pair of socks for her husband, Silas. She looked like a painting, rocking slightly back and forth, lost in her own thoughts.

"Phoebe?" I said in a soft voice. "Am I interrupting?"

"No, of course not." A smile spread across her shapely lips and reached her eyes. She looked surprisingly like her mother only a little taller.

"You looked lost in thought." I took a seat in the rocker across from her.

"Wallace is down for a nap, so I was taking advantage of the time to ponder

97

over a case I am working on *there*." She kept her voice low knowing Katie was in the kitchen and not entirely out of earshot.

"Anything interesting?" I wasn't entirely fascinated by the law, but criminal law was somewhat intriguing.

"My client is accused of murdering his business partner because the victim had extorted money from the business accounts and then lost all the money gambling." She absentmindedly continued knitting while she talked.

"I take it he has no alibi."

"Not really. On the night in question he claims he was driving up to his cabin in Vermont. Problem is, at the time of the murder, he had not yet reached his cabin. He says he pulled over in a rest area and took a nap, but of course, there are no cameras in that particular rest stop to prove he was actually there."

"Do you believe him?"

"As an attorney, it is not my job to believe him or not."

"But do you?"

"Personally, I am not sure. A part of me does but I have learned to stay detached in any way, shape, or form from my clients. I make a better attorney if I do not know anything about my clients but the facts pertaining to the case."

"That must be hard."

"Trust me, it is for the best. Most of the people I represent I do not wish to know." She shook her head slightly.

"It must be exciting though."

"Exciting? Yeah, I enjoy meeting people in the county jails awaiting trial or high-powered executives who believe they are above the law because of the amount of money they have." Phoebe chuckled. "I really should not complain. I am good at what I do and make a very good living at it."

She and I spent the better part of the afternoon discussing various scenarios to prove her client was innocent. It sounded to me like the victim's wife killed him. She had more of a motive than his business partner, but the wife had activated their home alarm system at ten in the evening and according to the alarm company, it was not deactivated until the police arrived to notify her of her husband's murder at seven thirty the next morning giving her an airtight alibi.

As I walked back home in the early evening hours I was intrigued by Phoebe's case. It was much more interesting than I would have previously thought. I had never considered going into law and still honestly wasn't, but it was entertaining to discuss with my sister-in-law instead of our typical conversations about family, relationships, and idle gossip around town on who was doing what and with whom.

* * *

Jackson was still barely speaking to me. He wasn't exactly being rude, but there was a noticeable chill in his words. I knew how upset he was about the idea of his mother and I traveling to Boston and there didn't seem to be enough reassurances I could express to make him feel any better. I had tried reasoning with him, pleading with him, and promising him everything I could think of under the sun, but to no avail. I had finally reached the point that I was upset with him for being such a negative pain in my ass.

Shortly before heading upstairs to retire for the evening, I found Jackson in his office buried behind a pile of papers. His hair was tousled from his nervous habit of running his fingers through his wavy locks. When he looked up at me, I noticed the dark circles under his emerald eyes. He was truly exhausted.

"Are you all right, darling?" I walked around behind him and wrapped my arms around him hugging him tightly.

"Yes, I am tired is all." He looked back at me with a weary smile and patted my arms giving me a loving squeeze. "Did you happen to read the paper today?"

"No, I spent the day with Phoebe. She was telling me about a case she is working on *there*. It was pretty interesting, a murder trial," I told him.

"Well, it is a shame she is not an attorney *here*. Perhaps she could figure out who is behind these attacks." Jackson handed me the newspaper he had been reading earlier when he arrived home. "This is why I do not want you out by yourself."

"Another attack," I asked as I walked over to the rocker beside the fire and sat down with the paper in hand.

"Yes, and this one was much worse than the last one," Jackson pointed out.

"But I had thought they had caught the man responsible?"

"Apparently, they were wrong," he told me.

I unfolded the paper and looked at the headline: Chicago Slayer Strikes Again. A cold chill ran down my spine and I looked over at Jackson. He had already started reading whatever legal document that was in front of him. I returned my focus back on the paper and began reading the top story.

It seemed a woman named Kelly Robertson had been found dead in an alley between a brothel and a tavern last evening. It was speculated that she had been raped but being that she was a woman of unfortunate means, they could not be certain. She was a well-known madam at the brothel who had run the establishment for the last twenty years or so. It said she was in her mid-fifties and was known for having a harsh tongue with the ladies and patrons alike. It seemed when the body of Ms. Robertson was found, her face had been disfigured, her nose and lips removed, and she had been stabbed forty-two times. The paper called it an unnecessary and vicious case of overkill.

"Oh, my goodness," I said, setting the paper aside and looking back at my husband. "That is horrible."

Jackson rose from his desk and walked over to me. He sat down in the rocker across from me and took my hands in his. "Now do you understand why I worry about you being out without an escort?" I nodded numbly at him. "The police now believe that there are at least two assailants because of the direction and type of wounds found on the body."

"Are they only attacking women like ... her?" I wasn't sure what to call her.

"No, but Ms. Robertson was the sixth victim. Three of the others were young women who worked in her establishment—that's how I knew who she was and what she was. But the other two ladies were simply women who happened to be in the wrong place at the wrong time. One was married with a young daughter and the other was engaged to be married this summer." Jackson shook his head slightly. "These men are monsters. And until they are caught, I want you to be extremely careful. Even if you are just going across the street to my parents' house or next door to yours, I want you to have Davonte escort you."

"All right." I had to admit this new development scared me.

"I am not trying to be overprotective, Jocelyn. I simply worry about your safety."

"How do you know who Ms. Robertson is?" I had to ask.

"I never met her, but I read the police reports where she was interviewed when her employees were murdered," Jackson explained.

"What she did have to say about them?" I couldn't fathom what type of woman she was.

"She seemed horrified by them. I did not know her, and I try not to be judgmental of her. I have no idea what circumstances brought her to where she was." He shrugged. "But she seemed to care about the ladies that were murdered."

"Still, I cannot imagine why someone would commit such a heinous crime, removing her facial features clearly is sending a message. Do you think the assailants believe she knew who they were and that she informed the police during her interview?" I inquired.

"That is the theory at the moment." Jackson smiled. "Are you sure you are not interested in pursuing a career in law? You certainly have the mind for it."

"I suppose recently I have been considering it. After spending so much time with Phoebe discussing her cases, I admit it has piqued my interest," I confessed.

"Really?" I smiled into his eyes feeling wonderful that we were connecting again after our recent disagreement.

"I am thinking about it." I reached out and touched his hand.

"Well, I think it is wonderful. And sort of a Chandler family tradition at this point." Jackson got up and kneeled in front of me holding my hands in his. "You know, Jocelyn, I would do anything in this world for you. I simply want you to be happy and safe. So please try to understand my concerns."

"I do, sweetheart. I do." I leaned forward and kissed him softly.

"I need to finish up some paperwork and then I will join you upstairs." He rose to his feet pulling me up in front of him. I wrapped my arms around his neck, kissed him again with a little more intensity, and then hugged him tightly.

"Do not take too long." I gave him a sly grin, letting my hand linger on his before I left his office.

* * *

Jackson came to bed a good hour after I had retired for the evening. However, I was still awake, laying on my side and staring out the window. I couldn't sleep. I heard him fumbling around in the dark getting ready for bed. I felt him crawl into bed beside me and his back pressed against mine. I rolled over and wrapped my arms around him, feeling the warmth of his body spread through mine. He placed his arm over mine and intertwined our fingers. Despite our differences as of late, I couldn't imagine my life without him.

CHAPTER NINETEEN

TUESDAY, April 13, 2010

Jackson and Zak sat on the bleachers beside the softball field watching as try-outs began. The air was cool, with just enough of a breeze to make it feel colder than the actual sixty-three degrees. I was wearing fleece hoodie and sweatpants with my cleats and tossing the ball with Caitlyn, trying to warm up my arm. So far, neither Jenna nor Hilary had made an appearance.

Our coach for the last two years had been Mr. Brenton Kane. He was a twenty-six-year-old blond, blue-eyed cutie that had been hired straight out of college as our gym teacher and girls' softball coach. We had christened him with the nickname of Candy Kane behind his back although we were sure he was aware of it. Of course, he also had a beautiful girlfriend with legs up to her armpits that came to our games.

Over thirty girls showed up for try-outs. Only fifteen would make the team. I always hated try-outs. They would last the next four afternoons and be fundamentally demanding. It made me feel horrible for the girls that didn't make the cut. Most just slumped off to the locker room, but some cried. Not a wailing cry but those silent tears that would escape before they could retreat from the group. Even after three years of playing on the high school team, I was still afraid I would be one of them.

Coach Kane glanced down at his clipboard and blew the whistle. "Okay, everyone over on the bleachers," he hollered.

Caitlyn and I, along with all the other hopefuls, jogged over to the bleachers where Jackson and Zak were seated on the top rung. We filled up the bottom four rows and tried to keep the whispering down to a dull roar.

"All right, all right ... please calm down." Coach Kane tapped on his clipboard impatiently. "Thank you all for coming out today. I know you're all a little excited. I am too, but we need to get organized before we can begin. Coach Smith and Coach Minnick were kind enough to offer their time to help me out this week. I'm going to put you in three groups, so we can evaluate your skills."

The coaches put us into three random groups and of course, I was put in the group under the watchful eye of Coach Smith. Caitlyn got to spend her afternoon in the company of Coach Kane. Coach Smith took our group over to the batting cages for some practice. I hadn't picked up a bat in over seven months. Luckily, it all came back when I held it in my hands. I relaxed, stepped into it, and swung. It felt fabulous. All the built-up frustration in both my worlds exploded when that bat contacted the ball. I had to bite my lip from screaming out with joy at the release.

We spent the final hour fielding and running bases. I was hot, sweaty, and covered in dirt by the time we finished up for the day. Jackson and Zak climbed out of the bleachers to join Caitlyn and me on the field and walked with us back up to the school.

* * *

I threw on a pair of flannel pajama bottoms and a long-sleeved T-shirt after a long hot shower. I walked back into our bedroom and collapsed across our bed. I was completely exhausted. I closed my eyes and listened to the voices of my husband and in-laws below in the kitchen. I was just about to drift off when I heard the doorbell ring. I rolled over snuggling up with our duvet when footsteps on the stairs brought me back to reality.

"Sweetheart. Are you awake?" Jackson sat down on the corner of our bed. "Your dad is here. He wants to speak with you."

"All right," I mumbled, not wanting to move.

"Come on." Jackson stood up and held out his hand for me. I reached up, taking it and allowed him to pull me to my feet. "Nice hair," he grinned.

"Shut up." I knew I looked a mess, but I honestly didn't care. Every muscle in my body was sore.

My dad was sitting in the family room talking with Jackson's parents. He stood up when I entered the room and wrapped his arms around me.

104

"Ethan told me you went to try-outs today. I am so proud of you." He kissed me on the cheek before we sat down on the couch together.

"Caitlyn wouldn't let me not try out. She can be very pushy when she wants to be." I tucked my stocking feet up under me to keep warm.

"I am glad she is. Ethan said neither Jenna nor Hilary tried out for the team."

I shook my head. "They never showed up. I was surprised. They have always played before."

"Well, I probably shouldn't say anything, but I think Jenna is going through a rough time right now. Her parents have split up. Craig moved out over spring break and got an apartment in the city. I spoke with him briefly before he left, and he said their house was going up for sale in another month or so. They are trying to hold out at least until Jenna graduates," he told the four of us.

"I had no idea. Jenna must be devastated." I looked over at Jackson.

Despite everything, Jenna had been my best friend for eighteen years and I hated the thought of her going through such a difficult time.

"Why did they split? Did Craig say anything else?"

"That's where it gets a little touchy."

"Why?" I had always thought of Jenna's parents as rather normal and boring individuals. Nothing could have prepared me for the words that fell out of my father's mouth.

"It seems her mother … ummm, Melinda decided to come out of the closet so to speak."

"What!"

"That's what I said when Craig told me. I never would have guessed that one in a million years," he said.

"Me neither. I cannot believe this. Jenna must be devastated." I leaned back against Jackson and the couch.

"That explains a lot about her recent behavior. Jenna is taking all the anger and hurt feelings over her parents' separation and mother's sexual revolution out on you," Robert observed.

Emily looked sideways at her husband with a strange look before she added. "Yes, dear. I believe so."

"Yes. I stated the obvious. What I was trying to express to Jocelyn was that Jenna's anger was not truly directed at her. I was only trying to make her feel better. I realize it did not come out right," Robert grinned.

"Perhaps. But still, Jenna is doing everything she can to make my life at school miserable. I was thrilled when she and Hilary did not show up at try-outs. I realize that might sound terrible, but it's still true," I explained.

"Maybe you should try talking to her," my dad suggested.

"No, I don't think so. If she wants to talk with me, she knows where I am." I was not willing to put myself out there to be her punching bag again.

"Jocelyn, Jenna is your best friend," my dad began.

"Was … Jenna was my best friend," I interrupted.

"Jocelyn don't be a child," he lectured. "She is going through a really difficult time. I am sure she needs your support. Can't you try and be the bigger person?"

"And exactly how do you suggest I do that? Every time I get near her, she starts throwing insults at me and snide comments."

"Why not try reaching out to her outside of school when she is less likely to be on the defensive? Perhaps you should go over to her house and try talking to her," Emily suggested.

"I will think about it," I muttered, wanting to drop the subject. I turned towards my dad. "So how is Ethan handling Corbin's situation with Hailey?"

"I heard about that. Ethan was rambling on about it the other night. I cannot imagine what their parents are going through. I mean, I had a hard time accepting your marriage and you're legally an adult and not pregnant."

"It was all anyone could talk about today at school, but I never saw the happy couple. I don't think they were there," I observed.

"Can you blame them? They are probably dealing with a lot right now. It must be very difficult on both families," Emily stated.

"I would imagine so. Ethan hasn't even spoken with Corbin since he broke the news this weekend. Your brothers tried to call him but hasn't been able to reach him. He's worried about him. He said Corbin's parents went ballistic. From what he explained, they took it worse than Hailey's," my dad remarked.

"It's not too shocking. I know she is not a prostitute, but she certainly wears the uniform. They can't be all that surprised." I half chuckled.

Robert and Emily looked at Jackson and I confused.

"She dresses a little skimpy," Jackson explained.

"That is an understatement," I muttered.

"Oh, I see." Robert tried to hide his smirk while Emily did the same by dropping her head a bit.

"Ethan told me a while back when Corbin had started dating her that Hailey's parents had gotten divorced when she was in junior high and she had a real messed up relationship with her dad and hated her mom. But he said her parents let her pretty much do anything she wanted." I looked over at my dad and shrugged.

"That explains her attachment to Corbin," Jackson stated.

"Worse than that, her mom actually lets her spend the night at his house. How messed up is that?" I added.

"Well, they cannot be surprised by her pregnancy then." Robert shook his head slightly. "I cannot imagine allowing Phoebe to do that when she was a junior. That is just asking for teenage parents."

"Ethan said that Corbin's parents always thought Corbin wasn't into girls, so they really didn't care if Hailey stayed over." I half chuckled. "I always thought Corbin had a crush on Ethan. I used to tease him about it all the time, even after Corbin start dating Hailey."

"Maybe he bats for both teams?" My dad smirked. "Who knows?"

All four heads spun around and stared at my dad for a moment before all of us busted out laughing. I couldn't believe those words fell out of his mouth. I had never in my life ever heard him say anything like that before.

Emily invited my dad to join us for dinner and he happily accepted. I knew he wouldn't give up the opportunity for a home cooked meal. It was wonderful having him with us and sitting down as a family. We talked a lot about our trip to New Orleans, the things we saw, the food we ate, and the places we went. Of course, we all failed to mention our little stop at Uncle Nicholas's.

I really wish I could have shared that part with him. I truly wished I could explain to him the amazing thing that was *EVE*. I wanted him to reconcile his relationship with his younger brother since he had become such an important part of my family as of late.

But as I looked across the table and watched my dad eating his dinner and smiling with ease, I knew *EVE* was not something that he was ready to learn about. And I had to accept the fact that he might never be. I couldn't really blame him, and I didn't. I knew explaining *EVE* and all it entailed was difficult enough for someone who was experiencing it firsthand, but it would have been completely impossible for anyone else.

CHAPTER TWENTY

FRIDAY, April 18, 1879

I was still sitting at the dining room table reading the newspaper after Jackson left for the office when someone knocked on our front door. I put the paper aside, wondering who in the world would be here so early in the morning. Muffled words came drifting from the foyer, but I couldn't make out whose voices they were.

Two seconds later Emily rushed into my dining room holding a folded envelope. She sat down in the chair her son had occupied a short while ago and thanked Tamesha as she poured her a fresh cup of hot coffee. Emily's eyes stayed on Tamesha until she returned to the kitchen.

"I apologize for stopping by so early, but this was delivered to me last evening after dinner. I didn't want to stop over while Jackson was still here since it was strange." I tried to look at the cover from where I was seated, but I couldn't make out the handwriting on the front.

"What do you mean? Who is it from?"

"That is what is so strange. Barnaby answered the door and the young lady there insisted that she give this envelope directly to me and no one else. When she handed it to me, she told me the letter was for you, that I was not to open it and to only give it to you when no one else was around." Emily looked as confused as I was.

"That is strange." Emily handed me the sealed envelope.

I turned it over to see if there was anything written on the other side. There wasn't. On the front was nothing more than my name. I glanced over at Emily again and she shrugged. So, I tore open the side and slipped the letter out. I read aloud:

Dear Jocelyn,

I apologize for so much secrecy, but I am sure you can understand why I am taking such precautions. I know this will come as a surprise to you, but how could I ever forget our visit to Uncle Nicholas's house on spring break when I learned all about our unique gift? While we were sitting at that table and Jackson forbade you to visit me, it occurred to me that I could come to you.

So here I am in Chicago. My husband, Keifer, and I arrived on the train yesterday morning and are staying at a little B&B off of Washington Street called Marigold's Bed and Breakfast. I am so excited to see you. I promise I will not discuss anything that might get either of us into trouble. Of course, I can't. Keifer knows nothing of EVE even though two of four of our children inherited the gift from me. I can tell you that after all these years since that day we sat in that kitchen (and yes, I know it's not even been a week for you … talk about strange), Uncle Nicholas was right in warning us. EVE is very tricky, and I will abide by Jackson and Uncle Nicholas's wishes. However, I could not pass up the opportunity to see you and put a little bit of your mind at ease with how I am coping.

I will make reservations for lunch at Dawson's on the corner of Washington Street and 42nd Street. I look forward to seeing you and Emily at eleven o'clock.

Love always,
   Sidney

I put the letter down and looked over at my stunned-beyond-words mother-in-law. It took Emily a second or two to recompose herself before she could respond.

"I had no idea," she muttered. "I cannot believe she's here. Did she mention anything to you before she went back to Northwestern?"

"No." I shook my head still in shock by what I'd just read. "She said nothing about this."

"Well, she's had some time to think about it, as she pointed out." Emily smiled. "What would you like to do?"

"Meet her for lunch, of course. Wouldn't you?" I ran my fingertips across the letter wondering what Sidney must be like. It was impossible for me to imagine her fifty years old and in this time period.

"Yes, if you would like me to join you. I would love to come." She watched me for a moment and sipped her coffee. "Are you all right?"

"No." My whole body felt numb. "My mind is still trying to process everything."

"I believe it would be best if we keep Sidney's visit just between us. Even though Robert wasn't exactly against our trip, I feel we shouldn't say anything to him or even around the staff," Emily said in a low voice.

"I understand." I nodded in agreement.

"I need to take care of a few things at home before we go to lunch." She stood up and put her hand on my shoulder. "Will you be all right?"

"Yes, thank you." I placed my hand over hers and gave it a gentle squeeze. "I will be over at ten thirty."

"All right, dear, I will see you then." Emily rose and headed for the door. Just before she left the dining room, she turned back towards me. "Oh, and Jocelyn." I looked back up at her from the letter. "Toss that letter in the fireplace." I nodded, and she left almost as abruptly as she arrived.

I sat there for a little while longer rereading Sidney's letter looking for clues to something I'd missed. I couldn't find any. I tried to place myself in Sidney's shoes and imagine what she was thinking by coming all this way knowing all she did. I was torn between excited and terrified to see her. Cora and Tamesha came in separately to make sure I was okay and ask if I needed anything. I told them both I was fine. I just wanted to be alone for a while. I got up slowly and walked into the parlor where Davonte had a low fire burning just to take the chill out of the morning air. My eyes reread her words one final time before I laid the letter and its envelope down on the burning logs. I stood there watching the edges catch fire and the letter begin to curl in on itself. I stood there until the entire letter was nothing more than ashes. All evidence of its existence was gone.

I made it upstairs to my room and rummaged through my armoire seeking out the perfect attire for our luncheon. As silly as it seemed I wanted to wear something special and look my best. I finally decided on my pale blue satin skirt and jacket with the white lace blouse. It was sophisticated and elegant with a classy feminine style that I loved.

Cora came in and helped me get ready. She curled my hair before she took my long locks and pinned them up in a stylish bun at the nap of my neck. She left a few stands hanging loosely to accent my face. She then helped me into my outfit and gave me my bonnet and shawl. I told her that I was going into the city with Emily for lunch and to do a little shopping and that I would be back before dinnertime.

* * *

Emily and I followed the waitress to a table for four in the corner of the busy restaurant. Sidney had not yet arrived, so we sat down to wait patiently for her and browse through the menu. The air was filled with such a combination of deliciousness that I was sure my stomach was going to growl. It was a nice place, not overly fancy or flashy, but simple and homey. The tablecloths were blue and white checkered, and each table had a small vase in the center filled with fresh daisies. I liked this place immediately.

"Nervous?" Emily asked.

"Yes, very," I confessed.

"Just remember, this is your sister Sidney. She's the same person you recall from your *other* plane. Granted, she'll look a little different, but it's still her nonetheless." She repeated the same words I had been repeating to myself all morning.

"Jocelyn?" I recognized her voice immediately. My eyes spotted her without effort amongst the busy lunch crowd. This woman, this version of Sidney was still every bit as lovely as her twenty-year-old self. Her golden blond hair was now white, but it was still long, and she had it pinned up in a bun like my own. Her bright blue eyes had slightly paled over the years, but they still held their vibrancy. She was also every bit as tiny and petite as her *other* self.

The man beside her was at least six feet tall. He had broad shoulders, thick white hair with a matching mustache and goatee. His eyes were a deep green and when he smiled at us, I noticed he had beautiful dimples in both cheeks that made him look years younger than his actual age.

"Sidney?" I stood as she approached.

"Oh, my goodness." She threw her arms around me and held me tightly. "I cannot believe it. You ... you're so young." She took a step back and looked me over. "You are so lovely."

"So are you!" I exclaimed. "You are so beautiful. I would know you anywhere." I hugged her again brushing the tears off my cheeks.

"My word, where are my manners? Hello, Mrs. Chandler, how are you? You look wonderful." Sidney embraced my mother-in-law briefly, which took us both by surprise. "I would like you both to meet my husband, Keifer Marshall." She turned towards him. "And dear, this is my niece, Jocelyn. She's my brother Patrick's daughter. And this is her mother-in-law, Mrs. Emily Chandler." We each shook his hand.

"It is a pleasure to finally meet you both. I have heard so much about you." He smiled warmly.

"Please, call me Emily," Emily said in greeting to Sidney's husband.

We ordered a light lunch, but the only one who bothered to eat was Keifer. The rest of us were too busy chatting about Sidney's children, their life in Boston, and everything that we could cover without discussing anything inappropriate.

I couldn't believe how this Sidney was so like the other Sidney. Her laugh was the same, her mannerisms, her facial expressions. It was fascinating and weird at the same time. I tried my best not to continually stare at her, but I found it difficult not to. I also discovered that her husband was quite charming as well. Keifer lacked the serious and often dry nature of most the physicians I'd encountered. Instead, he had a hearty laugh, a warm smile, and was quick to see the bright side of any situation.

The hours flew by and I was so disappointed when Emily pointed out that it was already five o'clock. No wonder the waiters had been giving us dirty looks. I was surprised they hadn't said anything to us. But I had noticed that the dinner crowd was beginning to roll in.

We parted outside on the sidewalk with a promise that we would meet up tomorrow mid-morning and spend the day shopping. I hugged Sidney tightly, hating to let her go. I hugged Keifer too and told him what a pleasure it was to finally meet him.

"That went very well," Emily stated as we climbed into their carriage. "How do you feel?"

"Wonderful. That was so amazing," I said, taking a seat beside her. "I couldn't believe how similar this Sidney is to the one in my memory."

"Yes, very similar, but different as well. I must confess I was a bit taken aback when she hugged me. I am not sure if that was for her husband's benefit or if our relationship has changed in the upcoming years because I have only met her twice in passing."

"I found that a bit odd too. Perhaps, well I guess not perhaps, because we know she knows some things we do not." I laughed and shrugged. "This is too weird."

I turned towards the window and watched the storefronts give way to houses as Barnaby guided us out of the city. It was such a lovely clear evening and all I wanted to do was go home and tell Jackson all about it. Unfortunately, that was the last thing I could do. He would be furious if he had a clue that Sidney was in town and that his mother and I had spent the day with her. I'm not even sure which of us he'd be more upset with since he had adamantly refused to even discuss the subject with me any further. I hated sneaking around. I hated keeping things from him. But right now, it was necessary.

Jackson never made it home for dinner. I played around with the food on my plate but never took a bite. I wasn't hungry. Between the elation I felt after spending the day with Sidney and the tension between Jackson and I, my stomach was in knots. Eventually, I gave up hope of Jackson joining me for dinner and asked Cora to draw me a hot bubble bath in hopes that it would help me clear my head.

I sank down in the oversized porcelain tub until the hot water reached my chin. My muscles began to relax and let go of some of the tension that they had been holding onto for the last several days. I closed my eyes and let the heat overcome me. I needed this.

I thought about the softball try-outs my *other* self was participating in after school each afternoon. I could almost feel the heavy bat in my hands and the joy it released in me when I contacted the ball. It was such an amazing feeling. I wished I was able to experience that *here*, but I knew that would be impossible. I thought about Caitlyn and how different she was from Olivia and Elizabeth. I couldn't help but smile, thinking about how humorous it would be if the three ever met. Caitlyn's overzealous personality, the flamboyant outfits she wore, and the lack of filter on her mouth that caused her to say whatever popped into her head without regard to whoever was within earshot would floor Olivia and Elizabeth.

I soaked in the tub considering what it would be like if my brothers *here* ever encountered Ethan *there* and how they would react to one another. Even my relationship with Ethan was something I couldn't imagine having with any of my brothers, even William—especially our physical altercations. It was fun considering how drastically different they all were. Thinking how I behaved between the two planes seemed odd and sometimes out of place.

Each day the fog between my two realities faded a little more. Clarity was both a blessing and a curse. The Chandlers' warnings regarding mannerisms, speech, pronunciation, and behavior were slapping me in the face almost daily. I had to consciously watch every little thing I did and said on *this* plane. It wasn't nearly as bad on the other since most people attributed the change in my speech patterns and enunciation to being around Jackson and his family.

But *here*, *here* was more challenging tenfold. Jackson had remarked on numerous occasions that I needed to watch myself, be more aware of my mannerisms, my language, my attitude, even my facial expressions. He had pressed it to the point that now I was almost afraid to react or say anything without thinking about it first and seeing if my response was era appropriate. His constant nagging was both helpful and irritating.

I dried myself off and wrapped a towel around my wet hair. I slipped into my nightgown and sat down at my vanity. The reflection looking back at me looked tired. I thought about the subtle difference between my two selves—the length of my hair was several inches longer here, my waist was thinner, my legs and arms were not nearly as toned or tanned as my other self. There were also other small differences such as the scar on my knee from sliding into second base and the small scar on my right bicep from where I got it cut on the fence when I was eight.

I brushed out my hair until it was almost dry. It shone beautifully in the dim light from the oil lamps and fireplace. I loved how long and thick it was with its gentle waves. I finally set the brush down, turned down the oil lamps on the mantle, and crawled under the thick blankets. I curled up in a fetal position facing the window and closed my eyes. The bed felt huge and empty without Jackson lying beside me. Despite our seeming reconciliation, Jackson had still been distant with me.

"Jocelyn?" I heard Jackson enter our room and close the door behind him. "Are you awake?" He came over and sat down on the edge of the bed.

I considered for a moment remaining silent and pretending I had already fallen asleep. But I couldn't. My heart ached from his lack of affection and refusal to communicate with me. "Yes." I rolled over to face him.

"I was not sure if you were asleep yet or not." He fidgeted with the corner of the duvet.

"I took a long bath. I just came to bed." I sat up and wrapped my arms around my knees.

"Your hair looks beautiful."

"Thank you." I noticed his body language was stiff and he looked uncomfortable. "Jackson, are you all right?"

"I hate arguing with you. I hate not talking with you."

"Me too." I reached over and placed my hand on top of his.

"Sometimes it is difficult for me to adjust to the differences between you and your *other* self, especially when your *other* personality bleeds through to this plane." He wouldn't look me in the eye, but rather stared down at the duvet in his hands.

"What do you mean?"

"When you talked to me and defied me, took a stand against my judgment, I could see your *other* personality breaking through. It was not you I was dealing with, it was your *other* self," he said, trying to explain.

"Would you contend that you have two distinct personalities?" I challenged.

"I do not believe so." Jackson's face held a quizzical expression as if he didn't understand what I was asking.

"If you do not, then why do you believe I do?" I questioned.

"You were raised drastically different by two separate sets of parents in two diverse families. How could you not be altered by them? I was raised by the same parents on each plane with the same morals and values." For the first time in our marriage I felt like smacking him.

"So, what are you saying, that having the same set of parents on both planes makes you somehow superior?" I really hoped I was misunderstanding him.

"No, not at all." He looked surprised by my words and quickly put his hands on my forearms. "I promise. I was not implying that. What I meant was that because your families are so varied across time, it is expected that you would behave differently. *Here*, you were raised by a very traditional family of the nineteenth century. Your position was laid out for you ... marriage, hosting parties, becoming a mother, and running your husband's household. Correct?"

"Yes." I couldn't wait to see where he was going with this.

"But *there*, *there* your role in life could not be more different. You have been raised to be an independent, goal-oriented, free-thinking, strong-willed, career-minded woman, who can take care of herself. A husband and children are more of an after-thought or bonus rather than a desirable status," Jackson attempted to explain.

"Are you saying that you do not care for or like my *other* self? That I am too different from the me you fell in love with *here*?" I wasn't sure what to think.

"Oh, Lord no, no sweetheart. I am not saying that at all. I love you more than anything in this world, more than anything in both our worlds." Jackson reached over and took me in his arms. "You must believe me. I love you for who you are on both planes. I only meant that sometimes when your *other* self-shines through into this world, it is hard for me to adjust as quickly to your behavior. But I would never change anything about you on either plane. I love you just the way you are."

"I love you, too." I held him tightly to me.

Jackson took my face in his hands and brought his mouth to mine. I devoured him with fire, pulling his body closer to mine, wrapping my arms tightly around him. Grabbing him, pulling him, caressing him. We fell together back on the bed, pulling one another's clothes off. I couldn't get enough of him.

CHAPTER TWENTY-ONE

FRIDAY, April 16, 2010

Jackson and Zak took their usual spots at the top of the bleachers to watch Caitlyn and me, run through another grueling workout to make the school softball team. I wasn't sure why they found it necessary to hang around, but they did. They claimed they were showing their support. But honestly, I figured it was because neither of them played baseball and didn't have anything better to do after school.

At the end of practice today Coach Kane would be posting the new team roster. This was our last chance to make any sort of impression on him before the final cuts were made. Each girl was trying her best and some were even resorting to flirting with the man. It was ridiculous.

We were broken up once again into the same groups we'd been assigned to on Tuesday. So, I followed Coach Smith back to the batting cages and pounded every pitch that came at me. It wasn't long before we were fielding, running bases and, as a bonus at the end of practice, sliding. Thankfully, it had been a dry week and the fields were dusty instead of muddy, but even with that little break, I was covered in dirt and sweat before I walked off the field with a few new bumps and bruises to go along with my skinned knees.

"Please gather around, ladies," Coach Kane bellowed and blew on his whistle. Once everyone was seated on the bottom rows of the bleachers he continued. "I want to thank you all for all your hard work this week. You've all done a great job. Unfortunately, there are only fifteen positions on the team and narrowing it down has been no easy task. Therefore, the final roster has been posted on the bulletin board in the girls' locker room. For those of you who did not make the team I want you to keep playing, work on your skills, and I strongly encourage you to try out again next year. And for those of you who made the team, congratulations! Our first practice will be tomorrow morning right here at eight. Have a great evening everyone. Dismissed."

"Well, let's go see if we made the cut," Caitlyn muttered as we made our way down the bleachers.

"You made the team, Caitlyn. I know it." I playfully bumped into her shoulder.

Jackson and Zak descended the steps with everyone else and caught up with Caitlyn and me. The four of us made our way across the student parking lot to the school building. The air was warm, but it felt stifling under all the dirt and sweat. The sun was just starting to sink off into the horizon. Our days were getting longer, but the sun was still disappearing well into the sky around seven.

"What do you guys plan on doing this evening?" Zak asked over the sound of our cleats on the asphalt.

"Celebrating these two making the team." Jackson put his arm around me.

"Ew, sweetie, I'm gross." I shrugged his arm off me. "And you don't know we made the team just yet," I reminded him.

"I have full confidence that you both did." Jackson put his arm back around my shoulder and this time I let him.

"Well, I'm still nervous," Caitlyn said.

"Me too," I agreed.

We left the guys standing outside the building as Caitlyn and I made our way into the locker room. The noise was almost deafening. Some girls squealed with excitement having found their name on the list, others were in tears of disappointment. I took a deep breath and made my way over to the board. The names were listed alphabetically, and Caitlyn Buchanan was listed right before Jocelyn Chandler. I spun around and jumped happily into Caitlyn's arms.

"We made it!" I sang out.

"Like there was ever a doubt? You two have been on the team for years." Liang smiled over at us. I hadn't even noticed she was standing there. "I made the team too this year!" She beamed.

"Congratulations!" I smiled over at her.

"That's only because Jenna and Hilary didn't try-out. If they had shown up, you wouldn't have," Jessica announced, glaring at Liang.

"Sour grapes, Jessica. You're just upset because this time, the coaches went by talent, not whose parents work for the school. I guess they learned their lesson after volleyball season," Caitlyn retorted, causing Liang, me, and all the girls around us to laugh and nod in agreement.

Jessica turned beet red and stormed out of the locker room without bothering to retrieve her things from her locker first.

"You're going to do great, Liang. Don't worry about her. I saw you during try-outs and you are awesome. You deserve to be on the team," I assured her before making my way over to my locker.

"Thanks!" she hollered after us.

"What's gotten into you? You were actually nice to your brother's girlfriend," Caitlyn observed.

"I just stated the truth. I may not care for her taste in men, but she's a great catcher. I can't deny that." I shrugged and retrieved my bag.

"Be careful, Mrs. Chandler. You just might grow to like the enemy," she laughed.

"Liang's not my enemy. Granted, her upbeat cheerfulness is a bit on the annoying side, but there are worse traits to have I suppose." I slammed my locker shut. "Ready?"

"Yep." Caitlyn closed her and followed me back outside to our guys.

After a long hot shower, I threw on a pair of skinny jeans, a teal tank, and a royal blue sweatshirt that zipped in the front. I slipped on my grey booties and pulled my hair up in a loose ponytail. Then I added a little make-up to slightly enhance my features. I guessed spending so much time with Sidney over spring break had rubbed off on me just a smidgen.

Jackson and I picked up Zak and Caitlyn over at Caitlyn's house shortly before nine. Caitlyn, whose blond hair was flowing beautifully across her shoulders, was wearing a cute little jean skirt with hot pink leggings, matching tank top, and an oversized buttoned grey sweater with a pink design. Her purple high-top Converse with their bright pink laces looked adorable with her outfit and made it look cute and casual.

The four of us piled into Jackson's CRV and headed out to the theater across town. The guys wanted to go see *Date Night* staring Steve Carell and Tina Fey. It had released over a week ago and Zak had heard it was hilarious. Neither Caitlyn nor I wanted to see it but there really wasn't much out. The guys had given us a choice between that, or *Clash of the Titans* and we really didn't want to sit through that. So, *Date Night* was the lesser of two evils.

I must admit, I was glad we went. *Date Night* turned out to be amusing and Caitlyn and I were both big fans of Mark Wahlberg. The guys enjoyed the movie as well. As we walked out of the theater the cool night air was a brisk awakening. I shivered, and Jackson put his arm around me pulling me closer to him. It was a cloudless night and the sky was alive with twinkling stars.

Caitlyn and Zak walked beside us holding hands. It seemed their turbulent relationship had finally calmed a great deal along with the ceasing of Zak's previous antics. Caitlyn credited Zak's change in behavior to Jackson. She was fully convinced that now that the two were spending so much time together Jackson's manners, his thoughtfulness, and his approach to any given situation had greatly influenced Zak. I wanted to deny her claim and tell her that perhaps Zak was simply maturing into the man he's supposed to be, but it was obvious that Jackson had contributed to many of these changes.

"I am so tired," Caitlyn complained from the backseat.

"Me too. Practice wore me out," I agreed.

"Do you want me to pick you up in the morning?" she offered.

"I don't know." I turned towards Jackson. "Are you coming to practice in the morning?"

"Sorry, love, but I have a prior engagement I cannot break." Jackson smiled slightly.

"Really? With whom?" I inquired.

"My pillow. We have not spent nearly enough time together lately and I am afraid it is feeling a bit neglected." A cheesy grin slipped across his shapely full lips.

"Oh please." I rolled my eyes at Caitlyn.

"Now that is strange, Jackson. You seem to have a date with the same lady as myself," Zak added.

"Good grief." Caitlyn playfully smacked his arm. "You two are pathetic."

"Well, why should we go? You guys are the ones who made the team, we didn't. Therefore, sorry about your luck, but you get the prize of waking up at the butt crack of dawn for the next month," Zac stated.

I turned around to look at Zac and said, "Butt crack of dawn? Very cute, Zak."

"I'm very poetic. It's a gift." He smiled smugly.

"You must be so proud of it since you show it off every chance you get," Caitlyn teased.

"I am," he responded.

* * *

I lay in bed, wide awake, thinking about Sidney. I hadn't dared say anything to Jackson about her visit, but I was dying to speak with Emily. Unfortunately, our day was so busy I couldn't get two minutes alone with her to discuss it.

I could see her image clearly in my mind's eye. She was older. Her hair was almost white, long, and she was still thin, petite, beautiful. Her eyes were the same bright blue, her smile sparkled, her dimples still prominent on her slightly lined face. It left me with the oddest sensation I couldn't explain. I was so anxious to get back to sleep just to be with her again.

I reached over on my nightstand and picked up my cell phone. Scrolling through my contacts, I found Sidney's number ... a number I rarely used in the past. I touched the icon for message and glanced over my shoulder to make sure Jackson was still sleeping soundly. With my back towards him I quickly typed in, *Hello, how are you?*

Good, you? appeared almost immediately.

Are you sleeping? I typed.

No, finals.

That sucks.

I'll be glad when they're over.

Are you coming home soon? I inquired.

Yeah, for your graduation, she replied, followed by a smiley face icon.

Fabulous, I typed back.

Everything okay on the home front?

Exciting as ever, lol

Not to be mean, I'd love to chat, but I must study. We'll catch up when I'm home. Love you.

I understand, no worries. Good luck, you'll do great! I quickly responded.

Thanks, sweet dreams, XOXO.

Goodnight, sis. I smiled and set my phone aside.

I wanted so badly to tell her about her visit, about how she looked, her life, how amazing she was, but I knew I couldn't. I wanted desperately to describe the whole day to her, tell her about how I'd met her gorgeous husband, Keifer Marshall. I closed my eyes picturing all like a scene out of a movie. I knew she had no recollection of any of it because for her, it had not occurred to her yet. Her only faded and blurry memories of *EVE* and her life in the nineteenth century only contained her at the age she was now, and I did not yet exist in her world *there*. Hell, our uncles *here*, her brothers *there*, were barely school children. I let out a deep breath and tried to fathom the bizarre nature of this new world we were suddenly thrust into. Just when I thought I could finally get my bearings in it, something this twisted changed every perception I had.

I curled up beside Jackson and rested my head upon his bare sculpted chest. I could feel the warmth of his skin radiating off him. His heartbeat was strong and steady. I loved listening to the sound of it. It was like my own personal lullaby luring me off into my *other* world.

CHAPTER TWENTY-TWO

Saturday, April 19, 1879

Jackson left for the office directly after breakfast. He said he had some briefs he needed to take care of before Monday and felt that he would get a lot more accomplished at the office rather than at home. I told him I had planned on going shopping in the city for a while with his mother and he simply nodded. His thoughts were already on the work he had to complete. He kissed me briefly and promised to be home early.

I took a long hot bath, savoring in the warmth of the water. I relaxed and closed my eyes, thinking of the vast difference in my two worlds and wondering what would happen if I asked Sidney all the questions that Jackson and Uncle Nicholas had planted deep in my subconscious. Ever since I was forbidden, I couldn't help but be curious about my future in the twenty-first century. What major did I finally decide upon? What career path did I take? And my children ... what were they like? Were they athletes? Honors students? Hellions? I couldn't help but wonder. I had yet to speak of our children with Jackson on this plane. I remembered their little angelic faces smiling up at me from the faded photographs, but I wasn't sure Jackson realized that. Was I happy? Were Jackson and I still happily married? Successful? Did we stay in Boston or come back to Chicago?

I could understand why Jackson and Uncle Nicholas felt the way they did. These questions could be dangerous. The answers could alter the course of my future. But the intrigue was there, and it was powerful. I couldn't deny that.

However, I knew I was playing with fire. Hell, I was dancing in the flames. But that still didn't mean I had to come out charcoaled. Thankfully, I was a decent dancer and knew how to manipulate the flames.

Still, the back of my brain was all too aware of the uncertainties and the rampant instabilities of the twenty-first century. And it terrified me. Marriages were disposable, sex was casual, and love rarely existed off the big screen, as Jackson called it. The concept may have been unreal to me, but the sentiment wasn't lost. That much was translatable across time. In such a time of uncertainty, the *not knowing* was killing me.

I soaked in the water until it was cold. I thought of every possible way to discover the truth without asking for it. There was only so much I could do, and I knew it. I had to keep my word to Jackson, and I would. I just wanted some sign, some indication that ours was truly an epic love story that survived two time periods.

* * *

Dressed in a lovely cornflower blue skirt, white lace blouse, and matching blue jacket, I carried my parasol and small ivory bag with a little bit of play money in it over to my in-laws across the way. The late morning air was crisp, clear, and filled with the smell of fresh cut grass. The sound of birds singing from the treetops muffled the sounds of my heels on the cobblestone walkway. Up and down our road I saw people outside on their porches, tending their gardens, and children enjoying the renewal of warm weather. It was a refreshing sight after the long winter months of hiding inside.

Barnaby greeted me with cheerful spirits. He took my parasol and showed me into their parlor. A low fire was burning softly in the hearth. I stared around the room flashing back and forth between time periods. Their house, so unlike mine or my parents' home in the twenty-first century, held onto the essence of both periods. The subtle differences such as the missing flat screen television above the mantle, the lamps on the end tables, and Jackson's laptop that was normally left on the coffee table when not in use, gave me great comfort. Even the color schemes were similar as were the furniture styles. Emily had even somehow managed to keep some of the family portraits in the same place in both periods.

"Good morning, Jocelyn. I apologize for keeping you waiting. It has been quite busy around here this morning." Emily walked in gracefully. She was elegant in a pale gray gown with a soft white lace shawl draped around her shoulders.

"Is there anything I can do?" I turned towards her.

"No. But thank you. Everything is fine." She picked up her parasol and change purse. "Shall we get going?"

"Yes." I followed her and Barnaby out to the carriage.

"You seem nervous. Are you feeling all right?" Emily asked once we were underway.

"I guess I am. Yesterday, her husband was there so it was more of an introductory meeting. Today feels more like a final exam." I fidgeted with my bag.

"She is still the same Sidney you grew up with. You must remember that. She is your sister," Emily assured me.

"I wish I could recall more of my relationship with her. Jackson told me we aren't close and that I do not see her often." I hated admitting it even though I was certain she was already aware of it. "I recall most of our trip to New Orleans and our time together that week. But this Sidney, my Aunt Sidney, I know next to nothing about her."

"Then this is the perfect opportunity to learn. I am sure she feels just as odd about seeing you in this capacity as you do her. This cannot be easy on either of you." Emily put her arm around me. "Just remember that in your *other* world this is the same individual you grew up with, look inside yourself, trust your heart not your mind."

"Have you ever been in a similar situation? What about Elaina? Does she have *EVE*?" It felt like a loaded question, but I knew very little about Robert's and Emily's siblings or extended family and I couldn't help but be curious.

"Elaina does possess the gift of *EVE*. However, like Sidney, her husband Samuel does not. Her other husband Josh in her *other* time also does not. It was her example that my oldest two children followed."

"Where is her *other* time?" I inquired.

"Same as ours." She turned towards me.

"Why have I never met her before?" Her answer surprised me.

"She's still in Boston. And you did meet her. She was at your wedding *there*. Jackson introduced her as Aunt Lainey. She was sitting with her husband Josh. He was tall, white haired, handsome." She attempted to jog my memory.

"They were seated beside Phoebe and Carson during dinner." I vaguely remembered them. "They left early, if I remember correctly." That whole evening was still a little foggy to me.

"Yes, they had to go to his family's that evening as well."

"Can I ask you a question?" A strange fact just hit me.

"Of course." Emily smiled warmly.

"Did you really write the necessary letters for our trip or did you speak with her on a telephone?" I was curious.

"Yes, I spoke with her on the phone, but for the sake of Samuel I also wrote the letter which she did promptly reply to." Emily laughed. "I figured you would think of that. You can see most things clearly now?"

"Most, but not all. It will be nice when both periods are completely clear. It makes me feel like a hindrance to constantly ask you or Jackson or your family for clarity."

"Not at all," she replied. "You know we are happy to help you in any way we can."

"Thank you, I truly appreciate it."

Barnaby halted the carriage in front of the place where Sidney and Keifer were staying. Sidney was already waiting for us outside in the garden. I took Barnaby's hand and climbed out of the carriage. I stood along the walkway watching her for a few moments not wanting to disturb her. She looked like a painting sitting under an old maple tree amongst the brightly colored lilies, tulips and varied greenery reading a book in her lovely sage green gown. Her hair was pulled up in a bun at the nape of her neck with just a few strands left slightly askew framing her face. It seemed to me that regardless of the time, Sidney's beauty and gracefulness truly transcended time.

Emily touched my arm bringing me out of my thoughts. I took a deep breath and walked with her into the little fenced-in garden off to the side of the house. The squeaking of the gate as I opened it caused Sidney to look up from her book. A delicate smile spread across her lips.

"Good morning, ladies. How are you?" Sidney rose and approached us.

"Wonderful, it is such a lovely day." Emily hugged her warmly like she was greeting an old friend.

"Jocelyn, you look beautiful." Sidney embraced me next.

"As do you." I hugged her tightly. "You looked so peaceful, I hated to disturb you."

"I had forgotten how much I loved the springs in Chicago. It has been many years since I enjoyed one," Sidney remarked. "Would you ladies care to join me? I took the liberty of ordering us some lunch in the garden. I thought this might allow us some privacy." She gestured towards a white wicker table and chairs in the far corner of the garden.

"That would be wonderful, thank you." Emily took my arm as we followed Sidney across the lawn.

The three of us sat down just as a short, portly middle-aged woman set down a lovely silver tray with tea, cups, and saucers, a small dish filled with freshly cut lemons, silverware, dessert plates, and a platter filled with cucumber sandwiches. My stomach turned. I had never developed a taste for cucumber sandwiches. I simply settled on a cup of tea with lemon.

"Thank you, Nadine. Could you please bring our entrees in a half hour?" Sidney unfolded her napkin and placed it gently across her lap.

"Yes, mam'." Nadine waddled back towards the beautiful old house.

"This place is very quaint," Emily observed. "I like it."

"As do we." Sidney poured each of us some tea. "Keifer and I stayed here before a long time ago when we visited Chicago about a year before the Civil War began."

"You were here before the Civil War?" I was dumbfounded.

"Yes, we came out for a visit with my brothers for Christmas. You were only a few months old. Tension was increasing across the country and I wanted to make sure they and their families were all right. I do remember holding you. You were such a beautiful baby. Everyone was so thrilled to finally have a girl in the family. It seemed for a long time that I was to be the last." Sidney added a dash of sugar to her tea.

"You saw me when I was a baby?" I was astonished.

"Yes, I saw you and your, I mean our, whole family." She smiled warmly. "Does that surprise you?"

"Actually, it does. Uncle Nicholas told me you two were not close," I tried to explain.

"Sadly, we are not. However, I do keep track of my little brothers. Lydia and I exchange letters occasionally, as do Annabelle and I. Nicholas was correct in saying that we rarely see one another. It can be difficult when we live so far apart. Plus, I hate to confess, but I am not very close with any of my brothers. I realize it must sound strange, but our grandmother, Marissa, raised me. Her husband passed away before I was born, and it was always just to two of us. I knew my father, Walter, his second wife, Bethany, and their sons, but we were never close. I do not believe Bethany cared much for me since I look so much like my mother Julia. My father loved her dearly, and I do not believe he ever got over her death," Sidney rambled.

"You do not believe he loved his second wife?" I asked.

"Oh, yes. He did. I did not mean to imply that he did not. What I meant was Julia was his first love and it was very difficult for him to even be around me most of my life. My grandmother told me it was because I looked so much like my mother and he almost died from grief when he lost her. Bethany never truly accepted me as part of her family. She loved my father and her sons dearly, but not me. To her, I was a constant reminder of my mother and my father's love for her. Bethany never made me feel very welcome when I would visit them. Therefore, I stayed away, which made it difficult to form a lasting relationship with my younger brothers."

"That must have been difficult on you, growing up without your family." I felt bad for even mentioning it.

"Please." Sidney waved her hand leisurely. "I had an amazing grandmother who loved me dearly. Plus, my mother's parents and siblings were very active in my life as well." Sidney took a sip of her tea. "So, you see I did grow up with a wonderful family. I had a delightful childhood and I married a man I love dearly."

"Keifer Marshall?"

"Yes, Keifer Marshall." Sidney's smile took a slightly mischievous appearance. "And Landon Harrison."

"You marry Landon?" Sidney nodded, and Emily shook her head at me letting me know I was flirting with the line I was not allowed to cross. "This coming from the woman who said that, 'marriage is not so much a ring around your finger but a noose around your neck'?"

Sidney laughed wholeheartedly. "I did tell you that didn't I?" I chuckled. "Thanksgiving Day when you were getting ready to go over to Jackson's for dinner. I had forgotten all about that."

"Sidney, I am sorry, but we need to not discuss such things," Emily warned.

"I did not tell her anything she did not already know or remember," Sidney defended her words.

"You told her you marry Landon. If I am remembering correctly, you've just recently become involved with him in *her other* time." Emily nodded towards me.

"She also knows we are involved in a serious relationship and she has met him. Jocelyn knows I would never bring home a man whom I am not seriously involved with," Sidney explained.

"Either way, it is a topic we should avoid," Emily added.

"My apologies," Sidney gracefully conceded. "Emily is right. I should not have said anything."

"Sidney, answer me this." I played with my stirrer. "How strange was it for you to see me yesterday, especially in this attire?"

"Very, although I am sure it was nothing in comparison to you not only seeing me in this attire but also as an old lady." Sidney laughed softly.

"I admit I was taken aback." I tried to shrug casually.

"It took me by surprise, and I am a bit more accustomed to the various oddities of *EVE*," Emily chuckled as Nadine returned with our entrees.

Before me was an inexpensive china plate with a marinated grilled chicken breast garnished by fresh spinach leaves topped with a wedge of lemon. Alongside it rested a large portion of broccoli spears and baked cheddar rice. Nadine had set a plate down in front of each of us and then added a basket of yeast rolls and freshly churned butter to the center of the table. It smelled heavenly.

"I didn't think anything could surprise you, Emily," Sidney said as she cut up her chicken and took a bite.

"I wish that were true. There are so many things we still do not know about this gift. Take you two for instance. I never would have fathomed the time difference yet the close interconnectedness of the two of you. I was told rumors of such things occurring with *EVE*, but I never imagined I would have the opportunity to witness it, let alone have it in my family," Emily told us.

"It is strange, I must say," Sidney stated.

"Strange, yes. But wonderful," I added. "To imagine that *here*, in the nineteenth century, you are my aunt, but in the twenty-first century you are my sister. I sit here looking at you and I cannot convince myself it is you." I couldn't even laugh at the absurdity of it all. "I mean, you sound like the Sidney I recall from my memories of my *other* world. You have her eyes, her smile, you even have her laugh, but I still cannot believe that the lady sitting beside me is the same one who is a pre-med student and cheerleader at Northwestern University."

"You think it's absurd? Imagine how I feel?" Sidney shook her head in disbelief. "I married physicians in both my lives. But only in one of them can my talents be utilized. Imagine, if you will, how frustrating it is for me to assist my husband, just as I am sure you have witnessed your mother do on countless occasions." I nodded. "But I cannot share with him any of my knowledge. Of course, I make subtle suggestions or nudge him in one way over another, but I feel practically useless."

Emily looked over at me with a knowing smile. "I understand," I told her.

"Understand what? Did I miss something?" Sidney inquired.

"When this all began for Jocelyn last fall, we had discussed with her why most individuals in our position do not typically go into the medical field … for the very reasons you just gave. It is incredibly frustrating and heartbreaking," Emily explained.

"I wish you would have had that discussion with me. It would have saved me a great deal of agony." Sidney rolled her eyes in the same manner I'd seen her do countless times before in another era. I couldn't help but giggle, thrilled in the knowledge that my sister Sidney was still there somehow in this older version that sat beside me.

"I believe I may have to reconsider my major," I said to no one's surprise. "I do not believe I would enjoy that kind of frustration on a daily basis."

"I do not, but I am too stubborn to change professions at this point in my life," Sidney remarked.

"Perhaps I will do something in the line of research," I said, thinking aloud.

"Probably not the best idea. I would imagine you would run into the same issues," Emily stated.

"Any suggestions?" I was open to anything at this point.

"I would stay away from engineering of any sort. Same issues in that area as well." Sidney shrugged.

"As well as the social sciences of any sort," Emily added.

"Wonderful." I took another sip of my tea and contemplated my options.

"You have time to think about it. Nothing has to be decided any time soon," Emily assured me.

"It would be so much simpler if you would just tell me what I decide upon." I looked over at my sister who held a knowing smile across her face.

"Jocelyn …" Emily gave me a disapproving look.

"You know I cannot do that." Sidney kept her eyes down at her plate while cutting her chicken.

"Yes, I know." *Of course, I know. I'm constantly reminded of it.*

"I wish I could help you, but you know I cannot. All I can say is …"

"Sidney," Emily interrupted, but Sidney held up her finger pausing my mother-in-law.

"All I can say is that whatever you decide, it will be the right choice for you, and you will be happy." Sidney smiled sweetly at Emily.

"I see you still love your little games." I shook my head at her, and Emily sighed with relief. "It is good to know some things never change."

"Not at all. I simply enjoy giving you a difficult time." Sidney smirked.

"Haven't you always," I teased. "That is the girl I remember."

"Some things are more difficult to erase than others, especially core personality traits." Sidney laughed wholeheartedly.

The luncheon was as pleasant as I had ever dreamed it could be. The three of us enjoyed a light, casual conversation, and we made sure to keep within the parameters set forth before us, steering clear of any topic that might be considered questionable. I quickly discovered that I really enjoyed this version of Sidney. She was the same as the one I recalled but also very different in many ways—subtle ways that only someone who had lived with her for years would notice.

Emily and I departed around four in the afternoon. I hated to leave Sidney, unsure as to when we would see each other again. We each promised to write one another and that we would see each other again soon. I hugged her tightly and kissed her lightly on the cheek. When I did so, she whispered, "Do not worry so much, little sister, you are happily married and have a wonderful life. I promise you."

Even though I knew she couldn't elaborate any further, just those simple words filled my heart with joy.

"Thank you," I mouthed the words back unseen to all but her and squeezed her hand tightly in mine.

Sidney smiled gently and squeezed my hand in return, her eyes telling me she knew what troubled my heart.

Our carriage ride home was almost tearful. I tried my best to stay my tears so that Jackson would not question my appearance once I arrived home, but my heart was truly breaking. I vowed silently to myself that I would make every effort to strengthen my relationship with my sister in my *other* life. If I couldn't be close to her *here*, I knew I would be *there*.

I curled up beside Jackson, draping my arms and legs around him. I listened to the sounds of him breathing softly along with the crackling of the wood in the hearth. The warmth of his skin soothed me after a long day of troubled thoughts. I ran my fingers lightly through his black waves and stared at his sculptured profile. His strong set jaw slightly softened by his full lips and the small cleft in his chin. He was beautiful.

My dear husband worked so hard to prove himself that at times there was little left of him for me. At times I felt very much alone here and couldn't help but wonder if our *other* life together would be much different after law school.

Balance in life between work and family was the key to true happiness. That much I knew. Finding it, however, still eluded us both. Jackson was always buried in work, consumed by it. He spent most of his waking hours poring over dusty books, papers, files, and letters. The once empty table in his office that rested between the bookcases beneath the front windows was now covered with mountains of 'stuff from the office' that I was not privy to. All Jackson and Robert would tell us about this case they were both working so diligently on was that it was of unspeakable crimes against humanity. Those words alone cured me of any curiosity I had of looking through them.

I couldn't wait until this case finally concluded and I would have my husband back ... at least until the next case came along. But Jackson had said the nature of this case was one that only occurs once in a lawyer's lifetime. I hoped he was right as I missed my time with him dearly.

CHAPTER TWENTY-THREE

SATURDAY, *April 17, 2010*

Jackson didn't even flinch when the alarm went off and I rolled my exhausted rear reluctantly out of bed. I sat on the edge and looked down at my sleeping husband. He looked so peaceful, so striking. His bare chest draped loosely with a soft blue sheet, his wavy black hair askew, his full lips slightly parted as he breathed softly. I wanted nothing more than to kiss him, see his emerald green eyes sparkle in the morning light, feel his arms wrap around me tightly and pull me to him.

But I turned away and left him sleeping. Instead, I climbed into a pair of gray sweatpants that came down to my knees and an old faded blue T-shirt. After I brushed my teeth and splashed some cold water on my face. I pulled my hair up in a long ponytail to keep it out of my face during practice. I didn't even bother putting on any make-up, there was no point. I grabbed a dark blue hooded sweatshirt that zipped up the front, and my flip-flops and made my way down the stairs.

The whole house was quiet as everyone else slept in. I was surprised that Emily and Robert were still in bed. Normally they were both early risers, dressed and fixing a home-cooked breakfast before any of us ever thought of rolling out of bed. The glorious smell of food and hot coffee was what usually lured us downstairs every morning. Today it was strangely absent.

I shrugged it off without a second thought and picked up my softball equipment bag containing my bat, the same glove I've used since I was twelve, a batting glove, softballs, and cleats. I walked out on the porch just as Caitlyn pulled up in the driveway in her little yellow bug. I closed the front door behind me and headed off to meet her.

The morning was cool, but it warmed up nicely as the sun gained its strength in the hours. Before long I was shedding my sweatshirt and wishing I'd worn shorts instead. Coach Kane insisted on conditioning us, much like Coach Smith. They were both staunch believers in stamina and insisted that with it we could beat out any opponent who may be more talented. I, on the other hand, was more certain that I was going to drop dead. Even though I was in prime condition for a high school athlete, I was not in the same condition as a professional athlete, which was what Coach Kane demanded.

I leaned against the back wall of the dugout finishing off the last of my frost Gatorade and wiped the sweat off my brow with the back of my hand. Liang trotted into the dugout and stopped when she saw me.

"Are all the practices like this?" She collapsed on the bench breathing heavily.

"He does lighten up a little. He's just trying to see what we're made of. He does this every year," I told her.

"And here I thought being on the softball team would be fun." She smirked.

"It will be. You'll see," I assured her.

Liang took a deep breath and closed her eyes for a moment. I watched her carefully, fully aware that she was dying to change the subject and working up her nerve to do so. "Jocelyn," she began. "I admire you and what you've done. I think it was a very brave thing to do." She looked up at me with her big deep brown eyes so full of kindness. "And I am sorry for the way Ethan and your mother are behaving. I just wanted you to know that."

"Admire me? Why on earth?" I chuckled despite my better intentions.

"You followed your heart despite familial opposition. That was brave, and I admire that. I could never have done such a thing." Liang smiled softly.

"You might have." I shrugged. I really didn't know enough about her to say such a thing.

"No, I wouldn't have. I was raised to listen and obey my father's wishes. He still holds the traditions of his heritage very firmly and I would never go against them," she told me.

"I thought your mother was an American." I was trying to remember what Hilary or Ethan had told me.

"Yes, she was. But my father is from Malaysia. I have been there many times. It is a very beautiful country, rich in its traditions."

"But you were raised here in the states, right? And your mother didn't have trouble with your father enforcing such views?" I asked.

"My mother died when I was twelve. She was very ill most of my life and I hardly remember much of her," Liang confessed.

"Oh, I'm sorry. I didn't know."

"My father remarried shortly thereafter to another American, a most unpleasant woman." She shrugged it off like it was nothing.

"Break's over, ladies. Grab a bat, Jocelyn. You're on deck, Liang." Coach Kane stuck his head in the dugout and bellowed.

"Of course." I pulled my bat out of my bag and took a few practice swings on my way to the plate.

I told Caitlyn of my conversation with Liang on our way home. She seemed as surprised as I was by the exchange.

"I never would have guessed. I always knew her to be very outgoing with everyone, and she's really sweet. I know she dates occasionally, but your brother is the first guy she's really gotten serious with. But I never knew she was raised with such strict traditions." Caitlyn rolled down her window to let the fresh air in.

"She actually sounded genuine about Ethan and my mother. It was weird." I leaned back in the seat and put my bare feet out the window.

"Who knows, maybe she can help fix your relationship with Ethan." I turned and scowled at her. "Don't give me that look." She shoved my legs playfully. "I know you miss him."

"Ethan's a pain in my ass and you know it." I rolled my eyes at her but smiled all the same.

"Admit it, you do. As much as he drove you up the wall, clung to your circle of friends, and harassed you every chance he got, you love him dearly and miss him every day. I know you. You've got this amazing heart that you hide under that tough exterior," Caitlyn said.

"You really think so?" Her words caught me by surprise.

"I know so ..." A slight grin spread across her perfect lips.

Caitlyn was one of the few people I knew that could make it through four hours of softball practice in the sun and still look amazing. During practice she'd had her hair pulled up in a loose bun on top of her head. Afterwards, she pulled out two pins and this glorious blond mane came tumbling down across her shoulders and down past her shoulder blades. Even without her make-up she was gorgeous. Her tall thin frame looked graceful in one of our old volleyball jerseys and cut off sweat shorts. Her bright blue eyes and perfect complexion glistened under the noon sun. I felt drab, fat, and clumsy in comparison.

"What are your plans for this afternoon?" Caitlyn asked as she pulled into the drive.

"I have no clue. Jackson was out cold when I left this morning," I informed her.

"Do you need his permission to go shopping with me? Prom is only a few weeks away and we don't have dresses." She put her bug in park and shifted in her seat towards me.

"I haven't even thought about prom." And that was the truth.

"So ... go, shower, doll yourself up. We need to do some shopping, girl before all the good dresses are gone."

"All right, all right. I'm going." I opened the car door. "What time will you be back?"

"An hour and a half." She shifted the car into reverse. "So, no time for hanky-panky, lady."

"You're just jealous." She grinned as I shut the door and ran up to the house.

"Yes, I am!" I heard her holler behind me.

Jackson was sitting at the island eating lunch in his pajama bottoms and T-shirt when I walked in. He was finishing up a tuna fish sandwich and still had half a pickle on his plate. He spun around on his bar stool trying to finish chewing the bite in his mouth, but it did not stop him from grinning at the sight of me in the doorway. My heart swelled.

"You finally rolled your lazy butt outta bed." I kissed him on the cheek before climbing on the stool beside him.

"About thirty minutes ago. How was practice?" he asked after swallowing before taking another bite.

"Rough, but good." Jackson slid an already made sandwich with its own pickle towards me.

"I figured you would be hungry."

"Thanks." I immediately dove in. "Caitlyn wants to go shopping this afternoon for prom dresses."

"Prom dresses? Are Zak and I invited too?"

"You really want to go shopping for prom dresses?" I raised an eyebrow at him.

"No, I was being polite." Jackson smiled at me and finished off his sandwich.

"I thought so." I tore off another piece and popped it in my mouth. "So, what are your plans for today?"

"I have not given it much thought. As I said, I only awoke a half hour ago." He stood up. "Are you going to shower?"

"Well, I'm not going to the mall like this." I finished off my sandwich and took my pickle. "Care to join me?"

"I thought you would never ask." Jackson reached over and tickled me. I took off running up the stairs with him playing grab-ass all the way to our room.

"Stop that," I swatted his hands away laughing. "I'm all sweaty."

"You love it," he teased.

I ducked into the bathroom, but I didn't quite get the door closed fast enough to keep Jackson out. He pushed his way past me. "I'm stronger than you," he announced.

"No kidding." I laughed and shook my head at him while I started the shower.

Steam began filling up the bathroom. I peeled off my clothes from practice feeling good to finally be free of them. Jackson stood across from me watching me intently.

"What?" I asked suddenly aware of his eyes on me.

"I love your body." A sly grin slid across his shapely lips as he slowly undressed himself.

"You are not too shabby yourself, Mr. Chandler." I smacked him on the ass and dashed into the shower. Jackson leapt in behind me.

"You think you are funny, don't you?" Jackson pinned me in the corner of the shower under the hot water tickling me.

"I'm sorry, I'm sorry!" Jackson tilted my chin upwards and pressed his mouth firmly over mine.

* * *

I barely finished getting ready when Caitlyn pulled into our drive and blasted her horn. I bounced down the steps and jogged to her bug. In the short time since we'd departed, she had managed to transform herself from student athlete to prom queen. She turned down the radio as I climbed in. Caitlyn was notorious for blowing the speakers out of every system she owned. In the short year and a half, she'd had the infamous bug she was already on her third sound system. Her dad had vigorously warned her that it was the last one he was going to pay to replace.

"Old habits die hard," I muttered once she could hear me.

"Yeah, I know," she smiled and put the car in reverse.

"Have you got any idea what kind of dress you are going to wear this year?"

"Not a clue." she looked over at me. "Zak did request something sexy." She rolled her eyes with a grin. "Shocker, I know. Did Jackson say anything?"

"I do not think he cares." I suddenly remembered the prom picture still tacked up on the corkboard in Jackson's room in Boston of him and Brittany. It made me nauseated to think about it. I knew he was simply going through the motions of high school with me at this point but thinking back at that picture… taken before *he* ever knew about *EVE*, when he had another life with her made me want to skip the whole charade.

"I think we should go for elegant but fun." Caitlyn broke my train of thought.

"Isn't that a contradiction in terms?" I leaned back in my seat and crossed my arms against my chest. I no longer had any desire to shop for prom dresses.

"Hey." Caitlyn nudged me a bit. "What's with the mood? You were fine a minute ago."

"I just remembered a picture I saw on the corkboard in Jackson's room in Boston of him and his ex-girlfriend, Brittany when they went to prom last year." I sort of lied, but not really.

"Ouch! That sucks. What did she look like?"

"You," I laughed. "She's blond, tall, thin … legs up to her armpits. A complete nightmare and the exact opposite of me," I muttered with disdain.

"She's his past, Jocelyn. He married you, not her. Besides, Jackson and Danny are complete opposites as well," she pointed out.

"Okay, I get it." I tried to shake off the image of them imprinted on my brain. "We all have a past of some sort."

"Do you guys want to go in on a limo with us? We could go downtown and have dinner at a nice restaurant before prom," Caitlyn asked as we pulled into the mall parking lot.

"Sure, we would love to."

With that settled, Caitlyn and I wandered into the mall. We checked out some of the smaller retailers that had only a few racks of prom dresses and either laughed or rolled our eyes at their selections. For the first couple of hours our trip appeared fruitless. We stopped by the pretzel shop in the food court and got a soda with a hot pretzel and cheese.

"I say we check a couple more shops before we call it a day. Who knows? We might get lucky." Her voice still maintained the same air of optimism she'd had all day.

"I think we should just head downtown and forget the mall. They have a much better selection," I suggested.

"If you're up for it I'll drive."

"Of course. Hopefully, we can find something original. The last thing I want to do is show up at prom wearing the same style dress as everyone else." I finished off my pretzel. "Where's the fun in that?"

"Does that mean we are looking for eccentric?"

"Definitely!"

"Lead the way." Caitlyn always loved finding things just a little out of the ordinary to shock people with, so I knew she was up for the challenge.

Back on the road Caitlyn turned up the stereo and the two of us sang loudly and off key to an old *Beatles Greatest Hits* album. Neither of us could carry a tune, but that tiny fact never deterred either of us from belting out the lyrics to every song. It felt incredible to be so carefree. We had the hum of the interstate beneath us, the wind in our hair, and classic music to pass the time. I felt better than I had in a very long time. I hated to think of what it would be like moving to Boston and leaving Caitlyn behind. I wanted so badly to take her with me, but I knew she was excited to be going to Northwestern in the fall for nursing.

Caitlyn parked over on West Ohio Street to avoid paying the outrageous mall parking fees and we walked the couple blocks over to North Michigan Avenue to the Water Tower Place mall. The popular mall stood just off the Outer Harbor of Lake Michigan and was filled with seven levels of stores, food, and entertainment. It was a beautiful mall but highly overpriced. We rarely made the trip since so many other options were widely available.

It seemed everyone had the same idea as Caitlyn and me. The mall was over-crowded, and it was a challenge just to maneuver through the walkways. We browsed through numerous stores working our way up floor by floor. I was beginning to become disheartened that we'd find anything. It seemed the most prominent style for this prom season was either grandma or slut and the print favorite was outlandishly bold, and bright, tacky, and tasteless.

We thumbed through the racks at Forever 21, PINK, and White House Black Market. Apart from a few gowns it was the same gaudy styles as we'd seen before. So, we trucked down to Macy's laughing and teasing over the scarce selection available, joking that we'd probably be better off creating our own gowns. Then it hit me ... Emily.

"Wait a minute, Caitlyn." I stopped in the middle of the walkway causing a couple behind us to run into our backs. "Sorry," I muttered and waved at them before turning to Caitlyn. "Emily loves to sew. She made those amazing costumes for Jackson and me for Halloween, remember?"

"Okay." Caitlyn looked confused.

"I bet if we find a picture or pattern or something, she would probably help us out with creating our own dresses for prom." I couldn't believe I hadn't thought of it earlier.

"Can she do that from just a picture?"

"She's amazing! We should ask her."

"Jocelyn, I'm an athlete, not Suzy Homemaker. I flunked sewing class in junior high, remember? I can't even put a button on a shirt let alone create a prom dress." She looked more than a little apprehensive.

"But she can. Don't get bent out of shape just yet. We'll talk to her when we get back. Besides, who knows? We may get lucky at Macy's." I rolled my eyes and pulled her by the hand towards the store.

We took the escalator up to women's apparel and searched until we came across the section of prom gowns in the back. Caitlyn pulled out a short purple strapless gown and held it up in front of her.

"Not too bad. What do ya think?" She turned towards the full-length mirror twisting and turning.

"Too dark for your skin tone. You would look better in pastels," I suggested.

"I know." she put it back where she'd found it. "How about this?" She pulled out a multi-colored satin one-shoulder mermaid gown that was tacky beyond words.

"Oh, Zak would love that." I giggled. "Maybe you should try it on?"

"Maybe I will. Maybe it's one of those dresses that looks better on than on the hanger." I couldn't help but admire the optimistic tone in her voice.

"Sure." I tried to stifle a giggle, but she noticed and put it back on the rack.

"Oh, I love this!" Caitlyn pulled out a gorgeous pale blush colored, sleeveless, chiffon dress with a keyhole neckline and beaded bodice. It was both elegant and fun. And it screamed Caitlyn. She held it up against her and twirled in the mirror. "I'm trying this on." She skipped back to the dressing room leaving me fumbling through the gowns trying to find something that would even make me look comparable to the beautiful creature Jackson escorted before.

I was the perfect average height, just a quarter inch shy of five feet six inches. Too tall to be short, too short to be tall. Perfectly average with stocky athletic legs, an average torso, and a medium sized chest ... and I was being generous to myself by saying medium sized. It was going to be damn near impossible to find something that could make me look half as elegant and beautiful as Brittany.

I didn't want to be jealous of her, even though Jackson married me, but it was almost impossible not to be. She was cut straight from the Barbie mold. She reminded me a great deal of Sidney. I tried to dismiss the negative thoughts and find a dress I could live with. Going to Emily was a last resort. I didn't want to put that on her when I knew she was busy working on her new book.

"How do I look?" Caitlyn reappeared from behind the blue velvet curtain. She waltzed over to the full-length mirror and spun around looking at herself from every angle.

"Wow." I was truly speechless. She looked gorgeous. That gown was perfect for her. It fit her like a glove. Her dress had a beautiful sheer chiffon overlay that went three quarters around. The back was open down to her waist and showed off her flawless skin.

"I know," she squealed and jumped over to me. "I'm going to get it. Zak is going to flip when he sees me in this."

"Yes, he is, along with every other guy there." I was happy for her.

She twirled around a couple more times in the mirror standing on her tip toes before she turned back towards me. "Okay, let me change and we'll find something fabulous for you. We need something that's gonna make Jackson's jaw drop." She winked at me then disappeared behind the curtain once more.

I absentmindedly shook my head at her and went back hunting for a dress. I glanced over several more gowns when something different caught my eye. It was a two-piece gown. The top was sleeveless with a nude underlay. The overlay was delicate, almost see-through, with white and pale blue specks and a floral lace appliques. The bottom half was a full billowing skirt designed in the same fashion as the top, except the floral lace design was scattered more sparsely the further down it went.

I quickly scanned through the three that were still there and found a size three. I grabbed it up and darted straight for the dressing room. I almost collided with Caitlyn who was on her way out.

"Did you find something?" she asked eagerly.

"Cross your fingers." I headed into the small room.

I slipped out of my clothes and climbed into both pieces of the ensemble. I stood on my tiptoes in the small dressing room mirror and twirled around. I had to admit it was fabulous. I absolutely loved it. I swished the full skirt back and forth with both hands smiling at my reflection. The fullness and the weight of the skirt reminded me greatly of the skirts I wore in my *other* life. Although I wouldn't have been caught dead in this skirt in that time, this was my prom dress.

I walked out from behind the curtain and did a full spin for Caitlyn. She squealed and leapt over to me. "Oh, my God! I love it!"

"Me too!" I checked myself from top to bottom in the larger full-length mirror in the area.

"Jackson is going to love that."

"I want it to be a surprise." I spun around to face her. "Can I keep it at your house until prom?"

"It's not your wedding dress, Jocelyn. Why all the secrecy?"

"Because I never got to surprise him with a wedding gown on our wedding day. I got married in one of his sister's evening gowns. It was lovely, and I was grateful for it, but I never got to see his face when he saw me for the first time. I know it's not the same." I gave her a halfhearted smile with a shrug.

"Does that mean that we get to get our hair, nails, and make-up done for this as well?"

"Of course." My smile got a little bigger. "But first we need to find some accessories … bags, jewelry, and most importantly, shoes!"

"That's my girl." Caitlyn hugged me tightly.

It was dark before we returned home. Caitlyn and I had grabbed something to eat on our drive back and stashed all my things in her bedroom closet before she took me home. Zak's car was parked on the curb in front of my house when we pulled up.

"Are we in trouble?" Caitlyn looked over at me and snickered a bit.

"I don't know," I shrugged. "Were we supposed to be home at a specific time?"

"Not that I was aware of." She turned the car off and opened the door. "Let's see what they're up to."

We found Zak and Jackson sitting on the couch screaming at each other and at the television playing *Halo* on the Xbox. It was so normal, it was weird. I'd never seen Jackson play video games. I knew he had them, he'd mentioned them casually, but I'd never witnessed the action or the intensity of his game. It was humorous. Jackson was acting … normal for the first time since I'd met him in the twenty-first century.

I stood in the doorway between the kitchen and the family room watching him but not believing what I was seeing. Caitlyn stopped beside me, confused and glanced between the guys and me. "What's wrong?"

"Nothing." I shook my head a little just to clear my thoughts. "Nothing at all." I walked into the room and greeted the guys. "We're back." I flopped down beside Jackson, playfully bumping into him.

"Hello, sweetheart, how was shopping? I was expecting you to return with a mountain of bags." Jackson leaned over and kissed me on the cheek.

"Oh, don't worry. I put a nice dent in our bank account today," I assured him.

"Did you already take it upstairs?" He paused the game making Zak yell at him. "Just a second." He turned back to me. "Did you find a dress? Let me see it."

"You can't. Not until prom."

"Why?" He looked over at Caitlyn for an explanation, but she just shrugged and continued telling Zak about her dress.

"I know it is silly, but I want it to be a surprise. I did not get to surprise you on our wedding day. So, this is sort of the next best thing."

"It is not silly at all. I think it is sweet and very romantic." Jackson reached over and squeezed my hand lovingly.

The four of us ended up spending our evening at home. The guys returned to their world of *Halo* and Caitlyn and I disappeared into the kitchen to make some chocolate chip cookies for them. Caitlyn seemed almost as determined as my mother-in-law to teach me how to bake. The funny thing was I had the best time that evening. Even though the first batch of cookies I made, and I swear I followed the recipe to the letter, turned out disgusting. The second batch, however, were perfect. And even though they were, I didn't think the three of them, nor my in-laws, would ever let me live them down the horrible taste of that first batch.

* * *

After Jackson fell asleep beside me, I watched him sleeping and smiled to myself. I loved this man. I loved his playfulness, his kindness, his intelligence, and his strong love for his family. I could no longer imagine my life without him in it. And day by day, my life before *EVE* was feeling more and more unnatural to me. Phoebe's words still haunted my thoughts: "We really do get to have it all, the best of both worlds." I was beginning to believe she was right.

In the last six months my life had been turned upside down and inside out, rearranged, redesigned, and painted purple. Everything I had ever known and loved about my life had disappeared overnight. But what I gained was some-thing I never believed existed in this time, a strong, loving, supportive familial unit and a husband that I shared a transcendent love with across time.

I closed my eyes and took a deep breath feeling completely at ease with the world. Jackson unconsciously tightened his hold around me. I looked back up at his beautiful face and couldn't help but wonder if his soul was still here with me, inside him, or if it had already wandered off to the world where technology didn't exist, where family still meant everything, and where I would surely be sleeping beside him ready to awaken to a much simpler life.

If only I had known what I was about to experience, I never would have opened my eyes.

CHAPTER TWENTY-FOUR

Sunday, April 20, 1879

I awoke abruptly to the thunderous sounds of someone beating on our front door. I felt Jackson jerk away from me and saw him leap from our bed. He climbed into his britches that were draped over the trunk at the foot of our bed and threw on his shirt trying to button it as he rushed out our bedroom door. I could faintly hear his footsteps on the stairs over the continuous racket being wreaked on my front door.

I reluctantly climbed out of bed and pulled on my robe and slippers. I grabbed my pocket watch out of its little blue gift box on the mantle and held it open close to the dying embers still smoldering in the hearth. It was four o'clock in the morning.

Who would be pounding on our door at this ungodly hour?

The noise stopped, and a deafening silence took hold on the house. I sat down on the corner of the bed and waited. Such a call at such an hour never meant something good.

Anxiously, I tied my robe closed, ran a brush roughly through my hair, and headed downstairs. I wasn't sure if I should or not, but I had to know what was going on. At the top of the stairs I could hear two male voices, but their words weren't clear enough for me to make out what they were saying.

With a knot in the pit of my stomach I descended the front stairs. The soft glow from the parlor told me where they were.

"Are they sure?" Jackson asked.

"Yes, Uncle Nicholas confirmed it was him."

"How?" I could hear the skepticism is Jackson's voice.

"His engraved pocket watch. Monte always carried it with him. Vivian had it engraved for their tenth wedding anniversary." I recognized William's voice.

My feet carried me swiftly the rest of the way down the stairs. The parlor doors were left ajar only by inches. I could see the two gentlemen standing by the hearth. My brother looked almost as disheveled as my husband. His hair was askew, his chin showed his morning scruff, his shirt was untucked with the top two buttons opened, and he was absent a jacket and tie. He must have had his sleep interrupted as well.

"William, what is going on?" I asked as I entered the parlor.

"Jocelyn, I apologize for the late hour or rather early hour. What time is it anyway?" William ran his hand through his dirty blond hair.

"Four in the morning," I answered, walking over beside them.

"I apologize for the rude awaking. I know how unsettling they can be having just received one myself." William slumped down on the chair beside the fire.

I joined Jackson as he sat down across from my brother on the lounge. Jackson reached over and took my hand making the anxiety in my stomach reach its full height. "Could someone please tell me what is going on?"

"I am afraid there has been an accident. Uncle Monte is dead," William said solemnly.

I looked between the two gentlemen feeling completely light-headed, numb, frozen in my body. I couldn't move. I couldn't cry. This couldn't be happening.

"I don't understand. How?" I managed to squeak after several long moments of silence.

"There was an accident with the carriage and horses." William didn't elaborate.

"Oh, my goodness." It simply wouldn't register in my brain. Uncle Monte couldn't be dead. I'd just seen him a couple days ago at my parents' home.

"You two should probably get dressed. We need to get over to Uncle Monte's house. Uncle Nicholas, Aunt Lydia, and our parents are already over there." William stood up and we followed suit. "I will come back in a half hour to pick you up. You can ride over with Olivia and me."

"Thank you." Jackson shook his hand and followed him to the front door. I trailed slowly behind them still feeling as if I were walking in a fog.

I stood in the parlor entryway and watched my brother leave. Jackson closed the front door and returned to me. "Jocelyn, sweetheart." He put his hands gently on my shoulders. "Are you all right?" His green eyes were full of concern.

"This cannot be happening." I stood there shaking my head. "How does something like this happen?" I looked into his piercing green eyes. "First Mimi, now Uncle Monte?" And the bubble of anxiety that I had held tight in my stomach finally gave way. Tears rolled down my cheeks and a loud gush of air sobbed from deep in my chest. I wrapped my arms around Jackson's neck and pulled him to me. I buried my face in his shoulder and cried. Jackson scooped me up in his muscular arms and carried me up the stairs to our room.

He laid me down gently on our bed as Cora walked in with a silver serving tray. "I's sorry 'bout your uncle, honey." She put her hand lightly on my arm and squeezed it tenderly.

"Thank you, Cora." Jackson handed me one of his handkerchiefs, so I could wipe the tears away.

"I brought you some tea with lemon." She gave me a soft smile. "It will help settle your tummy."

"How did you …?" Of course, she knew. Like her mother, Cora always knew what was going on beneath our roof. Plus, we'd both just lost her mother and she knew about unsettling anxiety knots.

Cora nodded and moved gracefully pouring the hot tea. "Sip it slowly. No need in it coming right back up."

"Thank you," I whispered and took a sip. I could feel the hot liquid flowing through my body and work its magic.

Cora set the tray aside and walked over to my armoire, picking out something for me to wear. Jackson silently brushed my hair away from my face as I watched Cora pull out the black gown I'd practically lived in when her mother had passed only a short while ago. She laid my dress and other essentials out on the bed beside me and went to work gathering Jackson's attire.

"Are you all right?" Jackson asked in a low voice.

"I just cannot believe this is happening." I hastily brushed my tears away and took another small sip.

"I know. Me neither."

"How could something like this happen?"

"I am not sure of all the details. I only know what your brother told me, which was that a snake spooked the horses." He helped me up. "We need to get ready. William will be here shortly and neither of us are dressed. I do not want to keep him waiting. I think we are all in for a long day."

* * *

We arrived at Uncle Monte's just as the sun was beginning to break over the horizon. The sky was filled with the soft hues of pink, purple, and orange. I stepped up on their front porch and turned to gaze out at the sky. It was showing signs of being a lovely spring day with mild temperatures. To me, it felt like the sky should be gray and filled with black heavy clouds dumping big fat raindrops upon our heads. The world should be mourning the loss of such a loving man.

Yet, somewhere in the back of my mind, I recalled Uncle Monte saying that he wanted to live his life in such a way that people would celebrate his death knowing that he had passed away having experienced a wonderful life. The memory brought a small smile to my face. I reached out and took Jackson's hand and followed him into the house.

All the oil lamps were unlit. The foyer was so dark I stumbled into William when he stopped in front of me. There was only the soft glow from the low fire in the hearth illuminating the parlor in the front of the house. I could hear the soft sobs of muffled tears throughout and the smell of coffee was so strong it made me wrinkle my nose.

My uncle's home was a modest one, larger than most, smaller than ours. He always believed in simplicity. Their home was elegant, sparkling clean, and cozy. It was a five-bedroom estate about two miles from our home with a vast lawn littered with mature trees and a lush garden. Monte and Vivian's eldest son, Floyd, and their second son, Charles, had their own bedrooms. Their youngest sons, Matthew and Zachary, shared a bedroom. The fifth room in the back of the house was occupied by Russ and Susan, a married couple, who had lived and worked for my uncle and his family for as long as I could remember.

Most of my family as well as members of Vivian's were gathered in the parlor. Some were scattered throughout the other corridors and rooms. All were speaking in hushed tones and whispers. The four of us walked quietly into the parlor scanning over the mournful faces. It was a heartbreaking scene. I approached my parents and hugged each of them tightly. Both were red-eyed and full of tears. I had never seen my father so distraught.

Friends, neighbors, colleagues, church, and family members drifted in and out all day long. My mother and Aunt Lydia did a beautiful job at welcoming everyone and accepting their condolences on behalf of our family. Aunt Vivian never surfaced from her bedroom. Occasionally, I would see one of her sons drift about the house. Floyd seemed to be focused more on making sure his mother was attended to. He had just turned sixteen and was now thrust into the role of man of the family. His younger brothers were a mere fourteen, ten, and six years old. My heart broke in my chest when Zachary emerged only to play with the lunch Susan gave him. He moved it around his plate staring blankly into space and talking to no one. His eyes were red and swollen. He cheeks still streaked with tears.

I went over and sat down beside him at the dining room table. I put my arm around him and gave him a gentle squeeze. "I am so sorry, little man." I leaned over and kissed him on the cheek.

He looked up at me and gave me a smile that made my chest ache deep inside my heart. But he said nothing. He simply went back to moving the food around his plate. I remained beside him for the next half hour when he finally got up after not taking one bite of his food and returned to his parents' bedroom to be with his mother.

I was in the dining room alone when I heard my Uncle Nicholas's voice drifting through the kitchen doorway followed by another gentleman's voice. It took me a moment to realize my uncle was speaking to Dimitri's father, George Donaldson. I stood up from my spot at the table and crept over to stand just beside the swinging door, so I could hear what they were discussing.

"I do not understand this. My wife came in from the mercantile this morning in tears saying Mr. Timmons was killed last night in some freak accident. How did this happen?" Mr. Donaldson inquired.

"I got a call shortly after midnight from my nephew Patrick. He was the physician on call at the hospital last night. He told me a man was brought in badly mangled from a carriage accident and needed me to come to the hospital immediately because he thought it was Monte. So, I rushed down there, but by the time I got there the man had already passed away. From what the eyewitness told Patrick, the gentleman was saying goodbye to lady, hugged her one last time while his driver was standing there with the carriage door open. Monte had his arm resting on the door and his sleeve or something, must have caught onto something in the door. Apparently, a snake came out of the gardens and crossed the pathway in front of the horses spooking them. The driver turned to grab the reins, but the horses both reared and then took off at a sprint dragging the gentleman along. He must have somehow got caught beneath the back wheel and been dragged for a several blocks. By the time the driver caught up with the carriage, the gentleman barely had a pulse."

"Oh, my God!" Mr. Donaldson exclaimed in a low voice.

"The driver was Russ, but the hospital could not legally accept his claim or his identification of the victim. That's why I was called. Patrick couldn't identify the gentleman a hundred percent or even ten percent for that matter. Neither could I to be honest." I heard my uncle sigh heavily. "I didn't share this with Vivian or the rest of the family for obvious reasons, but when Patrick pulled the sheet, I couldn't believe the thing lying there used to be a man, let alone my brother. The man lying there had no face. No face at all."

"What do you mean no face?"

"I mean he had no face. I mean it was taken off by the road. When he went under the carriage he must have been face down. The only way I knew for sure it was Monte was the engraved pocket watch that Vivian had given him on their tenth wedding anniversary. He always carried it in his front jacket pocket and that's where I found it."

"What was Monte doing out that late in the city? You said he was with a woman? Was he ..."

"No, of course not. But I did inquire as to who brought him in. You can imagine my surprise when I went out to the lobby and saw our older sister, Sidney, sitting there with her husband. She told me they were taking a trip to visit a friend of hers in Indianapolis and stopped over in Chicago because she wanted to surprise her brothers for the weekend." My entire body was frozen where I stood. My heart was pounding so loudly I was sure one of them could hear it. I could not believe what I was hearing. My throat went dry and I couldn't even swallow. My palms began to sweat, but I couldn't move.

"I wasn't aware you had an older sister," said Mr. Donaldson.

"Yes, she is my half-sister from my father's first wife, whom he lost during childbirth. Sidney was raised by our grandmother, and I do not know her very well. She remained in Boston when our father was transferred to Chicago," Uncle Nicholas explained.

"I understand."

"Naturally, I was surprised to see her. She and her husband Keifer are staying at Nadine's Bed and Breakfast over on Fifth. She said they had just arrived and were out sightseeing when they ran into Monte. So she invited him to join her and her husband for a nice evening in the garden catching up over a nice fire and warmed citrus tea."

"Why didn't Patrick call his father?" The same question was running through my mind.

"He did, but Annabelle said he was out on a call over at the Cain's residence.

Apparently, Quintin has an ear infection and Patrick was called over there to look at him. So, my nephew called me."

"This is horrible. I spoke to Monte yesterday. I cannot believe this has happened." I could hear the sorrow and disbelief in Mr. Donaldson's voice.

"Are you two going to hide in the kitchen all day? Come on." I heard Aunt Lydia usher the two men out through the other kitchen door back into the parlor.

I leaned against the wall barely breathing. *He knows Sidney's in town.* If Monte hadn't run into her none of this would have happened. He would have been home with his family. I knew it was some freak accident but somehow it all felt like my fault. If I hadn't pushed to see Sidney, she never would have sought me out *here*. Then everyone would have been fine. My curiosity and Sidney's initiative cost my uncle his life. Tears rolled down my cheeks. I sat down in the nearest chair and rested my head on the table, sobbing into my arms.

Countless minutes passed, and the tears continued to fall over my arms and puddle onto the table. I didn't care. The guilt I was feeling was eating away at me from the inside out. I felt like I was going to be sick. My head was pounding, my heart racing.

"What are you doing sitting here alone?" I lifted my head up to see Jackson standing beside me. "Are you all right?" He reached out and rubbed my shoulder.

All I could do was nod. I didn't trust my voice enough to speak. I feared I would make a full confession of everything that had happened in the last seventy-two hours.

"Uncle Nicholas is looking for you. He said it's important."

"Where is he?"

"Sitting on the front porch. And he is not alone. Is there something you would like to tell me?" Jackson sat down in the chair next to mine.

"Jackson, please." I didn't even know where to begin.

He leaned into my ear and whispered. "Care to explain to me why your much older sister, Sidney, is here with her husband?"

"I did not know she was coming. I promise." I looked him in the eye.

"I know. She told me. However, I am upset that you did not tell me about her visit."

"I did not know how to tell you," I confessed, brushing the tears off my face. Jackson reached into his pocket and handed me his handkerchief. "Thank you."

"Time to face the music." Jackson stood up and offered me his hand. I reluctantly took it and followed him out to the porch.

Uncle Nicholas was sitting in the rocker on their extended porch with Sidney and Keifer sitting in the swing across from him. I stopped in front of Sidney and knelt in front of her and hugged her tightly. Both of us held onto each other and cried. Keifer, Jackson, and Uncle Nicholas each tried to console us with gentle touches and words of comfort. All I could feel was this horrible guilt.

Jackson led me over to the double rocker that rested between them. I felt like I was on trial. Sidney was also wearing a black gown she must have just bought. Keifer was wearing a dull black suit like the rest of the gentlemen.

I had grown to hate the color black in recent months.

Sidney's face was tear streaked. Her make-up was smeared, and her hair was not nearly as stellar as it was yesterday. But neither was mine. It had been a long night and I hated to think that Sidney had witnessed this tragedy. I was impressed she was even out of bed after the night she must have endured. Keifer kept his arm tightly around his wife's shoulder.

"Jocelyn, I am so sorry. We tried. We all tried to stop the horses. Keifer and Russ chased after the carriage until they finally stopped. Keifer did all he could as we rushed him to the hospital," Sidney sobbed.

"There wasn't much I could do," Keifer said in a low voice.

"This was not your fault. It was a bizarre accident. No one could have prevented it," Uncle Nicholas assured her before turning his gaze on me. "I cannot express to you how disappointed I am with you."

"Nicholas, Jocelyn did nothing wrong. She did not know I was coming. I practically showed up on her doorstep uninvited," Sidney interjected. "Honey, would you please get me a fresh cup of hot tea?" She patted Keifer's knee.

"Yes, darling." Keifer smiled lovingly at his wife. "Please, excuse me," he said to us as he rose and disappeared into the house.

"Little brother, you have to understand I am not a child. I realize that you are recalling the terrified young lady I was thirty some years ago, but that is not the woman sitting before you. I stayed within a scope of topics that caused no harm to anyone. I only wanted to see my ..." Her eyes fell upon me and she smiled softly. "Niece and know that she is doing well. I understand that you do not know me well *here*, but I assure you, I would never do anything to ever jeopardize her future or any of ours."

"Jocelyn knew how against we were of the two of you getting together. I cannot help but feel you deliberately went behind our back to see her," Nicholas explained.

"Of course, I did. I found out about *EVE* before you ever learned to read, little brother. And I will not be told what to do. That said, I do respect your opinion and judgment, but you also need to trust me in that I have all of your best intentions at heart," Sidney said in a gentle voice.

"I would never question your integrity or your love for your family. I simply wish you would have come to me when you arrived here. The way events played out it feels to me like you all were being deceitful." Nicholas took the pipe out of his jacket pocket and began packing it with the tobacco from the little pouch he carried with him.

"And for that, I do apologize. I was unsure as to the reception I would receive if I had done it that way." Sidney poised herself with a grace that I envied.

Uncle Nicholas lit his pipe and stared out over the lush green lawn. Leaves were filling in the spaces on the branches that had sat bare throughout the last season. The gardens surrounding the vast porch were now in full bloom. An array of colors danced brightly in every direction. The sky had turned to a brilliant blue in the afternoon sun. It had warmed up nicely and was indeed a very beautiful day.

The four of us sat there listening to song of a blue jay singing loudly from the maple tree. It was lovely and mournful at the same time. I didn't have any words to break the uncomfortable silence that hovered over us. Keifer returned with a cup of tea and handed it to his wife before sitting back down beside her.

I remained there until evening watching the sun float across the sky and eventually sink behind the pasture in the distance. I watched people I'd known my entire life drift in and out all day long paying their respects, offering to help, bringing food that no one wanted to eat. It was thoughtful and kind of them. I knew that. However, I always found it strange, people's reaction in the time of an unexpected death. There was no written protocol on behavior. No one knew what to say, because there wasn't anything to say that could make loved ones feel any less pain. It was overwhelming.

Reverend Jacobs sat down with Uncle Nicholas for a while after he came out from the house just after twilight. I listened to him tell my uncle about God's greater plan and how Monte was at peace now. I squirmed in my seat a bit causing Jackson to place his hand firmly over mine. I knew it was his way of telling me to remain silent and I knew I had to despite how much I wanted to say something to the reverend.

After hearing him call William and Olivia's baby an abomination, I had lost all respect for him. For a man of God to say such a thing was unforgiveable. He was supposed to be God's representative on earth, and I couldn't fathom how he could say such cruel things and harbor such moral righteousness. The sight of him comforting my loved ones left me with a bitter taste in my mouth. I looked over at Jackson and rolled my eyes before I got up and went into the house to find my family.

* * *

Sidney, Keifer, William, and Olivia followed us back to our house to join us for a late supper. None of us were hungry, but it was time for us to leave the gloomy household. My head was hurting from crying so much and not eating all day, but I still did not want to consume anything. I felt like crawling into bed and drifting off into my *other* world just to escape the pain for a little while.

Tamera and Cora whipped up a light supper for us as we gathered around the dining room table. I sipped on my hot tea with lemon and moved the food around on my plate. The one thing I dearly missed here was Ibuprofen. I closed my eyes for a brief second and willed my headache away.

"So, you live in Boston?" Olivia asked Sidney.

"Yes, my husband has a practice there at the hospital."

"I have always wanted to see Boston. Are you going to be staying in Chicago for a while?" Olivia questioned politely.

"We were planning on leaving tomorrow, but our plans have been changed. I don't want to leave my brothers right now. I just cannot believe this has happened. I feel horrible." Sidney's voice was soft as she wiped a tear off her cheek with her napkin.

"I am glad you are staying for a while. It will give me the chance to get to know you better." I reached over and took her hand in mine.

"Where are you two staying?" William inquired.

"At Nadine's Bed and Breakfast on Fifth," Keifer replied.

"Why don't you stay here with us?" Jackson offered, smiling at me from across the table. I had wanted to ask them as well, but I was unsure because of Jackson's earlier reservations.

"We do not want to impose." Keifer glanced over at Sidney who nodded her head. "Well, thank you. We accept. I will fetch our luggage after we eat."

156

"I am so happy you are staying." I squeezed her hand.

"Me too." Her bright blue eyes lit up a little bit.

Later that evening after William and Olivia retired to my parents' home and Keifer and Sidney were tucked in nice and cozy in our guest room, Jackson and I finally got two minutes alone. It had been an extremely long day and I was exhausted.

"You surprised me this evening, inviting them to stay with us. Thank you for that." I crawled into bed beside him and kissed his full lips. "It means a lot to me."

"And that is why I did it. You know the risks. I trust you." Jackson's emerald green eyes sparkled up at me.

"Did you see Vivian at all today?" I asked.

"No. She stayed in her room all day. I only saw Floyd and Zachary a couple of times, but I never saw Charles or Matthew."

"Me neither. I wish I could have seen them, but I have no idea what to say to them. I cannot imagine what they are going through losing their father that way. Vivian must be losing her mind with grief. They were so happy together." I curled beside my husband and rested my head on his chest. Jackson wrapped his arms around me and held me tightly to him. "Promise me you'll never leave me." I looked up at his angelic face. "I could not bear to live without you."

"I promise I am not going anywhere." He leaned down and kissed my forehead. "But Jocelyn, you know what also gives me comfort?"

"What is that?" I continued watching his face.

"That if something ever did happen to me, I know you would be fine ... both *here* and *there*. You are so independent, strong, and such a fierce spirit, you could survive anything this world throws at you and come out swinging." He chuckled.

"Thanks," I muttered. *I'm not as strong as you think.*

"Goodnight, sweetheart. I love you," Jackson whispered and kissed me one last time on the forehead before he closed his eyes.

"I love you too."

CHAPTER TWENTY-FIVE

Sunday, *April 18, 2010*

Jackson awoke early and had his day well underway before I even considered opening my eyes. I could hear everyone moving about in the house as I rolled over and pulled Jackson's pillow over my eyes to block the sun from reaching them. My body felt drained instead of rested. I snuggled down under our thick downy comforter and replayed my day over at Aunt Vivian's. A physical ache gripped my chest and shortened my breath. I couldn't believe my Uncle Monte was dead. I had now lost him on both planes of my life.

I heard our bedroom door creak open and footsteps on the hardwood floor. I peeked from beneath Jackson's pillow and saw him walking towards the bed carrying a tray. "Wake up, sleepy head. It's almost noon."

"Really? Hell, it's early. Let me sleep." I groaned and pulled the pillow down tightly over my eyes. The sunlight was way too bright.

"Sorry, not today. We have things to do. Plus, I brought you breakfast in bed and fresh coffee." I hated to admit it but the coffee smelled fabulous. "Come on, sit up." He sat down on the edge of the bed and waited for me to sit up before he placed the breakfast tray on my lap.

"Wow. What's all this?" The plate was filled with cinnamon French toast sprinkled with powdered sugar, my personal favorite, a slice of ham and a small bowl of fresh fruit along with an oversized mug of coffee and a small glass of orange juice.

"I was not sure how you would be feeling this morning after what happened *there*."

"It was the first thing that entered my mind when I woke up. I cannot believe Uncle Monte's dead. It still doesn't feel real to me." I poured a little of the maple syrup over the top of my French toast.

"I know, and for it to have happened that way. I don't know what to say."

"I know ridiculous things happen every day in this world, but how do you explain getting your sleeve caught on the door, the horses getting spooked by a snake and then taking off at a sprint, and then getting sucked under one of the back wheels, face down, no less, and dragged for three city blocks." I had to stifle a giggle that was fighting its way out.

"You know you are going to hell, right? I cannot believe you are laughing." He chastised me even though the corners of his mouth were twitching involuntarily as he did his best not to smile.

"I am not laughing." But I was. I couldn't help it. "It is absurd! Completely and utterly absurd!" I gestured wildly with my hands for emphasis. "You can't even make that shit up. It's too ridiculous!"

"And here I was worried you would be all distraught this morning and I would have to spend my day calming you down. It is nice to see you handling your uncle's death so well." He smirked.

"Jackson, that is not fair. You know I loved him dearly. My heart breaks for Aunt Vivian and their boys. I hate to imagine what they are going through." I wiped away a few stray tears off my cheeks. "I do not know whether to laugh or cry at this point."

"I know, darling. Monte would laugh about it too I am sure. He was just that kind of man."

"Yes, he was."

After I finished my breakfast and got myself ready for the day, I joined Jackson and his parents in the family room. They were watching an old black and white Cary Grant movie. I knew Emily loved Cary Grant. She had a weakness when it came to Grant, Clark Gable, Jimmy Stewart, Henry Fonda, and Gregory Peck. She would turn TMC on in her office when she was writing and spend hours locked in there typing away on her romance novels. She told me once that movies made during Hollywood's heyday knew what romance and story lines were about. She hated all the CGI and special effects that dominated the film industry today.

"Good afternoon, sleepy. How are you feeling?" my mother-in-law greeted me as I joined Jackson on the sofa.

"All right. More in shock I think than anything else. I'm still trying to process everything."

"I understand. It was a shock to us all. I knew Monte for many years. He was a good man," Robert emphasized.

"Thank you." I wasn't sure what to say.

"I know it must be hard and confusing since you lost Monte *here* so many years ago and having those emotions cross the barrier can be difficult to adjust to at first," Emily said.

"As horrible as it sounds, it was harder for me *here* as far as the emotional aspects of losing Mimi than it has been with Monte. I feel bad about losing him, don't misunderstand me, but Mimi was like a second mother to me." Just the memory of her brought tears to my eyes. "I miss her every day, even *here*. With Monte, I knew him. I loved him both *here* and *there*. He was a wonderful brother to both my fathers, and I feel horrible that Patrick and Uncle Nicholas are grieving his death. I feel even worse for Aunt Vivian and their boys. But I'm not sure what I feel," I attempted to explain.

"It does not sound horrible at all. I understand. People touch our lives in different ways," Emily said.

"Uncle Monte was different, I suppose. Oddly, I feel very close to the man I read about in those journals, the soldier who was not sure if he would ever see his true love again. That version of Monte will haunt me forever. But the man I knew, strangely, was nothing like the soldier. Perhaps the war changed him, or he was not comfortable with expressing his emotions openly to those whom he loved. I am not sure which, but he was not a warm and loving man towards me. He loved me. I know he did. I also knew if I ever needed him, he would be there for me. All I am saying is that he was not what I would call an outwardly affectionate man. Does that make sense?" I asked as I struggled to convey the right words.

"Yes, it makes perfect sense." Jackson put his arm around me.

"No. No, it doesn't." I felt so foolish. "But I don't know how to put it into the right words without sounding stupid." I chuckled. "So, instead I make myself sound like an idiot."

"Not at all. We know what you mean," Robert said, and Emily nodded in agreement.

We sat silently and enjoyed the rest of the movie. I snuggled into the nook under Jackson's arm and lost myself in the throes of Cary Grant's velvety voice. As the score and credits began our attention was interrupted by deafening screams that came from somewhere out in front of the house.

"What in the world?" Robert said as he rose to investigate. Moments later he hollered from his spot behind the living room drapes. "I guess Jenna and Kyle are having an argument."

"Huh?" I glanced over at Jackson before joining Robert, who had lost interest and was returning to his seat on the lounge beside his wife.

I pulled the drapery back just enough to see Jenna standing in the middle of my old front yard screaming at Kyle through her tears. "I said leave me alone!" she shouted.

"Calm down, Jenna," I barely heard Kyle reply.

"Don't tell me what to do! I'm sick and tired of people telling me what to do!" she screamed back at him. Kyle approached her slowly holding out his arms to her, but Jenna smacked him hard enough that I jumped.

"What is going on?" Jackson came up beside me.

"I'm not sure, except she just hit Kyle," I answered, still watching them.

"You should go talk to her," Jackson suggested.

"You are kidding, right?" I turned towards him. "She hates me, remember?"

"Jenna is hurting. You should try at least." I wrinkled my nose at him. "Be the bigger person here, Jocelyn."

"This should be fun," I muttered, crossing over to the foyer and stepping into my flip-flops.

"Be nice," I heard him holler as I walked out the front door.

"Yeah, right," I muttered to myself as I began my journey down the driveway. "Easy for you to say, you're not the one she's been treating like crap for the last five months." I shut up as I crossed the street and into my parents' front yard where the two of them were still arguing.

"Great!" Jenna said as I approached. "What the hell do you want?" She glared.

"Nothing. I just wanted you to know that your little spectacle is entertaining the whole street," I said a little too harshly.

"Do you really think I give a shit?" Jenna fired back.

"No, I don't think you care at all, but it doesn't look like Kyle is too comfortable participating in it," I pointed out.

"Like I care." She rolled her eyes and folded her arms across her chest. "This is none of your business so why don't you just trot back over to your hubby and continue playing house."

"What the hell is your problem, Jenna? This whole charade is old, and everyone is tired of it. Don't you think it may be time for a slight attitude adjustment?"

"What do you care what I do or say?" Jenna shouted at me.

"I care because I love you despite the fact that you've been a bitch for the last five months!" I said angrily.

"I've been a bitch? That's rich! You're the one who ran off and got married without even inviting me! I was supposed to be your maid of honor and you stabbed me in the back!" Jenna fumed with her hands balled into fists at her side.

"Well, excuse me. It wasn't like I had planned it or anything. I didn't even know about it until right before it happened."

"Like I believe that!" she shouted back.

"Believe what you like. I couldn't care less. I only came over to tell you that all the neighbors are watching you throw a tantrum in my parents' front yard." I turned towards Kyle. "I'm sorry."

"No, I'm sorry," he said in a small voice, looking uncomfortable.

"Why are you apologizing to her? She is the one who barged over here and interrupted our conversation." Jenna turned her glare on poor Kyle.

"Conversation? It was one loud conversation," I muttered loud enough for her to hear me.

"Butt out and mind your own business, will you? Just go home." Jenna shifted her weight taking on a defensive stance between Kyle and me.

"Jenna, I didn't purposely stab you in the back. I didn't betray you. I never meant to hurt you. Jackson and I eloped to get me out of my house because of my mother and Ethan. It had nothing to do with you. I'm sorry if you got upset about missing my wedding." I calmed down and attempted to explain.

"You never meant to hurt me?" She scoffed at me. "You were my best friend my entire life. We shared everything. Then this guy moves in across the street and you turn into this person I don't even know." She gestured her arms wildly. "Jocelyn, you were all about books, and school, and college, and dreams of what you wanted to be. And then you go and throw away your entire life on a guy you've known for ten minutes. What the hell!"

"I know how this appears. I am not stupid. But I do not regret marrying Jackson," I told her.

"Maybe not yet, but you will. I can guarantee it. That day will come when you are going to be sitting in some crappy little apartment with a kid or two and he's out running around with the guys or cheating on you and you'll be regretting that you didn't even finish your bachelor's degree because you got pregnant. And you'll be stuck, either on welfare or in a shitty marriage or both." Jenna stepped a little closer and stated directly in my face.

"When did you start having premonitions?" I couldn't stop myself from asking. "Besides, single girls get pregnant all the time and so do girls who have boyfriends," I reasoned. "You do not have to have a husband to get pregnant, Jenna."

"Jesus, Jocelyn, look at the statistics. You don't have to be psychic to see what's coming. Have you lost all your common sense? He's going to leave you. Everyone always leaves. That's just life!" she spat.

"Contrary to what you believe, not everyone leaves, Jenna," I said in a lower voice.

"Don't worry, you'll find out I'm right and then it will be too late for you." I couldn't believe the hostility in Jenna's voice.

"I am sorry you feel that way." I shook my head over at Kyle who looked like he was at a crossroads between sympathy for Jenna and being fed up with all her crap. I couldn't blame him. "Have a good afternoon, Kyle." I turned and headed back towards my home.

I made it across the street and a few steps into my yard when I heard steps approaching me quickly from behind. The next thing I knew fingers gripped my arm roughly and flung me around. I almost lost my footing and barely caught myself from falling flat on my rear.

"Don't you walk away from me!" Jenna shouted in my face. "I wasn't done talking to you."

"I am done talking to you, Jenna." Now I was mad.

"What are you gonna do? Attack me like you did Taylor? Go ahead, try it. I dare you!" She sneered.

Kyle came rushing up between us and put a hand on each of our shoulders. "Stop this!" He faced Jenna. "What are you doing? She's your best friend and you're treating her like crap. This isn't you." His voice softened a little, but he stood his ground between us.

I heard our front door slam and saw Jackson trotting down the front steps and across the yard towards us. He came to a halt between Kyle and me and put his arm protectively around my waist. "Is everything all right?" he asked.

"And Jackson comes to save his princess. Typical." Jenna rolled her eyes.

"Enough, Jenna. I mean it!" Kyle responded.

"Explain to me why you're taking everyone's side but mine." Her eyes narrowed on him.

"I'm not taking anyone's side." Kyle exhaled audibly. "You're so angry with everyone in the world because your parents are getting divorced. So, what? Parents get divorced. Shit happens. It sucks, but its life. You're lucky to have had them married for the last twenty years. Most kids don't have that."

"You don't understand. You've never been through this!" Jenna yanked her hand off my arm.

"Jenna," I started.

"Just get the hell out of my face!" Jenna glared at me through gritted teeth.

"Come on." Jackson pulled me back away from her. He took my hand and walked me back up to the house. Neither of us turned around.

"Wow! That was a great idea," I said after he closed the front door.

"I am sorry. I had no idea she would react that way." Jackson followed me into the kitchen. "I was afraid you were going to hit her."

"Oh well, it wouldn't have been the first time." I shrugged and poured myself a glass of tea from the fridge.

"Are you serious?" He chuckled and climbed up on the barstool.

"Not like that." I took a sip and put the glass down on the island. "When we were kids. It's been a good decade since we had a physical fight."

"I cannot believe you ever had a physical one. What were you two fighting over?"

"If I remember correctly it was over a line-drive I hit. We were bickering before practice over something stupid I can't even remember what it was now, but during practice I hit a beautiful line drive and it damn near took her head off." I giggled. "She thought I did it on purpose, which I didn't, but anyway, she came up and punched me after practice. So, I hit her back. We laughed about it an hour later."

"So violent." Jackson moved out the other bar stool with his foot for me. "I knew you had an occasional scuffle with Ethan, but I had no idea you were so ornery," he teased.

"I'm not ornery. And I only went out there today because you asked me to," I pointed out as I sat down beside him. "So, this one is all on you, baby. Besides, I did not hit her." I nudged him playfully.

"You wanted to," he pointed out.

"But I didn't."

"If I had not come out, would you have?" Jackson asked.

"I would be lying if I said it didn't cross my mind, but no. I would not have. I am a married lady and ladies do not engage in such activities." I spoke in a prissy voice.

"A lady? Since when?" He laughed and picked up an orange out of the fruit bowl in the center of the island.

"Hey, I resent that." I shoved him hard enough that he had to catch himself by putting his foot down on the floor.

"Don't you mean resemble?" Jackson started peeling the orange.

"When did I get my head on the chopping block? I stayed calm today ... for the most part. And I never threatened her. She threatened me," I pointed out.

"She's dealing with a lot. Her parents' divorce is obviously taking a toll on her. Try to put yourself in her shoes for a moment," Jackson suggested.

"Are you kidding me? I would be thrilled if my parents got divorced."

"No, you would not."

"Yes, I would. My dad might discover happiness. They have been miserably married for twenty-five years. Perhaps once they were happy and in love, but that died a long time ago." I rested my head on the island for a moment and Jackson rubbed my back tenderly. "Their marriage is so bad that Sidney and I talked about it over Thanksgiving. Our parents' relationship has actually turned her against marriage." I lifted my head up and looked at him.

"Well, it must be some comfort to know that the damage was not permanent. We know she gets married." Jackson always managed to find the right thing to say. "And we know that it was successful."

"We do not know that for certain. We barely know anything about her relationship with Keifer."

"True, but now that you have met him do you not feel certain that Sidney is happy?"

"Well, I do like Keifer. He seems to be a wonderful man who loves her dearly," I admitted.

"I agree. And look at us. Do you believe that we will be unhappily married in twenty-five years?" He popped an orange wedge into his mouth and grinned.

"From what I saw in the photo albums, no I do not." I reached over and stole one of his wedges and took a bite of it. "But then again, pictures can be deceiving. No one would know by looking at our family photo in front of the Christmas tree last year with our plastered smiles and carefully selected wardrobe that my parents were screaming at each other up until the photographer arrived that day. We were all miserable, but the picture shows a happy loving family just as my mother had ordered us to be that day." I climbed down off the bar stool and walked over to the doorway. "Sometimes divorce can be a good thing. It can give everyone a chance to be happy. Everyone deserves a chance to be happy," I finished in a low voice.

I paused for a moment and looked in the family room at my in-laws. They were sitting on the lounge closely together. Robert had his arm around his wife and Emily rested her head on his chest, her legs draped over his. I smiled thinking about how lucky I was that my husband was brought up with such a strong example of a loving marriage. I knew Robert and Emily's marriage wasn't perfect, but it was the closest thing to perfect that I'd ever witnessed.

I headed upstairs to our bedroom and pulled out one of Uncle Monte's journals. I sat down on the bed and turned to the page I'd left off at several months ago. I ran my fingers lightly over the words as a single tear ran down my cheek. It was hard to imagine that the soldier who wrote with such passion and vigor was now gone from my life forever. Although I didn't know the man who was my uncle all that well, I did love him and would miss him terribly. I wish I had gotten to know him better *there*. Now I would never have the chance.

CHAPTER TWENTY-SIX

TUESDAY, *April 22, 1879*

The sound of thunder rocked the house in the pre-dawn hours. I jerked awake and sat up in bed. Jackson was still snoring softly beside me. I pushed the heavy blankets aside, threw my legs over the edge of the bed, and slipped my feet into my slippers. Our room was chilly and the fire in the hearth was smoldering. Sometimes I really missed central heating. I pulled on my robe off the end of the bed and tossed it across my shoulders.

I walked over to the window and pulled the drapes aside. Rain was pouring down upon the world outside as if it were weeping my uncle's passing. I leaned my head against the cold glass dreading the funeral that was only hours away. I hated funerals. I had attended too many in my young life already. I was now recalling modern medicines without any difficulty, which made these losses so aggravating knowing they could have been prevented. Perhaps not Monte's, but others I loved. I could not help but think that if Mimi had received regular medical check-ups, her problems may have been detected and prevented and she would still be with us.

I still had not seen Aunt Vivian. Emily and I had gone over to their house yesterday and she would not emerge from her room. We spoke with Floyd and Vivian's sister, Violet, who told us that she was refusing to eat or get out of bed. They were hoping they could get her to the funeral, but thus far, she was refusing it. Floyd told me a little later that his mother was refusing to believe it was him since she never saw his body and that he was only identified by his pocket watch. I didn't have the heart to tell Floyd the full truth of the condition of his father's body. He didn't need to know.

I curled up on the lounge over by the window and wrapped an afghan around me. I tucked my feet beneath me trying to keep some of the cold away from me. I looked over at my beautiful husband sleeping peacefully. My heart was overwhelmed with the love I felt for him. I could not imagine the agony my aunt was experiencing. I couldn't fathom the thought of losing Jackson. I loved him more than I had ever believed possible. He was my soul mate, my lover, my best friend. My world would be shredded without him.

Time passed without notice. My mind was lost in deep thoughts of my *other* life and all the bizarre things happening there. But as the sun fought to break through stormy skies unsuccessfully, I heard movement arousing from the far corners of the house below me. I pulled my cramped legs out from beneath me and stretched. I looked back out the window and saw the rain hadn't slowed at all. Jackson rolled over pulling my gaze from the dark cold world beyond my window. I really hated funerals.

We rode to the church with Robert and Emily. Everyone was silent. There simply were no words to say. The sound of the rain beating on the top of the carriage competed with the pounding of the horse's hooves on the cobblestone street. There was a procession of carriages leading up to the church filled with family, friends, and all the lives that Monte touched during his time with us.

The first several pews were reserved for immediate family. Jackson and I joined my brothers in the second row behind my parents. Sidney and Keifer sat beside my parents looking lost and uncomfortable. Jackson's parents and siblings sat directly behind us. The church was standing room only. In the first row sat Aunt Vivian, her sons, my parents, Uncle Nicholas, and Aunt Lydia. I could only see Aunt Vivian's profile. Her face appeared pale and gaunt.

The church was filled with flowers and the aroma was overwhelming. I could not get over the gaudy display. Uncle Monte rested in the large cherry oak casket on the right side of the pulpit. Thankfully, it was closed and there was a large wreath of spring flowers resting upon it. It was a mournful sight and diffi-cult to even look at. I could not seem to shake the horrible guilt I was feeling in the pit of my stomach.

Reverend Jacobs began his service paying tribute to the life of Mont-gomery Floyd Timmons. He talked about his service during the Civil War, the time he spent in college, his career, his marriage, and his sons. Then my father got up and spoke about his brother and the type of man Monte was, how much he touched the lives of all who knew him, and how he would be missed every day. It was a beautiful service and there was not a dry eye in the house.

Jackson kept his arm tightly around me as I wept for the loss of a man I loved, who we all loved. Even my in-laws had their hands on my shoulders trying to comfort me. I held onto Jackson's hand with a handkerchief in the other, but the tears wouldn't stop. The beautiful words Monte had written in all those journals haunted my mind. I wrestled with the thoughts of how a man could write with such passion and be very different in reality.

We stood side by side under the big tent at the gravesite. Aunt Vivian was inconsolable. My father held her up as did her son Floyd on her other side. It was a horrible scene. I knew there was nothing any of us could do for her.

After the funeral services were done and Uncle Monte was lowered into the ground in our family plot, we gathered at Aunt Vivian's house. Everyone talked in hushed tones and quiet murmurs. I helped my brother James' wife, Rachel, pass out hot tea and finger sandwiches simply to give me something to do. I felt I had to keep myself busy or I'd scream.

Later that evening Jackson and I followed my parents back to their house. My father was solemn and spoke only when spoken to. My mother never left his side. Sarah whipped up a quick dinner although no one felt like eating. My father just stood beside the hearth staring off into the flames.

"You really need to eat something, my dear." My mother gently touched his arm.

But he shook his head without looking at her.

"Patrick, you need to keep your strength. You will get sick if you do not eat."

"Annabelle, I told you earlier, I am not hungry. I will eat when I am." His words were hard, but his voice was soft.

"Father, please. Eat something for me." I walked up to him and wrapped my arms around him.

"I cannot understand for the life of me how all this happened." He held me closely.

"It was a tragic accident," I whispered.

"I need a drink." My father let me go and walked over to the bar in the corner of the room. He picked up the decanter of brandy and poured himself a healthy amount. "I know. I only wish I could have been there. I wish ..." He didn't bother finishing his sentence. Instead, he downed the contents of his glass.

"Patrick, I know this is hard." Sidney approached her younger brother. "But Monte would not want you doing this." She took the glass from his hand. "Let's eat something." She took him by the hand and turned toward us. "Let's all go eat something." The rest of us followed the two of them into the dining room.

* * *

Cora helped me out of my heavy dress and into my nightgown. I sat down at the vanity chair and she began to brush out my hair in long strokes just has her mother had done for years before her. I watched her carefully in the mirror. She reminded me so much of Mimi. She even resembled her a great deal, except for her smile. She had her father's smile. An ache swelled up in the middle of my chest just thinking about all the hours I'd spent with Mimi and realizing they were gone forever.

I patted Cora's hand gently and smiled. "It has been a long day, Cora. I think I'm ready for bed. Thank you."

"Sleep tight, Ms. Jocelyn," she said as she left my room.

"You too, Cora."

I brushed my hair off my shoulders as Jackson walked in our room, closing the door behind him. He began removing his tie and unbuttoning his shirt. I rose from my seat and walked over to help him. He smiled slightly showing off a hint of his dimples. I moved my fingers down his broad chest slowly and with deliberation. He reached up and ran his fingers though my long, thick, auburn hair. His eyes caressed mine. My stomach still filled with butterflies at the smallest touch of his hand. I loved that about him.

Once undone I gently brushed his shirt off his shoulders and let it drop to the floor. Jackson gave me a wicked smile and lifted me off my feet effortlessly. I wrapped my arms around his neck and giggled. He leaned down and kissed me firmly and carried me over to our bed. He put me down gently in the center of the bed and climbed in beside me.

CHAPTER TWENTY-SEVEN

TUESDAY, April 20, 2010

Seventh period, psychology class, my favorite class of the day. Mr. Rand was going over the material for our exam the next day covering research and statistics. Not a favorite topic of mine, but interesting none the less. Jackson looked bored out of his skull. I would imagine after taking college level courses over the same courses, an introductory high school psychology class would seem incredibly boring.

But he played his role. My twenty-two-year-old husband, a college graduate with a Bachelor of Science in psychology, holding onto his forged documents thanks to some talented attorneys, was continuing his charade as a high school student for my benefit. I knew he hated it. The thrill of returning to high school had long since died away and now he was left with the actual work and the monotony of it. And I loved him for sticking with it.

I knew how anxious Jackson was to get back to Boston, back to law school, back to the life he'd left out of his love for me. But he smiled. He went through the motions. He never complained. He cheered me on through volleyball and basketball season and would once more for softball. He played football and basketball for our high school teams. He attended class, took me to parties, and school activities. In my eyes, he was almost a saint for enduring so much in the name of love.

Jackson sat in the desk beside mine, drumming his fingers lightly on his notebook, glancing at the clock every couple of minutes. He seemed especially anxious today to escape the confines of our classroom. I reached over and placed my hand on his arm. "Stop," I mouthed to him. He half grinned and folded his fingers in his lap, but he continued looking at the clock.

"What is up with you?" I asked as soon as the final bell rang.

"Nothing." He scooped up his books. "Caitlyn is going to drive you home after practice. I have something to take care of." Jackson leaned over and kissed me quickly on the cheek and bolted out the door before I could even reply.

"Okay," I responded to the back of him knowing full well he couldn't hear me.

"Is everything all right?" Mr. Rand asked while my classmates followed Jackson out the door.

"I think so." I stuffed the rest of my things in my backpack. "He's up to something. I'm just not sure what."

"A surprise for you?"

"Well, it's not our anniversary or my birthday," I explained.

"Does a husband need a special occasion to surprise his wife?" Mr. Rand sat down on the corner of his desk.

"If I go by the example my parents set forth, I would have to say yes. But if I go by my in-laws, then definitely not." I chuckled.

"Your families are that much different?" he inquired, putting his foot up on one of the desks in the front row.

"Very much so." I propped myself on the edge of my desk. "Jackson comes from a very old school traditional type family that actually cooks and eats meals together. They spend time together and enjoy doing things together. His parents are still very much in love. My family is the exact opposite."

"Your family sounds more like mine," he laughed. "I found it strange when my wife's mother actually cooked. My folks divorced when I was young."

"Mine should have. They've been miserably married almost twenty-five years."

"Yet, you took the plunge right after turning eighteen. I find that ironic. Don't you?" He appeared to be amused by our conversation a little too much.

"Is this where you psychoanalyze me?" I laughed.

"No," he chuckled. "I'm just curious as to what would make someone who is a star athlete, an honor student destined for college most likely on a scholarship, get married on a whim over Christmas vacation?"

"Would 'for love' be an appropriate response?" I raised an eyebrow at him.

"I know you love him. Everyone can see that. And I don't believe that it's some high school crush, or infatuation. I believe you two sincerely love one another. But I also believe that there is more to your relationship than you two are telling anyone," Mr. Rand speculated.

"What makes you say that?" I smiled coolly, but a knot formed in the pit of my stomach.

"It shows in the way you two act around each other, like you share a secret no one else is privy to." He tilted his head and looked at me carefully as if he were studying me.

"And that arouses your curiosity?" I searched my brain for every face I'd encountered with *EVE* and nowhere was my teacher. I was sure of it.

"I would say it has something to do with the bigger scheme of things rather than the superficial. Am I wrong?" I couldn't tell if he knew something or was simply playing with me.

Two can play this game.

"But what if it is something you shared that you knew no one else, not even your closest friends and certainly not your family would ever believe. Does that make a difference?" I asked him in a coy voice.

"Perhaps, are you taking his word, or do you have proof?" Mr. Rand's eyes narrowed a bit.

"Proof was predestined. Jackson could not control that any more than I could have. He served more as a guide than an administrator." The confused look on Mr. Rand's face was priceless.

"Do you mean …" He searched for the right words.

"We are both married, Mr. Rand. I am sure you understand exactly what I mean." I smiled and leapt off my desk. "I am sorry, I have got to run. I am already late for practice." I headed out the door before he could respond. "It was nice chatting with you," I hollered behind me just as I left the room.

I couldn't stop myself from laughing out loud as I quickly went to my locker to swap my books around before hurrying off to the locker room to change for softball practice. Luckily, Coach Kane was in a good mood and didn't seem overly upset about my tardiness when I explained that I was kept after class by Mr. Rand. I jogged out to first base, thrilled that I didn't end up running laps.

* * *

The house was surprisingly empty when Caitlyn dropped me off. Jackson's CRV sat idle in the driveway. He must have gone somewhere with his parents. My suspicions were aroused by the time I jumped into the shower. It was highly unusual for Emily not to be here in the evening and it was past time for Robert to be home from work. I shrugged it off but kept an ear open for them.

Feeling better after my hot shower, I threw on a cute little outfit Sidney had picked out for me down in New Orleans. She had said it was flattering on me and showed off my figure. Sidney had spent most of our trip trying to redo my entire wardrobe. She said I needed to be more feminine and dress like a lady. Not an old lady, but a young one with style and class. What she wanted to do was dress me more like her. I obliged, if only to make her happy. I even fixed my hair more than I typically did and added a little make-up to surprise Jackson.

Afterwards, I headed downstairs in search of something to eat. It was dinnertime and I couldn't believe no one was home yet. It was unheard of for the kitchen to be left untouched this time of day. I rummaged around and fixed myself something to eat. I wasn't nearly as talented in the kitchen as Emily or Robert, but I was learning thanks to my in-laws.

I settled into the family room and turned on old reruns of *Supernatural*. I'd nearly got through a full episode when I heard a car pull into the drive. I hurried and put my things in the sink and straightened up the mess I'd made before the garage door opened all the way. I had just finished when the kitchen garage door opened and in walked three familiar faces.

"Hello, darling." Jackson walked over and kissed me on the cheek. "I have a surprise for you." He grinned widely.

"Really? What's that?"

Robert and Emily greeted me and placed their shopping bags down on the island. From the names on their bags I could tell they'd been to the mall in the city.

"Here." Jackson handed me a little ivory paper bag with a wide sage ribbon that served as the handle.

"What did you do?" I pulled a little black velvet box out. "Jackson, you shouldn't have." I opened it and gasped. It was an exact replica of the pocket watch he had given me for my birthday. I quickly flipped it over and there was the exact same words engraved in the sterling silver. *Time will reveal my Love.* "Oh, Jackson!" I wrapped my arms around his neck and kissed him fully on the lips. "How did you know?"

"The day you moved in here and we were packing up the last of your things I saw some of the pieces of it in your room. I knew how much you loved it, and I don't care how it got broken. I wanted to replace it."

"I broke it when you left," I confessed, holding my gift close to my chest. "I am so sorry."

"It's all right. I figured as much. It was a very difficult time for us. I understand."

"You have no idea what this means to me." I held the watch lovingly close to my chest and looked up into his piercing green eyes. "I love this!" I couldn't stop my eyes from welling up.

Jackson took me into his arms. "I love you," he whispered.

"I love you too." I gently brushed the tears from my cheeks.

"You look really nice. I like that outfit on you," Jackson remarked, taking a step back. "Are you going somewhere?"

"No, I simply wanted to look nice for my husband." I smiled coyly.

"I think you look beautiful," Emily added, emptying a couple grocery bags Robert had placed on the island.

"Thank you." I put the watch in my pocket and began helping her.

"Would you like to help me fix dinner tonight?" she offered.

"I would love to." I smiled over at Jackson and his father as they walked out of the room.

Emily and I busied ourselves preparing our evening meal. She told me all about the premise of her new novel. Her imagination astounded me. I couldn't fathom the patience it took to sit and write a book, keep numerous characters straight, and stream it all together. But she had written several successful series and a few singles. I admired her talent greatly.

"I have enough trouble keeping track of both my lives and here you not only manage that beautifully, you also string together incredible worlds of your own imagination," I said as I diced up an onion.

"Writing is my solace. I grew up in a house full of turmoil and I learned at a young age that writing was a way for me to escape into a world where I actually had some control," Emily explained.

"Were your parents divorced?" I realized I knew very little about her childhood. She never really spoke of it.

"No, but like yours they did not get along very well. My mother was a disturbed woman who did not have a kind bone in her body. Therefore, my father drank excessively." She sighed and busied herself seasoning the roast. "I truly believe my father could have been a wonderful dad if he had married someone else. As a child I blamed him for staying married to her and exposing us to her abuse. Even today I do not understand why he never left her."

"You never asked him?"

"No, he was not a very personable man. I do not believe we ever talked about anything more personal than the weather forecast. I always knew he loved me. I just do not think he knew how to show it," she stated.

"I'm sorry. That must have been difficult growing up that way." I could empathize with her.

"My parents both passed away several years ago and I cannot say I knew either of them very well. My father worked hard to take care of us. We always had everything we needed and most everything we wanted." Emily smiled slightly. "But my mother had *EVE* as well and despite having the support of numerous family members there to guide her she could never fully adjust to it. She was diagnosed with schizophrenia and put on heavy medications. They did not help at all. They made her worse. She spent the last decade of her life in and out of mental institutions."

"I am so sorry, Emily. I had no idea."

She set down her utensils on the counter and came over to me. She took both my hands in hers and looked me directly in the eye. I could see the depths of years of hidden sorrow and pain in her beautiful brown eyes looking back at me. "Jocelyn, that is why when we found out about you having *EVE* we dropped everything in Boston and came to find you. After witnessing firsthand how things can go terribly wrong with this gift, I had to make sure that you did not end up like my mother." She squeezed my hands gently then let me go.

But I grabbed her softly and embraced her. "Thank you for loving me enough to make sure I was all right. I surely would have ended up Lord only knows where without you and your family. Especially considering neither of my uncles was here to explain to me what was happening let alone guide me through it. I hate to even imagine what would have happened. I love you all so much."

"Oh, sweetheart, we would never let anything happen to you. You are like a daughter to me, not just my daughter-in-law." Emily squeezed me tightly.

"Thank you," I said before releasing her. It touched my soul to be so fortunate to marry into such a loving household.

Emily and I talked about Boston and how we were both excited to get back there shortly after graduation. She gushed on about the museums, shops, and all the historic places she was anxious to take me. She made it sound like such a mystic place, haunted by our founding fathers lurking in the dark shadows of the city. Considering how much historical research I'd done in the last six months I was excited to get back there as much as she was. I felt as if I spent half my time daydreaming about our new life in Boston where Jackson no longer had to hide and could be his true self… and age. And where I can finally spread my wings and fly without suffocating under the watchful eye of my mother. It was going to be a new beginning for the both of us and I could not be more thrilled.

* * *

I finished up the rest of my homework and closed my calculus text. I sighed audibly and peeked through the blinds at my childhood home sitting across the street. I couldn't help but wonder what was going on over there. It appeared dark and silent. The blinds were drawn giving only a hint of the light bleeding through the small openings. It left me feeling lonely. Although my relationship with my dad had improved greatly in the last several weeks, I still missed my brother.

I moved my books aside and sat on the top of the desk. I pulled the blinds up and leaned my head against the cool glass. I dearly missed my bay window seat and the comforting way the view from those windows had always made me feel better. Those windows were dark now with no signs of the life that had lived on the other side of them, the countless sleepovers, the secrets revealed, the tears, the laughter. There was nothing now but deafening darkness.

I couldn't take my eyes off the house that starred as the center of my universe for the first eighteen years of my life. It was both a heaven and a hell. I closed my eyes and tried to focus on all the good times that still lingered in those halls, but the last few months I'd lived there left a bitter taste in my mouth. What had once been my haven had turned overnight into a fierce battleground. The prize? Control over my future and my destiny. My mother had kept a firm hand on the back of my neck for as long as I could remember, and it had taken a crowbar to pry it off.

I climbed off the desk and slipped into my pajamas. It had been a long day. I crawled into bed and turned off the light on my nightstand. Jackson was still downstairs watching something or other with his father. I wrapped my arms around his pillow and inhaled his scent deeply. I dearly loved my husband more than anything else in this world. I knew that he wasn't perfect, neither was I. But all that mattered was he was perfect for me.

CHAPTER TWENTY-EIGHT

Friday, April 25, 1879

I found Sidney sitting at the dining room table enjoying her morning coffee when I came down for breakfast. She looked beautiful sitting there with the morning sunlight shining down upon her through the tall windows. She was reading the morning paper and absentmindedly stirring her coffee although I hadn't seen her put anything in it.

"Good morning, it is nice to see the sun finally made an appearance before you say goodbye," I remarked, taking a seat at the table across from her. She and Keifer were leaving that afternoon on a train back to Boston. I hated seeing her leave. I had really enjoyed having them here this week despite the horrible circumstances that had drawn out their stay. They had decided to forego their second destination after all that had happened.

Sidney had been instrumental in helping both her younger brothers recover in the unexpected death of Monte. My father and Nicholas would mourn the loss of Monte for the rest of their lives, but for a short time they had found great comfort bonding with their older half-sister. I had seen a side of her this week that I had never known before. The compassion she'd shown her brothers only made me love her even more. She was not the academic cheerleader that flooded my memories. Instead, she was a grown woman, a lady. A nurturing, loving, and compassionate mother, who was years beyond the carefree college girl in my head. The difference was astounding.

"Good morning, my dear niece. Yes, it should seem so. I do hate to leave. I feel so horrible about everything that has transpired since I arrived." Sidney finally put her spoon down.

"Uncle Monte's death was a tragic accident and you are in no way responsible for it," I explained to her for the millionth time this week as I fixed my own cup of coffee.

"I understand that. However, because he was visiting with me at the time of the incident, I cannot help but feel responsible for it," she explained.

"It would have made no difference who was with him. It was an accident. It could easily have been me or anyone else." I did not enjoy seeing her like this. "I, for one, am thrilled that you came to visit, and I hate that you are leaving." I reached across the table and took her hand in mine. "I wish I could visit you. Perhaps Jackson will let me now that he has gotten to know you better in *this* time."

"That would be lovely." Sidney smiled gently. "I would love for you to meet my children."

"You know how weird that sounds to me?" I leaned forward and whispered. "It is almost unimaginable to me. I am still not used to seeing you like this since in my mind I only know you as, well … the *other* you."

Sidney glanced toward the doorway to the kitchen and said. "Would you like to join me for a walk?"

"Of course." I finished up my coffee and returned upstairs to retrieve my shawl and parasol.

We stepped out onto the porch and were kissed by a warm breeze and a lovely spring morning. Sidney took my arm as we headed down the front steps. She looked over at my parents' home, her brother's home and a small smile slid across her shapely lips. "I have so many fond childhood memories of living there. It is such a beautiful old house."

"But it is not old," I remarked as we continued down the walkway to the cobblestone street.

"Yes, but for me, it will always be the place I grew up *there* just as it is for you." We turned in the direction of our childhood home and walked slowly past the gate. "It leaves me with such an overwhelming sense of deja vú. I feel sixteen years old again," she chuckled softly. "The first time I walked in there on this visit I stood there in the foyer waiting for our parents or Ethan to come walking out of the kitchen."

"I know what you mean. When the barrier began to crumble in my mind, I would flash back and forth between the two periods. It was the oddest sensation and really obscured my perception of reality. It still happens occasionally." We paused for a moment at the gate, both of us staring up at our childhood home.

The sun was shining down around the large house. The lawn was a plush green, and multiple flower beds were dressed up in a matrix of colors, while freshly awakened leaves that had recently budded into the new season danced happily in the breeze. The swing on the large wrap-around porch behind the columns swayed slightly in rhythm with the leaves.

"Which you do prefer?" Sidney broke my thoughts.

"What do you mean?"

"Which time period do you prefer? *Here* or *there?*" she inquired.

"That is difficult to say," I sighed audibly. "There are benefits and drawbacks to both I suppose. Each is unique and intriguing. The more I see and learn about *there* I love it. But I also cannot say I am overly impressed with our mother. She seems to be a hostile and cold woman." I rested my hand on the fence that no longer existed in my *other* time.

"I can understand why you would have that impression of her given the way she has behaved recently in your memory. However, you must know that she loves you dearly despite her inability to show it. I know she's a tormented lady who has not been happy in various aspects of her life for a long time," Sidney tried to explain.

"I realize she is miserable, but what I do not understand is why she finds it necessary to make everyone around her miserable as well."

"You know the old saying, 'misery loves company.' Some individuals feel better when they are making others feel bad." Sidney patted my hand and we began walking again along the cobblestone path.

"I have never understood that rational," I stated, trying to slow my pace to match hers.

"Me neither. I remember the fall-out between you two. It was upsetting to everyone in the family. I recall Ethan being especially harsh towards you and Jackson," she said as we continued on our stroll.

"Ethan was horrible. I was so angry with him."

"And you are not any longer?" Sidney looked at me with an eyebrow raised.

"Perhaps a little," I smirked. "But I do miss him. We used to be very close."

"I know. When we were little, I used to be so jealous of the relationship between you two. You were like twins. You did everything together."

"It was not like you think. I used to hate Ethan always being underfoot. He constantly tagged along trying to integrate himself into my group of friends. It used to make me so crazy," I explained.

"I remember watching the two of you playing basketball in the driveway for countless hours, riding bikes, watching movies, playing baseball in the backyard while I was practicing my cheerleading routines that you both ridiculed me about. You two had everything in common and were so much alike while I felt like the odd man out." Her smile faded.

"You were never interested in sports."

"Not true, cheerleading is a sport." A familiar smile slipped across her face.

"Keep telling yourself that." It was a statement we'd teased each other about for years.

"It is and I stand by it." Sidney nudged me in a playful manner.

"I believe you were very much like our mother whereas Ethan and I are more like our father," I said, changing the subject.

"Very much so." she stopped for a moment and tucked a loose piece of my hair behind my ear in a motherly way. "You were always Daddy's little girl."

"And you were mothers."

"She and I had a fondness for clothing, shoes, and accessories. Things you never cared about."

"That is not true. I love all those things, although perhaps not to the same degree as you and mother," I grinned.

"Is it rude of me to say I was happy to see you dressed like a lady when I saw you here?" I knew she couldn't help saying.

"Yes, but I forgive you." I could understand why she would say such a thing and I had to laugh to myself recalling my overly casual attire.

Sidney and I continued our walk, soaking up the day's warmth from beneath the shelter of my parasol. A million questions ran through my mind that I wanted to ask her. Does our mother ever forgive me for marrying Jackson? Do I reconcile my relationship with her and Ethan? What do I ultimately decide upon for my major? Do Jackson and I and our children stay in Boston after I graduate from college?

A thought crossed my mind that put a smile upon my lips. *I know what Ethan would be asking if he were in my position. Who wins the next thirty Super Bowls? World Series?* I knew he wouldn't be concerned with trivial things such as his own personal situation. He'd be more focused on sports and how he could make a killing knowing who to bet on just like Biff in *Back to the Future II.*

"You realize there are so many questions I would love to ask you," I said in a low voice.

"I know, and I understand. And I wish I could answer them all for you." Sidney stopped at the corner, taking my hand in hers and smiling into my eyes. "But I really cannot. However, I will tell you to trust your instincts in your interests in studying law because you, my little sister," she winked, "are going to make history and make a giant leap for workplace equality for all women."

"Are you serious?" I was baffled. "What do I do?" I couldn't help but ask.

Sidney tilted her head a little to the side as a sly smile slipped across her shapely lips. "You know I cannot tell you that. All I will say is that you should trust your instincts in every aspect of your life. It will take you far and never lead you wrong."

My curiosity was piqued to an all-time high. "How can you not elaborate on that? I mean, can you not even tell me what area of law I should specialize in? That information alone would be extremely helpful," I reasoned.

"I have already said more than I ever should have, Jocelyn. I wish I could answer all your questions, tell you anything and everything you want to know, but I am too fearful to elaborate further." She looked at me sympathetically.

"I know, I know," I sighed heavily and started walking down the cobblestone pathway, and Sidney followed. "This is all so frustrating," I complained.

"I probably should not have said anything, but I felt I had to. There are some things I could not leave up to chance completely. I felt I had to risk it by giving you a gentle nudge in the general direction," she explained.

"My kids?" I glanced over at her with a smile hoping for the slightest hint.

"Jocelyn," her voice took on that of a scolding mother and I couldn't help but smile all the broader by it. "You already know more about them then you should. All I will say is they are happy and healthy."

"Good." I nodded. "Good, I feel better just knowing that much," I added.

We rounded the block and headed back towards my home. Our time together was ending, and my heart was breaking a little more with each step. I didn't want her to leave. For the first time ever, I felt so close to Sidney. I knew we were gaining ground in our relationship in the twenty-first century, but I did not want to lose her on this plane. And I had no idea when I was going to get to see her again.

Jackson made it home shortly before we had to leave for the train station. Davonte loaded Sidney and Keifer's luggage and trunk in our flat board carriage.

I couldn't believe how much she traveled with, but it made me grin knowing that some things don't change across time.

My parents stopped by briefly to say goodbye. My father still had dark circles under his eyes, and it seemed the weight of his brother's passing had aged him in the last week. For the first time in my life I realized he was not a young man but rather at the far edge of middle age. His hair appeared to have grayed a little more around his temples and the rest of his hair was now more salt and peppered than I remembered.

My father hugged his older sister tightly, telling her how much he loved her and would miss her. It was hard for me to see him so vulnerable. I hated it. I always saw my father as a pillar of strength. I suppose most girls do. And it was hard with the passing of time to realize that the first knight in shining armor in my life was not invincible. I watched the two of them, thinking that they shared a past I knew very little about. Out of the three brothers, my father appeared to be the one closest to Sidney. Perhaps because he was the oldest, and I knew how important family was to him. He made that extra effort to keep in contact with her after they had moved to Chicago.

We waved goodbye to my folks and climbed into the carriage. Jackson and Keifer sat up front so Sidney and I could sit in back and talk on the ride. Davonte and Betsy followed us in the flat carriage with all their things. I rested back against the seat and held Sidney's hand. I knew eventually that this moment would come, and I'd dreaded it with every fiber of my being. I silently vowed to myself that I would make a true effort in my *other* life to have a real sisterly relationship with her. Granted, we were getting closer, much closer than ever before, but we still had a way to go.

"I am going to miss you so much." Sidney squeezed my hand gently. "I am so glad I got this opportunity to spend some time with you and your family."

"Don't you mean our family?" I smiled.

"Yes, our family. As strange as it may seem ... our family." At least I got her to smile.

Davonte unloaded their luggage with Betsy trying eagerly to help her father. She was an adorable little girl, who was always trying to prove she could do just as much as the adults. I hugged Keifer and kissed him on the cheek. He told me to keep in touch with them and that we were welcome to visit them any time. Keifer was such a kind man, and I was so happy that Sidney had found someone like him to share her life with.

Our husbands shook hands while Sidney and I embraced. Tears rolled down my cheeks as I held her close to me. She rubbed my back in a motherly way soothing my raw emotions. The train whistle blew interrupting our farewell. She tucked another loose curl behind my ear and promised to call me when she returned home.

Sidney and Keifer climbed aboard the train and waved to Jackson and me one final time before they disappeared into their car. Sidney sat down in the window seat and placed her hand on the glass. She smiled at me and wiped her own tears away with a handkerchief in her other gloved hand. My husband put his arm around my waist and led me back to our carriage.

CHAPTER TWENTY-NINE

Friday, April 23, 2010

Jackson and Zak sat in the bleachers munching on Red Vines, nachos, and popcorn, waiting for our game to begin. My dad and Jackson's parents were seated a few rows down from them across the uncomfortable metal stands. Ethan and a couple of his friends sat on the opposite end. I tried to make eye contact with him, but he refused to look in my direction.

It was a warm evening with just enough of a cool breeze to remind us that summer was not quite here yet. I sat in the dugout with Caitlyn and Liang, who I'd really taken a liking to after getting to know her better, waiting for the other team to return to their dugout so we could do the coin toss. Our classmates wandered around the ball diamonds killing time on this beautiful spring evening. I was surprised by the number of students that came out for the game. Softball usually didn't draw that much attention. There must have been nothing else going on that evening.

The game finally started, and it was neck and neck. Neither team could manage to score a single run by the time we hit the top of the seventh inning. We were playing our best and still felt like we were running face-first into a brick wall. Candy Kane was more frustrated than the rest of us. I had never seen him so flustered. It was almost entertaining just to watch him come unglued.

In the bottom of the eighth the pressure was taking its toll on all of us. I jogged out to my spot on first base and shuffled my feet around in the dirt kicking up dust. The first batter came up and hit an easy pop fly to Caitlyn at short stop, and she caught it with no problem. The second batter came up and hit a beautiful line drive right between our second basemen, Ashley and Caitlyn. Thankfully, the ball was retrieved immediately by Mallory in left center and thrown into Ashley, halting the runner at first.

Their third batter waltzed up to the plate full of cocky arrogance smacking the bat on her cleats. Our pitcher, Shelby, gave her two beautiful fast balls, rattling the batter just enough to make her swing wildly at the next pitch that was clearly inside. The ball contacted with the bat and popped straight up in the air. I found myself holding my breath watching Liang jump up, never taking her eye off the ball. The runner on first took several steps away from the bag waiting to see what would happen. I edged towards her, pushing her just a few extra steps towards second.

Liang stretched overhead, grabbing the ball, stumbling over the dropped bat. She landed on her ass with a shocked look on her face.

"Liang!" I screamed, breaking the dazed look on her face.

Liang rolled to her knees, throwing the ball at me from such an awkward position. I leapt to my right to grab it and tagged the first base runner before she could make it back. The bleachers went up in a roar as did our team as we rushed back into the dugout. It was a beautiful play and I seriously doubted we could have repeated it if we tried.

The game went into an excruciating twelve innings. My legs were going numb, my feet were killing, me, and I wasn't sure if I could even stand in the batter's box, let alone swing the bat with any strength. I collapsed down on the bench, thankful that there were five girls ahead of me in the batting order and I'd have a chance to breathe for a minute.

Our first batter struck out. The second hit a pop up and got out. I groaned out loud and picked up my mitt. Another inning … three up, three down. This was getting old and tiresome. Shelby stepped up to the plate. She tilted her cap visor against the setting sun, took a couple practice swings, and adjusted her feet to her batting stance. We all had our silly rituals.

I knew the girl had to be exhausted. Shelby had been pitching the entire game. I was sure she must have spaghetti arms by this hour. I held my mitt and stood up with the rest of my teammates along the fence of the dugout, anxiously waiting for the pitch. Per Shelby's ritual, she never swung at the first pitch. So no one flinched when the curve ball passed her by. The pitcher released the ball again and I knew Shelby was going to swing. She pivoted on her right foot as she stepped forward with her left and swung that bat with every ounce of strength she had left in her.

The sound of the contact between the ball and aluminum bat rang through my ears. The ball sailed over the infield and kept going. I held my breath as it disappeared into the sinking sun. The outfielders scrambled backwards, over and about, but didn't judge the trajectory accurately enough. The ball dropped just outside the left center field fence ... Homerun!

Everyone went ballistic. My teammates and I scrambled to get out of the dugout as Shelby rounded third and jogged her way down to home plate. We were screaming, hugging each other, and jumping up and down. We had never fought so hard for a victory in all the years we'd played together on a school team.

* * *

After a quick shower and a bite to eat, Jackson and I headed out to Mark's infamous property by the lake to celebrate. He had invited the team along with every teenager in attendance at the game. We parked in the makeshift parking lot amongst all the other cars. The bonfire was already roaring, and the music was blaring. The kegs were set up in their usual spot beside the iron trough filled with a mixture of sodas and beer.

I spotted Caitlyn standing beside Zak talking to a group of kids over by the bonfire. The night air was cool, hovering in the high fifties. I was glad I put on a long-sleeved shirt under my hooded sweatshirt as Jackson and I made our way through the crowd. He put his arm around me, knowing I got cold in any weather under seventy degrees. I smiled up at him, thankful he knew me so well.

We walked across the uneven trampled field trying to navigate through the dry areas hoping to avoid the mud. From the tracks that zig-zagged beneath our feet it appeared that Mark and his buddies had been out here recently riding their dirt bikes. They loved to get rowdy, drink a few beers, and raise some hell on the bikes every chance they got. They talked about their antics to anyone who would listen at school and had earned a reputation for being reckless.

I could feel the heat from the fire long before we reached it. We approached Caitlyn and Zak, who were talking with several of our teammates and their boyfriends. Everyone was in a festive mood and the drinks were going down easily. Jackson joined Zak on a trip to the keg, leaving Caitlyn and I alone for a few moments.

"I'm glad to see you finally made peace with Liang. I told you she was nice." Caitlyn tilted her cup in the direction to my left. Looking where she pointed, I saw my brother with his arm hung loosely around Liang's waist.

"I figured they would be here." I rolled my eyes. "I still say she can do better."

"Stop it! He's your brother."

"Exactly, which is why I am saying she can do better." I smirked.

As if on cue, Ethan looked up and made eye contact with me. He eyes narrowed into a smoldering glare. I rolled my eyes at him and turned my attention back to Caitlyn. "Okay, perhaps she can." Caitlyn saw Ethan's glare.

"I was hoping that things would get better before graduation, but it does not look like it is going to."

"I'm sorry." Caitlyn reached out and patted me on the arm. "Hopefully, it will. There's still time."

"Maybe." I shrugged just before the boys returned with fresh drinks. Jackson handed me an electric lemonade. It was delicious and exactly what I needed, feeling the heat of the fire against our exposed skin. The other three were drinking beer from the keg.

"How soon are you leaving for Boston?" The sound of his voice caught me off guard.

"What?" I turned towards Ethan.

"When are you leaving?" he repeated.

"A couple weeks after graduation. Why?" Ethan stood beside Zak with his arm still around Liang and a cup of beer in the opposite hand. Liang looked at us apologetically and stood there nervously holding a soda.

"Just curious how much longer I have to look at you," Ethan sneered. Liang stepped away from him just out of his arm's reach and shook her head slowly at him.

"How can you say that to your sister? Whether you agree with her choices or not, it's her life. Not yours. Get over it already. I'm tired of hearing about it." Liang looked at him with disappointment.

"You don't understand—" Ethan began, but she cut him off.

"No, I do understand. I've been around since last fall and witnessed everything. At least your dad has the kindness in his heart to make amends with his daughter before she moves away, which is more than I can say for you and your mother. I would be devastated if my mother said and did half the things your mother has done to Jocelyn," Liang told him.

"But she caused ..."

"She made a choice. It was her choice. And if you can't find it in your heart to accept it and make peace with her then we cannot be together. I can't be with someone who would cut me out of his life and treat me that way if he didn't agree with something I did." Liang put her hand on her hip and waited for Ethan's reaction.

The harshness in Ethan's face melted away as the five of us stood there staring at him. No one said anything during the awkward exchange. No one knew what do say. Ethan fidgeted with the rim of the cup of beer he was holding as if debating his response. He finally exhaled audibly, looking none too happy but ready to concede. It was a look I knew well with him.

"Fine, I'll keep my mouth shut." Ethan's voice was so low I barely heard him.

"That's not what I said." I tried not to smirk as Liang strong-armed my little brother.

"All right, I will make an effort." I could tell he was struggling hard to maintain his center, and I hated to admit I was enjoying the spectacle a little too much.

"Thank you." Liang took a step back towards Ethan and placed her hand in the middle of his chest. "Now, apologize to her like you mean it." Ethan swallowed hard.

"I'm sorry, Jocelyn," Ethan muttered. "And you too, Jackson."

"Thank you." I tried not to smile at Liang's control over my brother.

"Thanks." Jackson extended his hand as a peace offering. Ethan reluctantly shook it.

"I need another beer." Ethan turned and headed towards the kegs.

"I'm so sorry, Jocelyn. I hate it when he acts like this," Liang said.

"Don't worry, I'm used to it. This isn't our first argument. Granted, it's our longest, but," I shrugged, "what can you do?"

"He can be such a brat when he wants to be." Liang's voice held an annoyed tone. I'm guessing this wasn't the first time she'd experienced Ethan at his finest.

The rest of the evening went off without a hitch. I did spot Jenna, Hilary, Cody, and Kyle on the other side of the bonfire. I was hoping that maybe we'd get a chance to talk, but Jenna made sure she stayed clear of me, even when Cody and Kyle walked by and said hello to us. I made several attempts to make eye contact with her, but she either didn't see me or pretended not to see me. Either way, our issues were not going to be so easily resolved. I knew they weren't entirely with Ethan either, but at least it was a small step in the right direction.

CHAPTER THIRTY

Saturday, *May 9, 1879*

I sat in the back garden, which was alive with a flamboyant display of colors, and tried to concentrate on the book in my hands. But I couldn't. My mind kept returning to my *other* life, the softball game, the way the bat felt in my hands, the thrill of contacting with the ball, the double play, and the party afterwards. It flooded my brain with adrenaline and made me want to jump up and holler. My life *there* was so exciting in comparison to the dull hum of my daily life *here*.

I kept thinking about the prom that was only a matter of hours away. The amazing gown that was hidden in Caitlyn's closet that showed just a hint of my stomach, the delicate matching shoes, and the elegant accessories that Caitlyn and I had picked out during our shopping excursion. I was so jealous for no reason whatsoever. I knew she was me, and I was her, but I was still wrapping my brain around the concept of *EVE*, and when I concentrated on it too hard, I was always rewarded with a headache.

Jackson was across the street at his parents' house going over some case file with Robert and I had no idea when he was likely to return home. His career was even more demanding now that he was gaining a reputation as a fair, knowledgeable, and spirited attorney. I was so proud of him, but I also hated the way it took precedence over me and consumed his life outside of regular office hours.

Finally, I gave up and set my book aside. It was pointless. All my friends were spending this lovely spring day with their beaus, putting the final touches on their wedding, and excitedly discussing the future children they hoped to start having immediately. I felt so disconnected from them. I felt as if I was merely surviving on this plane while my *other* self-fulfilled all her goals and chased her dreams. Somehow it didn't seem fair.

I walked across the back gardens unable to shake the anxiety I was feeling. Davonte had done an amazing job in the last month transforming our oversized backyard into a beautiful menagerie of flowers, shrubbery, fountains, benches, and a trail of brick walkways that merged in the back corner near the big evergreens opposite the stables at a beautiful white gazebo. When he had approached me at first thaw asking about what I envisioned doing with the large open space, he confessed that he had some creative thoughts. I welcomed them all and only asked that he include the gazebo, the rest was his to play with. What emerged was more astonishing than anything I could have imagined.

I wandered about the grounds aimlessly touching the shrubbery and the delicate petals. The sunshine warmed my arms and my neck, but today I seemed to be especially aware of the weight of my gown, the restrictiveness of it, and the way it seemed to absorb the heat from the sun. I stopped my stroll for a moment and closed my eyes thinking once more about what lay ahead once this day was finally over.

I took a deep breath. There was nothing I could do to speed up the time. I made my way around to the front of the house and crossed over into my parents' yard. I figured I would see if anything interesting was going on next door since nothing was happening at my own.

I knocked briefly on the door before I opened it and entered. "Mother?" I called out to let her know I was here.

"Jocelyn?" my mother replied from the parlor. I poked my head in the door and found her and Olivia working on their needlework.

"Good afternoon, Mother. Olivia. How are you ladies doing today?" I asked as I entered the room and took a seat on the lounge.

"It is such a lovely day. Have you been outside?" my mother asked.

"Yes, I was just strolling around in our gardens in the backyard."

"I noticed Davonte has been spending a lot of time out there. Even little Betsy has been out there digging in the dirt," Olivia said.

"You both should really come over and see what he has created. It is a wonderland in and of itself," I told them.

"Perhaps after some tea you can show us. Sarah was just fixing us some,"

Mother said as she got up from her rocker. "Please, excuse me. I will see if it is ready."

"How have you been?" I asked Olivia once my mother disappeared into the kitchen.

"Very well, thank you. How are you enjoying married life?"

"It would be better if I actually saw my husband occasionally. He is so consumed with building his career I never see him." I sighed.

"I know how you feel. William is absorbed with his studies. Even when he is home he is buried in his books, like now." She nodded towards the stairs. "Who knew married life was going to be so exciting." Olivia giggled.

"Here we are, ladies, hot tea with honey and lemon." Mother reentered the parlor carrying the silver serving tray. She set it down on the coffee table and poured three cups. Olivia set her needlepoint aside and accepted the saucer and plate my mother handed her.

The three of us talked for the next hour about the upcoming wedding season and how busy it was going to be. Most of my friends that I had grown up with were all getting married in the next few months. My Christmas Eve wedding was completely out of the norm simply because most brides wanted to take advantage of having a beautiful reception party outside in the gardens following the church ceremony.

I gave Olivia and my mother a tour of Davonte's creation and they both could not believe how talented he was. My mother kept going on and on about how gifted he was and eventually inquired whether I would be opposed to her hiring him to do some work on her yard. I told her it was fine with me and she should speak directly with Davonte. However, I knew that Davonte loved working outside and being creative, therefore, he would welcome the opportunity.

The afternoon slowly faded into evening and Jackson finally returned home just as Tamesha was putting dinner on the table. He looked exhausted. He set his briefcase down on the other end of the table, walked behind me, and kissed me on the cheek before taking his seat at the head of the table.

"I am so sorry about the hour." Jackson placed his napkin in his lap. "Did you have a nice day?"

"Yes, I spent the afternoon with Olivia and my mother. I showed them what Davonte did to the backyard. They both loved it. How was your day?"

"Stressful. I spent the whole day in my father's study with him pouring through law books looking for a specific precedence," he explained.

"Did you find it?"

"No, which means we will have to search some more tomorrow." Jackson rubbed his temples for a moment before he started eating. "I am sorry, Jocelyn. I know I promised you we would spend some time together this weekend."

"I understand," I replied without looking at him. I honestly did understand, but I also did not want him to see the disappointment in my eyes.

We didn't talk much the rest of the meal. And what we did discuss was mainly chitchat since what I really wanted to discuss I couldn't because the walls had ears in an open dining room.

An hour later I found myself sitting at my vanity in my nightgown brushing out my hair. The anxiety I felt earlier in the day had only intensified as the hours dragged on. Jackson walked up behind me unbuttoning his shirt. I watched him in the mirror. He caught my gaze and smiled broadly at me.

"What are you thinking of?" he asked.

"Prom?" I smiled mischievously.

"That was not the answer I was expecting." He pulled off his shirt and laid it over the footboard of the bed. "Things must be getting much clearer."

"Yes." I put my brush back on the vanity and spun around on my stool to face him. "Tell me about prom. I can see my gown, shoes, and I know I am over at my friend Caitlyn's house," I said excitedly.

"The two of you decided to have a sleepover last night since you two were going to spend the day at the spa before prom," Jackson explained, taking off his pants and laying them on top of his shirt. "I do not know what your gown looks like. You want it to be a surprise."

"And I am still not going to tell you." I stood up and wrapped my arms around his neck. "But I do know what it looks like." I leaned up on my toes and kissed him firmly.

"That is not fair. You realize that, do you not?" Jackson's emerald eyes narrowed on me.

"No one ever said life was fair," I taunted.

"Aren't we the little devil?" My husband laughed and scooped me up in his arms, carrying me over to the bed.

Jackson climbed up beside me and supported his weight over me. He looked so incredibly handsome it took my breath away. He stared down at me for a second tracing my face lightly with his fingertips and making goose bumps spring up along my arms. He brushed my hair away from my face and then leaned down, pressing his lips firmly against mine.

I ran my fingers across his sculpted chest and moved them over his muscular back. His skin was soft and warm under my touch. I moved a hand up and wrapped my fingers through his black, wavy hair, pulling him closer to me. I loved the way his body felt against mine, the way he tasted, the brush of his five o'clock shadow rubbing against my chin. I closed my eyes and melted into him.

CHAPTER THIRTY-ONE

SATURDAY, *May 7, 2010*

I spent the night at Caitlyn's house after our game and Mark's bonfire by the lake party. She and I stayed up half the night eating horrible pizza, cookie dough, red vines, and so many Skittles we made ourselves sick. We watched sappy chick flicks, made humorous inappropriate remarks, and basically behaved like a couple of twelve-year-olds. But it was the night before prom, and we wanted to make the most out of the limited time we had left together to behave immaturely.

Caitlyn's mom, Jodi, woke us up at noon. We had crashed out in the living room and had littered the room with blankets, pillows, empty soda cans, and an assortment of wrappers. She playfully chastised us as she stepped over the mess we'd created and picked up trash along the way.

"Come on, ladies, time to get up. You both need to shower before we head to the salon," Jodi reminded us.

"Go ahead, Jocelyn. You get in the shower first and wake me when you're done," Caitlyn grumbled, pulling the blanket over her head.

"I hate you," I mumbled, climbing out from beneath the warm blanket and stumbling towards the bathroom.

I turned on the hot water and waited for the shower to steam up the bathroom while I brushed my teeth. I had no idea what time we'd fallen asleep, but I knew it was late. I felt like hell from eating so much junk food. All I wanted to do was sleep for another four or five hours. But Caitlyn and I were having facials, our hair and make-up done, and mani-pedis at one o'clock. We'd promised the guys we'd be ready by five o'clock when they were due to pick us up for a nice dinner in the city before going to prom.

* * *

I felt refreshed and revived after our afternoon of being pampered and spoiled. I simply closed my eyes and melted away under the touch of their skilled hands and let them work their magic. I could feel the stress and tension dissolve from my muscles. The result was stunning. Caitlyn and I looked like models. Her long golden hair was swept up into a French roll with white pearls barely visible, yet perfectly accented on the clip. She had a few skewed curls that framed her face elegantly. Her make-up was soft, giving her a more natural angelic look with her prominent deep blue eyes.

My long thick auburn locks cascaded down my back in large loose curls. The stylist had swept up the sides, leaving my long bangs to frame my face, and pinned the strands meticulously with the butterfly clip in soft shades of pink and green Emily had given me. My make-up was also done in subtle tones of browns and pale pink. I couldn't believe it was my reflection staring back at me in the mirror.

Caitlyn and I got dressed at her house. We hid away in her bedroom, music blaring, dancing around like fools in various stages of dressing. For once there were no worries, no grief, no arguments, no parental disappointment, no barrier, no stress ... and no *EVE*. Tonight, there was only our senior prom. Our final high school dance. A time to be young and let tomorrow's worries wait until tomorrow. This night belonged to us.

We spun around in front of Caitlyn's full-length mirror admiring how beautiful we looked. I truly felt like Cinderella heading off to the ball to meet my prince charming. We giggled and oohed and aahed over each other and ourselves. Jodi finally came in and fussed over us some more, fluffing skirts, adjusting curls. She kept on until the guys rang the doorbell at five o'clock.

When we came downstairs, we discovered that not only had Zak and Jackson arrived, but with them in a separate car was Jackson's parents, Zak's parents, and my dad. All had cameras in hand waiting to capture our senior prom on film. So we all headed out to the garden and spent the next thirty minutes taking an assortment of pictures in every possible pose our families could think of.

"Oh, Jackson, it's beautiful. Thank you." I turned my wrist admiring its beauty.

"You look breathtaking." Jackson leaned down and kissed my cheek. "Here." He slipped on my wrist a corsage with tiny, pale pink rose buds, greenery, and a splash of baby's breath. It was so delicate and lovely. "I got this for you." His emerald eyes sparkled.

"I love your gown." Jackson twirled me around on the soft spring grass. "I can see why you wanted to keep it a secret." His full lips turned into a smile that reached all the way to his eyes.

"You look incredibly sexy." I pulled him into my arms, kissing his luscious lips. "Just wait until later." I smiled up at him mischievously.

"Is that a promise, Mrs. Chandler?"

"Definitely." I playfully smacked him on the rear before joining Caitlyn and Zak in front of the flower garden. Jackson laughed and trotted up beside me.

Finally, with plastered smiles still in place the four of us climbed into the black stretch limo and headed to dinner before prom.

Prom was being held in the Marriot Hotel ballroom on the north side of Chicago. There were students milling about outside talking and ogling over how beautiful everyone looked. We pulled up in front and the driver let the four of us out. We immediately saw the other half of our former group make their way in just ahead of us. Jenna turned around for a moment and rolled her eyes in our direction before taking Kyle's hand and disappearing into the building. It made me a bit sad thinking about how she and I had talked so excitedly about our senior prom ever since grade school. And now that we were here, we weren't even speaking to each other.

The ballroom was decorated with metallic black and silver helium balloons across the ceiling, soft yellow lights, and a low glow from the silver candles that rested in the center of each black linen-draped table on the outskirts of the dance floor. A mediocre band called Secret Squirrels were playing on the stage at the back of the room. Off to the side there was a tacky backdrop of a starry night done up for our pictures. On the wall opposite the stage stood a long table with a large bowl of punch and an assortment of snacks, sweets, and goodies to munch on.

The four of us decided to get our pictures done first before we got all sweaty from dancing and our hair fell out of their perfect and carefully styled dos. We joined our classmates in the long line and waited for our turn. I scanned over the room looking at everyone dressed up in their finest. It was hard to believe that these were the same people I'd seen almost daily for the last twelve years sporting jeans, T-shirts, and every sort of casual attire. And there they were in gowns and tuxedos looking glamourous enough to walk on the red carpet.

"Mind if we sneak in line with you?" Liang walked up wearing a long, gorgeous, royal blue silk gown that hugged her body like a glove. Her long black hair was swept in a crown of curls accented with sporadic blue sapphires. Ethan had his arm draped loosely around her waist. He was wearing a black tuxedo with tails along with a royal blue bowtie and a cumber bun. I had to admit my little brother cleaned up nicely.

"Of course." I scooted over and let them slip in line in front of Jackson and me, receiving a few dirty looks from several people in line behind us.

"Thanks." Ethan tried to smile at me. It wasn't his best, but it warmed my heart immensely. It was the only act of kindness I'd received from him in the last six months. "I was thinking, Jocelyn, that since this is your last school dance and because you'll be leaving soon, it would be nice if after we got our pictures taken with our dates, we had one taken of us together."

"Are you serious?" I couldn't help but wonder if Liang had put him up to this. Either way, I didn't care. I would love to have a prom picture of my brother and me together. "I would love that." I reached over and hugged him tightly.

After pictures were done, the six of us had some punch and tea cakes before we hit the dance floor. I danced with Jackson first and then Zak. And then Ethan surprised me by taking my hand and asking me for the next dance. I glanced over at Jackson who smiled. Ethan twirled me around like a doll and then placed his hand on my waist. I hadn't realized how much Ethan had filled out in the last six months. He had bulked up and even looked like he'd grown another inch or so.

"You seem really happy," Ethan noted.

"I am." I rested my head on his shoulder. "Thank you for this."

"You know, I am going to miss you so much once you move to Boston."

"Really?" I chuckled. "I find that hard to believe."

"Who else am I going to fight with?" he asked.

"I'm sure you'll find someone," I assured him.

"But you know you're my favorite person to fight with." A devious grin slid across his lips.

"Screw you." I couldn't help but laugh at him. It felt so good to let go of all the months of tension between us. For a moment it felt like nothing had come between us. This was the young man whom I loved dearly, the one who'd shared my youth, knew the intimate drama of our household and survived them with me.

"You know you love me," Ethan said proudly.

"Always." I shook my head at him with a grin.

Finally, back in my husband's arms, I held him tightly as our bodies moved in perfect rhythm with the music. I loved the smell of his cologne and the way our bodies fit perfectly together. I rested my head into the crook of his shoulder and closed my eyes savoring this moment in my memory.

"Thank you for doing this for me." I looked up into his deep green eyes.

"For doing what?" Jackson asked.

"Taking me to prom."

"Why would I not? After all, it is my senior prom as well." He winked.

"You know what I mean."

"It is my honor and my pleasure to escort you to your senior prom. I would have done it even if you had decided to finish your senior year in Boston. Prom is an important event in your life on your journey to becoming an adult. I would not want you to miss out because of me."

"You, Mr. Chandler, are too good to me." I leaned up and kissed him.

"Besides, how could I miss out on my wife looking so gorgeous? You truly do." He kissed me again a little harder.

"Thank you." I held him a little tighter. "You look incredibly sexy in that tux. I will not be held responsible for my actions later."

"Promise." Jackson raised an eyebrow at me.

"There you are." Caitlyn rushed up beside us. "Cody's having a big after-prom party at his house. Want to go?"

"Do you really think that is a good idea? You know Jenna and Hilary are going to be there," I said.

"Cody came over and personally invited us. And he said to bring you and Jackson. Ethan and Liang are going as well," she said.

"I don't know. This night has been perfect. I do not want to ruin it by having another altercation with them," I told her.

"Cody promised that they'd be on their best behavior." Caitlyn was shifting around anxiously. "Oh, come on, Jocelyn. This is our senior prom. You've got to go."

"All right," I said reluctantly, looking up at Jackson and hoping he'd step in and tell her we had other plans, but he didn't.

"Yeah!" Caitlyn bounced up and down. "We're going to leave in about ten minutes. I think Ethan and Liang are going to ride with us in the limo."

Before I could even respond, she was halfway across the floor closing in on Zak. "That girl has way too much energy," I told Jackson.

"Yes, she does," he agreed, watching her bounce away from us.

The driver had pulled the limo around and was waiting for us as we exited the hotel. Caitlyn, Zak, Liang, and Ethan were already standing under the awning before the driver opened the door. Once inside, we all settled back for the forty-five-minute drive to Cody's house.

"How come you guys are riding with us? Didn't you drive?" I asked my brother once we reached the interstate.

"No, we rode with Corbin and Hailey. They left after about an hour because she wasn't feeling well. I guess she's had really bad morning sickness," Ethan responded.

"Are they still getting married?" Caitlyn asked.

"If her parents have any say in it, they will be," Liang replied. "I don't think Corbin is to happy about it."

"He's not. She's making him miserable, even more so than before." Ethan rolled his eyes.

"I feel bad for him," Zak piped in. "I couldn't imagine being stuck with someone as clingy and needy as Hailey. She would drive me bonkers."

"The girl is just plain annoying," Liang added. "Sorry," she told Ethan, "but she is."

"You're not telling me anything I don't already know." My brother shrugged.

"It must be hard. They have got to be terrified," I stated.

"Corbin is," Ethan admitted. "He doesn't want to get married, even if they are having a baby together."

"If he does not want to, then he should not do it. A marriage under these circumstances could only impact their already unstable relationship negatively. Plus, they cannot force him into marrying her," Jackson pointed out.

"Hailey's parents are pushing for it, hard," Liang said.

"Legally, Corbin does not have to marry her. He can even petition for a paternity test once the baby is born and have the court set up child support if it turns out to be his kid. Does he believe there is a chance the baby is not his?" Jackson inquired.

"If he does, he's never mentioned it to me." Ethan shrugged.

"I think she got pregnant on purpose," Liang shocked us all by saying.

"Seriously?" Caitlyn looked surprised. "Why in the world would she get pregnant on purpose? She's seventeen years old and has another year of high school. Is she really that stupid?"

"Yes," Ethan, Liang, and I all said in unison.

"Okay," Caitlyn laughed. "That's just plain sad."

It was almost eleven thirty by the time we reached Cody's house. Cars were lined up and down the street and we could hear the music as soon as the driver opened the door. He reminded Jackson once again that we only had the limo until two. Jackson shook his hand and promised that the six of us would be back around one thirty if not sooner.

The after-party was in full swing when we arrived. There were more people there than one of Cody's usual parties and people had begun spilling out onto the backyard. Thankfully, it was a warm evening and the temperatures remained hovering in the low sixties. I couldn't believe Cody's neighbors didn't complain more than they did.

Walking into the house, I immediately understood why people were hanging out outside. The house was stifling from too many bodies. The sounds of *Imagine Dragons* were blaring through the speakers, vibrating the floor. Most of the guys had shed their jackets and they lay in a pile in the corner with a colorful array of bow ties, while the floor was littered with various girls' high heels.

People were making the rounds talking with everyone, dancing off-beat in the family room, and doing Jell-O shots in the kitchen. I saw Taylor and Dakota grinding on Mark and Tray in the dining room. Then I spotted Jenna and Hilary standing over by the back door noticing that our little group had just arrived. They were leaning over and whispering to each other in an obvious way purposely trying to make me feel uncomfortable.

They succeeded.

I stood in the corner of the family room wishing I was anywhere else. This was not exactly how I envisioned ending this wonderful evening.

"Are you all right?" Caitlyn nudged my arm.

"I really don't want to be here," I confessed.

"Don't worry about them. They like to believe they are important." She nodded in Jenna and Hilary's direction. "Sadly, they are mistaken." I laughed despite myself. "Come on, let's get a drink."

The next hour crawled by. All I wanted to do was escape the crowded room, the noise, the glares. I wanted to be anywhere else. Thankfully, Jenna and Hilary steered clear of us most of the evening, but it still didn't deter them from sending hateful looks in my direction every chance they got.

For the life of me I could not understand why I had become the center of their hatefulness. My actions and behavior had nothing to do with them or affected their lives in any way, shape, or form. Frankly, I was so sick and tired of their petty attitude. And honestly, it still hurt that they were treating me this way after all we had gone through together and the friendship we'd shared.

The night finally ended and was graciously salvaged once the six of us left Cody's. Since we still had time with the limo, we cranked up the music, sang off key at the top of our lungs out of the open sunroof, and acted like immature juveniles. It was the perfect way to end the evening ... or at least I thought until Jackson and I got home, and he took me upstairs.

CHAPTER THIRTY-TWO

Friday, May 29, 1879

I woke up early and immediately realized that Jackson was no longer in bed beside me. My mind assumed he must have gotten up early and retreated into either his office or was already over at his parents looking for the case they were still searching for.

Jackson had promised me last evening that he was going to take the afternoon off and go out to the lake on the edge of town and have a nice picnic with me, William, Olivia, Elizabeth, and Lee. Due to the long hours he was putting in I had expressed to him I felt it necessary for not only his sanity, but for mine as well, whether he liked it or not.

Cora came in a short time later and helped me prepare myself for a delightful afternoon with our friends and family. However, I was a little surprised when I asked her if Jackson was in the study and she shook her head and told me that his father had sent Barnaby over just after dawn, requesting his presence immediately. I knew their work was important, but that did not ring right.

"Did Jackson say where they were going? To the office?" I turned around from admiring my new pale pink dress in the mirror.

"No mam', Mr. Jackson didn't say anything before he left," Cora replied, straightening out the bottom folds of my gown.

"All right. Thank you, Cora." I picked up my shawl and wide-rimmed white bonnet with the matching pale pink ribbon and tied it carefully under my chin in the mirror. "Please let Bertina know that I am going over to Emily's to see if she knows where our husbands are."

"Ms. Chandler, your breakfast? You haven't eaten yet," Cora reminded me.

"I will eat over there." I picked up my gloves and headed down the stairs.

The morning air was heavy with moisture from last night's rain. The sky was littered with clouds, but I could see the sun fighting to make its presence known. The emerald green grass glistened with the morning dew. The flowerbeds were in full bloom of magnificent colors all reaching towards the early morning dusty sun. I picked up the front of my gown so as not to get the hem damp in the morning dew and hurried across the street. A sick feeling in my stomach told me something was very wrong. I could feel it in my bones.

Barnaby opened the door on my second knock as if he was expecting me. I nodded and hastily handed him my bonnet before finding Emily pacing around the parlor. I immediately went to her.

"Emily, what is going on? Cora told me Barnaby fetched Jackson before dawn this morning on Robert's behalf," I said as I approached her.

"Sheriff McGuire woke us up before dawn and summoned them. While Robert got dressed, he sent Barnaby to retrieve Jackson. I am afraid that is all I know." Emily stopped speaking and started pacing again.

"Wonderful," I muttered, sitting down on the lounge.

Jackson and Robert arrived a short while later, both looking haphazard and worn.

"Jackson, what is going on?" I jumped up and rushed over to him with Emily directly behind me.

"Darling," he said gently, causing a knot to form in my stomach. "Please, have a seat." Jackson took my hand and led me back into the parlor.

Emily and I sat down on the lounge with nervous hesitation. Jackson kneeled in front of me taking both my hands in his. Robert went straight for the mantel and began packing his pipe with tobacco. He fidgeted around buying himself a few extra moments trying to find the right words.

"Robert?" Emily sighed audibly.

"Yes?" Robert seemed startled for a second, coming out of his own thoughts. "I apologize." He looked over at us and inhaled deeply off his pipe letting out a slow ring of smoke. "I am afraid I have some rather disturbing news. There was another attack last evening right here a few blocks from our front door and this time they targeted someone we all know and love."

"What? Who?" My eyes darted from Jackson to Robert.

"Christina and Thomas," Robert stated in a low voice.

Tears rolled down my face. I reached out and wrapped my arms around Jackson's neck. His arms engulfed me tightly. I buried my face in his shoulder and sobbed.

"How badly?" Emily asked, her voice was barely a whisper, her hands visibly shaking.

"Christina was murdered. Thomas was stabbed more than a dozen times, but he is miraculously still alive." Robert thumped his fist a couple times on the mantel displaying his frustration. "I have no idea how, but he is."

"His parents and Reverend Jacobs are with him now. Your father is doing everything he can to keep him alive," Jackson said in a mournful voice.

"How? Where?" I whimpered.

"Thomas told her father that they were approached by two men and forced into the alley at Central Avenue and Washington Street. He said they were armed with both knives and pistols. They demanded his cash. He said he handed it to them, but when they asked for Christina's engagement ring, she refused to give it to them. They became irate and ..." Robert's voice trailed off.

I didn't want to hear any more. I couldn't believe this was happening. These two men deserved nothing less than the same they had given to others. I got up and walked out of the room. I needed a moment to process what I'd just learned.

I walked out the front door and leaned against the porch railing. I angrily brushed the tears off my cheeks. I wanted to scream until my voice was raw. The air was clearing, the sun finally broke free from the clouds and was gaining strength with the passing hours. But it had lost its luster, as had the countless flowers swaying in the breeze to draw attention to their brilliance. Instead, they were a dull gray ... game over.

Time slowly passed while I stood frozen in my sorrow. I had known Christina since before I could remember. We had all grown up together. She was a carefree spirit without a mean bone in her body. She was quick to smile and ready to laugh. She had fallen in love with Thomas before we had even hit adolescence. And he was every bit as smitten with her. From that moment forward they were inseparable. I recall during that time Jackson seeming only a dream of mine for he was dating Sue Ellen and me being envious of her and Thomas. They had gotten married one spring afternoon in a makeshift ceremony performed by Theodore. Laura had been her maid of honor, just as she was to be again this summer in the real one. Olivia and I had been bridesmaids.

"Are you all right?" Jackson's voice asked softly from the doorway.

"No," I squeaked.

"Jocelyn." I felt his hand on the small of my back. "I understand how you feel. And I promise you these men will be pay dearly for what they have done."

I turned and looked my husband in the eyes. "Make sure they do."

* * *

The four of us went up to the hospital that afternoon. Christina's and Thomas's parents were sitting silently in the hallway. Christina's mother, Brenda Bowden, started crying when she saw me and immediately rose to embrace me. She was a slightly older version of her daughter and I had never fully realized how much the two of them truly resembled each other until that moment. I held her tightly while she cried on my shoulder. Her father, Gene, sat quietly on the hard bench looking defeated. His eyes were red and swollen. The top button of his shirt of was undone and his hair was disheveled, obviously from running his fingers through it. I had never seen him look so beaten before.

A few minutes later Christina's older sister, Callie, and her husband, Jordan, came around the corridor. Brenda gave me one final motherly squeeze and went to her daughter who couldn't restrain her hysterics any longer. As soon as Callie was in her mother's arms, she fell apart.

I walked over to Jackson and slipped my arm around his waist. Robert was off to the side speaking with Thomas's parents, Albert and Mary. I could not make out what was being said, but I could tell the update on his condition was not good. I turned and buried my face in Jackson's shoulder. His arm wrapped protectively around me gently soothing me. I wanted this day to end.

Friends, family, classmates, and neighbors wandered in and out throughout the remainder of the day as news of the tragedy spread through the community. Laurie, Theodore, Elizabeth, Lee, and their folks had taken up vigilance with the rest of us. It was a mournful day, a tearful day, a day of stunned disbelief. The ladies cried, the men swore vengeance.

My father emerged from behind a closed patient door leading into Thomas's room. There was a thin line of sweat above his brow and his face looked tired and full of concern. He motioned for Thomas's parents to join him and without a word to any of us, the three of them disappeared back into the room.

Tension filled the hallway. A deathly silence hovered over all of us. I dreaded to contemplate what was being said or occurring behind that closed door. I held my breath praying for the best, expecting the worst. No one was sure how Thomas had managed to hang on this long. The extent of his injuries was substantial, and I knew if he recovered, it would be a very long, difficult, and painful recovery. And that was only physically. I could not imagine the emotional turmoil he was going through after witnessing the woman he dearly loved being murdered. I recalled the damage that Sean's death had done to Olivia and his had been from illness, nothing as brutal and horrifying as this pointless attack.

Thomas's door slowly squeaked open. My father walked out wiping his hands on a towel. His white physician's coat was wrinkled and smudged from hours of wear. His eyes scanned over the group that had gathered in support and concern of Thomas. His eyes rested on my mother who approached him and gently placed a loving hand on his arm. A tear escaped out of the corner of his eye as he slowly shook his head.

Brenda let out a low moan that was followed by an onset of tears from everyone. Thomas was gone. The vibrant young man who was easy on the eyes, quick to laugh, sweet beyond measure, and kind to all was now at peace with the woman of his dreams. It was poetic in a sense that at least they were together once more. Still, it did not make losing him or Christina any easier.

It was after twilight before Jackson and I returned home. Neither of us had an appetite as we numbly climbed up the stairs to our room. We undressed and prepared ourselves for bed without saying a word to each other. I felt so drained. We had already lost too many loved ones in our lives in such a short period of time. Too many lives cut short due to senseless tragedy. It wasn't fair.

Jackson turned down the oil lamp on the mantel and crawled into bed beside me. I rolled over and rested my head down on his chest listening to the sweet lullaby of his heartbeat. He arms engulfed me. I closed my eyes, feeling the safety and security that only being in his arms gave me.

CHAPTER THIRTY-THREE

Friday, May 27, 2010

Last day of my senior year. Only two final exams stood between me and that final bell … AP psychology with Mr. Rand and AP Biology with Mrs. Neal-Beliveau. I was at least thankful that I got to end my high school career with my two favorite teachers. Our last three days of school we took two finals a day and were released by noon.

Jackson had helped me prepare for both exams and I felt ready to kick some butt. I walked down the hall beside Jackson headed to bio class. I got the strangest feeling in the pit of my stomach. It finally hit me. This was it. Never again would I roam these halls, slam my locker shut, enjoy our seemingly pointless lunch conversations, wear another school sports team uniform, see these faces that had cluttered my vision for the last twelve years of my life. In a few short hours I was going to walk out of this building a high school graduate. It was the oddest sensation.

I took my seat at the table beside Jackson and listened to Mrs. Neal-Beliveau give instructions for our final. I exhaled audibly and turned over my exam.

I couldn't help but notice how quickly Jackson moved through his exam. Suddenly, I felt very inept. I tried to refocus on my own test, but I could still see Jackson's hand moving rapidly down the Scantron sheet out of the corner of my eye. It was more distracting than anything else. Finally, I put my elbow up on the table and propped my head in my hand just to block my view of his movements.

Jackson was already done with his exam when I moved to the back of the room to complete the fill-in-the-blank section for the lab portion. In fact, he was the first person to turn in his paper. By the time I finished, I was somewhere in the top ten. It made me feel incredibly self-conscious even though I felt fairly confident in the material.

The rest of the class finished up ten minutes before the bell rang so Mrs. Neal-Beliveau let us talk quietly amongst ourselves. I took advantage and got out of my seat. I walked up to Mrs. Neal-Beliveau's desk and leaned on the side of it.

"Are you excited?" my teacher asked.

"About?" I stupidly inquired since I wasn't sure if she was referring to my move to Boston, Boston University, or graduation.

"Graduation tomorrow." She smiled.

"Yes, very. It seems strange though, but in a good way."

"I understand. I remember when it finally hit me that I was never going to have to return to that building, walk those halls, and look at the same faces every day for years on end. It was so odd." She laughed a little.

"It is weird," I agreed.

"How long before you move to Boston?"

"Two weeks." I felt weird even saying it.

"Have you started packing yet?"

"Not yet. I figured I would start packing after graduation. I have been too busy preparing for finals to even attempt packing anything." I shrugged. "But I did want to thank you. I have really enjoyed having you for a teacher and especially for what you did for me earlier this year."

"Jocelyn, I know you're a great student. You work hard, you're a talented athlete, and you care about your studies and your future. I didn't want to see your future derailed because of a typical high school mean girl." Mrs. Neal-Beliveau rolled her eyes in a comical fashion that I couldn't help myself from giggling.

"Well, I do appreciate your help." I leaned in a little closer. "You saved my rear."

"You're welcome. Just promise me that you'll behave yourself once you get to BU."

"I promise." I leaned down and hugged her. "I am going to miss you."

"I'll miss you too." She hugged me back. "And make sure to keep in touch with me."

"I will, I promise." The bell rang, and I headed back to my table to gather my things. I turned and waved goodbye one last time to my favorite teacher. She had been an amazing mentor to me, and I was going to miss her so much.

Jackson and I headed back to our lockers and picked up our psychology textbooks to turn back in. I pulled out the rest of the loose scraps of papers and junk from my locker and dumped it all in the trash can. I double-checked my locker to make sure it was completely empty. This had been my assigned locker since my first day of my freshman year. It was strange closing it for the last time. I shut it firmly and ran my fingers lightly over the cool grey metal.

I joined Jackson at the end of the hallway. He was chatting with Caitlyn and Zak about what we were doing after the final bell.

"I don't think there's much going on this afternoon or tonight because of graduation tomorrow. Most people are doing their open houses on Sunday," Zak was saying as I approached.

"Do you guys have any plans?" Caitlyn asked Jackson and me.

"I haven't made any." I looked over at Jackson unsure if he had or not.

"No, our schedule is wide open." I nodded in agreement with him.

"Fabulous! Follow us down to the park after the final bell," Caitlyn said just as the bell rang.

"Sounds good." I grabbed Jackson's hand and dragged him off with me down the hall.

"Any idea what she is up to?" Jackson asked, taking the stairs two at a time.

"Caitlyn? Who knows, but it's definitely something you can bet on it."

Mr. Rand was in the process of closing our classroom room when Jackson and I rounded the corner.

"Wait, Mr. Rand ...," I hollered, closing in on him.

"Mr. and Mrs. Chandler, last day of class and you can't even make it on time?" He shook his head at us with a cheesy grin.

"Sorry about that." I slid in the small opening.

"Me, too." Jackson stepped in after me.

We hurried over to our desks and sat down. I couldn't help but laugh. All eyes in the class were turned towards us. It was just like me to be tardy for my last class in high school. Perfect way to end my career. I placed my backpack under my seat and got out my pencil and extra eraser.

Mr. Rand spent the first ten minutes collecting our books before he began the same speech, we'd heard five times before from each of our teachers. He passed out our final exams and Scantron. The entire exam consisted of a hundred multiple choice and true and false questions that covered every topic we'd studied since January.

Our teacher sat back down at his desk and told us we could begin. I flipped my test over and started on the first question. I was pleasantly surprised and eased my way through each question. Thanks to Jackson and his advanced understanding of psychology and his relentless drilling, the exam was much less complicated than I had feared.

Shortly before our time was up Mr. Rand approached Jackson and me. He leaned against Jackson's desk in a very relaxed manner. He was such an easy-going man. He reminded me a great deal of Jackson's brother Alex ... *here*.

"Mr. and Mrs. Chandler, I must say you two are two of the best students I've ever had the pleasure of teaching."

"Well, thank you. I studied hard this semester," I replied.

"I appreciate that, Mr. Rand. You are an excellent teacher. And most importantly, you were entertaining and made the material interesting," Jackson told him, causing Mr. Rand to beam.

"Thanks! I try. It's not always easy to hold the attention of a bunch of high school kids," he told us.

"I think you have done an amazing job. I loved your class and learned a lot too," I told him.

"Any idea what you are going to major in at BU?" he asked us.

"Political Science, maybe. I was considering law school," Jackson said casually, and I tried not to smile since he had already completed his Bachelor of Science in psychology.

"Interesting." Mr. Rand tilted his head in consideration. "I think you would make a great lawyer, and Lord knows, we need some more of those. Good, honest ones are extremely rare in this day and age. What about you?" His gaze shifted towards me.

"Currently undecided, but I am also considering law." I shrugged. "But I figure I have at least a full year of general prerequisites and required generalized classes before I have to make a definite decision, so I plan on taking full advantage of that while I decide."

"I think that is wise." Mr. Rand nodded slightly in agreement. "Sometimes it's best to get the sample plate before paying full price for one entre and regretting your investment."

"I could not agree with you more." I smiled coyly at Jackson.

"Are you excited about the move?" he asked us.

"I am excited to get back home. I like Chicago, but Boston will always be home to me," Jackson admitted.

"I am excited, nervous, scared." I let out a nervous chuckle. "It's going to be very different. I really enjoyed Boston when I was there over Christmas," I told him.

"I've been there a few times. It's a great place. I love the historic buildings, the museums, the architecture. I think it's one of the most incredible cities in the states," Mr. Rand told us.

"I could not agree with you more," Jackson stated. "I believe Jocelyn is going to be very happy there."

"I believe so too," I agreed, taking Jackson's hand in mine.

"Well, I certainly wish you both the best and I hope you guys keep in touch with me." He offered Jackson his hand.

"We will." Jackson shook his hand.

"Yes, we definitely will," I promised.

"Good," Mr. Rand said as my classmates began counting down the clock like it was New Year's Eve. I couldn't help but join them in the excitement. Our high school career was now officially over.

The bell echoed through the school followed closely by an uproar of cheer. We grabbed our belongings and filed out of the classroom as quickly as we could. I was holding onto Jackson's hand and grinning widely. I had been dreaming of this moment for years. It was almost surreal that it had finally arrived.

The parking lot filled up fast and soon became a traffic jam nightmare from every direction. The sun was scorching down upon us and Jackson turned up the air conditioner in the CRV as we waited. I was so giddy I was bouncing around in my seat. I turned up the radio and sang poorly along with-it making Jackson crack up at my antics.

"You realize people are looking at you?" Jackson asked, shaking his head at me.

"I just graduated high school. Do you think I care?" I shrugged him off.

"I do not believe you do." He rolled his eyes playfully.

"Nope, not a bit," I giggled and continued.

Slowly, but surely, we made our way out of the parking lot. I couldn't help but notice a caravan of vehicles all seemingly headed in the same direction to our small-town park, the site of Pee Wee baseball games and our Fourth of July Extravaganza. It was sort of two layered being built into the side of a large hill.

The top part had the baseball diamonds, the basketball courts, the large open fields, the picnic areas, and the enormous playground equipment. The bottom half was more wooded, filled with trails, and a beautiful old bridge across a babbling little creek. There were also scattered picnic areas under the trees and one main group with about six tables under an old shelter just off the side of the lower level parking area.

That seemed to be the destination site of our little afterschool escapade. Cars were lined all through the lower level roads, the parking lot was full, and the cars were spilling over onto the top level. There had to be at least fifty cars all from the high school parking lot. I had no idea what was going on when Jackson finally parked halfway down between the two levels. We climbed the rest of the way down to the lower level. Parked several cars up were Zak and Caitlyn. She came bouncing up the hill carrying a plastic bag.

"Hurry up." Caitlyn couldn't contain herself. "You guys are so slow."

"We arrived two cars behind you," I replied. "What's in the bag?"

"Supplies." She linked her arm with mine, and we practically skipped. Jackson and Zak trailed behind us. "We need ammunition."

"Excuse me? Ammunition?" I asked.

"Yes." She stopped just shy of the lower level and waited for the guys to catch up. Caitlyn reached into the bag and pulled out multiple cans of silly string and shaving cream. "Here." She handed the four of us a can of each. "Be prepared. This could get ugly." A devious smile spread across her lips.

"Why didn't I know about this?" I inquired.

"Liang and I cooked this up with a few phone calls last night. I guess word got around," Caitlyn explained. "We thought this would be a fun way to celebrate the last day of school. I can't believe how many people showed up." Liang and Ethan popped out from behind a row of cars as we hit the parking lot at the bottom.

"Hello," Liang rang out. "Isn't this great! Can you believe this?" She spread her arms wide as the masses of people milled around everywhere.

"How in the world did you spread the word that fast?" I asked.

"Oh, that was easy. I posted it on Facebook last night." Liang laughed and shrugged. "I figured that was the best way to get the news out."

"It worked," I noted.

Liang, armed to the nines, linked her arm through mine in the same fashion as Caitlyn and skipped along with us. In pure juvenile fashion the three of us simultaneously began singing *We're Off to See the Wizard*, and I could hear the three guys behind us laughing and couldn't have cared less. Today was amazing.

We rounded the corner to the sheltered picnic area when Mark and Trey jumped out from behind some thick shrubbery amongst the huge trees. "Got ya!" they yelled and nailed us with a barrage of silly string and shaving cream. The three of us screamed and ran in different directions, reaching for our own arsenals.

From out of their hiding places, students sprang up from everywhere. Suddenly I was caught amidst a hellfire that was wet and sticky. I was laughing so hard it was almost impossible to duck, find cover, or escape. My hair was saturated with the nasty gooey mixture and my clothes were drenched in it. I realized the ground was completely covered making the concrete under the sheltered picnic area treacherous.

My peers were all screaming, laughing, running in every direction trying to escape. But there was no escape. There were too many of us. It was almost a blessing when supplies began to dwindle. When my ammunition ran out, I simply dropped the cans while dodging this way and that. Thankfully, amongst the chaos Liang found me and handed me a fresh can of each.

Freshly armed, I returned to the scene of the battle. I ducked behind a support beam and tried to locate Jackson. He was off to my far-right drenching Caitlyn in shaving cream. She was laughing so hard, she turned her head at the wrong moment and got a mouth full of it. I couldn't stop laughing at her expression as she tried to spit it all out.

With my attention focused on them, Ethan had the perfect opportunity to sneak up behind me and ambush me with his own stash. He doused my hair with shaving cream, grabbed the back of my shirt as I screamed and ducked away from him, filling up the back of my shirt with silly string.

"Ethan! How could you?" I screeched.

"I had to," he said, trying to catch his breath. I took full advantage and returned the favor. I yanked the front of his shirt and held down the top of the aerosol can of shaving cream emptying its full contents.

"Jocelyn! You're going to pay for that!" Ethan screamed.

I took off at a dead sprint to try and escape the wrath of my little brother. But it was pointless. Even in my top physical shape, Ethan was still stronger and faster than I could ever hope to be. He caught me easily tackling me to the ground. He pinned me with his knees on my shoulders and emptied the remaining contents of his silly string in addition to the shaving cream mess already in my hair.

"Okay! Okay! I give! Uncle! Uncle!" I cried out, squirming beneath his weight on my chest.

"Fine," Ethan laughed and climbed off me. He offered a hand and pulled me to my feet. "You look gorgeous, darling."

"You too, my dear." It felt amazing to be this way with him again.

The chaos around us was beginning to die down a bit. People were running out of ammunition and just trying to dodge those who still had it. Everyone was caked in a mixture of shaving cream and silly string. I bent over and tried to shake some of the goop out of my hair, but it wasn't working. My clothes were stuck to my body. I was a sticky mess.

Jackson, Caitlyn, and Zak finally made their way over to us on the lawn by the shelter. Fellow junior and seniors were turning up from every which direction all looking in the same condition as myself. Everyone was still laughing, teasing and carrying on through their excursions. Liang and Caitlyn made a good call. This was the perfect way to end our last day of high school.

We all hung around for a little bit longer, trading stories, goofing around, but soon everyone headed home to shower and clean the shaving cream out of body parts that were not meant for shaving cream. I was afraid to climb into Jackson's perfectly clean CRV, but he grabbed a couple of old towels he kept in the back and laid them out across our seats first.

Caitlyn, Zak, Liang, and Ethan were all going to meet us over at our place after we'd all cleaned up. But I realized once we were in the car and I was watching everyone else pack it up and leave too, that nowhere in the mess of people did I see Hilary, Jenna, Kyle, or Cody. It made me sad that they weren't there and that our friendship had strayed this far.

It took three washes just to get all the gunk out of my hair. I even had to have Jackson help me with it. It was ridiculous. Almost as funny as the look on his mother's face when we walked in the front door. She sent us directly upstairs to clean up telling us we were not allowed to have lunch until we were decent enough to enter her kitchen. And I was starving by the time we returned home.

Emily was sweet enough, however, to have lunch prepared for Jackson and I by the time we returned downstairs. We both sat down at the island and gave her a recount of the day's events. Jackson mentioned that we were waiting for our friends to come over and we weren't sure yet what our evening plans entailed.

"Well, I do not mind if your friends come over, but I need you both to stick around here for the evening," Emily said as she continued to clean her already spotless kitchen.

"Why?" Jackson seemed just as surprised as I was. Emily rarely said anything about what we did.

"Because you are graduating tomorrow, and your siblings are coming into town to see it," she answered as if it was no big deal.

"Seriously? I think we all know this is just a charade." Jackson seemed a little irritated.

"It may not be your high school graduation, Jackson, but it is Jocelyn's, and I am fairly certain she only plans on doing this once." Emily winked at me.

"Oh, definitely." I smiled back at her.

"Your siblings are coming down for her, not you, son. Sorry." She walked by Jackson and touched his shoulder in a motherly way.

"I did not know they were coming. When did you find out?" he asked.

"Phoebe and I talked about it a couple weeks ago. I figured that was a given." Emily shrugged.

"But can't we see them tomorrow? I am sure they will understand," Jackson reasoned.

"No, that is rude. There is no reason you and your friends cannot hang out here for this evening," she added before she left the kitchen.

"I hate it when she does that. She makes plans involving me without considering if I already have other engagements," he complained.

"It is not a big deal. I am sure everyone will not mind at all. They like hanging out here." I rested my hand on his. "Plus, they will all get to meet your siblings. It will be fun."

"I suppose," he muttered under his breath. I wasn't sure why it was bothering him so much. We'd all probably end up hanging here anyway.

It was another hour before Liang and Ethan wandered over from across the street and close to two before Caitlyn and Zak turned up. I explained to them what was going on and none of them cared about having to stick around the house. In fact, my fellow graduates extended their desire to retire early to get some rest before our graduation ceremony the next afternoon.

Emily was kind enough to make sure we were fully stocked in snacks and sweets as the six of us settled into the family room to watch movies. I put in the first *Lord of the Rings* movie, *Fellowship of the Ring*, a favorite of all of ours.

Jackson's parents left us alone to get some of their work done in the study. Robert claimed he had some briefs to go over and Emily was working diligently on her latest masterpiece. I couldn't wait to read it.

It was almost nine o'clock before Jackson's siblings, spouses, and children arrived. They had traveled together in Alex's wife, Leslie's, minivan that seated the seven of them comfortably. They appeared tired and worn. The children were cranky after such a long ride and I couldn't blame them. I'd made that trip myself and knew exactly how they felt.

Their mothers gave them quick baths while I helped Emily in the kitchen to whip them all up something to eat. It wasn't long before Cindy, Charlie, and Wally were bathed, fed, and tucked in for the night and their parents joined us in the family room. I introduced my new family to my friends and they happily snuggled in to watch the movies with us.

Everyone got along beautifully, and Phoebe was a huge hit, especially with Caitlyn. They had a great deal in common and spent the evening discussing clothes and shoes. I noticed Ethan hung on Phoebe's every word. It was almost cute the way he constantly watched her. But I cannot say Liang was so amused when she noticed his attention was not on the movie. I saw her not so gently elbow him and her eyes narrow when he looked at her. I stifled a giggled as his eyes returned to the television.

I walked out on the veranda to get a little bit of air. I sat down on one of the cushioned chairs and propped my feet up on the stone fire pit. The living room was buzzing, and people were lounging around everywhere. But all those bodies and all the commotion had made me want to slip away for a few minutes to gather my own thoughts. Christina and Thomas had been haunting me all day.

"Are you all right?" Ethan walked over and sat down in the chair beside mine. "What are you doing out here alone?"

"I just needed some air. It's a little stuffy in there with so many people," I explained.

"A little," he agreed, fidgeting with his hands. "I can't believe you're graduating tomorrow."

"Me neither." I smiled over at him. "This year has been a blur."

"A lot has happened that's for sure." Ethan shifted in his chair towards me. "Hey, I am really sorry for being such an ass and ruining your senior year. I just ...," he mumbled, trying to find the right words. "I just always thought your senior year would play out much differently." He sighed audibly.

"So, did I," I admitted. "Do you think I ever thought I would get married before I graduated?"

"No," he chuckled. "If I had even mentioned the notion to you a year ago you would have scoffed at me after you hit me."

"You're right." I laughed. "But things never seem to turn out the way we envision them. This year has been both wonderful and trying and amazing. But honestly, I would not change any part of it." Then I thought for a moment. "Well, maybe some of it ..." I smiled over at my little brother.

"I am sorry for the way that I treated you and Jackson. He really is a good man, Jocelyn. And I can see how much he loves you. You'd just better make sure he takes care of you in Boston."

"He will, and I will take care of him," I promised.

"Good, I'm glad you're happy." We sat in silence for several minutes simply enjoying the warm night air and the peace beneath the stars. Ethan reached over and took my hand in his squeezing it gently. "I am going to miss you," he whispered.

"I am going to miss you too." I glanced over at him. "Do you think Mom with ever speak to me again?"

"You know how stubborn she can be," he noted. "But I am sure with time she will come around."

"Yeah, after I graduate from grad school." I chuckled because we both knew there was some truth to the statement.

"Probably, and only if you don't have a kid first," Ethan added.

"Don't worry, we have no plans for that," I told him with a smirk.

"Someday?"

"Yes, of course someday, just not now or any time in the near future." My mind drifted back to the infamous photographs of my children.

"Good." He squeezed my hand again. "Well, we'd better get back in there." He rose from his seat and pulled me up beside him. "You know, I am glad we're okay." Ethan shocked me by pulling me into a hug.

"Me too. I do love you." I kissed him on the cheek before I let him go.

"I love you, too." He held my hand as we walked back in to join the others.

True to their word, the night ended about eleven. Everyone departed, exhausted from the long day of exams and hijinks. I was anxious myself to crawl into bed. I said a quick goodnight to our family and excused myself for the evening. I felt like I was moving in a fog as I climbed the steps to our room. The day had been long, endearing, joyous, and overwhelming. It still did not feel real to me. It was hard to fathom that my high school days were now behind me.

I changed into a pair of pajama shorts and a tank top before brushing my teeth and crawling into bed. I lay there watching my husband go through his normal routine. He washed his face and brushed his teeth before stopping at the end of our bed and slipped out of his clothes. The slow glow from the lamp on the nightstand, left long shadows on the walls and added soft hues to Jackson's muscular physique. His long arms and sculpted torso looked edible. I watched him for a second standing there in his dark blue boxer briefs. The sight of him took my breath away.

"Well, how does it feel?" Jackson asked, climbing into bed beside me.

"How does what feel?"

"Being a high school graduate?" He leaned down and kissed me softly.

"You should know. You've done it twice now." I grinned up at him.

"I love you," he whispered softly.

"I love you, too," I replied, pulling him on top of me.

CHAPTER THIRTY-FOUR

*S*ATURDAY, *May 30, 1879*

A small smile spread across my lips before my eyes even opened. I could vividly see everything that had transpired on my last day of high school *there* and it was so exciting. The contrast between my final day of school *here* in comparison to *there* was truly comical. The contrast between my two worlds was comical. The difference was night and day.

I stretched and yawned and reluctantly opened my eyes. Jackson's pillow was empty beside me. Most likely he was down in his study buried beneath a pile of papers just as he always was. I tossed the blankets aside and climbed out of bed. I put on my robe and walked over to the window. It was a beautiful spring day. The sun was shining brightly, fluffy clouds were drifting slowly across the sea of pale blue and the dew was glistening upon the emerald blades beneath me.

Then reality smacked me in the face. The joyful images from my other life faded quickly as I remembered what had happened yesterday. My dear friends, Christina and Thomas, had been brutally attacked and murdered. My smile quickly faded, and tears filled my eyes. I felt so guilty for my moment of happiness.

Cora knocked on the door and came in carrying a breakfast tray. "Good morning, Jocelyn. How are you this morning?"

"Good, Cora. How are you?" I asked as she put the tray on the nightstand.

"Well, thank you. I brought your breakfast this morning, but first we need to get you dressed." She hurried over to the armoire and started pulling out a dress without even looking first, which she never did.

"Cora, what is wrong?" I slipped off my robe and walked over to her.

"Mr. Jackson did not want to wake you, but he was called out late last evening after you both retired and he has not returned yet." She started pulling on my corset strings until I couldn't breathe.

"Where did he go? Who came and got him?" I managed to squeak out between breaths.

"Sheriff McGuire came by and said that Mr. Donaldson was requesting his assistance." I grunted as she finally tied the stays.

"That makes no sense," I muttered more to myself then to Cora as she helped me into my gown. "Which Mr. Donaldson?"

"I am not sure." She straightened the gown and smoothed it out before fastening it.

Dressed, I sat down at my vanity and Cora brushed my hair out and began twisting it up into a bun at the nape of my neck without going through the entire ritual. Her haste only enhanced my concerns and deepened by fears.

As soon as she was finished, I grabbed my bonnet and parasol and rushed down the stairs. I left my breakfast on the tray untouched.

Susan answered my in-law's door before I even finished knocking on it. "Good morning, Mrs. Chandler."

"Good Morning, Susan. Is my husband here?" I asked, taking off my gloves and handing my things to her.

"Yes, he is in the study with Mr. Chandler."

"I thought I heard your voice." Emily walked out of the parlor to greet me. "Come, join me for a cup of coffee." She took a hold of my arm and practically dragged me into the parlor. "Susan, more coffee please," she said before closing the door behind us.

"Emily, what is going on?" Her behavior was quite out of the norm.

"Just a moment." She held up her index finger and listened. A minute later Susan reappeared with everything we needed on a silver tray. She set it down on the table and left the room, closing the door behind her. "Sit down, Jocelyn."

"Emily, what is going on?" I was getting scared and tried not to show it.

Emily fussed about fixing our drinks as I waited impatiently for her to join me on the lounge. Finally, she returned and handed me a cup and saucer and sat down beside me.

"Last night Jackson showed up here a little after one in the morning. Barnaby alerted us to his presence saying it was urgent. When we joined him in the study, he told us that Mr. Dimitri Donaldson was arrested around nine that evening."

"Dimitri? What on earth for?" I couldn't imagine my childhood friend doing anything to get arrested. Dimitri was a kind and gentle man who worked hard alongside his father as a carpenter.

"For attacking Maryanne Kendrick."

"What?" I jumped up completely shocked. "That is absurd! He would never—"

"I know." Emily took my arm and gently pulled me back to my seat. "It seems right before eight o'clock last evening Maryanne started pounding on the Cain's side door, the home door, not the entrance to the store. Mr. Cain said she was disheveled, her hair was skewed, and her dress torn. She was crying uncontrollably. Of course, he helped her in, set her on the lounge, and Molly brought her some hot tea. Once they got her calmed a bit she told them that Mr. Donaldson attacked her and tried to force himself on her. She claims she managed to fight him off and make her way to the Cain's store. She said that when Dimitri saw her pounding on the door, he ran off."

"Maryanne is a liar," I claimed. "How can anyone believe her?"

"Mr. Cain believed her enough to get Sheriff McGuire. After he spoke to her Sheriff McGuire went over to the Donaldson's house and took Dimitri into custody. He requested Jackson for his attorney." Emily shook her head in disbelief.

"What are they going to do about it?" I knew she understood I was referring to our husbands.

"They are working on it. They have been since Jackson arrived. Unfortunately, it is Maryanne's word against Dimitri's."

"Did anyone see Dimitri attack her?" I asked.

"Not that anyone is aware of."

I took a deep breath and tasted the warm coffee. It was a welcomed necessity. I didn't know what else to say. I knew Dimitri's family must be in chaos this morning. I was also positive that Dimitri would never do what he was being accused of. It simply was not in his nature.

Emily and I scurried about for the next several hours in and out of Robert's study trying to help, feed, and attend to our husbands. They both looked worn out and very sleepy, but neither of them would stop long enough to rest. The study was cluttered with papers and law books scattered about that were bookmarked and dogged-eared. They were on a quest and their lack of finding some useful precedence was making them both irritable.

After we picked for an hour or so at the lunches Carley had served the four of us in the study, Barnaby came in to tell us that the Donaldson's and the Brice's were waiting for us in the parlor. I looked over at Emily, unsure as to whether we should follow or stay behind. She just took my hand and gently pulled me along behind the men.

Dimitri's parents, George and Corrine, were pacing anxiously about the parlor alongside Dimitri's girlfriend, Evelyn Brice, and her parents, Vincent and Jessica. It was clear by the look of them none had gotten a wink of sleep.

"Jackson, Robert, please tell me you can prove her a liar and we can put this entire nightmare behind us," Mr. Donaldson said.

"Rest assured, George. My son and I have been up all night working on this. And I can promise you we will not stop until Dimitri is exonerated of all charges." Robert shook his hand firmly.

Mr. Donaldson let out a deep sigh and flopped down heavily on the lounge. His oversized frame shook the house. He was pale and glistening. I looked over at Emily.

"Please give Mr. Donaldson a glass of cold water. I am going to get my father." I touched her arm and she nodded.

Without bothering to retrieve my things I rushed out of the house and trotted across the street. I opened the front door without knocking and headed straight to my father's study. He wasn't there. I ran to the kitchen and found Sara preparing things for dinner.

"My goodness, child, what's wrong?" she asked when I collided with her as I rounded the corner.

"Where's father?" I gushed.

"Reading on the veranda." She nodded towards the backdoor.

"Thank you." I kissed her cheeks quickly and took off again.

I found my father resting on a chaise lounge under an old maple tree reading the newspaper. "Father," I ran over to him and grabbed his arm. "Come quick, I believe Mr. Donaldson is having severe chest pains."

My father leapt to his feet. "Where is he?"

"The Chandler's," I hollered after him as he ran for his bag.

I hurried after him, but he arrived across the street before me. He was already kneeling beside Mr. Donaldson when I returned to the parlor. My father asked us all to clear the room, so he could assess Mr. Donaldson.

Emily ushered us all outside to her own veranda and Sara followed us with tall glasses filled with ice and a pitcher of lemonade. But no one was interested. I knew Mr. Donaldson had, had what my father called mild chest pains early last fall. After that, my father had advised him to take some time off from work and to avoid stressful situations. Since then, Dimitri had practically been running his father's business and it turned out he was very good with numbers as well as being gifted in carpentry.

The silence was making matters even more tense. The only noise was the mournful sound of birds nesting at the top of the trees and our shoes on the cobblestones. Evelyn and Emily were doing their best to comfort Mrs. Donaldson but were having little success. I leaned against one of the columns, observing everything and everyone ... waiting with them for the nightmare to end.

I am not sure how long we baked in the afternoon sun before my mother joined us. I was surprised when she walked out. Her beautiful hair was swept up neat and perfect, her elegant light purple gown looked lovely in the late spring sunlight, but her face betrayed her. Her eyes were red and swollen, her face was ashen. All eyes rested on her.

"George is resting comfortably. He had another episode with his heart, a much bigger one, but Patrick said he needs to rest and not be disturbed." Corrine rushed to her and embraced my mother.

"Can I see him?" she asked.

"He is very weak, Corrine. Let us allow him a little time to rest." Corrine nodded and returned to her seat.

"How is he, Mother?" I took her away from the others and whispered.

"Not well." She sighed heavily. "There was some cognitive damage as well this time. Your father does not know to what degree and most likely will not for the next several days."

"When did you get here?" I asked.

"Just a few minutes after you left. Sara came and told me what happened, so I came right over." My mother wiped her brow with the end of her apron. "I hope this heat wave is not an indication of how bad this summer is going to be. I feel like I am melting, and it is not even June yet."

* * *

I finally got Jackson home at sunset. He was dead on his feet and would not listen to reason. I was ready to strangle him. Thankfully, his father stepped in and insisted Jackson go home and get some sleep. Cora had a steaming hot bath ready for him upon our arrival.

While Jackson soaked in the bath I got undressed and slipped into bed. My mind was still in disbelief over everything that had occurred in the last twenty-four hours. My head was throbbing. I closed my eyes and tried to think about being *there*. I wanted so desperately just to be *there*. I wanted to drift away from this horrible mess and experience once again that magical night called prom. I wanted to get all dressed up, dance with my husband, and for one night enjoy myself and save all my trouble for another day.

CHAPTER THIRTY-FIVE

Saturday, May 28, 2010

Jackson woke me up just before ten. He set a tray filled with French toast, scrambled eggs, bacon, orange juice and coffee down on the nightstand before leaning over me and kissing me gently on the forehead.

"Good morning, sleepy head."

"Hmmm … I don't want to get up," I complained, but I wrapped my arms around him pulling him down on the bed.

"No time for that." Jackson laughed and climbed off the bed. "You need to eat, shower, and get ready for graduation."

"What time is it?" I sat up and rubbed my eyes.

"Ten," he replied, opening the blinds and filling the room with bright sunlight.

"Aw, why did you have to do that?" I groaned and buried my face in his pillow beside me.

"Come on." Jackson pulled me back into a seated position and put the tray on my lap. "Eat up and get showered. Everyone is downstairs waiting for you." He kissed me on the forehead and disappeared back downstairs.

I ate, showered, and shaved my legs. I stood there in the bathroom mirror in my pink lace bra and matching panties. With my hair still up in a towel I began putting on my makeup and thinking about what I was going to wear. Now I wished I had gone shopping and bought something special for the day. When

Emily had asked me last weekend, I had politely declined, citing that I needed to study for finals.

I finished up my makeup and shook my hair out of the damp towel. I added a little mousse to it and started blow-drying it. I figured I would curl the ends and pull the sides up under my graduation cap.

Once dry, I brushed it out in long strokes. The amber waves cascaded over my shoulders spilling down my back. It was at least a good six to eight inches shorter then my hair was in my *other* life. But still, I loved how it glistened in the sun with its golden highlights. I picked up the curling iron but paused when I heard a knock on the bedroom door.

"Yes?" I poked my head around out the bathroom door and hollered through the bedroom door.

"It's Phoebe, can I come in?" my sister-in-law replied from the other side.

"Of course," I said before turning back to my hair.

Phoebe stuck her head in the bathroom and chuckled when she saw me. "I know it's warm outside, but don't you think you should wear a little more under that gown?"

"Do I have to?" I smiled at her through my reflection in the mirror and continued working on my hair.

"I suppose not." She shrugged, leaning against the doorframe.

"You know how stuffy these things are. It just seemed practical."

"I was thinking you should wear something a little less practical." A clever grin slipped across his lips.

"What are you up to?" I spun around and confronted her.

"I found this a couple weeks ago when I was shopping with my girlfriends in New York, and I thought it would be perfect for you today. So, don't be mad. I had to get it for you." She turned towards the garment bag that she must have laid down on my bed when she arrived.

"Phoebe, you shouldn't have," I protested, but I approached the bed all the same filled with curiosity.

"Yes, I should have. You are my sister and I can splurge on you when I feel like it. Besides, today is a very special day that requires a very special dress." Phoebe unzipped the faux plastic and pulled out a strapless cream-colored satin gown with a black Victorian design around the top and a black oval design in the same fashion at the bottom. It was simply elegant.

"Try this on." She handed it to me.

I was giddy. Phoebe was notorious for her taste in fashion. She always dressed in a classic sense of style and grace. She had an impeccable eye for design. It seemed to me she had missed her true calling in life. I knew she was an amazing criminal attorney, but I couldn't help but believe that she should have been in New York, Paris, or Milan.

I took the dress of the hanger and unzipped it. The fabric was so soft and sensuous. I stepped into it and Phoebe zipped it up. "Well?" I twirled around in front of her before looking at myself in the mirror. "What do you think?"

"I think I would lose the pink bra." She laughed at my reflection.

"I don't know. I think it adds a little something." I giggled.

"Don't you have a nude strapless bra?" she asked, unzipping the dress to my waste.

"Are you serious? Do you honestly think I have a nude-colored strapless bra? I think I have a white one." I started searching through my panty drawer.

"Stop. Please, stop." Phoebe walked over and touched my arm. "I had a feeling you might not have the kind of bra required for this type of gown, so I picked you up this." She picked up a small Victoria Secret's bag off the corner of my bed I hadn't even noticed was there. "Try this on."

Inside the bag was a strapless, pale nude bra. It had similar wires in the front that reminded me a great deal of one of my corsets that I recalled all too clearly in my *other* world. It rested in the front at the top of my navel and dipped down under my arms at my sides and went down my back to meet in a one-inch strap. Phoebe had guessed my size correctly. It fit me perfectly.

* * *

The football stadium was packed full of families and friends anxiously waiting for the ceremony to begin. The school had set up little white chairs across the football field for the graduates to sit in. We waited around in the field house that still smelled of sweat socks and body odor. I stood beside Jackson rocking back and forth on the black strappy heels that Phoebe had purchased to match my dress.

"Will you stop fidgeting?" Jackson put his hands over mine where I was playing with my honor cords.

"This is ridiculous. Why are they making us wait around in here?" I complained.

"I am melting in this box," Caitlyn chimed in.

"They really should have aired this place out." Zak stepped in front of a couple people and joined in. "It smells ripe in this joint."

"Yes, it does," Jackson agreed.

"Okay everyone, settle down," hollered our principal, Mrs. Cosgrove, as she clapped her hands at us. "I know you're all excited. Now if you'll all just line up the way you did during rehearsal."

"But no fanny grabbing this time," Caitlyn whispered to Zak before he snuck back to his place in line.

I tried not to giggle as Mrs. Cosgrove shushed us all one more time before opening the door. The warm air from outside washed over us, but with it came the sticky humidity that was slightly ahead of schedule this year. Sitting outside in this unseasonably warm weather was going to make this ceremony more pleasant and long.

At two o'clock sharp the Graduation March song began playing over the loudspeaker as we walked onto the field in two single file rows. Our graduating class consisted of seven hundred and twenty students. All of us were wearing royal blue caps and gowns representing our school colors of royal blue and gold. In the past they used to have the girls wear the gold and the guys wear the royal blue, but our class had voted in the fall when it came time to order our graduation gowns to be rid of the gold gowns. They were hideous looking since they resembled a shade of color somewhere between vomit and baby diarrhea.

My class filed into our assigned rows and sat down. Mrs. Cosgrove stepped up to the podium and began her speech. It was the same one being said at every single high school across America this time of year, just varied slightly to make it fit the personality of the graduating class. But essentially, they were all the same. Then our valedictorian, Tristan Phillips, stepped up to the podium and rambled on excessively about our future, our goals, and what we should all hope to achieve in life. She was not only our class valedictorian, but she was also the student council president, science club president, and chess club president, and on our school debate team. To say she was wicked smart was a mild understatement. It was rumored that she was graduating with a 4.8 grade point average, but I couldn't swear to it.

My eyes drifted off to the bleachers to see if I could find my families. I knew Jackson's parents and siblings were up there amongst the masses somewhere, but for the life of me I could not spot them. It was a blurred sea of faces staring down at us. It made me feel like I was sitting in a fishbowl on display. I knew my dad and Ethan were up there somewhere and most likely, Liang too. But I couldn't find them either. I wondered if my mother was here. Certainly, she would want to see me graduate, even if she was still mad at me. I was her daughter, and this was a huge milestone in my life. However, considering her recent attitude and behavior towards me, I had my doubts as to whether she'd shown up.

Forty-five minutes of baking in the sun and sweating in the humidity was not fun. I shifted in my seat again, waiting for them to start calling our names. If we could have at least moved, we might have felt a bit better. I felt sorry for our friends and families sitting in the hot metal bleachers under the direct sun. Those bleachers absorbed the heat and literally baked under intense rays. I was ready to take off my graduation cap just to use it to fan myself with, but Phoebe had pinned it into place since it refused to sit right on my hair.

Finally, sixty minutes in our vice principal, Mr. Acton, stepped up to the podium and began calling our names. We did as instructed and each row stood up as the one before it hit the end of the aisle before walking across the makeshift stage. Once we reached the podium, Mrs. Cosgrove handed us our diplomas and shook our hands. Then we shook hands with Mr. Acton and our school counselors, Mr. Sutherland, Mr. Mills, Mr. Davis, and Mrs. Karmen.

Jenna was one of the first students to graduate. She looked so pretty with her blond hair hanging down loosely and a big smile on her face as she accepted her diploma. I admit I felt a small pain in my chest even now for not being able to celebrate this day together.

Caitlyn, Jackson, and I were in the second row of students to walk the stage. I stood right behind Jackson and followed him down the row of chairs. He took my hand and pulled me to walk at his side. "I am so proud of you," he whispered.

"Thank you for doing this for me," I whispered back to him. "All of this."

"I would do anything for you." He leaned down quickly and kissed me on the cheek just as we came to the end of our row.

Jackson held my hand all the way up on stage until it was time for him to accept his diploma and shake everyone's hand. I held my breath and waited on the top rung of the steps for my name to be called next.

"Jocelyn Alyssa Chandler," Mr. Acton announced.

I walked slowly but steadily in my new strappy heels across the stage to Mrs. Cosgrove. She handed me my diploma and shook my hand. "Congratulations, Mrs. Chandler."

"Thank you." I happily accepted it and continued down the line.

I followed Jackson off the stage, back down the aisle, and returned to my seat. I opened my diploma and looked at it. It was so pretty. Jocelyn Alyssa Chandler was written in big letters under our school name. It still looked foreign to me. I was only now becoming used to signing Chandler instead of Timmons. A part of me had considered hyphenating my name, but knowing it wasn't an option for me in my *other* life, I figured it would be easier for me to keep it the same across time.

One of the downsides of having a last name at the beginning of the alphabet was going first. Now all we could do was sit in the sun and bake while the rest of our class crossed the stage.

That took another ninety minutes.

When the last student in our class crossed the stage, Mrs. Cosgrove stepped back behind the podium. She thanked everyone for attending and rambled on until Layla York, the last student to receive a diploma, returned to her seat so she could finally announce us the graduating class of 2010.

A deafening roar erupted from the field as we all stood and screamed. It was official. We were finally high school graduates with diplomas in hand. I threw my arms around Jackson's neck and leapt into his arms. My lips devoured his with hunger and happiness. He hugged me tightly before releasing me. I turned and hugged Caitlyn, then Zak, and several of my surrounding classmates. Congratulations all around.

Minutes later, families, friends, and graduates reunited all over the school grounds. It didn't take long for Jackson's family to spot us, bringing emotional greetings, hugs, kisses, and praise. I embraced them all. I was so truly blessed to marry into such a family. Emily gushed with pride overhearing our names called and couldn't stop hugging us numerous times.

"There you are." I heard my dad's voice from behind.

"Dad!" I spun around and jumped in his arms. "I'm so happy you're here!"

"Are you kidding?" He chuckled, holding me tightly and swinging me back and forth slightly. "I wouldn't have missed this for the world. I am so proud of you!"

He finally set me down, and I noticed Ethan and Liang standing beside him. I grabbed Ethan and wrapped my arms around him. "Congratulations, sis." My little brother hugged me and even kissed me lightly on the cheek.

"Thanks!"

"You must be so happy." Liang stepped forward and hugged me as well. "Congratulations!"

"Thank you, and thanks for coming."

I looked over at my dad, who was talking with Robert and Emily. I smiled to myself happy that at least most of my family was here.

"Don't I get a hug too?" My smile broadened as I saw Sidney and Landon approaching holding hands.

"You came!" I squealed.

"Of course, we did!" She wrapped her arms around me. "I couldn't miss this."

"Thank you." I brushed back the tears of joy that decided to appear.

Even Landon hugged me with congratulations before he shook Jackson's hand. Sidney hugged my husband next and kissed him on the cheek. I was so thrilled they had made it. I reached out, taking my brother's hand and squeezed it gently. "I am so glad you are here." Ethan just beamed.

I took a deep breath and looked around. "Mom didn't come," I said rather than asked.

"Oh, she's here," Ethan replied.

"Where?" I looked around again but did not see her.

"As soon as the ceremony was over, she walked back to the car," he informed me.

"Then why did she even bother?" I shook my head in disbelief, but Ethan only shrugged.

My newly expanded family stood around taking pictures and making plans for the next day. I knew we weren't having a traditional open house like most graduates, but the Chandlers still wanted to do something special to celebrate the occasion for me. They decided upon a big family barbecue at home for the following afternoon. I noticed that Emily made a special point to tell my dad to invite my mother as well, although we all knew she would never show.

It was six in the evening before we made it back home. Jackson and I had made plans to meet up with Caitlyn and Zak around eight to hit the bonfire graduation party out at Mark's. But first we needed to eat something and change out of our dress clothes.

Jackson chased me up the stairs trying to tickle me. I wasn't exactly hard to catch considering I was only beginning to walk a little more gracefully in heels. I swatted his hands away trying to dodge him, laughing at him, but he picked me up as soon as we hit the top floor landing.

"You really think you can escape me?" He chuckled before leaning down to kiss me playfully.

"No, and I have tried," I teasingly remarked as he carried me into our room.

"And I believe I have proven the lengths to which I will go to find you." He laughed deviously.

"Do you know how creepy that sounds?" I replied.

"That is devotion, my dear." Jackson put me on the bed and climbed up beside me.

"I think it's called stalking." I laughed, but then he leaned over and kissed me deeply.

Jackson's body hovered over mine. His mouth consumed mine. His fingers brushed through my hair, then down my shoulders. His lips caressed my neck. I arched my back towards him and pulled the back of his dress shirt out of his suit pants. My fingers ran over the hot muscular skin across his back and then I traced them across his chest.

I knew I would never get enough of this man.

Jackson and I reemerged downstairs a little over an hour later. A buffet-style dinner was already underway when we arrived. The little ones were seated around the table with their parents and grandparents. But the adults struggled to hide their grins or snickers as we fixed our plates in the kitchen before joining them all in the dining room.

"Trouble finding your clothes, little brother?" A sly grin slid across Alex's lips.

"Or just celebrating?" Phoebe teased.

"Shut up." Jackson rolled his eyes at them before he held out my seat for me at the table.

We sat down and dove right into our food. We were both starving, and our little escapades had only increased our appetite substantially. And the food was delicious. Emily never ceased to amaze me how quickly she could whip up the most incredible dishes in record time.

We talked nonstop about the move, all the preparations, and the packing. I was surprised to learn that Robert and Emily had decided not to sell the house in Chicago after all. Robert stated that he felt fortunate to have had the opportunity to reclaim the property and wanted to keep it in the family since he was the one who originally built it. Therefore, he and Emily had decided to close it up like what they had done with their home in Boston for the last year.

"Did you hire a property management company to care for it while you are gone?" I inquired.

"No, we got someone we trusted to take care of it in our absence." Robert smiled over at me. "I spoke with your dad about taking care of it for us. He said he would be happy to."

"Really?" I was shocked.

"Shane was happy to help. Plus, Ethan volunteered to take care of the lawn and flowerbeds. Of course, I told him we would pay him which seemed to sweeten the deal for him." Emily chortled.

"I am sure he was thrilled." I shook my head, knowing my brother a little too well.

We finished up dinner and moved into the family room for some coffee and conversation. I sat next to Phoebe and talked about all the stores and malls around Boston she was dying to take me to. From all she was saying she was going to keep my schedule full until the fall semester kicked in. I was already nervous about learning my way around a new city and starting over in a new place. Not to mention with everything becoming so clear between the eras, it was a lot of changes in a short period of time. I was just glad I was going to have so much help along the way.

Jackson and I left to pick up Zak and Caitlyn just as twilight settled in. It was a gorgeous warm evening. The luminous moon was high in the sky casting amazing hues across the ground below. We rolled the windows down and turned the radio up. *Linkin Park* was blaring through the speakers. Caitlyn and I were belting out the lyrics along with them. The wind was blowing the warm night air through our hair, reminding us that we were young and alive.

Most of the upcoming senior class and the newly graduated seemed to have turned out for the celebration. As a nice touch, there was a table of food set out by the beer kegs and alcoholic beverages. There was also a barrage of streamers, balloons, and a huge banner hanging between two trees that read Congratulations, Class of 2010.

Jackson parked his CRV amongst the dozens of other cars. Thankfully, we had been having a dry spell recently and the ground was dry. So tonight, unlike before, we didn't have to dodge mud holes. I looped my arm though Jackson's and the four of us wound our way through the makeshift parking lot to join the others.

Our boys took off to find drinks leaving Caitlyn and I standing alone on the outskirts of the party. She looked over at me and shrugged her shoulders and then literally pulled me into the party. "Come on, graduate. It's time we had some fun."

"I couldn't agree with you more." We trotted off together to find some trouble.

Caitlyn and I managed to snag a couple of unopened hard lemonades from Derryck, one of the upcoming senior football players. He simply rolled his eyes at us and returned to the alcohol tub for some more drinks. We just laughed it off and pressed forward. We made our way through the crowds of people we'd known for years, laughing, telling stories, reminiscing about past antics.

And somehow it seemed that Derryck had turned into mine and Caitlyn's personal bartender. For whatever reason, and I think it was because he'd always had a crush on Caitlyn, he was very attentive in making sure that she and I were never without a drink no matter where we roamed. Jackson and Zak kept a distant eye on us while they too were busy enjoying themselves. I really enjoyed watching Jackson cut loose a little bit and have a good time.

After I'd just finished my third hard lemonade, I was feeling particularly jovial until I heard someone behind me calling my name. I recognized the voice without a second thought. I should have. I'd heard it almost every day of my life for eighteen years.

"Yes?" I turned around after she called my name for the third time.

"Can I talk to you for a moment?" I couldn't believe there was no hostility in her voice for the first time in six months.

"Sure." I nodded back at Caitlyn and stepped away from the crowd with Jenna.

We walked a short distance to where some of the cars were parked. She stopped next to her car and leaned against the hood. "I don't even know where to begin." Jenna ran her finger over the rim of her plastic cup awkwardly. "I know I've been horrible to you."

"Yes, you have." I stood there feeling extremely uncomfortable. I didn't know what to say to her, so I just stood there looking at her. "What do you want, Jenna?"

"I don't want you to move away or us to start college with things like this between us. I know I said and did some unforgivable things in the last six months." She fumbled with her words. "And I know I have no right to ask you for forgiveness, but I am. We've been the best of friends for far too long to let that friendship die now. You're like a sister to me, Jocelyn. I love you."

I didn't respond. I didn't know what to say.

"Fair enough." She took a deep breath before she continued. "I'm sure you found out about my parents' divorce."

"Yes, my father mentioned something to that effect," I told her.

"Then I guess you also know why?"

"Yes," I barely whispered.

"Have you told anyone?" she immediately inquired.

"Jackson was there when my father told me," I admitted.

"Wonderful." Jenna sighed audibly.

"He would never tell anyone."

"Does Caitlyn or Zak know?" she asked, sharpness returning to her voice.

"No, of course not. Neither of us has breathed a word."

"It's humiliating. I can't believe this has happened to my family." Jenna rolled her eyes with impetuous flare.

"Honestly, Jenna. I understand why you are upset, and you have every right to be. But this is not the end of the world. Don't you want your parents to be happy?" I tried to reason.

"They were happy." She rolled her eyes again. "Well, at least I thought so. Nothing like finding out your entire life has been a lie." Jenna hastily brushed a tear off her cheek.

"It was not a lie. I know your parents love each other very much. Just not in the way that you want them to." I tried to sympathize with her.

"My mother has a girlfriend. Did you know that?"

"No." I failed to mention that I had seen a new car over there recently.

"Her name is Carla. She keeps trying to get me to like her. She buys me things and she's always trying to get me to go places with them. She even has two kids from her ex-husband. Her son is a year older than us and her daughter is two years younger. Thankfully, I haven't met them yet, but Carla keeps pushing for it." Jenna took a big gulp of her beer. "I hate her."

"How is your dad?" I had always liked her father, Craig.

"As best can be expected, I guess. He's so angry all the time. I feel horrible for him."

"I am sure he is dealing with a wide range of emotions right now."

"Not really, just hate mainly," Jenna snorted. "I can't say I blame him. Everything that has happened to our family is her fault."

"Have you decided where you are going in the fall?" I tried to change the subject.

"I was going to go to Northwestern, but I changed my mind. I'm going to Indiana University with Hilary."

"That's wonderful. I am so happy for you. I think it will do you good to have her with you next year." I tried to sound genuine.

"When are you leaving for Boston?"

"Two weeks." I took a sip of my hard lemonade. "I haven't begun packing yet," I admitted.

"Jocelyn, I …" Jenna stuttered. "I'm sorry I was such a bitch to you this year. I just want you to be happy. I admit I was a little leery that you and Jackson got so serious so fast." I looked at her, raising both my eyebrows and chuckled. "Okay, I was a lot leery."

"Jackson is a wonderful man, Jenna. I love him more than anything in this world."

"It's just, well …" She took another long drink. "I always got the impression that he was hiding something and then it was like you were both hiding something. Like you two were in on this big secret that no one else was privy to." Jenna brushed another tear off her cheek. "You and I used to be that way. We had secrets, we shared everything. It was always you and me against the world and that all changed the day he entered our lives. You changed …"

"Jenna, I haven't changed." I took a couple steps closer to her. "Well, perhaps a little, but we all change and grow as we get older. That is a part of life."

"You realize you speak like Jackson and his parents now?" She snorted again.

"I suppose so. I guess that you do adapt to your surroundings and considering I do share a home with my in-laws and my husband, it is only natural," I told her.

"I know that." She rolled her eyes again at me. "You just seem different."

"Jenna, I am happy. That is the difference." I stepped closer to her and put my hand on her arm. "Seriously, Jenna, I am so happy with Jackson. I don't worry about the future and you know why? Because I have Jackson and I know whatever comes at us in this world, we will face it together."

"How can you say that? People get divorced every day. Look at my parents." Jenna loved to be dramatic at times.

"Well, first of all, both of us are straight." Thankfully, she giggled at that. "Secondly, I know what the statistics say, but contrary to popular belief, some marriages do make it. Besides, I believe in our marriage."

"I hope you're right." She threw back the rest of her drink. "God, I've missed you." She wrapped her arms around me.

"I missed you too." I hugged her back tightly.

Kyle walked up with a cup of beer for Jenna and handed me another hard lemonade. We both thanked him as he grinned widely. He had that soft glow about him that only came from having one too many drinks.

"I'm so happy you two reconciled," he stated.

"Me too." Jenna smiled. "I've been a bitch and I apologized for it."

"Don't worry, we are good now." I reached over and hugged Kyle. "And congratulations, graduate."

"Thanks, congratulations to you too." He kissed me lightly on the cheek.

Jackson came up behind me and wrapped his arms around my waist. "Is everything all right," he whispered as he leaned down to kiss the side of my neck.

"Everything is wonderful." I reached up and kissed his full lips.

For the rest of the evening, peace fell over our little group. We were all together to celebrate one of the most important days in our young lives. Maybe it was the alcohol. Maybe it was nostalgia. Or perhaps the realization that our high school days were behind us and when fall rolled around three months from now, we would all be sitting in new classrooms on campuses scattered across the country from each other. Whichever the case it may be, I was delighted to make amends before we moved.

The music was loud, the fire was roaring, the liquor was flowing, and the atmosphere was festive. We danced, we laughed, and we had the night of our lives. I knew this was most likely the last time I would ever see most of these people, at least for a very long time. It was heartbreaking ... thankfully, the alcohol made it easier for all of us. I never wanted it to end.

CHAPTER THIRTY-SIX

Sunday, May 31, 1879

I could feel the sunlight beating down on me through our bedroom window. I didn't want to open my eyes and let go of the magical evening I had just experienced. I was thrilled that things seemed to be on the mend finally in my life *there* and not just with Ethan, but with Jenna also. Instead, I was forced to open my eyes and face the horrors awaiting me. I rolled over into a fetal position and tried to will myself back to sleep.

My efforts proved futile.

Cora came in a short while later to tell me that Jackson was back over at his parents' house, working with his father. He did leave a message for me insisting that I accompany his mother to church services. I understood why he wasn't going to be there, but I couldn't understand why he insisted that Emily and I attend. However, I didn't question his decision and got myself ready.

My mother-in-law picked me up in their carriage with Barnaby at the reins. Emily looked beautiful in her soft green gown with matching bonnet and gloves. She slid over a bit and patted the spot beside her in the carriage.

"Good morning. How are you?" She was all smiles.

"Wishing I was *there* instead of *here*," I whispered after I'd climbed in and sat down.

"I understand, I feel like my husband and son have me doing recon work for them," Emily whispered back.

"Excuse me?"

"I thought you understood why our men insisted we make an appearance this morning. They want us to pay attention to what people are saying, get a feel for what other people believe occurred. With there being no witnesses to the alleged attack, the perception of the community is vitally important if this should happen to go to trial," she explained.

"Do you really believe it will come to that?" I was stunned.

"It may, they are just not sure at this point."

Barnaby stopped the carriage in front of the church steps. He opened the door and helped each of us out of the carriage. I stood at the foot of the steps and took a hold of Emily's arm. She smiled over at me and patted my hand. Her small gesture urged me forward.

Just as Robert and Jackson feared, the church was in a state of near chaos. I had assumed there would be various groups of ladies speaking in hushed whispers. After all, it was a town that prided themselves on knowing everything about everyone's life, but I had not expected this level of upheaval. Community members who normally abstained from idle gossip, rumors, and hearsay were actively, openly, and loudly discussing the details that had made it quickly through the grapevine.

Emily and I stood in the back unnoticed for several minutes, absorbing the words that were flying in every direction. It seemed an overwhelming majority believed Maryanne to be lying about the attack and the only ones defending her story were her parents and her immediate family. Mr. and Mrs. Cain were diligently squashing the rumors that Maryanne was beaten and raped. They repeatedly stated that she had been crying, her hair had been slightly out of place, and the shoulder of her dress had been torn. Nothing more.

I knew the details of the story by heart at this point, having gone over them time and again with Jackson and his parents looking for certain inconsistencies in Maryanne's account of events. Dimitri had told Jackson that he had been walking home after having dined with Evelyn and her family. He'd left her house and had been headed down the main street towards his family's store and their residence above it. Dimitri said that Maryanne approached him from behind, calling out to him. He had stopped to inquire what she needed, and she had initially made small talk with him and asked how he was and what he had been doing. Dimitri said he tried to be polite and excused himself, but Maryanne grabbed his arm and demanded to know why he was being so abrupt to her. He said he shook his arm away from her and tried to walk away, but she grabbed him more forcefully and yelled at him for turning his back on her. When he attempted to pull away a second time, Maryanne slapped him across the face. At that point Dimitri turned and left her standing alone, unharmed, on the walkway three shops from the Cain's Mercantile.

Dimitri's account differed greatly from Maryanne's.

"Mrs. Chandler." Mr. Cain approached, taking Emily's hand and kissing it softly. "And Mrs. Chandler." He proceeded to do the same to me. "How are you ladies doing this morning?"

"Upset, Mr. Cain. I am very distressed over these wild accusations and outright lies," I told him.

"Yes, I must agree with my daughter-in-law. This entire situation is quite disturbing," Emily stressed.

"I could not agree with you ladies more. I am afraid the story has been altered so that no one present even knows the truth of what happened," he stated.

"And the general consensus?" I couldn't help but ask.

"That Maryanne is a liar." Mr. Cain shook his head slowly. "But how to prove it?"

"Robert and Jackson are working diligently on it," Emily told him. "I've known Mr. Dimitri Donaldson since he was a child. I grew up with his parents and they are kind and loving people, just as their son is. I cannot imagine that young man ever doing something so heinous. He has always been a gentleman of the highest quality. I certainly cannot believe he would ever do such a thing."

"I have to agree with you. I cannot fathom Dimitri ever behaving in such a manner. I watched that boy grow up, saw how distressed he was when he ended his relationship with Maryanne, and I know how manipulative Maryanne can be. I have seen it firsthand in the way she has treated my own daughter. She is exactly like her mother." Mr. Cain turned his head and scanned the crowd slowly. "And I told your husbands yesterday, Maryanne did not behave like one would expect a woman who had experienced such an attack. Her tears were forced, her body language was all wrong. But that is just my opinion and I am afraid without a witness, things for Dimitri are not boding well."

The organ music began, ending all conversations. Everyone moved about finding a place to sit. Emily and I slid in the row beside my parents and tried to get comfortable on the hard-wooden pews. We settled in for a long service. Reverend Jacobs never failed to take full advantage of current news to fully exploit it to his advantage.

Three long and excruciating hours later, Reverend Jacobs finally concluded his sermon. The heat in the church was stagnating. I had been fanning myself since the moment we walked in and it had only gotten worse. I felt like I was melting. I honestly believed that Reverend Jacobs made it his mission to torture us all in this enclosed space on days he knew we would be miserable.

I followed my family and friends to the green grasses surrounding the church. The heat outside was not much better than inside. The gossips were anxious to pick up their previous conversations right where they had left off before services. It amazed me how some individuals had so little tact. I noticed that neither the Brice's nor the Donaldson's were in attendance. I knew Mrs. Donaldson would be staying at my in-laws for the foreseeable future, while Mr. Donaldson was convalescing. My father had highly recommended that Mr. Donaldson not be moved until he was strong enough to climb stairs on his own. And from what I understood that was quite some time off. He was incredibly weak and frail from what Emily told me. I hated to think how hard this situation must be on both the Donaldson's and the Brice's.

I accepted my parent's invitation to a family dinner while Emily returned home to ensure our husbands took a break long enough to eat. I rode with my parents and listened to my mother ramble on about the menu she had given Sara this morning. My mother had invited all my brothers to attend and all had accepted. I sat back against the seat and rested my eyes. I wasn't sure if I was ready for a full house. I was only happy that I wasn't the hostess.

I picked at my food and kept involved in conversations with Lizette and Rachael. They were both excited about Rachael's pregnancy. Truthfully, at six months along Rachael was radiant. I was so happy for her and my brother. We discussed baby names for both a boy and a girl although she was certain she was having another daughter. I swallowed hard and tried not to envision the faded photographs tucked neatly in the hope chest at the foot of my bed *there*.

The afternoon drifted into evening and everyone was trying to avoid the obvious question on everyone's minds … what was going to happen to Dimitri? I couldn't shake it. I wanted to go see him, but Jackson had forbidden it. He wouldn't even discuss it with me, citing that a county jail was no place for a lady. Unfortunately, Robert and Emily both agreed with him. However, I was happy when Emily dropped by briefly to let me know that our husbands had visited with him that morning and Dimitri was doing well, all things considered.

So, I was even more surprised when she returned less than an hour after she'd just left. She gracefully entered the parlor and requested that I follow her back to her house saying that Jackson wanted to discuss something with me. I made my apologies to my family, excused myself, and followed Emily outside. She stopped short on the porch, reaching out and touching my arm.

"Jocelyn, I came and got you out of courtesy to my son. There is one thing you need to always remember as a lawyer's wife. We hear and witness much, but we never speak of it. Greta Larkin and Reverend Jacobs just arrived at our home. They are seated in the parlor waiting for us. I asked Carley to hold off getting our husbands for a moment, so I could get you," Emily explained.

"But they will see us." I wasn't sure why that was a bad thing.

"No, they will not." A coy little smile slipped across her perfectly shaped lips. "Follow me."

The sun was fading into the distance as I took Emily's hand and let her lead the way. We circled around behind the trees and followed the worn path between the fence line and the shrubbery. We crossed the road between our houses and went up the side of the property around to the veranda. She was right, we had crossed unseen.

We entered through the back entryway where Carley was waiting for us. She handed each of us a clean handkerchief to wipe our brow. Emily nodded at her and she scurried down the hallway to retrieve our husbands and announce our guest. We waited in the kitchen for Carley to return and heard the men's footsteps down the hall.

"Slowly," Emily whispered to me. "Carley, you go first with the lemonade. We will follow you."

Carley picked up the silver tray with the pitcher of iced lemonade and glasses upon it and walked steadily out of the kitchen. Emily placed her hand on my arm, and we followed a few steps behind her.

"Good evening, Reverend." We heard Robert's voice before we entered the parlor. "What can I do for you?"

The men were finishing their pleasantries when Emily and I made our appearance. We greeted our guests while Carley served the lemonade. Once everyone was seated, I noticed how uncomfortable Greta looked. She was wearing a pale, yellow dress trimmed in white lace. Her mousey brown hair was curled and pinned back away from her face. Her eyes were red and slightly swollen. It was obvious she had been crying recently. She had never been here before, to my knowledge, and I was positive she had never been to my home. I had no idea why she was here with our church's reverend asking to speak with my husband.

"I apologize for interrupting your evening, Mr. Chandler. We went by your home and Cora told us you were working with your father this afternoon," Reverend Jacobs began.

"Yes, we have been taking care of things for Mr. Donaldson." I knew Jackson was being deliberately vague.

"I believe we may be able to help you with that," Reverend Jacobs said.

"I am not sure I understand." Jackson had never liked Greta and his tone reflected as much. He held her in pretty much the same category as Maryanne.

"Ms. Larkin came by my home this afternoon, very upset, and told me the most disturbing news. I figured it was best to talk with you, being as you are Mr. Donaldson's attorney," Reverend Jacobs informed us, either not picking up on Jackson's tone or simply choosing to ignore it.

"All right." I could hear the speculation in Jackson's voice.

"Ms. Larkin was with Ms. Kendrick on Friday evening. She witnessed the altercation between Mr. Donaldson and Ms. Kendrick." A dead silence fell over the room. "Ms. Kendrick..." Greta shifted uncomfortably in the chair.

"Maryanne and I were taking a walk after dinner to get some air when she saw Dimitri walking home from Evelyn's house. She wanted to follow him, so we did. We walked a distance behind him without him noticing. Finally, Maryanne said she wanted to talk with him. I told her no, to leave him alone. But she ignored me and called out his name. Dimitri stopped. When Maryanne left me to speak with him, I sat down on the bench outside the lumber mill. I was in the shadows and I do not believe Dimitri knew I was there. I heard their exchange. Dimitri tried to be polite and excuse himself, but Maryanne grabbed his arm and wouldn't let him leave. When he did shake off her grasp the second time, she slapped him across the face. Dimitri said nothing. He just turned and walked away."

"Did you ever see Dimitri put a hand on Maryanne?" Jackson asked.

"No, sir." Greta finally looked Jackson in the face.

"Then how did she end up at the Cain's with her dress torn and in tears?" Robert inquired.

"Maryanne was angry when Dimitri left her standing alone in the street. She watched him walk away before she found me on the bench. She was screaming about 'how dare he treat her this way' and 'she was going to make him pay for it.' When she finally said she was going to ruin him and started ripping the shoulder of her dress I told her she needed to stop. When she messed up her hair and picked up some loose dirt to smudge her face and her dress, I told her I was leaving. I told her I did not want any part of this, and I left her on the porch of the lumber mill. I did not realize she went through with it until Saturday morning. After Dimitri was arrested, I knew I had to say something. That is when I went over to Reverend Jacobs this afternoon," Greta said, concluding her story to her captivated audience. I was baffled by Maryanne's naivety regarding Greta's sense of right and wrong. No one, no matter how good a friend if they had any sense of moral decency, would stand by and let someone be framed for a crime they didn't commit.

Jackson leaned back in his chair looking as if someone had punched him in the stomach. He let out a deep breath and ran his fingers through his hair. I had seen that look many times before. I knew he was trying to control his temper. I gently put my hand on his arm to calm him down before he said something he would certainly regret later.

"Well, thank you very much for coming forward and telling the truth, Ms. Larkin. I believe we need to contact Sheriff McGuire and see what our next step is going to be for Mr. Donaldson," Robert said.

"I agree." Jackson stood up. "Reverend, would you mind waiting here with Ms. Larkin?"

"Of course." Reverend Jacobs nodded.

I stood up with my hand on Jackson's arm. "I will accompany you," I said softly.

"Thank you." He nodded, and I followed him to the door.

Barnaby was already waiting outside with the carriage. Jackson helped me in before settling back beside me. At least he waited until we were away from the house before he exploded.

"Can you believe this shit?" he said, his voice rising.

"Jackson, language." It made me nervous when ears were within hearing distance.

"I don't care! Dimitri has been sitting in jail for two days, three if we can't get him released this evening. I always knew Maryanne was a bitch, but this is beyond my imagination," he shouted.

"I am not surprised." A sad truth.

"Neither am I to be honest. I knew Maryanne and Greta were horrible, but this … this is inexcusable. Even for Maryanne. This is beyond despicable."

"I am thankful that at least Greta's conscience got the better of her," I admitted.

"Still, to even contemplate doing such a thing to another person just because they see your true wicked self. I cannot image having a heart like that," Jackson stated, raking his fingers through his hair again.

"Because you could never have a heart like that. You are a loving, honest, faithful man who would never deliberately hurt another person. It is not in you to carry such hate." I leaned over and kissed his cheek. "It is one of the things I love most about you."

"You could not do it either." He grinned a little and shook his head. "And I love that about you too."

We arrived at Sheriff McGuire's house just after dark. The air was cooling down and there was a slight breeze in the air. Jackson wrapped his arm around my waist as we walked up the pathway to the porch. I knew where Sheriff McGuire lived, everyone in town knew that, but I had never been to his house before.

Jackson knocked on his door and we waited anxiously for someone to answer. Finally, we heard approaching footsteps on the hardwood floors. Mrs. McGuire answered the door.

"Good evening, Mr. Chandler, Mrs. Chandler. What can I help you with?" She greeted us with a friendly voice.

"Good evening, Mrs. McGuire, is your husband home? I need to speak with him urgently," Jackson replied.

"Yes, please come in." She stepped back and held the door open for us.

Sheriff McGuire was a tall, robust man with graying hair, large blue eyes, and a bushy mustache and goatee. Despite his large frame was incredibly light-footed. I didn't even hear him enter the room as we waited for him in the front parlor.

"Hello, Jackson, Mrs. Chandler." He shook my husband's hand. "Please have a seat. What can I do ya for?" We sat down on an old lounge and the sheriff took a seat in a rocker beside the fireplace. His wife came in with some hot tea and sat down in the rocker on the other side of the hearth.

"I am afraid I just heard the most troubling story," Jackson began.

"Oh, son, you are young. Just give it time. I have almost reached the point after thirty years in this job that nothing surprises me anymore." Sheriff McGuire laughed whole-heartedly.

"I have no doubt." Jackson smiled. "This evening I was over at my father's house working on exonerating Mr. Donaldson when Reverend Jacobs stopped by my house with Ms. Greta Larkin." He continued to recount what Greta had told us she witnessed.

By the time he was done Sheriff McGuire and his wife were completely stunned and horrified. Neither could believe someone would deliberately do something so malicious to another person, especially someone they claimed to love. I understood completely how they felt. Maryanne's actions were beyond my comprehension.

"Where is Ms. Larkin now?" Sheriff McGuire inquired.

"She is at my parents' home with my parents and Reverend Jacobs," Jackson replied.

"All right, we need to collect Mr. Rhoads, Maryanne, and her parents and see if we cannot get this matter cleared up this evening so Mr. Donaldson can be released immediately." Sheriff McGuire rose from his rocker.

"Mr. Rhoads? That name is not familiar to me," I noted.

"Mr. Rhoads joined our community last month as our county prosecutor when Mr. Burns retired," Sheriff McGuire informed me, shaking Jackson's hand. "I will round up everyone and meet you all back at your house. If you do not mind, I would like to hold off on informing Ms. Kendrick of Ms. Larkin's testimony. I will tell her there were a few inconsistencies with her story that need to be cleared up."

"Very well." They walked us to their front door. "I shall meet you all there shortly. Again, I apologize for interrupting your evening, but I felt it necessary under the circumstances," Jackson told them.

"I am glad you did. Thank you, Mr. Chandler, Mrs. Chandler." Mrs. McGuire smiled softly and closed the door behind us.

Emily escorted Greta to the dining room to remain unseen when we heard the two carriages arrive at my in-laws' home. Carley poured her some coffee and stayed in there with her until we gave Maryanne the opportunity to be honest. Emily had asked that Mrs. Donaldson remain upstairs with Mr. Donaldson in their guest room, citing that those who were coming over were going to be discussing aspects of the case that she was not privy to. Both Robert and Jackson wanted to avoid Mrs. Donaldson's reaction to Greta's evidence in front of so many witnesses.

The Chandler's housekeeper, Susan, showed our guests to the parlor and then served all of us some tea. Maryanne looked extremely uncomfortable as she sat down beside her parents. She continually fidgeted with the small fan in her hands and kept her eyes on the floor.

"All right, Sheriff, you have us all here. Now will you tell us what this is all about?" Mr. Rhoads, a short, round, balding man asked. He was clearly not happy about having his Sunday evening disturbed.

Sheriff McGuire walked over to our hearth and lit his pipe. Leaning one arm on the mantle he angled himself in Maryanne's direction. "Well, as I already told you, Mr. Rhoades, I asked you all here to settle the matter of several inconsistencies in Ms. Kendrick's statement. Therefore, I wanted to get this cleared up before we go to court tomorrow morning with Judge Albertson and formal charges are filed against Mr. Donaldson."

"I do not believe my daughter needs to recount anything. This attack has been most upsetting to her, and I do not want her to have to relive it again." Mr. Kendrick placed a protective hand over his daughter's fidgeting fingers.

"I agree. Maryanne already told you what happened," Mrs. Kendrick said, agreeing with her husband.

"I am afraid it is necessary. Maryanne?" The Sheriff drummed his fingers on the mantle impatiently.

Maryanne finally looked up and scanned the room, realizing all eyes were upon her. She shifted slightly in her seat and did her best to give us a performance worthy of experiencing such an attack. She began recounting her story, conveniently leaving out that Greta was with her and that she was the one who had acted hostilely when she had grabbed Dimitri's arm and slapped his face. She was such a talented manipulator that she managed to even whip up a few tears as she described their alleged struggle and her narrow escape to the Cain's household.

"Ms. Kendrick, you stated that you were out walking alone just after dark, correct?" Sheriff McGuire asked, and Maryanne nodded in response. "Why were you out alone?"

"Are you suggesting that my daughter deserved to be attacked because she went for a walk after supper?" Mr. Kendrick asked angrily.

"No, not at all," the Sheriff assured him. "Did you ever strike Mr. Donaldson when you were struggling to break away from him?"

Maryanne's eyes widened just a smidgen. "I am not sure, I may have."

"Are you positive that everything you have told me about this event is the God's honest truth?" Sheriff McGuire asked.

"I do not appreciate what you are implying, Sheriff McGuire." Mr.

Kendrick's voice turned hostile as he put a protective arm around his daughter, who sat there dabbing her false tears with a handkerchief.

"I am only asking because when she goes before Judge Albertson tomorrow, she will be giving sworn testimony. Do you understand what that means, Maryanne? Because if there is evidence shown that disproves your account of the event then you can be charged with perjury," the Sheriff said.

"Yes, of course. I wouldn't lie about something like this," Maryanne said, continuing her charade.

"All right, then, Mr. Chandler?" Sheriff nodded to my husband who left the room for a moment and returned with Greta.

The look on Maryanne's face was priceless when Greta walked into the room. Initially, her eyes widened in disbelief and fear. Then they narrowed in a leer, an almost threatening manner as they rested on Greta. I couldn't help but notice the distressed look in Greta's eyes as she stood awkwardly in the corner away from Maryanne.

"I do not understand. What is *she* doing here?" Maryanne asked through gritted teeth.

"Ms. Kendrick, would you care to revise your statement?" Jackson asked, trying not to smile.

"Whatever outlandish story Greta has told you is an outright lie!" Maryanne spat, jumping to her feet.

"It is time to tell the truth, Maryanne," Greta said as she stared her down.

"I am telling the truth!" Maryanne's face was crimson.

"You claim you love Dimitri. If that is true, why would you want to destroy his life this way? Don't you get it? Your lies caused his father to have another heart attack. How can you live with that knowledge? I can't!" Greta fired back in a much more civil tone.

"What is she talking about, Maryanne?" Mrs. Kendrick asked, rising to her feet.

"She is lying! I swear, Mother. She is lying just to hurt me. I have no idea why," Maryanne insisted.

"Young lady, Ms. Larkin's story matches Mr. Donaldson's account of what transpired perfectly, and I am positive that they have not been together to collaborate a story," Sheriff McGuire told Maryanne.

"Oh, Maryanne, how could you do such a thing?" Mrs. Kendrick was clearly surprised. Her father looked as if someone had slapped him across the face.

"In light of this information, I feel we should go release Mr. Donaldson immediately." Mr. Rhoads rose to his feet. "Ms. Larkin, I appreciate you coming forward no matter how long it took for your conscience to haunt you," Mr. Rhoads's voice was dripping with sarcasm. "As for you, Ms. Kendrick, I expect you to be in my office at nine tomorrow morning to discuss your pending charges."

"Charges?" Maryanne's jaw dropped. "But I ..." Her voice trailed off.

"She will be there." Mr. Kendrick took a firm hold of his daughter's arm. "Don't you have anything to say for yourself?"

"I apologize," she said, crying real tears.

"Sheriff McGuire, Mr. Rhoads, Mr. Chandler, Mr. Chandler, ladies, I sincerely apologize on behalf of my daughter. Until tomorrow." Mr. Kendrick led his daughter and his wife to the front door.

Once the commotion settled down, Reverend Jacobs took Greta home for the evening. Mr. Rhoads, Sheriff McGuire, and Jackson left shortly thereafter to release Mr. Dimitri. I helped Emily and Susan tidy up the parlor. It had been a weekend filled with emotional turmoil and everyone was utterly spent. I said good night to my in-laws so that the two of them could go upstairs and have a long talk with Mr. and Mrs. Donaldson regarding the evening's resolutions. I was happy to forego my participation in it.

I headed directly upstairs once I returned home. I got myself ready for bed and then paced our bedroom. I felt elated that Dimitri had been exonerated of all charges and wished I could be there when Jackson told him, but I wasn't allowed to go. I checked the window periodically, hoping that Jackson would be home soon.

CHAPTER THIRTY-SEVEN

SUNDAY, May 29, 2010

I had no clue what time we'd finally made it home last night. All I knew was my head was screaming and the little bit of light that was bleeding through the blinds was only making it worse. I could hear the rest of the family downstairs moving about. The noise was only compounding my headache. I pulled Jackson's empty pillow over my face and rolled over. I wasn't sure what time it was, but I did know it was way too early for me to be awake.

So, I drifted back off once again.

Jackson gently rubbed my back sometime later, trying to arouse me from a deep slumber. I felt his weight as he sat down on the bed beside me. "Hey darling, it is past time you got up."

"Go away." My head was still killing me.

"Sorry, I cannot do that. Our barbecue is beginning in an hour." He pulled the blanket off me. "I will start the shower for you. I put some aspirin and a Bloody Mary on the dresser. Phoebe swears by it. She said you will feel like a new lady."

I reluctantly dragged my exhausted rear out of bed and made my way over the dresser. I put the aspirin on my tongue and then gulped down the Bloody Mary. It tasted so nasty. I hated tomato juice, always had and always would. I outwardly shuddered and joined Jackson in the bathroom.

"How much did I drink last night?" My beautiful husband was adjusting the water temperature for me. "I think you drank your body weight in hard lemonades." Jackson flipped the switch, turning the shower spigot on.

"I thought you were drinking too?" I leaned against the wall with my eyes barely open.

"I stopped after my second beer. I figured it was truly your graduation with your friends and I wanted you to enjoy yourself." He walked over to me and helped me get undressed. "The shower will help clear your head." He took my hand and helped me into the shower. "I will be downstairs. Holler if you need me."

"Thank you, honey," I said before he closed the bathroom door behind him.

I emerged from our bedroom an hour and a half later feeling like the new lady Phoebe had promised me. She was right. The Bloody Mary and aspirin had worked wonders in combination with the hot shower. I curled my hair, did my full makeup, and even put on this adorable spaghetti strap navy blue summer dress that Sidney had picked out for me in New Orleans. It was tight across the bodice but then flared into a full skirt that rested just above my knees. Jackson loved it and teased me about it being my June Cleaver dress. The top of the dress had a cream paisley design crocheted into it with similar patterns scattered throughout the skirt. I stepped into my matching cream sandals that had thick ribbons that wrapped around my ankles, which I tied in a bow on the back of my lower calves. They were darling.

Our families were already enjoying themselves in the veranda out back. Robert was grilling steaks and barbecue chicken and having a beer with my dad. Landon and Sidney were sitting with Phoebe and Emily around the seating area. The children were running around the yard chasing Alex, and Leslie and Carson were having a conversation with Ethan and Liang.

I stood in the doorway watching my family and feeling very proud. But my eyes did not find the one I knew would be missing … my mother. Even though I knew she would not be here, it still upset me that even after all that had happened, all she had put me through, she could not find it in her heart to celebrate my graduation from high school with me.

Before anyone noticed my presence, I backed up into the house and out of their line of vision. I walked directly out the front door and began walking across the street to my former home. I wasn't sure what was running through my mind or what I was even hoping to accomplish by walking over there. I only knew that I was upset and felt it necessary to finally voice my opinion on it.

The air was hot and sticky, the humidity high. There was only a slight breeze struggling to penetrate the stifling sauna. The grass had lost some of its luster and moisture and was starting to feel harsh. I could hear the blades breaking from dryness under my feet. My mother's car was parked in its usual spot, so I knew she was home and had not been called away by the hospital. I walked steadily with determination before I could change my mind.

I walked in the front door without even bothering to knock. I came to a halt in the foyer with my hand still on the doorknob. The house was dead silent. My mom had to either be in her room or her office. I scanned over the area and decided to check her office first. I closed the front door and walked through the kitchen to my parents' office. The door was open, and my mother was sitting on the small couch reading a book. She didn't even notice my arrival.

"That must be some book," I said, clearly catching her off guard.

"It is," she said coolly, barely glancing up. "What do you want?"

"I want to know why you are not across the street with the rest of the family celebrating my high school graduation."

"We have been over this, Jocelyn. I have nothing further to say on the matter." My mother continued looking at her book instead of me.

"No, what I believe you said was you were not going to participate in or attend my wedding. You never stated that you were boycotting my graduation as well." I leaned against the doorframe and crossed my arms in across my chest.

"I went to your graduation yesterday. I saw you walk across the stage under *his* name instead of your own."

"You are mistaken. I graduated under my legal name, Jocelyn Alyssa Chandler," I replied.

"Then you are a fool and I have no time for fools." She shook her head ever so slightly but still would not make eye contact with me.

"And I think you are horrible, truly horrible," I spat.

"And I did not raise my daughter to talk to me that way." My mother tossed her book aside and stood up. "Why are you even here, Jocelyn? You got what you wanted, you're married, you're going to Boston for college. Why are you here?" she demanded.

"Because you are my mother and across the street is a barbecue celebrating mine and my husband's graduation from high school. If you ever cared about me, if you ever loved me, you would join me and the rest of my family in celebrating this milestone in our lives." I tried to remain calm despite the fact that my stomach was churning so badly I wanted to vomit.

"You expect me to break bread with the people who allowed my high school aged daughter to get married under their care? These people who talk you into applying to a school fourteen hours away from your home? I think not." She put her hand on her hip trying to control her anger.

"I know you are miserably married, and you have been for years. But that is your marriage, not mine," I started to explain.

"And do you really think yours is going to be so different, young lady? Don't you think we started out just like you and Jackson? All flowers, chocolate, and wine. We couldn't keep our hands off each other. But then our careers started taking off, we had children, and suddenly there were not enough hours in the day to get everything done. And we were tired, God, we were exhausted. Then one day I realized that we just didn't talk anymore or do anything else," she said hotly.

"Really, Mother, you are going to blame your career and your children for the failure of your marriage? Our presence had nothing to do with the success or failure of your marriage. A marriage is work, hard work ... daily work and you are right, it is not easy, but I have also learned that open communication is vitally important to the relationship," I scoffed back at her.

"Seriously? You've been married for fifteen minutes. Trust me, little girl, you know nothing!" she mocked.

"You know, I honestly do not know why I even bothered to come over here." I rolled my eyes at her with disbelief. "I cannot believe I thought you might actually miss me or care about me."

"That's where you're so wrong. I do care about you very much." She shifted her weight from one foot to the other. "Damn it, Jocelyn. I love you ... more than anything in this world. You are my daughter. Your happiness and your future are all that matters to me."

"Then why can you not understand that I am happy, and that Jackson is my future? My happiness is irreparably tied to his," I explained.

"Good grief, Jocelyn, grow up. Life is not a fairy tale. You need to learn that now before you wake up in five years and don't recognize the stranger in your bed."

I took a deep breath and tried to count to ten before responding. "Mom, I only came over here to invite you to join me and my family in an afternoon barbecue to celebrate my high school graduation. That is all I wanted. You are more than welcome. I love you and I hope you decide to join us." I took a step back from the doorway. "Goodbye, Mother. I hope to see you soon." And before she could say another word I rushed out of the house, so she would not see the tears welling up in my eyes.

I paused on the front porch, trying to catch my breath. I brushed the tears off my cheeks and did my best not to smear my makeup. I wasn't sure what I'd been expecting to accomplish by going over there. I only knew that I needed to try and mend the bridge between us. My mother and I had never been close, or even friends, but she was my mother and even though I did not particularly like her very much, I did love her.

I slowly descended the steps and walked down the walkway back to my home. The heat was still stifling, the air … sticky, but everything felt a little different. I felt proud of myself that at least I'd ended our heated discussion by rising above it and leaving with a true sentiment. Despite how truly difficult it was for me to even cross the street and enter that house again, I felt all the better for having done it.

I stopped in the bathroom in the hallway downstairs and double-checked my makeup before heading outside. I didn't want Jackson to know I'd been crying. I knew it would only upset him and this was supposed to be a party. I dabbed my eyes with a tissue and freshened my lipstick. I looked myself over in the mirror.

You can do this.

I took a deep breath, opened the door, and joined the festivities.

There was an enormous amount of food, dishes, appetizers, and desserts displayed across numerous folding tables for all the guests to consume at their leisure. In the center table was an outlandish bouquet of flowers in our school colors with multiple helium balloons attached. Sitting in front of it was a full-sized red velvet cake that had cream cheese frosting, a picture of our school mascot in the upper corner, and had *Congratulations Jackson & Jocelyn, Class of 2010* printed across the top. When it came to hosting a party my mother-in-law never missed a beat.

The afternoon passed by smoothly into the evening hours. As twilight set in Alex lit the bonfire, which was enclosed by stone in a pit in the center of the veranda. Several friends from school had made appearances while they made their rounds to classmates' open houses. Caitlyn and Zak arrived around four and stayed. Jenna and Kyle brought Hilary and Cody with them before seven and stuck around.

I snuggled on the double rocker with Jackson, sharing stories and munching on various foods. I was so happy to be right there surrounded by those I dearly loved. Then it felt like a bucket of ice water got thrown on our bonfire and all that was left was a smoldering mess of damp wood hidden beneath a cloud of smoke.

"Amy, how nice of you to join us." Emily rose to greet my mom as she awkwardly entered our backyard from between the houses.

My head jerked around so quickly my temple collided with Jackson's cheekbone. "Mom?"

"Hello, sorry to interrupt. May I join you?" she asked in her forced pleasant voice that I knew she only broke out with when she had to be around people she would rather not associate with.

"Of course." Emily smiled genuinely and led her over to a chair that Robert set next to my dad.

"I wanted to stop by and congratulate our graduates." My mom stopped a few feet in front of the double rocker. "Jocelyn." I stood up and embraced her tightly.

"Thank you," I whispered.

She didn't reply but instead patted me softly on the back before releasing me.

"Congratulations, Jackson." Much to my surprise my husband stood and hugged my mom.

"Thank you, Dr. Timmons."

I made the introductions between my mom and Jackson's siblings, their spouses, and children. Everyone shook hands and exchanged pleasantries before my mom took her seat. An uncomfortable silence lingered amongst the group. My dad reached over after a couple minutes passed and took my mother's hand in his own. It was a simple gesture, but it filled my heart that despite their flawed marriage there was something still there no matter how hidden it seemed.

It took some nudging, a lot of nudging, but everyone eventually relaxed under the watchful eye of Dr. Amy Timmons. The atmosphere wasn't nearly as lively as before, still, at least for the first time since my surprise eighteenth birthday party, everyone was together in the same place and no one was yelling. I considered that a tremendous progress.

* * *

Once everyone had retired to their respective homes and Jackson and I were alone for the first time since he'd woke me that morning, we finally got the chance to talk. I got undressed in the bathroom and slipped into the shower trying to rid my body of the thin layer of perspiration from the humidity that felt like a layer of film all over me. I stood under the hot water and closed my eyes just letting it rain down on my head and flow over my shoulders.

"Are you all right?" My gorgeous husband stepped in the shower beside me.

"I am exhausted." I rested my forehead against his chest.

"Today was interesting," he said with hesitation.

"I think it could not have gone better." I looked up into his piercing green eyes.

"When did you talk to your mother? I know she did not come over here of her own accord."

"I went over there after I got ready. I just walked in the front door and found her in her study reading a book." I leaned against him. "We had a heated exchange and said some nasty things to each other. Then I told her if she ever loved me or cared about me at all she would make an appearance."

"Whatever you said worked. I almost fell out of my seat when she walked through the gate," he admitted. "The look on everyone else's face was absolutely priceless."

"I know, especially my father's. I thought for a second he was going to have a coronary." We held each other and giggled under the water.

"Anyway, I think it is a wonderful start. I am proud of you for making the effort to made amends with your mother before we move." Jackson kissed the top of my head lovingly. "I know it was not easy for you considering all that she has done."

"No, it wasn't," I agreed.

We crawled into bed together. I curled up beside Jackson with my head on his chest and my damp hair flowing across his arm. I closed my eyes and listened to the sound of his heartbeat. It had been an incredibly long and emotional day. I was worn down and didn't even want to think about the next day when I knew I was going to have to start packing up our lives here. This was the only home I had ever known and as excited as I was about moving to Boston and starting BU in the fall, there was still a twinge of sadness in my heart to leave it all behind.

CHAPTER THIRTY-EIGHT

Thursday, June 3, 1879

Light rain continued to cover our already darkened world. Yesterday we'd said our final farewell to Thomas and Christina. They were buried side by side in a plot on top of the hill in the cemetery just outside of town. Over half the community had come out and stood in the rain to say goodbye to the beautiful couple.

I had gotten to the point that I hated this cemetery. It seemed like only yesterday that we were here saying goodbye to Uncle Monte and Mimi shortly before him and yet, here we were again, saying farewell to two lives cut short too early. It didn't seem fair.

I rolled over in bed and stared out the window. I loved the sound of the rain hitting the roof. It was soothing, comforting, and brought better memories of my childhood of playing in the rain with William. I knew Cora would be up here soon to rouse me out of bed. But today, I simply wanted to remain where I was ... snuggled down beneath the covers where all the terrible things that had occurred recently didn't reside.

Instead, it was Jackson who came bursting through the door. He was wet and flushed as he took his overcoat off and tossed it at the chair in front of my vanity. I sat up immediately wondering what was amiss. Jackson never wore his overcoat upstairs and certainly never tracked rain and mud through the house.

"Jackson? What in the world?"

"They caught them!" He sat down on the edge of the bed beside me. "Sheriff

McGuire and his deputy caught them last night. They were attacking another lady. Your father is attending to her now. She also worked for Ms. Robertson. Apparently, she was returning from a visit from someone in our area of town, she would not specify whom, but anyway, they dragged her into an alley and did horrible things to her."

"Oh, my goodness, that's terrifying. They were that close to home? They must have remained in the area after they attacked Christina and Thomas," I noted.

"Yes, they were," Jackson told me.

"Did Sheriff McGuire come by your office? How did you find out about all this if it just happened?" I wondered.

"That is the strange part. These two criminals requested me specifically to defend them."

"What!" I felt a chill run down my spine. "How do they even know who you are?"

"That is what you are not going to believe. And since they were apprehended in the act, there is no doubt they are guilty." Jackson shook his head and ran his fingers through his wet curls. "They want me to help them with a plea deal. And I simply cannot do it. I went down to the jail this morning with Sheriff McGuire and I still cannot believe it."

"I do not understand, Jackson." He wasn't making much sense. "You know them?"

"Yes, and so do you. One very well and the other you've met casually over the years. He was up here from Louisville, Kentucky visiting family."

"Louisville, Kentucky? I do not believe I know anyone from there." No one came to mind.

"Yes, you do. I know you do. Although you may not recall, or he may not have told you that was where he was from. But the other makes me so upset I am beside myself this morning."

"Who?" Curiosity was killing me.

"Theodore and his cousin, Peter." Jackson said flatly.

"Theodore Norris? Laurie's Theodore?" He nodded.

I sat there so stunned I couldn't find words to respond with. Theodore ... a man I had known my entire life. We had grown up together, were the same age, spent countless hours with our same group of friends. It couldn't be. This man was engaged to one of my closest friends. He had attended my wedding, every birthday party since I could remember, and I his. He had eaten at our table numerous times. There had to be some mistake. It just couldn't be possible.

"How could he ...? Are you sure?" A tear of sheer disbelief and horror slid down my cheek. "Does Laurie know?" I couldn't imagine what she was going through.

"Sheriff McGuire was heading over to the Cain household when we parted leaving the jail."

"Oh, my God. Poor Laurie," I mumbled.

"I know this is going to come as quite a shock to her and to the rest of the community once word gets out. I hate to think of what Mr. and Mrs. Norris are going through. They are such kind people," Jackson noted.

"I need to go to Laurie's." I tossed off my covers and climbed out of bed.

"Of course." Jackson stood up and went to the doorway, calling Cora to help me ready myself.

By lunch Jackson and I were in the carriage with Davonte at the reigns. The rain had increased in intensity and was pounding down upon us. The world outside was dark as black clouds hovered over the city. I leaned my head against Jackson's shoulder and sat there consumed in my own thoughts. I couldn't wrap my brain around the fact that Theodore did all those horrible things. I could not fathom that he had it in him to be so cruel as to harm, let alone torture, rape, and murder an innocent person. And how could be have ever done such despicable acts to Christina and Thomas. He had known them his whole life. What kind of sociopath could do such a thing to those he claimed to love? Yesterday, he had stood beside Laurie at the funeral and wept alongside all of us. The memory made me sick to my stomach.

Davonte pulled in front of the gate at the Cain's house attached to the mercantile. He climbed down and opened the carriage door holding an umbrella for Jackson and me. He was kind enough to hold it over us as we made our way to their front door to keep us from getting soaked in the downpour.

Mr. Cain answered the door. He looked defeated and worn. He nodded his head at us but never said a word as he stepped aside to let us enter. Laurie was on the lounge sobbing into her mother's shoulder. Sheriff McGuire was standing over by the mantel looking at if he'd rather be anywhere else then here.

"Mr. Chandler, Mrs. Chandler, nice of you to stop by. I was just explaining procedures to Laurie and her parents." Sheriff McGuire walked over to us and shook Jackson's hand.

"Of course," Jackson replied. I smiled at our Sheriff, nodded, and walked over to Laurie.

I sat down on the other side of her and gently rubbed her back. Laurie was distraught. Who could blame her? I couldn't imagine what she was going through learning that her fiancé was a serial killer. He had managed to fool everyone who'd ever met him.

"Mr. Chandler, I understand that you spoke with Mr. Norris?" Mr. Cain asked.

"Yes, Sheriff McGuire told me the assailants requested me personally. At that time, I did not know who they were," Jackson explained.

"Are you going to represent them?" Mrs. Cain spoke up.

"No, I told them I could not." Jackson shook his head. "Even my father refused to take the case."

"Good, I am happy to hear that." Mr. Cain walked over to the mantel and lit his pipe. "I cannot believe this nightmare. He made fools out of us all."

"Yes, sir," Jackson agreed with obvious distain. "I did tell them that their best bet was to plead guilty and throw themselves at the mercy of the court."

"They will be sentenced to death if they plead guilty, will they not?" Mrs. Cain inquired, still comforting her daughter.

"Yes, I believe so. Judge Albertson has no tolerance for murderers. I believe his judgement will be swift and harsh," Sheriff McGuire added.

"They deserve nothing less. If I had to be the one to pass sentencing, I would have done to them what they did to their victims. An eye for an eye. That's what the good book says." Mr. Cain inhaled deeply on his pipe.

A knock on the door ended the conversation. Mr. Cain walked over and answered it. To my surprise Judge Albertson was on the other side along with Deputy Martin. The judge did not wait for Mr. Cain to invite him in, he just waltzed through the door like he owned the place.

Judge Albertson was a large man with square shoulders. He was balding on top with salt and pepper hair, more salt then pepper. He had a very distinguished looking mustache and goatee that was also more salt then pepper. He wore wire rim spectacles that hid his unemotional hazel eyes. The very air around him commanded respect.

"Good afternoon, everyone, I thought I would find you all here." He handed Gracie his top hat and overcoat. "I just spoke to the suspects and I am happy to say that they both pleaded guilty and waved their right to a trial by jury."

"What does that mean exactly?" Mrs. Cain inquired.

"They both confessed to their crimes. Therefore, I found it unnecessary to drag out this nasty business and passed sentencing. Both declared they wanted things handled swiftly and were very stoic about it."

"And their sentence?" Mr. Cain asked the question we were all wondering.

"Death by hanging," Judge Albertson answered without missing a beat. Laurie let out a low wail. "I apologize for the blunt delivery, but I had no other choice considering what the two had done."

"When?" Jackson asked.

"Day after tomorrow," Deputy Martin spoke up for the first time. "Mr. and Mrs. Norris are with them now."

"This must be tearing their world apart," Mrs. Cain stated empathetically.

"This has torn more than one family apart," Mr. Cain said flatly.

I sat there in silence listening to the men discuss the legal aspects of the case and then they tried to contemplate how Theodore could have done such a heinous thing. No one knew much about his cousin Peter, who had acted alongside Theodore, but the previous encounters everyone present had had with him, he had given the impression of being a well brought up and polite young man. The fact that there were no indications leading up to this made it more difficult for everyone to even attempt to understand. Not that it was even possible to understand how someone could do something like this.

The afternoon slowly turned into evening and I realized I had yet to eat anything today. My stomach began to rumble, reminding me that I needed to eat something sometime soon or I was going to get a wicked headache. I glanced over at my husband hoping he was in the same predicament as me. I knew he had to be hungry as well.

We finally left by dinnertime. Laurie had retired to her room without as much as a word to anyone. She was exhausted and had just had her entire world destroyed in one day. There was nothing any of us could say to her to make her feel any better. I felt horrible for her. She had said she wanted to be alone and her mother had helped her to her room. I hugged her tightly and reassured her that I would be here for her for whatever she needed. I told her I would stop by tomorrow. She just nodded and left the room.

Jackson and I rode home in silence. The rain had finally turned to a light drizzle. Evening was setting in early due to the number of thick clouds that lingered about. I rested my head against Jackson's shoulder. My mind was a whirlwind of thought.

"When you saw Theodore, did you ask him why?" I couldn't stop myself from inquiring.

"Yes." Jackson turned towards the window.

"What did he say?"

"He said because he enjoyed the adrenaline rush it gave him." His voice was flat and hollow.

"What? That is the most ridiculous explanation I have ever heard."

"I agree," Jackson mumbled.

"Did he say anything else?" I asked.

"Like regarding Laurie or his family and what his actions must be doing to them?" his voice was seething with anger.

"Yes," I said.

"Actually, I asked him about them." He turned from the window and looked at me. "And you know what he replied with?" I shook my head almost afraid to hear his response. "He said he just made them famous."

"How ludicrous," I was disgusted.

"I told him no one would remember him except for those whose lives he destroyed." Jackson rolled his eyes and shook his head slightly. "I could not believe the sheer audacity of that man. And his cousin was even worse. He just laughed and smiled the whole time. I cannot say I was not tempted to strike them both."

"I can understand why."

* * *

Finally, in bed with a full belly, a heavy heart, and fear for what tomorrow might bring, I closed my eyes. I rested my head on Jackson's chest and took comfort in the strength of his beating heart. I wanted desperately to drift off into my *other* life just to escape the harshness of the world around me. I wanted to get in my car and drive with the windows down and the radio turned up. I wanted to feel the wind on my face, blowing through my hair, the sun beaming down on me. I wanted to shoot hoops with Ethan in the driveway, dance around with my girlfriends singing loudly and off key. I wanted to twirl around on the dance floor in my prom dress with Jackson again. I wanted to disappear from this world and float away to the *other*. Even for a little while just to ease the pain that was lying so heavy upon me.

CHAPTER THIRTY-NINE

THURSDAY, June 1, 2010

The house was still slumbering peacefully when I rolled out of bed. It was a good while before dawn and I was too restless to sleep. I snuck downstairs trying not to awaken anyone and started up a fresh pot of coffee. My heart and head were too consumed with the world I had briefly left behind, and sleep was not going to give me any peace.

I wandered out onto the veranda to watch the sunrise. I sat down on a lounge chair and immediately realized the cushions were cold and slightly damp from the morning dew. I slowly sipped my hot coffee and brushed a tear off my cheek. I was still in shock with what Theodore had done. My mind simply could not process the why of it all. He had grown up with Thomas and Christina. We were all friends and had spent countless hours together throughout our young lives. I was so angry with Theodore. I wanted to grab him, shake him, demand answers from him.

I couldn't seem to shake that horrible sense of loss for all those who had left my life in the last few months. Tears streamed down my face for Mimi, Uncle Monte, Christine, and Thomas. And even for Laurie. My heart went out to her as well. I know she was living in her own personal hell and there was nothing I could do to make her feel any better. She had been engaged to a monster, who had fooled us all into believing he was a gentleman.

I hated Theodore with every fiber of my being.

* * *

Sidney came by just before eleven to take me out to lunch. I was excited to finally get to spend some time alone with her. I was anxious to speak with her and see how she was adjusting to *EVE*. Our schedules permitted very little time for us to spend together although our phone calls and texting had increased tenfold since spring break. I knew she was still struggling with the concept. Hell, I was too, and I had several months head start on her. Not to mention I had Jackson and his family to lean on and help me adjust.

Sidney was wearing a white jean mini skirt, a grey cotton sleeveless shirt with a small ruffle along the neckline. She wore a long silver chained necklace with clear, white, soft pink, and dark pink jewels hanging loosely between her breasts. She had a shorter one with the same jewels around her neck except that silver chain had a burgundy ribbon intertwined through it. At the end of her beautifully tanned, shapely legs were stylish black sandals with multi-colored jewels across the tops. Her long blond hair cascaded down her back and across her shoulders. She was so elegantly styled she was stunning looking.

And for once, knowing my older sister was going to be dressed to the nines, I had put a lot more effort into my attire than I normally would. So today my hair was curled, my make-up was carefully applied, and I was wearing a soft blue sheer summer dress that flowed gracefully to my mid-thigh. The tan ribbon-adorned sandals added the perfect touch along with the beaded necklace and matching earrings. Jackson loved it when he entered our room. He twirled me around and kissed me deeply telling me how sexy I looked.

We decided to stop at a little café in the center of town. It was a cute little place that had the best coffee and paninis for miles. There was a long lunch counter, tables, booths, accented by various plants, tables of baked breads and desserts. It had a charming atmosphere with a relaxed feel about it. Sidney and I found a booth in the back corner and ordered our sandwiches.

"Where is Landon?" I asked after the waitress disappeared with our orders.

"Golfing with dad," she chuckled. "And Landon is so bad at golf."

"That's all right, so is dad." I shrugged.

"I cannot believe you are already out of high school. It doesn't seem like you should be old enough."

"I am married, Sidney."

"I know, I can't believe that one either. Although you did pick a very good man. I really do like Jackson. And his family is great. They are so supportive of you guys and they must have been invaluable to you when you first learned about *EVE*," she said.

"Yes, they were. I know we have been talking more and texting, but I feel badly that I could not be there for you more," I told her.

"Don't feel too badly, Uncle Nicholas has been amazing. I believe I have been driving him a little crazy as much as I have been leaning on him," she admitted.

"Really? I was unaware you two were talking. He never told me." I really shouldn't have been surprised, as caring a person as he was, I knew he'd be concerned about her at Northwestern all by herself.

"Yes, he has been so wonderful and patient with me. I call him for clarification when things aren't clear or don't make sense to me. He has helped me out so much. I know I would be lost without him," Sidney said.

"I love him so much. I just hate the fact that he is alone. I spoke with him about transferring up to a university near or in Boston," I told her.

"He told me he was considering it. I told him I thought it would be great for him." She smiled.

The waitress dropped off our lunch and we both dug right in. I was starving, and I absolutely loved the food here. Plus, their mocha lattes were to die for. I sank my teeth right into my panini and listened to Sidney ramble on about her summer classes and her relationship with Landon. I was surprised to learn that they had moved into a little apartment together on campus. A part of me wanted to tell her that they get married in a couple of years, but I knew I couldn't say anything. Instead of biting my lip I decided it was safer to change the subject.

"So, 1848 huh? What is that like?" I inquired.

"Different. Bizarre. Weird. Delightful. I have the most wonderful man in my life." Sidney's face lit up like a Christmas tree.

"Really? What is his name? Tell me all about the bum?" I playfully teased her.

"His name is Keifer Marshall. He is a couple years older than I am and he is hardly a bum. In fact, he is in medical school studying to be a doctor. He is almost finished, and I think when he does, he is going to ask me to marry him."

"That is great. I am so happy for you!" I exclaimed. I didn't want to tell her I already knew him well and that I thought he was more perfect for her than Landon.

"And he has the most beautiful green eyes with sandy blond hair and dimples. He's tall, muscular, and has the best sense of humor." She giggled. "He makes me laugh all the time. I never know what he's going to do next. So that keeps life interesting."

"He sounds wonderful."

"He is. I could not be happier with him, but I admit it is so strange now that things are becoming clearer. Imagine how strange it is to spend a fabulous day with Keifer, go to bed at the end of the evening with a smile on my face thinking about him only to open my eyes to Landon lying beside me in bed," Sidney said.

"I honestly cannot imagine it. I know Alex and Phoebe do it and they both seem happy with it, but I am so happy that I have Jackson with me on both planes," I admitted.

"It is a shame I did not meet Alex first," she laughed.

"True, but it would not have done you much good in 1848. He was not alive yet." I laughed with her.

"Damn, I cannot win this one." Sidney shook her head. "Guess I will have to keep the two I have then."

"Yeah, damn the bad luck. I am sure it is such a sacrifice having two extremely hot and sexy men to spend your days with. I feel so bad for you." My voice dripped with sarcasm.

"True, it is a sacrifice, but somebody has to do it." Sidney gave me a coy look and flipped her blond hair over her shoulder making me laugh all the harder at her.

"Seriously though, how is 1848?" I calmed down and asked.

"I'm adjusting, I suppose. It is so weird. The clothes, the styles, the mannerisms, the buggies, all of it. You honestly cannot tell me that you enjoy the weight of those gowns and do not get me started on the layers and the corsets. Dear Lord, it is ridiculous," she confessed.

"I know, I had such a hard time adjusting to those. But you have to admit they do wonders for our waistline."

"Okay, that much I will give you. But you cannot tell me you are entirely comfortable in all that garb. It is barely June and I hate to think about what this summer is going to be like without central air conditioning. Talk about miserable." Sidney took a long drink of her caramel latte.

"But don't you love the extreme difference in family dynamics? That, I think, was the most surprising aspect," I said.

"Well, considering I was raised by my grandmother, I rarely see my father or my little brothers, and my step-monster despises me for looking like my deceased mother. I believe my experience in that category somewhat differs from yours," Sidney said with one eyebrow raised.

"I am sorry. I had not thought about that. That must be difficult on you," I noted.

"Nonsense. I have the most loving, caring, and supportive grandmother anyone could want."

"And your grandfather? You have never mentioned him," I inquired.

"My grandfather, Ralph, passed away before I was born. Marissa speaks highly of him. She misses him dearly. I wish she would find someone else. There are several widowed men at church who have tried to court her, but she says that Ralph was the love of her life and she could never love another like she loves him. I have tried many times to tell her that she needs someone to be there for her, someone to talk to, spend time with ... someone who can be her companion. But she refuses to listen. Keifer and I have discussed it that after we are married, she will live with us. We will always take care of her," Sidney said with obvious love.

"I wish I could meet her. She sounds amazing."

"She is, and boy does she ever love Keifer. She thinks he is just adorable and so funny. She loves that he is so considerate of me and takes such good care of me." Her face radiated as she spoke of her love for her family *there*.

"I cannot imagine how strange it is to talk and see your little brothers *there* and *here* see them as grown men. That would be so bizarre." I shook my head slightly.

"Honestly, I'm still not sure what to think about that. I rarely see them, but when I do, it is truly inexplicable. And I hate to admit that I tend to favor Nicholas over Monte and Patrick. My dad, Walter, mentioned it to me once that I need to stop spoiling Nicholas over his brothers." She let out a small laugh. "I attributed it to him being the youngest. And he is so adorable which makes it easy for me to spoil him."

"It is hard for me to fathom what it must be like. Especially since you two have grown so close *here*. To see him as a child ..." I sighed audibly. "Must be amazing and unbelievable. I would love to be able to see him as a child. He must be so adorable."

"He is. He has the most incredible imagination and tells me stories about buggies that move without horses and people using devices to talk across locations. I honestly believe he is getting glimpses of his world *here* and is remembering them after he awakens."

"Really? Wow. There must be holes already developing in his conscious-ness," I noted.

"That's exactly what I thought. Whenever he tells me about them, I just laugh and add to it in a playful manner. I pretend along with him, but I also try not to elaborate too much to it for obvious reasons." Sidney let out a small snort with a sigh.

"I wonder if that is why he has spent his life trying to decipher *EVE*. I mean take Monte for instance. He resented it more than anything. I am not saying I do not understand his reasoning for what he did on this plane, but he never embraced it the same way Nicholas did," I observed.

"Monte is a peculiar child to say the least. I have not figured him out yet. He enjoys building things, odd things." She crinkled her brow. "He's odd."

"Sidney, he is just a kid." I giggled. "How weird can he be?"

"He makes Eddie Munster look normal," she remarked.

"Wow." I wasn't sure what to say.

"Anyway," I could tell she wanted to change the subject. "What do you think of all the free time on your hands now? I don't know about you but there are times when I feel like I am going stark raving mad from the silence. I believe I have read more books *there* than I ever have *here* and that includes college. There are times when I would give anything for my music or my iPad."

"I know exactly what you mean. The long hours during the day when Jackson is at the office are mind-numbing. And to be honest, I really suck at needle-point." I laughed. "All my brothers got to go to college and my father would faint if I even suggested it."

"I understand, but Jackson lets you study and learn new things, doesn't he?"

"Of course, but it is not the same." I shrugged.

"True, but at least it is something. Most women *there* don't even have that. The restrictions placed on us are stifling. I don't know how those women do it. At least we get the opportunity to go to college in one of our lives."

"Thank God for that. There are some amazing aspects of that world that I dearly love. I love my family and the closeness we share. I do love the clothes. I know they are heavy, restrictive, and uncomfortable, but they are so elegant and beautiful. I love the carriages, the peacefulness, and the closeness of the commu-nity. It is so different from the hectic, career-driven, everyone looking out for themselves mentality *here*," I pointed out.

"Not everyone is like that, you know. Some people are genuine, even on this plane. Granted, it is rare, but it does still exist. It's just a little harder to find."

"You know, I'm glad we're doing this. In my *other* life I have four older brothers who are so over-protective of me they don't let me breathe. My neighbor Olivia is about the closest thing I have to a sister. I was so thrilled when I found out I have an older sister *here* and then when I learned we weren't close it broke my heart. So, I promised myself that I would do anything to mend my relationship with you." I reached over and rested my hand over hers.

"I always wanted us to be close. I hated that we never had anything in common." Sidney smiled sweetly across the table at me. "Guess we cannot claim that now."

"Definitely not."

* * *

Sidney and I went from the café to the mall. We visited some vintage store we had never been to before and tried on some rather unique clothes. We giggled and teased with every ridiculous outfit we modeled for each other. Most of the clothes were from the 1970s, an era where styles were questionable at best. Sidney tried on the accessories to enhance each outfit and twirled around in front of the three-fold mirror.

For good measure, after an hour spent in the shop under the rolling eyes of the owner Sidney and I bought some tacky costume jewelry before we finally exited. We moved on to the next shop and another one after that. It was the first time in recent memory, if ever, that Sidney and I had been out alone and had so much fun together. I was truly going to miss her when I moved to Boston. I knew we'd talk, text, and hopefully visit, but days like this were certain to be a rarity. That knowledge made me a bit sad.

CHAPTER FORTY

SATURDAY, *June 13, 1879*

Jackson and I arrived at my parents' home for the celebration of my brother Patrick Jr.'s thirtieth birthday. My mother had outdone herself again. Half the town had shown up for the festivities. My mother had told me she wanted to do something spectacular to heal the wounds of our family as well as the community, which had suffered recently with the passing of Uncle Monte, Christina, and Thomas, the scandalous lies of Maryanne and the execution of Theodore and Peter. Thankfully, Maryanne moved to Charlestown to live with her aunt after she was forced to publically apologize the following Sunday to Dimitri and his family for all the harm her lies had caused.

Good riddance.

I was not sorry to see her go. She and the Nelson boys had been the focus of town gossip for the last couple weeks and finally, the subject had grown tiresome and people were hungry for the newest scandal to sink their teeth into.

People love drama regardless of the era.

I suppose it was not shocking. Everyone seemed to love a juicy story. Some things never did change throughout the ages. This past year had been filled with speculations, secret affairs, unexpected pregnancies, scandals, death, lies, and betrayal. No one ever said life was dull, even without social networking and modern technology.

My mother picked the perfect day to host my brother's party. His birthday had fallen on the previous Wednesday and she had gone back and forth about having the party before or after. Last weekend had been gray and rainy. She had chosen correctly. Today the skies were a brilliant clear blue with a few scattered fluffy clouds floating about. The temperature clung to the mid-seventies with a warm afternoon breeze, and little to no humidity. It was perfect.

Jackson looked perfect in his light gray suit, white shirt, black tie, and black suspenders. His boiler hat perched upon his crown of thick black wavy hair. I never tired of looking at him. The sun brought out the strong copper highlights in his hair and made him appear more irresistible. His emerald green eyes sparkled at me as he took my lacey-gloved hand in his.

The guests had spilled outside on the veranda and across the lawns. It appeared that the entire town had come out for the celebration. I would even venture to guess there were more people here than attended my eighteenth birthday party. Plus, I knew this display of attention was something that made my oldest brother most uncomfortable. His wife, Katherine, on the other hand, was sucking up all the attention she could get. She was practically making a spectacle of herself. The woman was shameless.

Jackson and I spotted Olivia and William mingling about in the backyard. Olivia was laughing with her arm linked through her young husband's. They really did look sweet together. I was thrilled to see them so happy together. Olivia was finally coming back to life after all she had endured this last year. She truly deserved to be happy.

William saw us across the lawn, smiled, and nodded in our direction. I loved my brothers, but William and I would always share a closely-knit bond. He was my first protector and my first knight in shining armor. William was the one who'd taught me to fish, teased me relentlessly, pulled my braids, let me cry on his shoulder, and spent countless nights watching over me during my night terrors. He was so incredibly special to me.

I held Jackson's hand and made the rounds, greeting guests, family, and friends. This was the single most important thing I loved the most about this era—the closeness of those near and dear to our hearts. For *here* there were no fast food restaurants, no impersonal social network that created the illusion of ties, no cell phones, no countless hours of mind-numbing television chipping away at brain cells. The world truly was bigger, more mysterious, wondrous, and enchanting on this plane. Family and communities worked together for the betterment of all. We knew our neighbors. They were our family, our friends. We didn't hear rumors about their successes, failures, triumphs, and tears ... we experienced it alongside them. Doors were seldom locked, a handshake was a stronger, more meaningful contract than a piece of paper and a man was only as good as his word.

I stood against one of the columns of veranda and considered all the changes to come about over the next hundred and thirty years and felt incredibly blessed to have the opportunity not to read about it in a textbook, but to live it. I knew my graduating peers in 2010 would never comprehend this world that I resided in. Most of what we were taught about this period in history, this time called the Industrial Revolution, didn't even begin to scratch the service of what it was truly like. Certainly, the world was changing rapidly around us and in that growth many of life's simplest joys had slowly started to decline.

It was difficult, if not impossible, for me to comprehend the existence of *EVE*. On both planes of my life I was no one special. I was simply a young girl in the final year of her primary education on the path that had been set out before me by my parents, whether it was going on to college to pursue a higher education or fulfilling the role of wife, mother, and running a household. Learning of *EVE* had altered every aspect of my young life, some for the better, some not ... depending on whom you asked.

In 2010 the evidence of *EVE* had brought about tremendous turbulence within my own household due to my growing relationship with Jackson. It had altered my college plans, tested bonds of friendship and family, and caused me to question my own sanity for a time. But what *EVE* had given me, taught me, far surpassed the initial cost. In exchange I found the man of my dreams, a family whose unconditional love was unparalleled to anything I had ever known, the friendship and love of an estranged family member, and the opportunity to develop a relationship with my sister. I'd also been given the ability to witness a life that was based on love, family, morals, and honor.

In 1879, the knowledge of *EVE* brought me back from the brink of hysterics, it delayed the growth of my family, while also reinforcing the importance of family, unity, and a deep appreciation for the simple thing's life had to offer. I got to witness the exceptional world that surpassed my wildest imagination. I was shown things that boggled my limited scope of reality. It allowed me to fulfill my thirst for knowledge, strengthened my independence, and had made me realize that the cost of all that was gained across the hundred-and-thirty-year time span was not worth all that was lost.

I rejoined the festivities, ate too much of Sara's delicious creations, and enjoyed the company of all those who existed in my little small corner of the world. It was days like this that proved to mean the most when I looked back on both my lives. I looked around at my friends and family together, talking and laughing, having fun, sharing their lives with each other, and I couldn't think of anywhere I'd rather be in either of my lives.

* * *

I wrapped myself around my husband and felt the familiar peace that washed over me when I heard the strong beating of his heart. Jackson held me in his arms and softly brushed my hair away from my face. His love, his strength, and his faith in our marriage offered me solace at the end of each day. I knew in my heart and my soul this was where I belonged.

"Thank you," I whispered to Jackson, running my fingers lightly across his sculpted chest.

"For?" I felt his head shift as he looked down at me. I looked up to meet his piercing green eyes.

"For this incredible life we share." I reached up and kissed my loving husband.

Jackson grinned mischievously and chuckled. "Trust me, you have not seen anything yet." He pulled me up to bring my lips to his. He kissed me hungrily, holding me tight against him. "I love you," he whispered, rolling over on top of me.

"I love you, too."

I fell asleep thinking of what was waiting for me when I was thrust into the twenty-first century reality. I was both excited and disheartened about leaving my family in Chicago and moving to Boston for college to begin my new life as Mrs. Jackson Chandler. My stomach was in knots thinking about all the new adventures that awaited us on the horizon the next time I opened my eyes. I snuggled in closer to Jackson and closed my eyes. I didn't want to miss a thing.

CHAPTER FORTY-ONE

SATURDAY, *June 11, 2010*

I leaned against our bedroom window, staring at the house across the street. I loved that home. I knew every nook and cranny, every squeak in the floorboards, every flaw, and every hiding spot. It was the center of my universe in every memory, both good and bad.

Jackson and I had spent all day yesterday over at Cody's house with Hilary, Jenna, Caitlyn, Liang, Kyle, Ethan, and Zak. They were kind enough to throw a surprise farewell pool party for us. We had such a great time, but it was sad as well. It was another goodbye I didn't want to have. All of them were family, and I loved them dearly.

But just as with everyone else our age, freshly graduated from high school, the time had come for us to all take that next step in life towards our futures, our dreams, our goals, and in becoming who we were destined to be. By the evening's end, we were all in tears, hugging and crying, carrying on as if we would never set eyes on one another again.

It was hard. It physically hurt. My chest felt hollow as we drove home. The not knowing when we'd all be together again. That option was no longer there for us to decide. The best we all could hope for was maybe Thanksgiving when we all returned home from school. It was an odd feeling, unsettling even, leaving them standing in front of Cody's house with no 'see you tomorrow' between us.

Jackson called my name from the bottom of the stairs breaking my train of thought. I took one last look at the house across the street and headed down to find my husband.

It was time to go.

I stood in the front yard, my feet wet with the morning dew, and watched the semi-truck pull away, carrying all our belongings. I wasn't sure if I wanted to cheer or cry that the day of our departure to Boston had finally arrived. I had been anxiously awaiting it for what felt like an eternity and all I could feel was numb.

Ethan and my dad walked out the front door of my childhood home. I watched them cross over to our yard, noticing that my mother had not bothered to join them in seeing me off. Somehow, I wasn't surprised and yet, it hurt all the same. I was her child and I was moving about a thousand miles from home and she couldn't even cross the street to say goodbye to me. Tears burned my eyes and blurred my vision. I quickly rubbed my eyes with the back of my hand.

"You're not allowed to start that." My dad took me in his arms and held me tight. "I am going to miss you so very much."

"I'm going to miss you too, Daddy." My tears soaked into his shirt.

"Make sure you call me as soon as you get there. Or you can call me from the road if you get really bored."

"Don't worry, I will," I assured him.

"I still don't like the idea of you driving all that way even if you are following Jackson and his parents," my dad said again for the millionth time in the last three days.

"I don't like it either." I let go of my dad and looked over at my little brother. "Which is why I've decided not to." I reached into my front pocket and handed the keys of my car to Ethan. "It's yours now. Take good care of it for me."

"Are you serious?" Ethan couldn't believe it as he stared at the set of keys in his hand.

"Yep." I pulled the title out of my back pocket and gave it to my dad. "I already signed it over to Ethan."

"What are you going to drive in Boston?" Ethan asked.

"Emily has a SUV that I can drive if I need it until I can save up for another car," I assured him.

"Well, thank you." Ethan stammered. "I am going to miss you so much." He embraced me. "Don't forget how much I love you." His voice was shaky.

"I love you, little brother. You better come and visit me." The tears rolled down my cheeks.

"I will, I promise." Ethan gave me a quick peck and let me go. "Just make sure Jackson takes good care of you."

"He will." I tried to smile and brushed the tears off my face.

"Ready?" Jackson walked up beside me. I nodded and reached for my dad again.

"Thank you for everything, Daddy. I love you so much!"

"I love you too, pumpkin. Call me if you need anything." Tears welled up in his eyes.

"I will." I kissed him one last time. "I'll see you soon," I promised.

"You can count on it."

I walked slowly to Jackson's CRV, waving one last time at the first two men in my life. Jackson opened the door and I climbed in and fastened my seat belt. Jackson closed the door while I searched my purse for a Kleenex. My husband slid in and started up his car. As he backed out of the driveway, my dad and Ethan stood there watching us, waving through their tears. I blew them a kiss and rested my hand on the glass. I mouthed, 'I love you' as Jackson headed south down the street. I turned and watched my dad and my younger brother fade away until I could no longer see them.

As we turned the corner out of the place I'd called home for the last eighteen-and-a-half years, I rested my head against the window and let the tears flow freely down my cheeks. It was time to begin the next adventure in my life —college, marriage, career, children. All waited on the horizon ahead of me. And as excited as I was to embrace it, it broke my heart into a million pieces for all that I was leaving behind me.

A thousand memories flooded my brain from both planes. Years and a lifetime of laughter, tears, happiness, and pain that all occurred in that single place I'd called home. My mind raced uncontrollably flashing on holidays, birthdays, sleepovers, hours shootin' hoops in the driveway with Ethan and my friends, the silly arguments with my family members. I knew we would come back to visit, but it would never be the same again. It would never be my home again. Not the way it used to be.

There's no turning back now.

Jackson followed his parents onto the interstate exit. In less than a year the world as I had known it had disappeared before my eyes. I had started my senior year in high school with aspirations of good grades, playing sports, and hanging out with my friends. Never in my wildest dreams did I ever think that the boy who moved in across the street and made me physically ill to be around would end up holding the secret to a world I was suddenly thrust into.

And although I was still adjusting to living dual lives on separate planes of existence, I couldn't imagine doing it alone. Jackson and his parents had saved my life in every way possible. Not only had they explained to me the truth about *Essence Voyager Era*, they showed me how to embrace it and even excel in it. Never in my wildest dreams would I have ever contemplated the existence of *EVE*. It still sounded absurd to me and I lived with it daily.

As I glanced over at my new husband and thought about all the changes that had occurred in the last year, I knew there was nowhere else I would rather be than with Jackson, right here and right now ... on the road that would lead to both our pasts and our futures. I reached over and took his hand in mine. A smile slid across his lips although he never took his eyes off the road. His profile was stunning. I loved this man more than life. I knew that our life wasn't always going to be red roses and wine, but I took great comfort in knowing that no matter what obstacles came our way neither of us would ever have to face them alone, regardless of which time we were in.

"I love you," I whispered to him.

"I love you, too."

UNTITLED

APPENDIX

2009

The Timmons

- Shane Douglas, VP Compliance of Chicago General
- Amy Marie, Pediatrician at Chicago General
- Sidney Harper, Sophomore at Northwestern University
- Jocelyn Alyssa, Senior in high school
- Ethan Jude, Junior in high school

The Chandlers

- Robert Abraham, Corporate Attorney
- Emily Jade, Novelist
- Alexander Nolan, Divorce Attorney in Boston
- Leslie, Alexander's wife
- Lucinda, Alexander & Leslie's six-year-old daughter
- Charlie, Alexander & Leslie's four-year-old son
- Phoebe Rochelle, Criminal Attorney in Boston
- Carson Adler, Phoebe's husband
- Wallace, Phoebe & Carson's one-year-old son
- Jackson Wyatt, Senior in high school/Studying law at Boston University

The Burks

- Craig, Jenna's father
- Melinda, Jenna's mother
- Jenna, Jocelyn's best friend/Dating Kyle/Volleyball & Basketball player

The Clausens

- Brett, Kyle's father
- Sonya, Kyle's mother
- Kyle, Jenna's boyfriend/Senior in high school
- Brandon, Kyle's brother/Freshman in high school

Friends

- Caitlyn Buchanan, Zac's girlfriend/Volleyball, Basketball, Softball player/Senior
- Zak Engling, Caitlyn's boyfriend/Quarterback & Point Guard/ Senior
- Hilary Wade, Cody's girlfriend/Volleyball & Basketball player/ Senior
- Cody Porter, Hilary's boyfriend/Wide receiver & Small forward/ Senior
- Mariah Jones, Ethan's ex-girlfriend/Junior
- Corbin Stewart, Hailey's boyfriend, Ethan's best friend/Junior
- Hailey Collins, Corbin's girlfriend/Junior
- Taylor Perry, Jocelyn's nemesis/Cheerleader/Senior
- Dakota Anderson, Taylor's sidekick/Cheerleader/Senior
- Liang Chi, Ethan's girlfriend

Coaches/Teachers

- Coach Smith, Volleyball & Girls Basketball Coach/Teaches English Lit 9
- Coach Shelburne, Football Coach/Teaches computer programing
- Coach Minnick, Boys Basketball Coach/ Teaches algebra
- Coach Kane, Girls Softball Coach/Teaches PE
- Mr. Rand, Teaches AP psychology
- Mrs. Neal-Beliveau, Teaches AP biology
- Mrs. Killian, Teaches Jocelyn's English Lit 12
- Mrs. Runyon, Teaches Jackson's English Lit 12
- Mr. Dunn, Teaches chemistry
- Mrs. Ulbright, Teaches history
- Principal Julia Cosgrove
- Mr. Acton, Vice Principal

1878

The Timmons

- Patrick Michael, Physician
- Annabelle Nichole, Married to Patrick/Jocelyn's mother
- Patrick Michael II, Physician
- Katherine, Patrick II's wife
- Jonathon Niles, Physician
- Lizette, Jonathon's wife
- Isaac, Jonathon & Lizette's nine-year-old son
- Louisa, Jonathon & Lizette's eight-year-old daughter
- Derek, Jonathon & Lizette's four-year-old son
- James Henry, Attorney
- Rachael, James's wife
- Abbigail, James & Rachael's five-year-old daughter
- Aiden, James & Rachael's three-year-old son
- Hannah, Housekeeper/Nanny
- William Arthur, Married to Olivia Adams/First year at Northwestern University
- Jocelyn Alyssa, Engaged to Jackson Chandler

The Timmons's Household

- Eddie, Stableman/Married to Mimi/Cora's dad
- Mimi, Manages the household/Married to Eddie/Cora's mom
- Cora, Housekeeper/Daughter of Eddie and Mimi
- Sarah, Cook
- Missy, Housekeeper

Timmons's Siblings

- Marissa Simone, Walter's mother/Patrick, Monte, Nicholas & Sidney's grandmother
- Walter Mitchell, Marissa's son/Patrick, Monte, & Nicholas's father
- Julia Rochelle, Walter's first wife/Sidney's mother/Passed away in childbirth
- Sidney Harper, Child of Walter & Julia/Raised by Marissa
- Bethany Carrie, Walter's second wife/Mother of Patrick, Monte, & Nicholas
- Montgomery Floyd (Monte), Middle child of Walter & Bethany

- Vivian, Monte's wife in the nineteenth century
- Floyd, eldest son
- Charles, son
- Matthew, son
- Zachary, youngest son
- Nicholas Tyrone, Youngest son of Walter & Bethany
- Lydia, Nicholas's wife
- Oliver, eldest son
- Ashton, son
- Quinten, son
- Tristen, son
- Jeremiah, youngest son

The Chandlers

- Robert Abraham, Attorney
- Emily Jade, Married to Robert/Jackson's mother
- Alexander Nolan, Attorney
- Veronica, Alexander's wife
- Casper, Alexander & Veronica's six-year-old son
- Wyatt, Alexander & Veronica's five-year-old son
- Kyra, Alexander & Veronica's three-year-old daughter
- Phoebe Rochelle
- Silas Monroe, Phoebe's husband/School teacher
- Wallace, Phoebe & Silas's one-year-old son
- Katie, the Monroe's housekeeper/Nanny
- Jackson Wyatt, Law School at Northwestern University

The Chandler Household

- Barnaby, Stableman/Married to Carly
- Susan, Housekeeper
- Carly, Cook/Married to Barnaby
- Norma, Housekeeper

The Chandler – Timmons's Willow Pines

- Jackson Wyatt, Criminal Attorney
- Jocelyn Alyssa
- (Gavin Harold, Eldest son/Not yet born)

- (Ethan Alexander, Youngest son/Not yet born)
- (Alyssa Nichole, Daughter/Not yet born)

The Willow Pines Household

- Cora, Mimi & Eddie's daughter/32 years old/Housekeeper
- Davonte, Married to Tamesha/Father of Betsy/Thirty years old/Stableman/Butler
- Tamesha, married to Davonte/Mother of Betsy/Thirty years old/Cook

- Betsy, Tamesha & Davonte's daughter/Eight years old

- Bertina, Tamesha's sister/Twenty-two years old/Housekeeper
- Horses

- Cheyenne
- Jasper

The Adams
- Benjamin, Banker/Married to Harriett
- Harriett, Married to Benjamin
- Olivia, Jocelyn's best friend/Married to William
- Kincade, Olivia's seven-year-old brother
- Oscar, Olivia's four-year-old brother
- Grady, The Adams's stableman

The Cains
- Henry, Owns the mercantile
- Molly, Married to Henry
- Laurie, Friend of Jocelyn's/Theodore's girlfriend
- Quintin, Laurie's five-year-old brother
- Gracie, the Cain's housekeeper

The Maddox's
- Elmer, Elizabeth's father
- Ester, Elizabeth's mother

- Easton, Elizabeth's twenty-year-old brother
- Elizabeth, Jocelyn's friend/Lee's girlfriend
- Edwin, Elizabeth's sixteen-year-old brother
- Elijah, Elizabeth's fourteen-year-old brother
- Elisa, Elizabeth's eight-year-old sister
- Sabina, the Maddox's housekeeper

The Donaldson's

- George, Carpenter/Married to Corrine
- Corrine, Married to George
- Josiah, Dimitri's twenty-five-year-old brother
- Dimitri, formerly engaged to Maryanne
- Calliope, Dimitri's sixteen-year-old sister
- Ingrid, Dimitri's fourteen-year-old sister

Friends

- Christina Bowden, Jocelyn's friend/Thomas's girlfriend
- Thomas Reynolds, Christina's boyfriend
- Theodore Norris, Laurie's boyfriend
- Maryanne Kendrick, formerly engaged to Dimitri/Jocelyn's nemesis
- Sean Preston, Dimitri's best friend/Died of pneumonia in Spring 2009/ Formerly engaged to Olivia Adams
- Lee Miller, Elizabeth Maddox's boyfriend/Architect
- Mr. Grahame, History teacher
- Sheriff McGuire
- Mr. Rhoads, County Prosecutor
- Evelyn Brice, Dimitri's girlfriend

UNTITLED

AUTHOR BIO

A. L. Waddington grew up in a small town in Indiana and always had a vivid and overactive imagination. She loves music, playing sports, and can be quite mischievous at times. She has been known to play practical jokes on occasion and is a firm believer in the theory of organized chaos. She has a slight addiction to coffee and when she's not hidden behind her laptop or buried in a book, she can be found exploring the Southwest region of the country and trying to lose that last stubborn ten pounds. She has a master's in military psychology and is currently working on her doctorate. She resides in Arizona with her husband, Eric, their girls, and two spoiled puppies.

UNTITLED

MORE GREAT READS FROM

SCARLETT INK PUBLISHING

THE EVE SERIES

Essence, Book 1

Jocelyn Timmons does not believe she is anything special. She's about to find out how wrong she is. Our minds often wander, but can our souls?

Enlightened, Book 2

Can Jocelyn Timmons have it all or will she lose the love of her life instead? Time stands still cause time can't heal.

Perception, Book 3

My hope, my dreams, and most of all me ... we will finally be set free. Perception, the gripping third installment in the EVE series, continues Jocelyn's quest of living in two worlds with her unique gift – but will she finally get answers to the many questions surrounding her double lives?

Scarlett
Ink
Publishing

COMING SOON

Coming this Fall
Don't miss the exciting spin-off to the *EVE* series.
The journey continues...

TRANSCENDENCE
THE SPIRIT QUEST SERIES
Book 1

TRANSCENDENCE

THE SPIRIT QUEST SERIES

WEDNESDAY, July 15, Present

The plane began to descend slowly in the Chicago night sky. I hate flying. Not so much the act of flying itself but crashing. I was terrified of crashing. Granted, crashing into Lake Michigan wasn't the same as crashing into the Andes, but still. Being horribly mangled and crushed doesn't ring good times for me. Instead, I tried to think of other things to take my mind off of where I was. I tried to recall my class schedule after our short break, but my mind was a blank.

Pet peeves, I closed my eyes and thought. What are my pet peeves? People who put the toilet paper roll on, so it rolls out from the bottom instead of the top. People who litter. People who don't respect others. Chaos. Double standards. Cold showers ... I truly hated cold showers, liars and thieves ... probably more than anything in this entire world.

Turbulence jolted the plane just enough to make me jump and grab my boyfriend, Landon Harrison's hand. He was sitting beside me with his headphones in watching *The Avengers* movie on his iPhone. He smiled over at me and squeezed my hand.

"You all right, babe?" he asked with a smile.

"Yeah," I grimaced.

Landon's eyes shifted back to his little screen. It amazed me how calm and collected he was. I was ready to come unglued and he was more interested in the

Hulk pounding on Loki. I shook my head and tried to focus on the words written on the page before me. I had brought along a copy of *Doctor Sleep* by Stephen King. I had fallen in love with *The Shining* years ago and was dying to read the sequel but hadn't quite managed to even put a dent in it yet. My fear of crashing was too overwhelming.

I leaned my head against the window and watched the Chicago skyline draw closer around us. The skyscrapers towered in the night sky twinkling like fireflies across the dark blue backdrop. It looked so beautiful and serene from this distance. The city resembled nothing of the sporadic outbreaks of violence advertised on the evening news.

As instructed by the captain Landon turned off all electronic devices in preparation for landing. He tucked his phone into the side pocket of his backpack and put his seat up straight. "For such a short flight, it feels like it takes forever," Landon complained.

"Remind me it is better than driving," I glanced over at him and said.

"Much better than driving." He chuckled. "Hell, we'd barely be out of New York in the time it took us to fly here."

"I know, I know," I muttered under my breath. "Still doesn't make me like it," I said with sarcasm.

"I know, my dear." Landon leaned over with a coy smile and kissed me quickly on the cheek. "But your dad appreciates you making the sacrifice for his wedding."

"Are you all right?" I felt my younger sister, Jocelyn's hand on my shoulder. She and her husband, Jackson, were seated right behind us.

"Yes, I am fine." I turned around and smiled reassuringly at her.

My sister was aware of how much I hated to fly. It had taken her and Landon several days to convince me that it would be easier, faster, and cheaper than driving. Personally, I thought a road trip with the four of us would be fun, but considering we were on a time crunch we wouldn't have been able to stop over in New York for a couple days or any of the other tourist attractions along our way across the Midwest.

Our parents had gotten divorced four years ago, the summer after our younger brother, Ethan, had graduated high school. Our mother, Amy, had taken a position as the head of pediatrics at some hospital in Seattle and neither Jocelyn nor I had spoken with her much since she'd transferred. She was a good mother, a little overbearing perhaps, career driven — definitely, and maybe even a little too judgmental, but we all knew she loved us and would be there if we needed anything.

Our father, Shane, was a lot more laid back than our mother. He was the type of parent that even if he didn't always agree with the decisions his children made, he accepted them without judgment and always supported us, had our backs, and loved each of us unconditionally. So, six months ago when we had all journeyed home for the holidays and our dad announced that he had proposed to Patsy, a child psychologist he had been dating for the last year and a half, the three of us couldn't have been happier for him. Patsy was so different from our mom, which I believe was her main appeal to my dad. She was like a duck, things just washed over her, and she handled anything stressful with grace, style and most importantly, humor.

Our mom was extremely feminine, whereas Patsy not so much. Mom never left the house without her hair and makeup fixed to perfection or looking anything short of ladylike. Patsy was a little younger than our mother, but not much. She looked professional in her work attire, but outside of the office she was a jeans and T-shirt kind of gal. She rarely wore makeup and her hair spent more time pulled up in a low ponytail than down, and I'm not even sure if she owned a curling iron. Patsy had more of a natural beauty about her that didn't require a great deal of effort and her radiant, fun-loving personality gave her a personal glow. I had to admit I liked her from the start.

The wedding was three days away and my sister and I were bridesmaids. Ethan was set to be the best man and Patsy's son, Donnie, who was twenty, was also standing up with them. We had sent Patsy our sizes and seen photos of the dresses we were supposed to be wearing but had not even tried them on yet. Hopefully, they would fit, and we wouldn't spend tomorrow doing alterations. It was to be an outside wedding by a lake at the country club my father golfed at frequently. I was hoping the weather would hold out but given the inconsistency of Midwest summer showers I wasn't sure what to expect.

I gripped Landon's hand as the wheels finally touched the ground. He rolled his eyes playfully at me but patted my hand, nonetheless. I let out a deep sigh as we taxied through the runway towards the gate. I could hear Jocelyn and Jackson discussing what they wanted to eat, and I remembered we hadn't eaten since brunch at Jackson's parents' house before we left and realized I was famished as well. His parents, Emily and Robert, were flying in Friday afternoon for the wedding. Robert was an attorney and had to be in court early on Friday morning. So, they were unable to fly in with the rest of us.

Landon grabbed our carry-on bags from overhead and waited impatiently for people to start filing out of the plane. He rattled his fingers on the back of his seat in frustration. He was slightly ADHD and always on the move. He hated idle time and couldn't relax if his life depended on it. His mother had said she'd wanted to duct tape his butt to a chair as a child. He wasn't much different as an adult.

I placed my hand over his, making him stop. He looked over his shoulder at me and gave me a coy smile. "Sorry."

"Patience," I whispered.

"My strongest suit." He slightly shook his head.

"I wish," I replied, elbowing him in the back.

Slowly but surely, we edged our way off the plane. The four of us walked side by side down the long hallway to the terminal. We'd each only brought carry-on bags in hopes of getting out of O'Hare airport in record time. Our dad was supposed to meet us outside and Jocelyn had told me she had texted him when we landed. He had responded back with a simple 'okay,' but instead of finding him on the curb as planned we were all surprised to see him and Patsy waiting for us as we left the secured area of the terminal.

"There's my girls," Dad exclaimed happily as soon as he saw us.

"Daddy!" Jocelyn was the first to reach him and throw her arms around him. She was a Daddy's Girl. "What are you doing here?"

"I missed my girls." He smiled and kissed her on the cheek before releasing her and hugging me.

"You just saw us a couple weeks ago." I smiled and shook my head at him. The four of us had come home for Ethan's college graduation from Notre Dame.

"How was your flight?" he asked.

"Good." I kissed his scruffy cheek.

"Hello, Landon." My dad shook my boyfriend's hand before shaking my sister's husband's hand. "Jackson, it's good to see you both. Are you guys taking care of my girls?"

"Always," Landon replied with a cocky grin. He and my dad got along extremely well for which I was truly grateful. Plus, he also got along famously with Jackson. However, that one had taken some time considering he'd eloped with my sister during their senior year of high school. My dad had punched Jackson for that one and I admit I wasn't too thrilled with them either, but after I knew the truth of why they did it I was truly happy for them.

. . .

No, she wasn't pregnant. Everyone initially thought so and speculated for a long time about it, but she wasn't. That would have been easier for me to accept than the real reason. Not to mention I never would have believed them in a million years if I hadn't inherited the same ability and experienced it firsthand. As insane as it sounds, my sister and I had inherited an ability called *Essence Voyager Era*, or *EVE*, from our uncles. *EVE* was the genetic gift of being able to live parallel lives on two very separate planes of existence. Jackson and his entire family had also inherited the same gift and my sister was fortunate enough to have him with her on both planes. I, unfortunately, was not so lucky.

This gift or curse or whatever it is, is quite unusual to say the least. How many people have it? Who knows? My Uncle Nicholas had spent his entire adult life doing research on it and had barely touched the tip of the iceberg as he put it. But what we did know was that the barrier in the consciousness remained intact until late adolescence or early twenties. When it starts to disintegrate the individual begins to have visions or experience episodes from their *other* life. To say that this can be slightly unsettling is a mild understatement. Personally, I thought I was going insane. And unfortunately, due to familial structures today, most individuals who reach this phase of enlightenment are diagnosed with schizophrenia if they do not have a close family member with the gift to help them through this difficult transition. With divorce being so prevalent these days and families spread out across the country if not the globe, the misdiagnosis is often made. When that occurs, and the person is placed on antipsychotic medications, it halts the barrier from full depletion and that individual gets "stuck" in that phase. Lucky for me, I had my sister, my uncle, Jackson, and his family.

My uncle had volumes of notes on research he'd conducted throughout his life as a professor of history. He speculated that *EVE* has always existed but is mostly mistaken as prophecy. It seemed that most cultures across time have had some form of it, from oracles to medicine men to most notably *Michel de Nostredame* back in the sixteenth century and his collection of quatrains. More recent "prophets" have even capitalized on their abilities and made names and money for themselves. True or not, my uncle's hypotheses were uncanny in their resemblance to what I experienced nightly when my soul drifted off from the twenty-first century to my *other* self, who wakes to a new day in the mid-nineteenth century.

Anyway, my sister Jocelyn was set to marry Jackson in the late nineteenth century when he and his family learned that she too had the gift. That sent them all on the journey from Boston to Chicago to aid her in the transition, and during the process she fell head over heels in love with him on this plane as well and the two of them eloped only a couple months after meeting. That alone tore our family apart and our mother barely forgave her, although true to their word, the couple had remained together and strong as ever for the last five-and-a-half years. My sister graduated last year with a BS in psychology and just completed her first year of law school at Boston University, just like her husband and the rest of his family.

The fall semester after I learned about *EVE*, Landon and I had transferred from Northwestern University to Harvard, citing that it was better for us when applying for their medical school, but the truth of it was I wanted to be closer to my sister, Jocelyn, Jackson, and his family. Plus, Uncle Nicholas had successfully procured a position at Boston University where Jocelyn was going to law school. It made dealing with this most bizarre and strange gift easier being surrounded by family and loved ones who understood its blessings and its curses.

"Hello, Patsy, how are you?" Jocelyn's greeting broke my train of thought.

"Good." Patsy reached out and gave us both a brief hug. "I'm glad you're all here. Now your father can stop worrying." She laughed easily.

"Is Ethan here?" I inquired as we started towards the airport exit.

"Yes. He arrived last week. I think he's having a little too much fun at Notre Dame." Dad put his arm around me and took my carryon.

"He's supposed to enjoy himself the summer before grad school. He's earned it. Besides, it's a great school for him." I knew how proud my dad was when Ethan got into school there and became part of their legendary football team after high school. He'd driven down for every home game throughout Ethan's undergraduate studies.

"Yes, it is," he agreed.

"What about Donnie?" I asked him while Jocelyn and Patsy made small talk about the wedding.

"He's out with his friends. He should be home later. He's not returning to the University of Kansas until the week before the start of the semester. We've turned the guest bedroom into his room," Dad replied.

"That's good." Even though none of us technically lived at home any longer I was glad none of our childhood bedrooms that still contained our stuff was offered to him.

We rolled the windows down on our ride home. Patsy talked a mile a minute about the rehearsal dinner, the wedding, the reception, the gowns, tuxes

... the woman was on a roll of excitement. I rested my head on Landon's shoulder in the crowed back seat and let the warm night wind blow through my hair. I was exhausted, and it felt like soft kisses from my childhood across my cheeks. I missed the smells of fresh cut grass and burning wood from a bonfire as we passed by.

I was home.